UNDER THE SHADOWS

Book 1: Shadows of Synd Series

E. ABRAHAM

For Lindsay.

I wish you could have seen what I've accomplished.
I'm still working on being famous for my words, but I made
them all spicy.
I know you'd approve.

Oh, and pick up your fucking dishes.

Trigger Warnings

Violence: Guns and Knives
Explicit Sex
Human Trafficking Scenes
Adult Language
Criminal Activities
Drugs
Kidnapping

If any of these are triggers for you, please visit the author's website for other works.

CONTENTS

ONE 15

TWO 25

THREE 33

FOUR 39

FIVE 49

SIX 59

SEVEN 65

EIGHT 75

NINE 81

TEN 87

ELEVEN 97

TWELVE 105

THIRTEEN 119

FOURTEEN 127

FIFTEEN 135

SIXTEEN 141

SEVENTEEN 153

EIGHTEEN 163

NINETEEN 173

TWENTY 183

TWENTY-ONE 193

TWENTY-TWO 202

TWENTY-THREE 214

TWENTY-FOUR 222

TWENTY-FIVE 230

TWENTY-SIX 240

TWENTY-SEVEN 248

TWENTY-EIGHT 254

TWENTY-NINE 264

THIRTY 274

THIRTY-ONE 282

THIRTY-TWO 290

THIRTY-THREE 296

THIRTY-FOUR 302

THIRTY-FIVE 313

THIRTY-SIX 321

THIRTY-SEVEN 331

THIRTY-EIGHT 337

THIRTY-NINE 349

FORTY 357

FORTY-ONE 367

FORTY-TWO 377

FORTY-THREE 385

FORTY-FOUR 393

FORTY-FOUR 401

FORTY-SIX 415

FORTY-SEVEN 425

FORTY-EIGHT 433

FORTY-NINE 441

FIFTY 453

FIFTY-ONE 461

FIFTY-TWO 471

FIFTY-THREE...477

FIFTY-FOUR...485

ABOUT THE AUTHOR 497

The shadows are my friend. My sweet spot. There, I can blend in, become a wisp, a trace of something else. Most people look forward, thinking the threat comes from the front.

They forget about the shadows. Which is exactly where I live.

Those shadows call out to me, begging me to slip into them-discover the secrets others hide away, and punish those who think they can shroud themselves in my shadows.

The shadows are the only place I feel truly like myself.

ONE

SAMANTHA

"Hurry up, Sammy. We can't be late to the gala." Mason pounds on my door, frustration seeping in his tone.

"And we don't want to be early, either," I call back in a sing-song voice as I slip on my heels. I don't want to wear them, but they're the only pair that goes with this dress. I sigh, knowing I'll have to play my part tonight. Mason has been drilling into my head all week how important this gala is, but I hate these parties. Every time I plaster on a simpering smile and make small talk with the city's elite, a part of my soul dies.

"I'm going to leave you behind if you're not downstairs in five minutes."

I scowl as Mason's footsteps retreat, clomping down the stairs. Our house is so big any sound echoes, making it hard to find the source. I hate that, too.

My brother wouldn't leave me, though, so I glance around my room for anything I've missed. At the last second, I grab the sheathed knife off my dressing table and strap it to my thigh. I may have to play the part of a mindless socialite, but I'm not going out without some way to protect myself. I've been adopting this persona so long sometimes, I can't remember the real me. The only time I'm at peace is when I'm alone, going to and from a job, but the role gives me something in return, at least. When no one expects anything out of me, it's easier to slip into the shadows and be forgotten. It's tiring, though. I glide down the stairs, trying to be silent, but my heels give me away. Mason twists, scowling, and I shoot him a cheeky grin.

"Mason, I think it unwise for Samantha to go with tonight. There will be important people there you need to make connections with, and I fear she'll be a distraction," Victor states, straightening the cuffs of his suit. Too bad he's all dressed up with nowhere to go.

"Why else do you think I'm going, Uncle?" I smile, tilting my head, already falling into the role of a blithering idiot.

"Perhaps we could find a better use for you, rather than flouncing around like a hooker playing at being important, dear," he retorts.

My skin flushes at the insult. I look down at the dress, trying to decide which part is most offensive to him. The color isn't garish but a plum satin. Sure, the plunging neckline is a little risqué, but my tits aren't falling out. They're contained by massive amounts of tape and the wrap-around ties that cross in the back. The double slits could maybe be lower, but I'll fit in with the other women at the event.

We have this conversation every fucking time, and every time, I grit my teeth, taking my uncle's insults and innuendos. He's not the head of the family, but he acts like he is—simply because he married into the Byrns's clan and buddied up to our father. I have to ignore the comments made in public; I don't want to embarrass my brother, but I'm getting sick of hearing it at home, too.

"Would you like to reword that, Victor?" Mason's words are cold, the voice of a boss at the head of a mafia family ringing through. I've been lucky to never have him use it on me, but I've seen grown men piss themselves when he's walked in a room and used it. Normally, they're strapped to a chair, facing some type of torture, but still.

"I'm merely worried that Samantha isn't living up to her potential. Surely, allowing men to objectify her in a slutty dress isn't what you're hoping for, Mason."

I roll my eyes, knowing he thinks marrying me off to the highest bidder is the potential he's talking about. Victor isn't normally so blatant about it, though. He must really not want me to attend this gala, but I can't imagine why. It's raising money for mental health resources for kids, for fuck's sake.

"Your assessment is unnecessary, Victor. Samantha is grown. You would do well to remember that." He strides to the door, a lackey barely getting it open before he barrels through to the limo. Victor disappears into the bowels of the house, intent of sowing whatever discord he can while we're gone. I hesitate, bracing myself to put my mask more firmly in place, when Colin, my brother's second, slides next to me and squeezes my hand.

"You ready?" he whispers, mussed sandy blond hair falling across his forehead.

"Why doesn't this seem to be getting any easier?"

He sighs. "Sam, as long as you remember who you are, inside where no one else can see, it doesn't matter what face you wear in front of everyone else."

I huff out a laugh. "When did you get so philosophical? I seem to remember you eating paste at one point when we were growing up."

"This is the problem with little sisters: they never forget anything." He grins, brown eyes twinkling.

"I'm not actually your little sister, you know." I quirk an eyebrow at him while he tugs me to the waiting car.

"Close enough."

Colin helps me in, and I settle against the seat opposite my brother, shaking my head as he tries to hand me a glass of champagne. It's hard enough dealing with the elite at these parties. More than a glass or two will have me saying whatever snarky thing pops in my head, and I'll ruin the carefully constructed persona we've crafted all these years. Colin nudges me, making a face, and I hide the grin behind my hand.

Mason clears his throat. "Sammy, couple rules tonight. This is a . . . shared event. A lot of influential players will be there, so I need you to steer clear of some of them."

"None of them talk to me anyway, unless they're propositioning me. I don't understand why tonight would be any different," I comment, rolling my eyes to peer out the window at the houses rolling by.

"These aren't your typical elite. They'll be there, too, but some others are attending."

"Spit it out, Mason. Who is coming that you're worried about?"

He scowls, muttering, "The Kings will be there. I don't know which one is coming, but at least one of them will be in attendance. You need to stay out of their way."

I blow out a breath, trying to find a response that won't set him off. The Kings are the other side of the coin to us, ruling the west side of Synd, while we control the east. Mason crosses their paths at galas and parties, but he's always made me stay home.

When I was young, I wanted to cross the river running through our city to see the other side. Mason shot me down every time. I never understood what the big deal was. We're all in the mafia, we're not even rivals, really. We each stay on our sides, controlling and protecting the people within, not bothering the other. I'm pretty sure Mason does business with them, but he holds those secrets so closely I couldn't guess what type of business they do together.

"I don't see how my meeting them will make a difference. I'm sure they know I exist by now."

"It's not about whether they know you exist. It's to keep you safe."

I snort. We can't have a candid conversation in front of Colin. We trust him with our lives, but there are still secrets Mason has never shared with him.

My safety is why I have to play the airhead role at these functions. My safety is the reason Mason keeps me on this side of the river. My safety is the reason Colin doesn't know what I do at night. Mason is convinced if anyone finds out my extracurricular activities of extracting information and taking out men who break the rules, I'll be targeted. He's probably right, but it still chafes to not be myself. It's a lonelier existence than I'm willing to admit most days.

We pull in the circular drive, and I wait for them to slide out before I scoot across the seat. I struggle every time to stand without revealing my thong to everyone. Flashes from cameras are everywhere, and I paste on a smile, taking Colin's hand to successfully exit. I want to rush inside and get this night over with so I can go home and put some sweatpants on, but Mason warned me we weren't leaving early, since there's a silent auction. I dutifully smile, linking my arm with Colin's. After an eternity, we're through the front doors, leaving most of the cameras behind. I silently thank whoever allowed only two reporters in here tonight.

Colin leans down, whispering in my ear, "Three rolled eyes, two trips, sixteen touches, and four blushes from Mason."

I choke on the bubble of laughter in my throat, thanking whatever made Mason decide Colin should be my date tonight instead of him. The game we play at these parties makes the night go faster at the very least.

"Seven numbers, two spilled drinks, five items, and one choking episode from Mason," I murmur, waving a hand at the mayor's wife, who looks like she got into the chardonnay way before the event started.

"How the hell am I going to bid and win on five items? You make sure Mason always outbids me."

"Same way I'm going to trip two people tonight: finesse." I flip my dark-brown hair over my shoulder, trying not to disturb the curls, then wiggle my eyebrows at him.

"Would you two knock it off?" Mason grumbles, handing me a champagne flute. The bubbles tickle my nose as I sip, pursing my lips at the dry taste.

A commotion behind us has me turning, but Colin covers my hand resting on his arm with his own and pulls me toward the ballroom filled with tables. I drag my feet, expecting to be front and center like usual, but he tugs me to the right side of the room, weaving us between tables laid with fine china and obnoxious crystal centerpieces with a single twig inside.

"Why are we over here? Did Mason piss someone off?" I ask when he settles me in a seat.

"They split us up. Apparently, the planner thought one of us would freak out and start shooting if we were put close to each other." He snorts, settling into his own seat.

"Who? The Kings?" I crane my neck around, trying to catch sight of them, but the room is mostly empty, with everyone still gathered in the foyer. Their arrival explains why I'm already sitting down for dinner instead of mingling.

"Yeah. No one believes we leave each other alone. They're always waiting for the other shoe to drop." He stands abruptly, stepping around me, holding out his hand. "Mr. Livingston, great to see you."

I glance back, catching the sight of shockingly white hair and a bazillion wrinkles, then spin back around. Mr. Livingston isn't my favorite person. Sure, he owns most of the banks in Synd, but he also can't figure out that my chest doesn't have eyes and that my tits won't talk back, but he keeps trying.

Thankfully, Colin leads him away, talking about some new business venture Mason hasn't told me about. I peek around and pick up the butter knife when it seems like no one is paying me any attention. Casually, I twist my arm and scratch the one spot on my back I can't reach, sighing when I hit it just right.

"Did you know hippos can't swim?" a deep voice says from my right. I flip the knife in my hand, striving for grace as I place it next to the fork. He grins, green eyes dancing beneath sun-streaked light brown hair, lounging in Colin's vacated chair. He scans the space, eyes narrowing before coming back to my face, the grin firmly back in place.

"I didn't know that. Did you know your nose never stops growing?" I tilt my head, trying to figure out why this ridiculously hot man is talking to me. His grin grows bigger, if that's possible.

"Well, well, well. I did not expect that," he murmurs, laugh lines creasing his glittering emerald eyes as he takes a sip from his drink— whiskey, I'd guess, from the color.

"Didn't expect what?"

He waves away my question, scanning the room again. I turn to spot whatever it is he's looking for. Mason is tucked in an alcove with another man, but I can't make out his features. Mason's face is tight, and his mouth is a slash across his face. I consider going over to run interference, but he'd shoo me away.

"What brings you here tonight?"

His question pulls my attention back to him. I'm mesmerized by his strong cheekbones and the tattoo peeking out of his dress shirt.

"Uh, doesn't everyone love a good party?" I try to paste on a simpering smile, but he raises his brow.

"You have no idea who I am, do you?" he asks and runs his fingers through his messy hair.

My brain scrambles, trying to place his face. There's no way I've met him before. I rarely watch the news, and I never talk to anyone who's in power unless they're attending these parties. I should pay more attention to who's who with the major players. I'll leave it to Mason and Colin to handle them.

"I'm sure you'll tell me." I giggle, hating myself just a little bit more. The more galas I attend and clubs I dance at and masks I put on, the more exhaustion settles in my bones. There has to be more out there than this.

"Are you going to bid on any items?" he asks, but most of the sparkle has gone out of his eyes. I sigh inwardly, knowing I'll have a dozen versions of this conversation the rest of my night before I can finally escape.

"Don't know. Nothing caught my eye."

"You didn't want the purse? Or maybe the spa package?"

"Nope, I have everything I need. You?" Honestly, I didn't even pay attention to what items were for bid. I look for the ones I can give away to someone else. I didn't lie. I have everything I need and more things than I want. Mason will buy something to keep up appearances or beat Colin, but he doesn't like these events any more than I do. Colin is the only one who likes to schmooze people, and he's good at it, which is why I stick to his side. He does all the talking, and I can pretend I'm somewhere else.

"Oh, there's one thing I think I'd like very much," he murmurs.

I whip my head back, but he's not looking at me. He's staring at the brochure that lists all the items for auction.

I lean in. "Which one?"

He tilts the pamphlet. "That one." He points at a first-edition book I've never heard of. I tilt my head closer and nod as I read the description.

"Hmm, you like to read?" I lift my head. I'm much closer than I should be. I pull back, aiming for casual, but he ticks up the corner of his mouth.

"Sure, doesn't everybody?"

"Uh, no. Most people would rather do anything else other than read, at least the people at these things are like that."

"I suppose. Do you like to read?" The sparkle is back, reminding me I'm supposed to be playing a part, and I'm not doing it well with whoever this guy is.

"I'm usually too busy, going to the spa or the clubs or shopping." I smirk. Part of me hopes he hears my sarcasm. As short as this conversation has been, it's arguably the most meaningful one I've ever had at a party.

"Of course"—he shakes his head—"Refill?" He stands, nodding at my full glass.

"I'm fine, thank you." I stare at my plate, trying to figure out who he could be.

I startle as he whispers in my ear. "Good to meet you, Bug."

I glance over my shoulder, but he's already striding away. Who the hell *is* he?

TWO

SHANE

I pinch the bridge of my nose, fighting back the creeping headache. Alex is striding away from Samantha Byrns. Other than the pictures in the media, I haven't seen her in ten years. She's no longer the gangly teenager peering out a second-story window. The back of her head is all I can see. Her hair is darker now, auburn curls cascading down her back.

I shake my head, fixing Mason Byrns with narrowed eyes. The last time we spoke was a clipped conversation at another event six months ago. Clearly, we don't know what the hell to do, since we've spent most of this conversation asking vague questions and giving one-word answers.

"When are you meeting with Helms?" I ask, getting to the point. I can't handle dancing around, hoping I can read between the lines. This is why Alex comes to these events. I can't handle dealing with inane small talk and innuendos.

He sighs, glancing over to his sister. "I don't know yet. Soon. Has he contacted you?" Apparently, I'm not the only one sick of this scene.

"A cryptic text message saying 'get ready'—whatever the hell that means."

"He's paranoid. Always has been. I don't have anything unusual going down on my side, so I can't imagine what he's reaching out for."

"Nothing on mine, either. Shit, the reporter just walked in." I try to squeeze into the shadows, but there's nowhere else to go. The last thing I need is to be photographed with Mason fucking Byrns and start a whole shitshow in the media. Mason peers over his shoulder, then pulls out his phone and sends a text before slipping it back in. Ten seconds later, Princess Byrns is waylaying the reporter, who throws her head back and laughs, touching his arm and guiding the blushing man away.

"At some point, we're going to have to set something up to sponsor together so we can put the rumors of a rivalry to bed."

"Did you just have your sister run interference?" I rub my jaw, watching her sashay out the room.

"Don't worry about it. She can talk a person's ear off."

I file away the information, like every other detail I come across about her. I can't figure her out. Other than what I've read online, I don't know what she does, and it drives me up a wall. Even Ren can't figure her out, not that he's as invested in it as I've been.

"If Helms has a problem, let me know," I tell Mason.

"You sticking around for the dinner?"

"No. Alex is, though," I answer, glancing around to find my second. The last thing I want to do is hang around here, glad-handing rich dicks, pretending I care about their opinions. I'd rather give the money or the resources directly to whatever cause their supporting at these fancy parties. The opulent spending is disgusting.

"All right, I'll let you know if I find something you need to know."

As much as the media presents us as rivals, I actually like Mason. Only Helms and Byrns understands what it's like to be in my position. Taking over for our fathers at a barely legal age sent us down separate paths, but I respect them more than I'd like to admit. Mason raising Samantha, like I did my younger sister, helps. Although, Mason's sister was halfway grown, while Emma was only three.

"Don't spend all your money on the gold hippo unless you're going to drop it off at Helms's front door." I smirk, skirting the wall.

Hopefully, I can make my escape without dealing with any more sycophants. The uproar I caused when I showed up in the first place was too much. I catch Alex's eye when I hit the lobby, ignoring the mayor's wife, who is frantically waving to get my attention. Alex laughs, clapping a man on the shoulder before weaving his way to me through the crowd.

"Well?" I ask, scanning the crowd.

"Lot of big names here tonight. You sure you don't want to stay?"

I narrow my eyes, and he grins. "The last thing I want to do is deal with this bullshit. Now, what's with Byrns's sister?"

"I'm not convinced. Anything from Mason?" He leans against the wall next to me.

"He's as clueless as we are. Helms is playing his cards close to the chest. He's meeting with Byrns soon, though, before he sets something up with us, I'm sure."

"You sure he'll meet with us? He always seems to favor the east side," Alex comments, drawing my eye to him.

"Ren tell you that?"

He smirks, shrugging. "Might have. He caught Emma trying to sneak out again, by the way."

I curse under my breath. At thirteen, she's taking needless risks, trying to be more independent. I'm powerful in this city, but I can't control every lowlife from hurting her. They probably wouldn't even recognize her. I keep her away from this life as much as I can.

"I'll have a talk with her, again. For some reason, she doesn't realize how much danger she's putting herself in."

"If you let her out every once in a while, she might get a clue."

"You make it seem like I lock her in a cage. She's fine. I'm going. Try to outbid Mason for the gold hippo."

"Hippo, you say? Wait, why do you want that thing? It's fucking ginormous."

I chuckle. "I don't want it. I want to drop it off in the Reapers' territory and blame Mason."

I slip out a side door, shoes scuffling on the stairs, but I slow when a heated argument floats up from the level below. I'm not getting involved in the staff fighting among themselves. Peeking over the rail, I see a woman's head bobbing, hands flailing as she shrieks in frustration.

"Would you keep your voice down?" A man answers. I can't see him tucked under the steps, but his voice rings with familiarity.

"If you didn't want me to make a scene, maybe you should have told me your wife would be here," she screeches.

"Of course, she's here. I'm not going to bring my slut to a function like this," he sneers.

"Slut? You weren't calling me a slut when you were fucking me in the back of your limo last night."

"That is typically where sluts are fucked. How did you even get in here? Surely, you weren't invited."

"Fuck you. You're a grade-A bastard. I'm sure the reporters outside will love to listen to all the juicy gossip you've been whispering about. They won't think I'm too dumb to understand what's going on."

She yelps, body jerking and skin hitting skin cracks through the air. She wails, cowering from the man.

"You'll keep your damn mouth shut if you know what's good for you," he growls between gritted teeth.

I've heard enough, descending quietly. The woman's eyes widen before she ducks her head, hiding her reddened cheek, as he grips her arm. It's pure coincidence I came across him, but I'll use it to my advantage. Ren is already outside, ready to ambush the commissioner, whenever he'd stepped out for a smoke, but I suppose I can speed up the plan.

"Commissioner," I say, straightening my lapels.

He drops his hand and steps around her, blocking my view. "Ah, Shane King, glad I caught you before the auction. Did you see the . . ."

"I'm not interested in talking shop tonight, Commissioner." I slip my hands in my pockets, rocking on my heels.

"Of course." He smiles, then lets out a high-pitched laugh.

"Aren't you going to introduce your friend?" I quirk an eyebrow.

"She's no one of consequence. You know how women are, always getting hysterical over nothing." He scratches his jaw, eyes bouncing around the room.

I nod, slipping my phone out of my pocket to text Ren. My phone buzzes almost immediately with his response, and I smirk.

"Alan, I do believe Ren has some information for you. He's out back waiting, if you would." I gesture him to the door. He doesn't acknowledge the woman behind him, striding for the door without a backward glance. That was easier than I thought. I track him until the door clicks shut. I shoot off another text, waiting until it's read before slipping it back into my pocket and turning back to the woman.

"I'm sorry, Mr. King," she whispers, tears filling her terror-lined eyes.

"No need to apologize. What's your name?" I keep my distance, not wanting her to run.

"Marcy. Marcy Tensmin."

"Ms. Tensmin, do you have a safe place to go tonight? Or are you in need of help?" It took me years to ride the line between mafia boss and benevolent leader. Most people I come across are terrified, like Marcy, having heard the rumors. I'm sure she thinks I'll make her disappear for the threats she made toward the police commissioner we installed.

"Um, I'll be fine." She shrinks, though I haven't moved.

"If you aren't, I have some resources available."

"Oh"—her mouth falls open and a dazed look crosses her face—"I'll be okay. I shouldn't have said those things. Do you think he's coming back?"

I follow her eyes over my shoulder, a vibration coming from my pocket, and I check my phone again, another smirk slipping through.

"Ms. Tensmin, you won't need to worry about the commissioner anymore. I'd appreciate if you would keep whatever you've heard from him to yourself. However, if you do feel the need to speak out, I have someone in mind. Do you know Alex King?"

She clears her throat, choking out a "yes."

"Good. He'll be more than willing to listen to what the commissioner has been up to. We can deal with any of the issues that might arise from his missteps. Now, if you'll excuse me, I have other business to attend to."

She nods, bewilderment plastered on her face. I exit the same door the commissioner did minutes before, but he's long gone, cloistered in a car with Ren. He'll be far from the city by morning, unless Ren discovers he's crossed us in some way. Regardless, I'm not going to allow the commissioner to continue in his current position. It puts more on my plate, trying to find a new commissioner who we won't have to break in, but I'm sure Ren already has a list of names. Alex will have his input, and we'll have a new one installed by the end of the week.

I fall on to my town car's seat, the tension falling from my shoulders, and I nod to the driver. Tonight only added more questions than answers. Some days, I wish I could push off the responsibilities and take a fucking vacation. Our family has controlled the west side of Synd for generations, but the last ten years have been especially hard. The attempted coup took out most of the leaders, and building us back to our former glory has fallen squarely on my shoulders. Emma used to ask when we were going to leave, take a vacation, like her friends in school. When I told her never, she lost her mind. I never want to repeat that experience.

"We're here, sir," the driver says, and my head snaps up, realizing where we are.

"Thanks. Go home, Knot. Tell your wife hello," I say, pushing open the door.

"Will do, boss."

As soon as I'm up the massive staircase at the front door, Emma's screeches ring from the second floor. I have the irrational urge to turn and make Knot take me with him, but I brace myself and trudge up to the third floor. Her door rattles as she kicks it, with a terrified Titus posted outside. Emma yells incoherently, and a thud hammers against the wood. I gesture to the newest guard, and he hustles off down the hall, intent on escaping her wrath.

"Emma."

A pause suspends in the air, but her heavy breathing comes from the other side of the door. I wonder how long she's been freaking out.

"I thought you were at the party," she spits out, sarcasm dripping from her tone.

"I was, and now I'm back. Want to tell me what's going on?"

"I will if you open the damn door." I narrow my eyes at her language.

"The door isn't locked, Emma."

The handle turns, but the door doesn't open, and she shrieks again. I don't know why she assumes I locked her in. There aren't even locks on the outside of her room. I shove down on the handle, but the door doesn't budge. I ram my shoulder into the wood, and it pops open, almost sending me to the floor.

"Oh," she mumbles, tucking her hands into her back pockets. Her blonde hair is a riot around her tear-streaked face.

"For fuck's sake, Emma, you trashed your room? Why didn't you just ask Titus to help you open the door?" I holler, throwing my hands up as I take in piles of clothes and shoes scattered across her floor.

"I didn't trash my room! It looks fine. I thought Titus was there to keep me in, so I wasn't about to ask him for help." She rolls her blue eyes that match mine, planting her hands on her hips.

I sigh, exhaustion settling in my bones. "Just clean it up. Then get to bed. I'm sure you're tired from having a temper tantrum for half the night."

"I'm hungry, though. I didn't have any dinner, since I was locked in my room, which was a perfectly acceptable reason to have a freak-out session."

"Fine, let's go get some food. You can tell me all about how it's all my fault your door got stuck."

I tuck her under my arm, leading her to the kitchen. Maybe I can salvage the night with dinner with my baby sister. I glance out the window, lightening flickering across the sky, thunder rumbling. I suppress a foreboding shiver, forcing its way through my body, intent to leave tomorrow's problems for tomorrow.

THREE

REN

The thud of the locks echoing through the car makes the police commissioner jerk. He reaches for the handle, but it doesn't open. A thrill sends a shiver through me, but I hold it back, keeping my blank mask in place. Alan isn't particularly bright, which I had warned Shane would be an issue in the long run, but he was a temporary solution to a long-term problem. I nod to the driver and flip the switch to slide the divider up, cutting us off from him.

"What's the meaning of this, King?" he demands as the car pulls away from the curb. I contemplate ignoring him, but he never did have any patience.

"You're going to tell me everything you've been engaged in since we installed you in your position. Please don't hide the dirty details. It will only piss me off."

I avoid his eyes, staring out the window as we wind our way away from the event center, cruising over the bridge separating the east from the west side of the city.

"I've already told you everything. Shane said you have information for me. Why are we leaving? My wife is back there."

"She'll be taken care of. Now, start telling me the things you haven't shared, or we'll have to make a detour."

"I don't know what you're talking about," he states, but panic laces his tone. A small smirk graces my face. He might play tough, but underneath all the bravado, he is terrified he'll lose his status. It's the reason he jumped at our offer to be in such a high position within the community. He wanted to ride our coattails for as long as possible. Somewhere along the way, he forgot his place, though. And now, he'll pay the consequences.

"Alan, now is not the time to be modest. How about I'll tell you the information I have, and you can tell me if I'm missing anything." The commissioner blanches, all the color draining from his face.

"I swear, I've told you everything," he hisses.

"Well, I've been monitoring your finances. It seems that quite a bit of money is coming in and not that much going out. I took the liberty of transferring the funds from your off-shore account in to the appropriate places. It was so kind of you to make such a hefty donation to the hospital in our name. Extortion was a bit much, though, don't you think? No matter, we returned the funds to those businesses you tried to double-dip from. They weren't very happy to have to be tithing twice, but I'm sure you knew that." He trembles at my implications.

"I didn't realize you were doing that. It must have been an oversight."

I narrow my eyes at him. "There was also the seizure of money and resources from certain individuals, mostly on the east side of the river. What was the next step in your plan? Were you going to facilitate a hit? Perhaps a couple of our shipments would disappear, only to pop up in Byrns territory? Doesn't matter. I'm sure you thought if you pulled enough strings, sewed enough doubt, the Kings would retaliate, and suddenly, we'd be at war. Then you could swoop in, save the day, and take over. The problem with your little plan is two-fold. One, you'd never be able to hold on to the city. It's laughable to assume you, alone, would be able to accomplish all that we do, and two"—I pause, watching the sweat slide down his face—"You're much too stupid to pull off such a stunt."

"Where are you taking me?" he whispers.

"Home. You'll be relieved of your duties as commissioner, of course, but there's no reason for us to dirty our hands with such unpleasant business."

We turn into his driveway. It's massive, not as large as the King estate but big enough to be ostentatious. Why he needs this much space when it's only him and his wife is beyond me. The lock thuds again, and he scrambles from the car, practically face-planting on the drive to get away from me. I reach over and pull the door shut, and we pull away slowly, heading for home.

He'll try to run—they all do. I wonder if he'll wait for his wife. He'll most likely try to leave her behind. Unfortunately, for him, his accounts have been frozen, and his cars have been disabled, so he'd be running on foot, if he could get that far. I wake my tablet and swipe on his security system, remotely watching as he sets the alarm. A few taps later, and it's turned against him, imprisoning him inside the house. Guess he won't be going on foot, either.

Another tap and Shane's face fills the screen, Emma in the background, stuffing her face with food. He walks out the back door and into the backyard.

"Is it done?"

I tilt my head, studying him, before answering. "Not quite. He's sequestered in his house for now. He's quite jumpy, but that's to be expected. I'd rather call in the Wraith, let them deal with him."

He nods, staring off screen. "Whatever you think is best. Check on his mistress, make sure she connects with Alex instead of running her mouth. I have a feeling Alan has been a little rough with his hands for a lot longer than just tonight."

"Do you have any more questions for Alan before they dispose of him?"

"I'm sure it'll be a bunch of begging. I don't like using the Wraith. I like to know who we're working with. Are you sure you can't ferret out their identity?" Shane asks, and I sigh, resigning myself to repeating this conversation every time I want to hire the assassin to do our dirty work.

"Shane, there are some necessary evils in our world. One of them is the Wraith. No, I don't know who it is. No, I don't really care. They are discreet, capable, and they keep their mouth shut, which is why no one knows who they are. If they left a calling card, their cover would be blown. The only reason we know of them, is because we're the ones that hire whoever they are. Unless you'd rather I take care of this situation myself, and in that case, I'll need to know now. I need to change before dealing with him."

He sighs, glancing back at Emma. "No, call them in. The last thing we need is a trail back to us. You'll need to go back to the gala, though, make an appearance." I scowl, though he's right. Alibis need to be provided, which is exactly why we use the Wraith in the first place; although, I'm not sure how my showing my face at the gala will help in this case.

"Fine, but I'm not fucking staying," I grumble. I hang up and slide down the glass, telling the driver the change of plans.

Ten minutes later, we pull up to the center. I didn't want to come in the first place, but we always need another route away from events like these. I straighten my jacket when I step out. Thankfully, most of the cameras are gone, but I duck my head anyway, striding for the doors. I swing them open, stepping into the brightly lit foyer. Dinner must have started, since the space is almost empty. I take a step when a hand on my arm has me jerking to a stop.

"Sir, do you have an invite"—the lady's face pales when I turn to her—"Mr. King, I'm sorry. I didn't recognize you. Did you need a seat? We'll get one for you right away." She gestures behind her at another worker, who steps back, panic on his face.

"That won't be necessary," I say, peeling her fingers from my arm. I keep walking, leaving behind the frantic whispers.

I slip through the main room's doors, the sound of cutlery grating my already frayed nerves. At least I'll get a meal out of this fiasco. A hundred people laughing and chatting overwhelms the space, making it hard to think. Alex is waving a fork around, laughing with the man next to him. Eyes follow me as I slip around the perimeter, skirting the tables, and slip in Shane's seat.

"Mr. King," the waiter says, placing a salad in front of me.

"Ren! When did you come in?" Alex booms, looking around, as if I've left a trail of destruction behind me.

"Shane suggested I attend, since something came up for him." I explain more for the guests' benefits.

He leans in. "The salad has walnuts and raisins in it."

I push it away, trying to keep the disgust from my face. The conversation around our table starts again, and I ignore the woman's suggestive glances, who's seated next to me.

"Did you see the hippo?" Alex asks, grinning.

"Hippo?"

"It's huge and golden. I'm going to buy it. Did you know hippos can't swim?" Alex smiles over the lip of his glass at the server, and she giggles.

"You're not going to bid on it. Where the hell would we put it?" I grumble, scanning the guests. Most are absorbed in their own conversations, but a few glance at us, their gaze skipping away when they meet my eyes.

"Oh, it'll be a gift. Don't get your panties in a twist. Interesting view on the east side of the ballroom," he comments, turning to engage the man next to him again while I zero in on where he's directed me.

Across the room, as far from us as possible, is the Byrns clan. I recognize Mason and Colin, but I almost skip over the woman seated between them, giggling at Colin, who's whispering in her ear. I haven't seen Samantha Byrns since we were kids, growing up in the same world but eons a part.

The memory of her tiny hand in mine makes my palm tingle. She helped me once, long ago, when I was hiding from my father. I shake the vision away. It was so long ago she probably wouldn't remember. I don't know why I do. Apparently, she grew up to be a socialite, so I never had the desire to meet her again. As I stare at her, though, her face drops, the dopey smile disappears, and her shoulders droop. Someone catches her attention, and the smile reappears but doesn't quite meet her eyes.

"Ren, maybe don't stare at Byrns's sister?" Alex mutters out the corner of his mouth.

I tear my eyes away, but not before she looks up, locking eyes with me. She whips back to her brother, cheeks flushed.

Interesting.

FOUR

SAMANTHA

I shuck off my dress, and it pools at my feet. I should hang it up, but I kick it into my closet instead. I'll deal with it tomorrow. Tonight was exhausting. Mason was in a mood all night after he spoke to whoever he cornered in the alcove. He also refused to tell me who it was, but I have a feeling it was Shane King. Colin tried to run interference, tugging me away every time we crossed paths with any of them—not that Shane stuck around. A rattling pulls me out of my head, forcing me to stop reliving the night. I grab my phone, but the screen is dark.

"Shit," I mutter, yanking open my bedside drawer and grabbing my other phone out. The last couple weeks have been weird, making me scatterbrained, and I keep forgetting to put it back. I never know who's going to go through my shit thinking I won't notice. The phone buzzes again, and I swipe it, putting in the metrics, which feels a little like hacking. Although, I have no idea how any of it actually works.

I chuckle when the messages pop up. I never know who is actually texting me, unless they're dumb enough to leave a name, but this guy is a repeat customer. He's always proper, giving me a bullet-point list of the reasons behind the hit, as if he's trying to convince me to take the job, before finally sending the name. I never answer, since that would be stupid, but he always leaves a riddle at the end. I showed the first one to Mason, but he didn't get it.

How many surrealists does it take to screw in a light bulb?

I tug my lip between my teeth, closing my eyes, and it comes to me. My finger itches to answer, but I sigh and grin at the screen. He'll send me the answer tomorrow, after the job is finished and the news hits the media. The money goes to another account, but the answers to his riddles feel like something just for me. My feet catch on the discarded dress when I walk into my closet. I kick it aside, slipping the phone into the hidden compartment. I pause, pressing my lips together, and snatch it out again before getting dressed and slipping it in my pocket. I'm pulling on a shoe when a knock on my door has me poking my head out of my closet.

"Sammy?" Mason pops his head in, scanning the room for me.

"What's up?" I shuffle to the bed and sit to slip the other ballet flat on.

"Got a job?" He closes the door before leaning against it.

"Yeah, came through, urgent for tonight. You heard about shit going down with the police commissioner?"

He ducks his head. "Yeah, I heard a little something about him. This a scare tactic? Or a full recall?"

"Full recall. I'll try to get some info, but I think he's already paranoid, so I probably won't get much." I wait, but he stares at his feet.

"I don't have to remind you to not tell anyone you're the Wraith, right?" he says, raising his head.

I jerk back. "Uh, no. I've been the Wraith for what, four, five years? I'm pretty sure I know the rules by now."

"I'm worried. Things feel weird around here, don't they?"

It's been years since my brother and I have talked like this. He usually goes to Colin when he gets like this. I've stumbled on them tucked away somewhere in the mansion, muttering about this or that, but he never comes to me anymore. It stung at first, but I'm used to it now. It doesn't make him any less of a brother or my friend.

"Something feels off, but I can't figure out what it is. I thought it was just me. Is anything coming up? Something big?" I ask.

His eyes flash, but he looks away before I can decipher the emotion swimming in his eyes. "I'm sure it's nothing. Listen, tonight is different. The commissioner lives in King territory. Remember to stay away from their estate. They especially can't know what you do after dark."

I scowl. "Why are you lecturing me about this shit? I've followed your rules, even though I think they're ridiculous. Stop babying me, Mason."

"Don't cross them, Sam, it's not worth it." He pauses until I nod before saying, "You got all your gear? His house is alarmed, so you'll have to deal with that. Don't forget your training. And for fuck's sake, don't take off your mask, even when you're in his house, not until you get home. Take the long way."

"Oh my god, Mason, I have done this before. Stop, before you induce a fit or something." I flip the lock on my window, making sure it's unlocked before going to the false panel by my closet. It clicks and pops open, revealing a dark landing and stairs leading down. "Close the door after me?"

"Sure, Sammy. Love you." His face disappears as he shuts the wall, but I'm frozen.

"Love you," I whisper into the blackness, knowing he won't hear me.

The trip through the tunnels is long and boring. I've made this trek so many times I don't register the twists and turns. I only stop once, grabbing the bag I've stashed down here to slip the various weapons and gadgets into the many pockets and sleeves in my clothes. The night air is crisp, promising fall around the corner, but it's still warm enough I'm sweating by the time I'm half a mile from home. The lots out here are huge, spanning several blocks, and it feels like I haven't made it anywhere when the trees fall away and the slightly pricier homes take over. Everything is quiet, most houses are dark. This is my favorite time of night, and I take my time. The commissioner isn't going anywhere, and I need this. I could take a car, but walking is easier. Less eyes and no witnesses.

I skip through a park, startling some animal who rushes off into the bushes. The streets change again, giving way to boutiques and shops, long since closed. I take the alley behind the coffee shop that always gets my order wrong and time myself racing across the street to a small two-story building. I skip up the fire escape stairs, the metal rattling through the night. I burst through the apartment's back door turned waystation. Four guns are pointed at me, but I clap before spreading my arms wide and grinning.

"Hello, boys! Miss me?"

"For fuck's sake, Sam, stop fucking doing that. One of these days, we're going to shoot you and then your brother will burn the city to the goddamn ground," TJ grumbles, tucking his gun away.

"Aw, don't be salty, TJ. I need some way to keep you on your toes, don't I?" I settle in the chair, watching one of the new kids deal the cards.

"What are you doing here? Pretending you're a ninja again?" he grumbles, his face souring when he looks at his hand. If he only knew.

"I had an errand to run. Thought I'd see if you guys needed anything before tomorrow." I study their faces, but I can't read TJ. He's still trim, though he's pushing fifty. I've never understood why he didn't demand a higher position when my dad died, but he said he was content running his area. I've known him most of my life. His territory is one of the few places where I don't need to put on an act. He wouldn't believe me if I giggled at him anyway.

"We're all set. Not our first rodeo. Well, for most of us." He eyes the newbie, who almost drops the deck, flushing as he shuffles again.

"Okay, got any water in this place or is it all whiskey?" I spin and open the fridge before grabbing a bottle out of the door. "Welp, see you boys later."

"Stay out of trouble, Sam," he says, raising an eyebrow at me.

I grin, slipping out the door again.

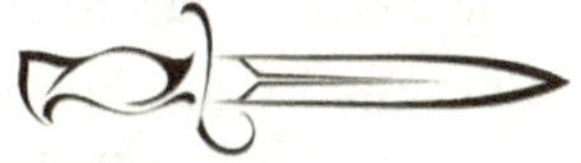

I'm huffing by the time I make it over the bridge to the west side of Synd. Usually, I detour through the Barrens, but after spending the night in heels, my ankles are throbbing. I'm cursing myself for taking this job, but if the commissioner really has been embezzling money, among other things, he needs to go. Mason didn't mention who would be installing a new one, but I bet the Kings will. I think it's their turn, but I can never remember; they leave me out of those meetings.

The commissioner's house is uppity. I'm staring at it from the tree line, and there's no other way to describe it. I swear I saw a peacock in the back. The windows are shaped like bullets, but I don't know if he put them in or if it was some crazy ass architect. I slip the mask over my face. I hate wearing it, but it keeps me anonymous. I skirt the yard, trying to assess whether to climb to the roof. There's a balcony hanging off the side of the house in a triangle, which doesn't seem very practical, but what do I know?

Halfway across the yard, I stumble into a divot in the grass, and I fall to my knees, the dew from the grass soaking into my leggings. Of course, I would trip. At least I didn't put a hole in my pants or get blood everywhere. I get up, rub my knee, and keep moving. The drain pipe up ahead looks sturdy enough, so I latch on, shimmying up to the second story. The door is glass, but it's dark in the room beyond. It's also the size of a postcard. Whoever designed this house must have been high on something. I roll out the lock pick kit and get to work. The lock pops, thudding into the quiet, and I put the kit back. I almost open it and step through but jerk back, cursing myself. I grab my blocker, flipping the switch and waiting until it lights up. I grin, reveling in the fact that I'll be a ghost now. Another button and a faint beep from the security panel fades out.

I step in, expecting a bedroom, but it's bare. Not even a rug is on the hardwood floors to quiet my steps. I skip to the door, inching it open. Outside the room, the hallway is bright, lighting my way to wherever the commissioner is holed up. My eyes fall closed, and I listen for any movement, but it's silent until . . . a crash and a bellow. Someone is raging below me. I slide down the wood banister and almost spill onto the floor, but I land on my feet.

"You're a goddamn professional, Sam," I whisper, grinning.

I follow the sound of furniture bouncing off bulletproof glass to an office. Usually, I slide in, sneak up on whoever I've been hired to take out, and slip back out, but this one is personal. I've never liked Alan. He always thought my ass was a handhold for him. When the Kings made him commissioner, I told Mason it was a mistake, but he brushed off my concerns. Seems I was right all along. The sister in me wants to rub it in, but I remind myself I'm an adult.

"Mr. Commissioner, you are not having a good night, huh?" I call over his shouting, leaning against the door jamb. He spins, horror etched on his wrinkled face.

"No," he gasps, holding his hands in front of him as if that will somehow stop me.

"You have definitely put on some weight, Alan. How you pulled a wife and a mistress is beyond me. You've been busy banging two women and embezzling money and extorting from businesses, not to mention trying to facilitate a war between the two major crime syndicates in the city. Did you really think they wouldn't find out?"

He blanches, a drop of sweat rolls down his face, dripping off his chin. He morphs before my eyes, going from pathetic and scared to drawing himself up to all five foot eight inches. He squares his shoulders and steps forward, wagging a finger at me. Thankfully, a desk sits between us. I'm pretty sure I can outrun this portly fellow if need be, but I don't fancy running after falling in the yard. My knee twinges at the thought. He'll brandish a weapon when he figures out he's not getting out alive.

"You're just a girl. Here, I thought the Wraith would be scary, but you're not him, are you? Why don't you run home, go play with your dolls? How did you even get in here?" His eyes whip back and forth at the cameras, but he doesn't know I've turned them off. I roll my eyes, though he can't see me. My lashes brush against the fabric, and I suppress a shudder. I hate wearing this thing.

"I came down in a bubble," I deadpan. They never believe I'm the Wraith. It's annoying. It's insulting.

"Go home, little girl, before I shoot you. You're breaking and entering. That's a felony."

"Why the fuck can't a girl be the Wraith? We're just as capable, if not more so, than a man." I throw my hands in the air and shake my head, leaning against the wall.

I should have kept that to myself. Mason was right, something is off lately. I'm off. Now isn't the time to have an existential crisis. Alan laughs, tipping his head back, turning back to the window to try to get out.

I'm thoroughly done with this night. It's gone to hell in a handbasket. I didn't want to do this anyway. I just want to put on my sweatpants and eat popcorn and watch some reality show where everyone ends up screaming at each other.

"All right, anything you want to tell me? Would you like to brag or go on a rant or something?" I slide my gun out, flipping off the safety, then look up.

He's focused on the window. I'm still debating whether I should make it look like a break-in or just a man pushed too far over the edge when his transgressions caught up with him, when a beep comes from above me. My head snaps up, and I eye the camera that's now panning back and forth, settling on the commissioner.

What. The. Fuck.

Alan whips around, narrowing his eyes on me, then he sees the gun in my hand. I lift my weapon and pull the trigger, cutting off his shout when the bullet hits him in the neck, ripping through his jugular. Blood spurts out, and while it wasn't where I wanted to shoot him, at least I hit the artery. This is where I gather most of my information, in those two to five minutes before they bleed out, but there's no way I'm moving from my spot. The live camera above me is freaking me out. Jammers aren't perfect, but I've never had a problem before.

Alan drops to his knees, pressing a blood-soaked hand to his wound. I can barely see him over the desk, but he's fumbling with something I can't see, even on my tiptoes. He can't call the police, which is ironic. I snort, which turns to a cough when the barrel of a gun rests on the desk. He's fighting to keep it steady; determination blazes in his glassy eyes. I crash to my knees, the sharp report ringing out. I don't know how he managed it, but the bullet is buried in the wall, right where my head was a second before.

I crab walk back through the door, away from him, who still looks intent on shooting me. I can't blame him. I glance up at the camera in the corner of the hall. It doesn't move, and I sigh but then it pings and swivels toward me slowly.

"You have got to be fucking kidding me," I mutter. Another shot rings out, but I'm through the door, and I doubt he'll be able to give chase.

I scramble around, crawling under the camera before it can get me in its sights. This house has so many goddamn cameras the chances of getting out without be spotted will be almost impossible. I settle for crawling. I can't stage the rest of the house, but Alan's tirade will have to be enough. I hate leaving things half done, but I'd rather have an unsolved case than be caught.

I drag myself around a door frame, peeking up to find the cameras in the room. There's one still frozen camera. I leap up and sprint for the window nestled between two alcoves in a library. I grab the jammer again, trying to figure out which button to hit or switch to flip or dial to twist to get this damn thing open.

A beep behind me sounds out, and my breathing shallows. I jam my fingers to hit anything I can, hoping one of them gets me out of here. I swear I can hear the camera panning slowly, searching for me. I shove the jammer into my waistband and grab my gun, smashing the butt of it against the lock over and over until it gives way. A sob of relief escapes me, and I burst into the night, cold wind zinging through me as I fall off the sill. After scrambling to my feet, I sprint for the trees, thanking whoever is watching over me I was able to get out.

The darkness swallows me as I stumble into the trees, then hang on to a trunk, trying to catch my breath. I gaze back at the house, still and silent. I'm already making up excuses in my head for when Mason asks how it went. It wouldn't be the end of the world if someone saw me, since I'm masked, but the thought of someone having proof I exist sends a shiver down my spine.

Who the hell hacked the cameras? The only person who knew I would be here is Mason and the person who hired me. My phone buzzes, and I pull it out, scowling when I read the riddle.

How many surrealists does it take to change a light bulb?

Fish.

FIVE

ALEX

Four in the morning is a terrible time to be awake. I keep my eyes fixed on the ceiling, counting the shadows over and over. My door slamming open doesn't even make me flinch. Rolling my head to the side, I see Ren framing the doorway.

"What?" I grunt.

"Got something for you to watch," he says, striding to my bedside and handing me his tablet. I pull up to lean against my headboard while he settles at the table by my window, tapping away on his leg.

"You good?" I ask.

He nods at the device in my hands before gazing out the window. This isn't anything new for him. Shane is the only one in the house who has a regular sleep schedule—well, him and Emma, but even his is fucked up most nights. The video starts, but it's grainy, like the camera it was pulled from is old. A figure trips on a lawn, then blackness.

"Uh, so you caught a ninja?"

"Keep watching," he mutters.

The screen lights up again, the police commissioner filling the screen, fixed on something below the camera, yelling incoherently and then a gunshot ricochets, then blood seeps from his neck. He falls to his knees, a gun, another shot, and the camera moves. The screen goes black again, then shows a hallway. Again, blackness, and a new angle in a dark room. The figure is hunched over something, then they bang the butt of their gun on the window lock until it pops open. This ninja isn't very good, tumbling out the window and fleeing into the night.

"What did I just watch?" I turn to him, baffled.

"I believe that was the Wraith."

He keeps staring into the darkness, fingers still drumming against his leg. "No way. The Wraith is like, badass. That person was—"

"Frantic. I believe that was my fault." He looks at me, but I can't read his face in the muted light.

"What do you mean?"

"I was curious. Shane questioned why we use them, how we don't know who they are, and I wondered if I could figure it out. So, I hacked the cameras. It took some time, but I was able to. I believe I wouldn't even have that, had the cameras been stationary. Someone trying to identify the Wraith would certainly make them nervous. I did . . ." He clears his throat, cracking his knuckles one at a time. "I made a mistake."

"Like an actual mistake? Or a Ren mistake?" I give him a look, and he scowls.

"I'm not sure," he admits.

"All right, what was the mistake?"

"They weren't able to get the window open. I didn't . . . I couldn't . . ." He shakes his head, surging to his feet and pacing back and forth. I let him go, waiting for the eventual slowdown in his steps. When he stops, his head hanging, I wave my hand for him to continue.

"I opened it for them," he mutters.

I hum. "Well, that seems like a Ren mistake. So, you got them out? Who cares? No one knows. Not like the commissioner will discover it;

he's dead. I'm not going to tell anyone. I'm guessing you're not going to tell anyone. Even if someone did find out, would they care?"

"They'd know we're in league with the Wraith. Not only that, but the Wraith knows. I might have exposed myself."

"Like you flashed them?" I chuckle, imagining Ren in a trench coat and bowler hat.

"Fucker. No, they know I'm the one who was looking for them. They'll put together I helped them."

"Okay, but the Wraith doesn't know you're you. Wait, how will they know you're the one who helped? How did you"—I swallow a snicker—"expose yourself?" Ren goes back to pacing, but he's shoved his hands in his pockets. Of course, he's still fully dressed at four in the fucking morning. Weirdo.

"I send them a riddle every time I hire them. The answer comes when the job is done. I may have sent the answer earlier this time."

I press my lips together, trying not to cackle. Leave it to Ren to add some weird shit onto what should be a simple job. He glares when he spots my smile.

"Dude, I have one question," I say, wiping the grin from my face, "Why?"

"The first time we hired the Wraith I might have been drunk, and it slipped. Then I felt like I had to continue." He groans, scrubbing his hands over his face. "It's fucked up. I know, but there's nothing I can do about it now. I need to know the fallout from this. Then I can handle it."

"No fallout. There's literally nothing wrong with them knowing you helped. If anything, it'll make shit better. Maybe they'll give us a discount."

"Fine, but I'm not telling Shane, so keep your fucking mouth shut."

"Tell me what?" Shane asks, strolling through the open door, still dressed in his tux.

"About the sleepover. Did you bring your pajamas?" I laugh.

He rolls his eyes. "Listen, I need you to go meet with Todd Munther tomorrow. Early."

"The assistant police commissioner? Tell me we're not putting him in charge," I demand.

Shane's head snaps up from his phone. "What do you mean?"

"He's dumb. Like, real dumb."

"Alex is right, he's not very bright. He blew up the microwave at the main office by leaving a spoon in it," Ren says, grabbing the tablet from where I tossed it on my covers.

"A lot of people make that mistake," Shane responds, but he doesn't look convinced.

"Five times," Ren deadpans.

"Let me talk to a few people, see where we can slot someone in. There's not many who want the job nowadays, and we need someone who won't get in our way. Apparently, going through three commissioners in two years is a little dodgy."

I lean back, closing my eyes. I'm tired now, but if Shane wants me on this early, I don't think I'll get much sleep. Maybe I can nap later. Samantha Byrns in that purple dress dances behind my eyelids. It was the first time I'd met her, but after all the articles on her, highlighting the belle of the ball, I felt like I knew her. I was wrong. She played the part well, but she slipped. The exhaustion in the slump of her shoulders, the tired look when she thought no one was paying attention, the glint in her eye when she snapped back at me, the ring of sarcasm in her voice points to someone who is a very good actress. I even caught her scratching her back with a butter knife. I grin, eyes still closed.

"Alex"—Shane's annoyed voice breaks my thoughts—"I need you to check on the southside. The gang down there said something about a shipment not being right. And you've got that lunch with Greggers."

"I don't have a lunch with Greggers. You have a lunch with Greggers. You're not pawning him off on me. He's insufferable, and I'm not putting up with his bullshit anymore. I say cut his ass loose. He doesn't do shit for us anymore," I mumble, wishing they'd get the fuck out.

"I agree. He's become an annoyance I'd rather not deal with anymore," Ren chimes in, striding for the door.

"Where the hell are you going, asshole?" Shane calls at his retreating back.

"I'm going to bed."

I sigh. "Get the fuck out, Shane. Go to bed. We're not going to solve all our problems tonight."

"We still need to talk about the Byrns princess."

"No, we don't. If you want to be obsessed with her, go right ahead, but there's no way we're getting close to her with Mason standing directly in between us and her." I peek at him, his face morphing from denial to frustration.

"I don't want to get close to her, but there's something about her . . ."

"Well, why don't you go to your own room and contemplate that? I'm going to sleep."

I shuffle down, flipping on my side, and he grumbles, shutting the door behind him. I'll get a solid three hours if Emma doesn't bust down the hall, banging on every door like she does most days. I sigh, pushing away all the shit I have to do tomorrow.

A crash startles me awake hours later. I grab my phone, groaning, when another boom echoes outside my door.

"I swear to fucking god, Emma, I'm going to throw you out the fucking window!" Shane's voice thunders. Emma giggles and her footsteps fade.

I drag myself to the bathroom, knowing I won't get back to sleep now. Twenty minutes later, I walk into the kitchen, where Shane is still lecturing Emma about respect and not waking the whole damn house up. Ren is leaning against the counter, sipping from a mug, looking all sorts of fucked up.

"Give it a rest, Shane. She's not even listening to you," he grumbles.

Her eyes widen, tucking away the phone stashed in her lap. "I'm going to school. Love you!" She skips out, grabbing her backpack by the door.

"She's going to be the death of me," Shane mutters, laying his head on the table.

"She's thirteen. She's going to be the death of all of us," I joke, pulling open the fridge.

"Wraith did the job last night. How much did that cost us?"

"Enough," Ren answers. "Anything new from Helms?"

"No, he won't answer me. Something is going down around here, but I can't figure out what it is. Anything you've come across recently?" Shane turns to me, raising an eyebrow.

I glance at Ren, but he's no help. "Uh, what exactly am I supposed to be looking for?"

"Anything unusual. I can feel something coming, but I can't put my finger on it."

"That's not vague at all. I have no idea what I could even point to, other than the shit with Helms, which I'm not dealing with."

He scowls, pulling out his phone and shooting off a text. Shane doesn't usually worry about shit like this. He lets me deal with those things, but his gut is rarely wrong. I'm staring at the milk carton in my hand, contemplating whether I have enough time to eat cereal, but Ren leans in, raising an eyebrow.

"What?" I shove it back in and slam the door shut before grabbing an apple.

"You're going to be late."

"No, I won't. I don't have to be there for"—I check my watch—"Shit."

"Don't fuck it up," Shane calls, laughter chasing me to the door.

"Tell Mason to say hi to his sister for me." I shout back, ducking as he throws an apple at my head, laughing as I leave to go ruffle some more feathers in our city.

The drive through the early morning is tedious, traffic seeming to appear out of nowhere. I spend the time noting shit Shane's piled on my plate in the last couple days. I'm late to the restaurant. Waving to the hostess, who giggles as I pass, I spot Munther in the back, pulling at his collar. Even across the room, I can see the sweat dotting his forehead. I slide in the booth as his head is craned over his shoulder, and he jumps, smacking his knees on the table and upsetting the salt. I set it upright before throwing a pinch over my left shoulder. Smirking at the distraught man, I fold my hands on the table.

"Todd, you seem upset."

He snatches a napkin and mops his brow before leaning in and whispering, "King, what the hell is going on? Is Alan really dead? They're saying he offed himself, but I spoke with him yesterday, and he seemed fine."

My eyes wander to the server lingering out of earshot, shooting glances at us. I nod, and he nods back, hurrying off to put in my order. Thank god Shane picked a restaurant where they know me. I debate how much to reveal, how much I need to play into the part the King organization expects of me.

"Alan was troubled, but he tried to hide behind many things, including taking things that weren't his. In any case, we're in need of a new police commissioner. We'd appreciate your input on who you believe would be best suited for the position."

He sucks in a breath, nodding. "Of course. I mean, not a lot of people are clamoring for the job. People are seeing it as a death sentence now."

Exactly what I told Shane. We might be forced to put this dumbass in Alan's place. A commotion at the door has me turning, but all I can see is a gaggle of people blocking the view. The manager rushes by our table, and I track him. It would be just my luck if Mason Byrns came in right now. My eyes bug out when Samantha Byrns slips through, yanking the sunglasses off her face, turning a dazzling smile at the manager, who looks to be gushing over her. Her hand flits out, waving away whatever he's saying, and her tinkling laugh floats over the din of other customers. It sounds forced, brittle. She disappears, following the manager up the stairs, but my eyes are fixed, lost in my thoughts.

Todd clears his throat, drawing my attention back, and I raise my eyebrow, watching him blanch, the blotchy redness draining from his face. Most people think I'm the nice one, the one they want to deal with, the one they think will help them when faced with Shane's wrath. But every once in a while, I remind them who I can be if they push me too far.

"Todd, let me get this straight. You've been the assistant commissioner for seven months now, involved in a lot of dealings, working with a lot of people, and you can't think of anyone who would like to step in to the position of police commissioner?"

"Uh, well, I mean . . . I'm sure I could come up with someone. Maybe," he says, pulling at his collar again.

"See that you do," I reply. The server sets a plate of food in front of me. I unwrap the silverware before pulling out my phone but glance up when the other man doesn't move. "You can go."

He scrambles up, tripping over his feet, upsetting the salt again. I tip more salt over my shoulder and dig into my meal before shooting off a text to Shane. My screen lights up, a string of curses fill the preview, but I ignore him. I knew he wouldn't be happy, but there's no way we're putting Todd in the position. I scroll through the headlines, seeing a new post from this morning, a picture of the restaurant I'm currently in, with Samantha Byrns front and center. Vultures. Every last one of them. I shake my head, killing the screen and shoveling the eggs into my mouth.

I have half an idea to go upstairs and slip in a seat next to her to mess with everyone's favorite socialite some more, but I dismiss the idea. Chances are, someone would take a picture, and there'd be hell to pay. My phone lights up again, Ren's name flashing across the screen, and I answer it.

"Shane is not going to be very happy with you when you arrive home, Alex."

"I'm not putting Todd fucking Munther in the position. We would be putting out more fires than it's worth," I grumble before stuffing a piece of toast in my mouth. I glance up, catching the server's eye, and he hops into action, an orange juice appearing before Ren answers. They don't usually do such simple food at this place, going for fancy shit, but thankfully, I've been friends with the chef here for years.

"Not the problem. Did you see her?"

"Samantha Byrns? Yeah, she came in a little after I did. Went upstairs. Why?"

"And did you see the article?"

I drain half the glass before answering. "I saw the picture. Would you get to the fucking point?"

"Read the article, dumbass. And get home before you piss him off more."

He hangs up, and I pull a face at my phone. Fucker. I still do as he said, reading the article quickly and then rereading. Goddammit, someone saw me come in. Thank god there's not a photo, but still. Now I'm linked to Mason Byrns's sister.

Shane is going to fucking kill me.

SAMANTHA

I don't want to be stuffed in the back of a car with my brother, going to a meeting I didn't want to go to in the first place, in a too-short dress and a knife strapped to my thigh. Unfortunately, I didn't have a choice. Usually, Mason lets me do my own thing, flitting in and out of the darkness as the Wraith, taking out enemies and ferreting out rogue secrets for our family. But tonight, he said he needed me. I don't know which face to wear, though: the mindless social climber or the secret assassin or just Sam—not that I know who that really is these days. All my identities are mixing together. I don't recognize the woman in the mirror most mornings.

I'm not going to lie, knowing he wants me at this meeting makes my heart leap. Whenever I give him advice on how to run things around here, he tells me I should keep my opinions to myself. The first time, he said it was like a stab to the gut. He's repeated the words enough now only a dull ache vibrates through my chest these days. No point wasting my breath when no one cares enough to listen.

I love my brother, and he's loads better than other men in his position, but I'm still a woman and his little sister to boot. It doesn't afford me much say in the way he runs the east side of Synd. It bothered me when I was younger, but now, I do what I want and ask forgiveness later, which Mason rails against, but he always lets me off the hook.

The last couple days, though, have been rough with him. First, the gala, where the stick was so far up his ass I swear he developed a hernia. Then my itsy-bitsy, tiny mistake on the job with the police commissioner, followed closely by the article insinuating Alex King and I were secretly meeting for breakfast. Mason tried to shut the rumors down, but him stepping in only made it worse. Now, apparently, Alex and I are secretly married with a love child or something. I stopped reading them, which doesn't stop Colin from teasing me every time we cross paths.

"Who are we meeting again?" I interrupt his tirade about the latest fuck-up our uncle got us into.

Mason sighs. "Ryker Helms. He's Prez for the MC in the north."

"I know who Ryker Helms is"—I roll my eyes, then glance at him—"I also worked out that he never takes meetings with any of the gangs in Synd. So, why is he suddenly keen on meeting us?"

"No idea. Maybe he's finally willing to play nice instead of lurking on the outskirts."

Mason shoves open the door and stalks to the restaurant. He doesn't wait for me, already shedding his big brother role and replacing it with ruthless leader of a crime family. Showing any type of deference to me only hurts us both in the end. I wish he would have told me how I'm supposed to act, though.

I keep my eyes on him as we make our way through the silent kitchen to the dining room. I don't bother scanning the space, seeing as how I scouted the place earlier. A restaurant isn't our usual place for meetings, my brother preferring the Depot for these types of things, along with a whole host of others. Inside the seating area are at least a dozen bikers lining the walls, all looking stereotypical in their patched leather jackets and tattoos.

Ryker is seated at a table in the middle of it all, eyes fixed on his phone. He glances up when we approach, and the chair scrapes across the wooden floor as he rises. He scans me and fixes his gaze on my brother, but in that second, his piercing blue eyes burrow into me, and I suppress a shiver. Ryker is only a couple years older than my own twenty-four years, but he radiates power. I'm sure he has no problem getting what he wants: women, deals, allegiances.

"Byrns." Ryker's voice vibrates through the space, deep and gruff as he nods to Mason and sinks back down.

"Helms." My brother nods back, pulling out a chair.

A hail of gunfire floods the space. Everyone in the room erupts: yelling, diving, drawing guns from concealed places. Tables are knocked over and used for cover as both the bikers and our guys return fire through the shattered front windows.

I'm frozen, though. I've been shot at before. Hell, I've been shot before. This is an ambush, though. A large hand jolts me out of my transfixed state, violently yanking me under the table. I have no time to school my features as I stare in horror at Ryker, who definitely just saved my life. His mouth is moving, but I can't hear him over the ringing in my ears.

"Gun! Do you have a gun!?" My hearing switches back on as he yells, squeezing my arm. I shake my head, unsure of what will come out if I open my mouth.

He shoves one in my hand and turns toward the fray. He fixes those blue eyes on mine over his shoulder and glares. "Just don't shoot me."

I nod again, even though he's turned back to the fight, shouting to his men. Muscle memory takes over, and my hands fly over the weapon, checking the magazine, and I search for a target. I can't make sense of who is on our side. Shadows race back and forth in the street, using cars for cover as they fire at us, sitting ducks in this room. I can find an exit, but I'm not leaving without my brother.

I glance behind me, trying to find Mason, but Ryker yanks me down again, a bullet hole right where my head was three seconds before. He eyes me, probably expecting me to freeze up again, but now, I'm pissed. Whoever the hell these people are have no idea what they've unleashed.

I brace my feet, grab Ryker's shoulder, and use him to launch up toward the low-hanging beams. I heave my body up and brace my feet to stand. I run along the wood, trying to get to the back door. If I can make it out the side exit, I can double back and flank them, making them scatter. I'm about to jump down when two silver canisters are chucked through the shattered window, pinging along and bouncing to a stop in the middle of the room.

"SMOKE!" One of the Reapers dives on top of them, trying to snatch them up and send them back from where they came. A gray cloud envelops him, sending the room into a chaos of shadows. Being above the worst of it, I see several shapes rushing the building. I plop down on the beam, wrapping my legs around it, and swing upside down, praying my legs won't give out. I hate shooting like this, but my training kicks in, and several men drop as they try to crawl through the window. They bolt to the pockmarked cars waiting across the street, peeling away as silence descends on us, a blanket thicker than the smoke bombs.

I wrap my arms around the beam, scooting until I'm on top of it again. I try to use my height to find my brother and the men we came with, but I only spot Ryker checking on his own men. Two of our guys are slumped against the wall, bullet holes through their heads, guns still strapped to their sides. They never stood a chance.

"Samantha," Colin, my brother's second calls from below. He cocks his head, confusion warring with concern in his eyes. He holds his arms up, helping me down. His face is bloody, but I can't find a wound on him.

"Where's Mason?" I ask, glancing through the smoke as the living check on the dead.

"He's not here." Colin won't look me in the eye, a pained expression on his face.

"What do you mean he isn't here? He wouldn't leave me."

"He got hit when it first started. I stuffed him in the car with Richie to take him to the hospital. I'm sorry, Sammy, but it's bad." Colin's eyes find me at last, lined with panic.

Numbness spreads through me as Ryker strides to us. Their voices rise and fall as my emotions float past, away from the pain and fear and doubt, until a single one remains: rage. Staring at the carnage around me, I wrap that fury around my heart, stoking the flames, letting the wrath feed my vengeance until it's honed into a sharp blade made of retribution and shadows.

SEVEN

SHANE

"Alex, what the fuck is going on?" I yell into the phone.

"I don't know yet. Some shit is going down on the Byrns' side. Stop fucking calling me!" He hangs up.

My phone pings over and over with incoming texts. Everyone from the new police commissioner to Big John down at the south warehouse is flooding my phone. I stride down the hall, taking the stairs two at a time. Emma steps out of her room, and I snag her arm, pushing her back in.

"Something's happening. Stay in your room." I signal Titus down the hall, and he jogs over. He's barely eighteen, but he's smart, which isn't always easy to find in our world. "Guard this door with your life."

He nods, nervously touching the gun tucked in the back of his pants, glancing at Emma. Her wide blue eyes meet mine, begging me for reassurance, but I don't have anything.

"You're not going to school tomorrow. I'll check on you later." I spin, intent on my office, when Emma calls for me. I peer over my shoulder.

"Love you," she mumbles, fear radiating from her.

"Love you, too, Emmie."

My phone is still going crazy when I reach my office. After I slam the door, it pops open, and Ren storms in. I collapse in my chair, tapping on my laptop to wake it up. The list of things I have to check to find out what the hell is going on grows each minute that passes, and I'm already exhausted.

"Tell me you've got something, Ren."

He falls in a chair and bounces his leg, eyes fixed on his own screen. He sets one tablet on his lap, phone in his hand, and another tablet makes its way to my desk.

"Ren," I bark.

"I don't have anything. Shut the fuck up."

I drum my fingers on the desk, silently cursing him and Alex. What's the point of having all this power if I can't find information when shit goes down? Scanning the headlines, it's all more of the same. A shootout on an empty restaurant. No one was inside, no one was injured. Something about a dispute with a customer. It's all bullshit. I scoff, closing the windows, then scroll through my texts. I latch on one from Quincy, our contact for the east side of the Barrens. He works for both the Kings and the Byrns', but he's an easy way to pass info to the other side of the river if need be.

Shit just got real.

I shoot off a message, asking for clarification. I throw my phone on the desk and lace my fingers behind my neck, waiting for his response.

"I think I got something. GSW came in to Memorial thirty-seven minutes ago. Critical. Entry in the head. Emergency surgery."

"Got a name?" I hold my breath, but he shakes his head, and I let it out with a whoosh. My eyes snap down when my phone vibrates.

Byrns shake up.

"Holy fuck," Ren mutters, his eyes meeting mine. "Mason Byrns was shot."

We sit in stunned silence for a whole minute, absorbing what this could mean for the city, for us. It's like the world stops for that one minute, and when time is up, we burst into action. I grab my phone, calling Alex. Ren is on the phone with his mysterious hacker, his fingers flying across the various screens in front of him.

"Alex, we need eyes down there. Now. Was anyone else killed we care about?"

"I don't know. I only heard about Byrns," he huffs. His pounding footsteps echo down the line.

"Find out who he was meeting. No way he was going for a late-night dinner. I'm assuming Colin is taking over while they figure out what the fuck is going on with Byrns," I bark.

"I know what to do, Shane. What do you want me to do about Samantha Byrns?"

"What the fuck do I care? Don't do anything with her. She's not our concern. Find out what the fuck went down and if it'll affect us. That's what I want to know, not which party Mason's sister was attending tonight."

I hang up before he can rile me up anymore. He's been bringing up Samantha more and more lately, ever since he distracted her while Mason and I spoke. I've been putting out fires since that fucking article about them came out. He's eating up the attention, but Alex doesn't have time for pampered princesses, so I don't know why he keeps pushing the subject. Ren's muttered curse has my eyes flying to him.

When he doesn't speak, I scowl. "Tell me what's going on, Ren."

"I can't pull the footage in that area. Someone is blocking it. I'll get Nemesis on it, but this doesn't feel like a random thing."

"You think it's another uprising?" I hold my breath, praying he dismisses my concerns. The coup ten years ago was bad; starting over again would be disastrous. At least now I have more experience, more loyalty than I did at eighteen, but it still would be a shitshow. I'd like to think we take care of our men and that they won't turn on us like the lower gangs did to my father, but there's always the possibility. I still don't know how I was able to pull off taking over and getting us back to where we were. I would have failed had it not been for Alex and Ren backing me up. Mason's ability to build the Byrns' family back with little support was impressive. With him out of the picture, at least for the moment, I'll have even more on my plate.

"It could be, but it might be an isolated incident. We'll have to wait and see. Alex will be able to find answers more than I will. Shane, this could be bad for us. We should double down. Make it clear we're not behind this, and our side of the river is secure."

"The media will say whatever they want. Right now, they're reporting it as a disgruntled customer." I click through the headlines again. "Nothing about Byrns being hit. I'm calling Helms."

"He could be behind this." Ren eyes me, and I pause.

I shake my head, saying, "No. Why would Helms try to take out Byrns? It makes no sense."

"It's a little curious after so long, with minimal contact with us, Ryker Helms, president of the Reapers, reaches out to both Byrns and us for a meeting. Not together but separately. I don't want to think it's him, either, but we have to be prepared for anything." My phone rings, and I snatch it up.

"Alex." I put it on speaker, setting it on the desk.

"Ryker Helms and Mason Byrns were meeting at the restaurant. Quite a few men were lost on both sides. Helms disappeared, but I'm assuming he's back in the Reapers' territory. Colin Ashford was there . . . and Samantha Byrns."

"Is Colin in charge? I need to talk to him. We need to bury any rumors that we're behind this."

"I still don't know. He's at the hospital with Samantha. They've got the place locked down. No way I'm getting in there. I'm going to see the new commissioner and tell him to keep his fucking mouth shut. Last thing we need is it leaking Byrns is in the hospital." A shout on his end has him cursing, and he hangs up.

"I hate when he does that," I mutter.

"I imagine he'd stop if you wouldn't bother him so much with things he already knows to do."

I glare at him, but he doesn't look up. My phone buzzes again, and a sigh escapes me. The last thing I want to do is speak to the mayor, but I know he'll keep calling regardless of whether I answer.

"Jamison, I don't have long, so get to the point," I snap.

"What the fuck is going on, King? I'm getting people calling me, and I don't know what to tell them." He honestly sounds like he's about to cry.

"We'll inform you when we want to, Jamison. Now isn't the time to think you're in charge here. If you want to keep your job, you'll remember that."

"Are you threatening me?" I roll my eyes at the indignation in his voice.

"If I wanted to threaten you, I'd put Ren on the phone. The fact that you're talking to me should be your first clue. Don't push me, Connor. You're on thin ice already with that stunt you pulled at the gala," I snarl, remembering the bullshit Alex told me he spewed.

"Well, reporters are calling my office. My assistant keeps telling me they're saying you took out Byrns. I just need—"

"We had nothing to do with this. If you push the line that we did, I'll personally see to it we have a new mayor before the night is out," I state, then hang up.

I pace to the window, unable to sit still. Lately, things have been off, just a subtle shifting in the air. I've tried to keep the feeling of walking along a knife's edge to myself, but with Mason going down and a possible regime change on the horizon, I wonder if this is the end of our problems or just the beginning.

"Ren, keep an eye out for Emma. I have a feeling this whole shitshow is going to become a major problem," I murmur, staring out the window.

"I can only do so much, Shane. I'm one person."

I glare over my shoulder at him until he nods. I trust he'll take care of Emma like I would. As much as she's my younger sister, she's theirs, too.

She might not always appreciate having three older brothers watching out for her, keeping her in line, but at some point, it will probably save her life, or at the very least keep her out of the trouble we got up to when we were her age.

"I've got something," he says, breaking into my thoughts. "The cameras around the area were blocked, but I got footage from the hospital. It's not much, but it was Mason. He's out of surgery. Looks like they induced a coma. There's nothing from the Byrns' side, though."

"At least we've got confirmation it was actually him. Anything on Colin? I'll need to talk to him as soon as possible. The last thing we need is for them to blame us." I turn back to the window, watching the men around the property double while Ren and I find answers.

"I doubt they will. There's no evidence to suggest we were at fault. No disputes to point to. If anything, we've been more friendly lately. The gala alone should point to our innocence in this."

Ren never did understand the politics behind things. He likes things black and white, with clear lines and definitions. He's great at being rational, but he doesn't understand emotions very well. This is why Alex does most of the glad-handing within the community. With his ever-present grin, people feel much safer revealing things to him rather than Ren or myself. The only reason I get information is because of my position. Ren forces information from the mouths of those who don't want to spill their secrets.

"Some people won't care about those things. The media will point fingers at us when they find out Mason is no longer running things on the east side," I explain, though I doubt he cares.

"We should reach out to some of our other contacts."

"I've reached out to everyone I trust to talk to right now. Alex is dealing with the community. You've got Nemesis. I don't know who else we could possibly call." I swing around, collapsing back in my chair, pinching the bridge of my nose.

"We should reach out to the Wraith."

I groan, not wanting to have another conversation about the psychopath Ren insists on using for jobs we don't want to be tied to. Rationally, I understand the reasoning behind why, but I hate using them. Not knowing who I'm working with rubs me the wrong way. I don't know why Ren is okay with it. He's the one who usually can't stand not having all the information before he dives in to something.

"Why?" I resign myself to at least hearing him out. As much as I hate using the assassin, we've never had problems. They get results, even if we don't know who they are, and they never ask questions. I don't think they know who we are, either.

"They run in the shadows, so it stands to reason anything going down there they would know about," he explains slowly, like I won't understand him if he rushes his words.

"Fine," I snap, "But don't be surprised when you don't get an answer."

He already has his phone unlocked, swiping at the screen, brows pulled low. He blows out a breath, then balances the device on the edge of my desk, eyes fixed on the darkened screen. We sit in silence, with only the occasional buzzing from my phone, which we ignore, waiting for the phone to do something. After a couple minutes, I give up, pulling my phone out to read through my own messages and checking the media sites again. Ren waits another minute but goes back to his tablet.

An hour passes, with both of us lost in gathering more information and connecting with people all over the city. An informant tells me Helms put the Reaper's territory into lockdown, no one in or out. Ren gets a cryptic message from some low-level dealer from the Barrens about an increase in activity. Alex calls once, twice, three times, before he finally says he's coming home, then leaves again just as quickly.

"What did you even say to the Wraith?" I break the silence, scanning the headlines yet again, with no change.

"I asked what the fallout would be if Mason Byrns dies." My whip my head up, eyeing him.

"What the fuck did you ask that for? I thought you were going to ask about who did it or something we could actually use."

"I have a theory," he says, and I know I won't get more until he's worked through it, solved whatever hunch he has brewing in his mind.

I scowl, turning back to the computer. A tentative knock rings out. Ren leans back, flips the lock, and opens the door. Emma pokes her head in, concern glazing her eyes. I try to smooth out my face, but the wince she flashes tells me I didn't succeed.

"Emma, you should be in bed. It's late," I murmur, coming around the desk and wrapping an arm around her shoulder.

"I heard something, but I don't want you to be mad." She pulls out of my hold, sinking into the chair next to Ren, still absorbed in whatever he's working on.

"Okay, I won't be mad," I assure her, leaning against my desk and crossing my arms. I have a feeling I'm not going to like this.

She clears her throat. "Uh, it was about that other guy, who's like you. He got hurt, right?"

Ren turns to her. "Where'd you hear that?"

"Some of the guards were talking about it. I didn't catch much, but they said it might be like before," she whispers.

"They shouldn't be saying shit to you. I'll deal with it," I growl.

Ren holds a hand up, stopping me from marching out the room and confronting every fucking person I can find.

"Emma, he was hurt. He's in surgery now, and they believe he has a good chance at surviving. What are your actual concerns?"

I glare, wanting to cuss him out for telling her anything, but she turns to him, eyes begging for answers.

"Do you think they'll go after Shane next?" she asks.

I suck in a breath, tucking my head to my chest. "No. I don't. We don't have a lot of information at this point, but everything points to an isolated incident. In fact, it might have been a coincidence he was hurt. I'll make sure nothing happens to Shane."

Relief floods her face, but it's taken over again by worry. "What about you and Alex?"

"I'm sure we're not even on the radar. Besides, everyone loves Alex. He's too happy to kill easily." He shoots her a small smile, but she doesn't return it.

"I love you, too, Ren. I don't want anything to happen to any of you," she says, getting up and wrapping her gangly arms around his shoulders. He pats her arm awkwardly, but his eyes have softened. She moves to me and pecks my cheek before walking out, letting the door click shut behind her. I fall into my chair again, wondering if it'll make it through the night with how many times I've collapsed into it.

I open my mouth, then shut it again when Ren's phone lights up on my desk, then fades to black. We're frozen, staring at the device. Ren reaches out and opens it, not bothering to pick it up. He spins it around, showing me the only message from the Wraith we've ever received.

Catastrophic.

EIGHT

ALEX

The pounding on my door has me flying out of bed, sheets wrapped around my ankle, and I plow into my nightstand. Shane flings it open, gun already in hand, and scans the space. His eyes settle on me, and he scowls as if it's my fault he barged in here, waking me up from a dead sleep. In the last week, I've gotten approximately four hours a night, and I'm running on fumes.

"What the fuck do you want? I just got to sleep," I complain, untangling myself and glancing out the window. Moonlight filters through my window, and I snatch up my phone. One fucking hour. That's how long it's been since I've fallen into bed without stripping my clothes off.

"Victor fucking Smith. What a stupid goddamn name," he grumbles, settling into a chair across the room as if he'll be here awhile.

"No, I'm not fucking doing this. Get out. I haven't slept in a week." I sink onto my mattress, resting my elbows on my knees, burying my face in my hands.

"We have to set up a meeting with him. The sooner the better. I'm not dealing with any bullshit he's going to pull. Fuck, I hate that man."

"Seriously, Shane. I'm trying. He's not talking to anyone right now, which makes sense. At some point, he'll reach out, or we'll force him to meet with us. You have to stop obsessing over this," I say, my hands muffling my words.

"The new commissioner, what's-his-face—he's been calling me nonstop. He has to stop, or I'm going to send him on a permanent vacation. The mayor looks like he's about to have a breakdown every time I see him. The media is having a fucking field day with this. We still don't know who's responsible for Byrns being shot. Oh, and apparently, someone at Emma's school told her I'll get what's coming to me. She won't tell me who."

I rub my temples, resigning myself to a therapy session. Maybe I can get some sleep if I rush through it.

"New commissioner's name is Oliver Whittler, I'll tell him to stop and redirect his calls to me. I'll visit the mayor, tell him to get his shit together. We can do a little something about the media, but honestly, most of the city doesn't care what they have to say unless it's something to do with Samantha Byrns. Leave the issue of Byrns to their side of the city. And I'll talk to Emma, teach her what to say when shitty people get shitty."

I huff, heavy eyes finding Shane, but he's still staring out the window. I can't possibly fix every problem we're facing, and it's overwhelming. We're all stretched to the max, and shit is starting to slip because of it. I never thought someone would try to take out one of us, the leaders behind the veil of polite society, but here we are. It shouldn't be surprising, seeing as how, ten years ago, underlings tried the same thing on a larger scale. Hell, that's how we came into power in the first place, but it's still shocking.

"The Barrens," he murmurs.

"What about the Barrens?" I tip my head back, feeling the weight of another task settling on my shoulders. He's going to drop something on me, and it might be the thing that breaks me.

"You hear from any of our contacts down there?" He turns, fixing his eyes on me. He looks exhausted, a new haggardness covering his face.

"Not since that night. They keep to themselves, though, so not surprising. What's happening in the slums?"

"Ren's contact, Jerry . . . Gary . . . whatever the hell his name is. He mentioned some shit. People going missing."

I sigh. "It's the Barrens; there's always people disappearing down there. It's not exactly a pleasant place to live. With it turning colder now, being butted up right along the river, a lot of them don't make it."

I turn my hands up, not sure what he wants from me. The Barrens skirts the river that snakes through the center of Synd, bisecting our territories. It's a maze of abandoned buildings, and blocked streets, running the whole length of the city. It's only a half-dozen blocks on each side, but it's not hard to get lost down there. They run their own shit, with the understanding that we don't fuck with them, and vice versa. I don't go there, though, so I don't know why Shane would be talking to me about it. I have one person who lives on the edge of the Barrens on the east side, who sometimes talks to me.

Shane shakes his head, turning back to the window. "This is different. At least, I think it is."

"You still off?" I think back to our conversation weeks ago, him trying to convince me some shit wasn't right. I figured it was just me, though, wondering when shit was going to get easier.

"I thought it would go away after Byrns went down, but it's still there. It's worming its way through my mind, refusing to leave."

"That's not fucking creepy," I mutter, and he snorts. "I don't mean to add to shit, but some of our supplies are wonky."

He swings back, glaring at me. "Wonky? What the fuck does that mean?"

"The shipment was off. Then the guns were late. I don't know if people are getting skittish or something, but I'm looking into it."

"We can't afford to have more shit go wrong." He sighs. "Let's deal with everything that's going to affect us now, leave everything else for later. Victor doesn't matter. I'll keep trying to get a hold of Helms. Just deal with the commissioner and mayor. Get them off my ass. I'll talk to Ren about helping dig in to the shipments. Maybe we have someone skimming off the top."

"Already done. I talked to him earlier." I yawn, rubbing my eyes.

He walks out without another word and closes the door. Our stress levels are going to get us sick or killed. I lay back, feet still hanging off the bed. I'm almost asleep when Ren waltzes in, and I let out a string of curses.

"Your feet are going to go numb like that," he remarks, taking the seat Shane had vacated.

"Fuck off, Ren. I have to sleep." I'm practically begging, but he ignores me, just like Shane.

"I'll make this quick. Our supplies are being rerouted somehow. Don't ask me anything more, since I don't have answers, but I figured you should know before you start busting our people."

"If that's all you wanted to tell me why the hell are you sitting down?" I stare at the ceiling, refusing to get up.

"I tried to get more information from the Wraith. I haven't heard anything. I don't believe they've taken any jobs. I wanted to make sure—"

"You're not the reason the Wraith isn't taking jobs. It has nothing to do with you but might have to do with no longer getting work from the Byrns' clan right now. I'm sure they do business with a lot of higher ups in the city. Might be laying low." I peek at him, and he's nodding, a contemplative look on his face. At least he's not freaking out this time.

"Samantha Byrns."

I sit up, eyeing him, before saying, "What about her?"

"She hasn't been seen in public."

I roll my eyes. "Of course she hasn't. Her brother was fucking shot. You expect her to show up at a club and dance the night away while he's in the hospital in a coma?"

"I expected . . . I don't know what I expected, actually. However, I was able to get footage from the hospital cameras. She's subdued, which makes sense. The curious thing is, Nemesis pulled footage from the slums bordering the Barrens. There aren't many, but I believe I've seen her walking the streets. She doesn't look like she normally does."

I scowl when he brings up his hacker. I hate using her, since I don't understand what she does. In fact, I'm not sure I like using the Wraith, either, but I leave that shit to Ren.

"Why are you stalking Samantha Byrns?"

His face tightens. "I'm not stalking her. Shane asked me to keep an eye on her."

I chuckle, running my fingers through my hair. Of course he did. "Oh, how the turns have tabled," I mutter before he raises an eyebrow at me. "He told me to stop obsessing over her, merely because I asked what we should do."

"I'd rather not be dealing with her at all, so if you'd like to take over, be my guest," he retorts, an edge creeping into his voice.

"I would if I could, brother. Now get the fuck out." I close my eyes again, hoping he'll get the hint, but when I crack a lid, he's still sitting, staring out the window. The tension inside my stomach eases, and my muscles relax. I'm on the edge of sleep in less than a minute, half in, half out of consciousness, when I pop my eyes open. I track Ren leaving, noticing as he flexes his fingers over and over. My stomach tightens again, tension flooding back into me. I sit up before he reaches the door.

"Want to wake Emma, sneak her ice cream, and watch a movie?" I call out, part of me praying he'll say no.

"I'll get her," he whispers, and I catch his grin before he shuts the door.

Ten minutes later, we settle in the room we've made into a theater, tucked under blankets, gorging on ice cream as the opening credits roll over the projector. I'm sure I'll be asleep before the end of the first scene, but being here with my family makes it worth it.

"For fuck's sake." Shane's voice floats in from behind us, and I glance over my shoulder, grinning. Emma ducks, hiding under the blanket spread across her lap between Ren and I. "I can fucking see you, Emma."

"No Emma here! Just a lump of blankets!" she squeaks.

Shane stomps around, blocking the screen, planting his hands on his hips. "Oh, you guys didn't invite Emma? That's a shame."

I'm about to call out a warning, but a chuckle leaves me as he spins, plopping right on top of her. Her peals of laughter mix with his. Shane pokes the blankets again, taking a seat next to Ren. Emma's head pops out.

"Shane, you made me miss the beginning! Ren, restart it."

They start bickering, but I tip my head back, watching them through tired eyes. Relaxing for the first time since hearing about Byrns going down.

NINE

REN

"Jensen, you'd better start talking, or I'm going to think you're double-crossing us," I state calmly, pulling my thin leather gloves higher up my wrists.

"Mr. Ren, I don't know what you're talking about. I wasn't nowhere near there. Promise."

I meet his eyes. He looks like he's about to cry, and I sigh. "You forget, I know where you live, Jensen. Are you telling me you haven't been home for two weeks?" I raise an eyebrow, and he drops his head, staring and shuffling his feet as if they'll have the answers I seek.

"Someone burned it down," he mumbles.

I glance around, making sure we're still alone. A shadow detaches from the alley, and I catch Alex's eye. He slips back into the darkness, off to another meet-up. Why he insisted on accompanying me to the Barrens is beyond me, but it's hard to deny him when he gets an idea in his head.

"So, someone burned your place down. Where have you been staying, then?"

"There's a warehouse over in Byrns' area. Been bunking with a couple other guys over there." He nods toward the bridge, and my eyes follow. The two sides look the same, both dark and dreary. The light rain obscures the buildings, but even when it's clear, the view is desolate.

"Any activity over there?" I ask, swinging back to eye him.

He purses his lips, and I'd normally assume he's hiding something, but Jensen isn't the sharpest crayon in the box. I wait, my patience wearing thin. I have at least four other people to see tonight. I don't have time to pull information from him. I wasn't even going to see him tonight, but when he literally dropped at my feet, falling out of a dumpster, he was hard to ignore.

"There's shinies everywhere," he says.

I close my eyes, pulling a deep breath in. The slang in the Barrens isn't hard to decipher, but it still irks me.

"Shinies?"

"Oh, yeah, uh, fancy cars. Like real fancy? I dunno what they are, though. Never really seen them before."

"Color?"

"Uh, black. Bad guys drive black cars, right?" His face scrunches in thought.

"I drive a black car," I deadpan, waiting for the realization to dawn on his face, but I wave away his sputtered apologies. "What are the cars doing? Where are they going?"

"I dunno. They just drive around. I dunno if they're really doing anythin' other than asking ta be jacked."

I nod, peering over the bridge again. The more shit goes down on the east side, the more I wonder if they're under attack. First Byrns goes down, then our shipments are being diverted, no one knows a fucking thing, the Reapers' territory is in lock down, and now, new people are trolling the east side of the Barrens. At some point, we have to consider these aren't isolated incidents contained to the east side of the river, and they might affect us sooner or later.

"If you come across anything else, you know what to do."

He nods, stumbling past me to take the bridge over the river.

"Jensen!" I call out when he's almost halfway, waiting until he looks back. "Whereabouts you staying?"

"Couple blocks from NightStorm," he yells back, then continues on.

I pull out my phone, making a note to send supplies to the warehouse. They'll never accept money. In fact, most of the time, they won't accept anything from us, but if a shipment of blankets shows up randomly outside their door, they won't turn it down. Jensen will probably know it's me, but hopefully, that will make him more willing to keep passing me info.

I slip into the driver's seat, making my way deeper into King territory. It's late, but when I hit club row, hundreds of people are milling outside, music rattling my windows. Traffic makes it hard to get anywhere quickly, and I glance at the clock, cursing. I hate being fucking late.

An alley next to a still-open restaurant has a space reserved for us, and I pull in. A burly man, tattoos covering half his face, swings open a side door for me, and I nod. The door clicks shut behind me, and I climb the stairs to the office above. It's one of the few eating establishments open this late, catering to the elite clientele who work more behind the veil than who the public sees. I doubt most people know it's here.

I stride into Marco's office. He jolts in his seat and spins to face me as I settle into one of the chairs facing his desk. We stare at each other for a full minute before a smile blooms across his face.

"Mr. King, I wondered if you'd show." He gives me a smarmy smile, one I don't return.

"What did you want, Marco? I'm a busy man, and I don't particularly like being summoned."

He sneers, trying to hide behind his hand. "I'm concerned with the amount of money I've been throwing at your organization."

I tip my brow at his choice of words, but I stay silent. Marco isn't the most pleasant man to deal with, but he has enough clout I can't just shoot him outright. The fact he owns half of the restaurants our lower gangs launder money through is enough for Shane to reconsider taking him out at least. I'd rather deal with his son, but I have a feeling Junior wouldn't be too happy if we took out his father. Marco leans his elbows on his desk, lacing his fingers and smirking.

"Seems things are changing over on the east side. I figured it might be time to renegotiate our terms."

"No."

He snorts, shaking his head. "You don't tell me 'no,' boy."

Marco may be a savvy criminal boss, but unfortunately, he's never rose to our level. His insult isn't the first of his mistakes, but it will be the last. I told Shane before I left I wasn't going to put up with his arrogance anymore. I will retaliate, regardless of the outcome. There are few times Shane will put a leash on Alex and I, understanding that some things are best taken care of without his approval. I'm glad I told him, though, so he's not surprised when Marco's body is found floating down the river.

"Frankly, I can tell you whatever I want. You don't even register on the map in Synd. I've wondered for some time now when you'd take the leap and try to fuck us over. I can't say I'm surprised. You have one chance to rectify this situation."

"And if I don't?" He sniffs, examining his nails. They're bitten down to the quick, which tells me much more than his words ever could.

"I think we both know the outcome of those decisions. Again, I don't have time to wait for your answer, so you'd better start backtracking. Now."

I cross my legs, wishing I was wearing something more than jeans and a sweater. I would be more comfortable in a suit, matching the energy swirling in this office. No matter what I wear, though, he should be more careful with his demands.

"Are you threatening me?" His false bravado is almost amusing, especially since a drop of sweat streaks his hairline. I have to give him credit, though; most don't make it this far into the conversation before they crack.

"I could say it's not a threat, it's a promise, but it's moot at this point." I push to my feet, leaning over his desk. "I'll be seeing you, Marco."

He stammers as I stride out the door, leaving it open in my wake, if only to hear where he actually goes with his tirade. Marco's gravelly voice booms into the hall, spewing dire warnings of how we'll regret this, how we'll never find someone willing to work with us, as if he's the only crooked businessman in this city. I hustle down the stairs, already late for my next appointment, when I find Junior at the bottom.

He's a spitting image of his father twenty years ago, minus the broken, bulbous nose. His dark eyes are fixed on the stairs, where his father is still shouting after me. Marco didn't even bother leaving his office. He's probably still seated behind his desk, huffing and puffing to pull himself out of his chair. He made the comment once he had some health problems, but he didn't trust doctors enough to seek out help. Hopefully Junior has a different view, since I'm pretty sure his issues are hereditary.

I stop in front of Junior, forcing his gaze to my own, and I wait. The emotions flitting across his face are too fast for me to track, and I wish Alex was here. He's always been better at reading people, especially when they're trying to hide something. I rely on facts to guide me, making sure the evidence matches our theories, but Alex has a sixth sense about these things. One look at a person, and he knows if they're lying. The jealousy is a dull ache in my chest now, after so many years of relying on him. Having Shane and Alex at my back allows me to focus on where I'm strongest, which isn't feelings.

"Mr. King," he murmurs, nodding.

"Junior."

He glances back up the stairs, sighing. "He went too far."

It's a statement not a question, but I answer anyway. "He's been on the edge for quite some time."

He nods again. "Well, I hope you'll still work with me when I take over."

I try to keep the shock from my face, but I'm not sure I succeed. Junior is in his twenties, barely old enough to run anything, yet he's been smoothing shit over for his father for years. I assumed it was out of respect and love for the man who raised him, but clearly, I was wrong.

He huffs, the corner of his mouth tipping up. "You thought I'd be heartbroken? Beg you to reconsider? No, I'm done mopping up his mistakes. That bastard has everything you're going to hand down coming to him. Just . . ."

"This is the only time you will have the opportunity to make requests, Junior, so think carefully what you ask of me."

"I have two." I raise my eyebrow, but he continues, "Please stop calling me Junior. I fucking hate it."

"Okay, and your second?" He glances past me.

"I want to watch," he whispers with conviction, and when his eyes find mine, they're burning with determination.

I step around him, not giving him an answer, since I don't have one yet, but I'll allow it if it's possible. When I reach the side door, I peer over my shoulder, finding him exactly where I left him.

"What do you want to be called now?" I call back to him.

"James. It's my middle name, the only thing he allowed my mother to give me," he answers without turning around.

Marco finally appears, eyeing his son, then me, before realization dawns on his face. He might be stupid, but he isn't dumb. A flush travels up his neck, and his hands ball into fists at his sides. James pivots, striding off into the kitchen, no doubt with the intent to lay low until the call comes in or the deed is done. I smirk at Marco before slipping out the door.

TEN

SAMANTHA

I crouch on the flat roof of the abandoned hardware store and peer over the edge at the four boys below in the alley: low-level gangbangers doing a quick deal in the shadows. I can tell they're young, since they keep glancing around. They wouldn't bother hiding in the dark if they knew what they were doing. The police don't patrol this area of Synd, preferring to stick to the suburbs and out of our areas.

We're smack dab in the middle of the Barrens, a couple of blocks on either side of the river but spanning the whole city, north to south. East of the river is ours, but the King family controls the west. Up north is the Reapers' territory, but it's such a small area the people in the Barrens don't bother with it.

Shane King, Ryker Helms, and my brother all came of age and took over after the attempted coup of every major crime family in Synd ten years ago. Most of the top guys, including our fathers, didn't survive, which left those three young guys not ready to take over. They were thrust into leading us through the smoke and chaos left behind. The only thing that saved us was that we were all in the same boat. I don't remember much of that time, but the flow of information between the families stopped. Protocols, rules, and boundaries were set and have been followed ever since, even after we'd fortified our empires again.

With the deal done, two of the boys slip off to the next block over. I shimmy down the fire escape to have a little chat with the two left, when they take off running. A sleek black car rolls slowly past the mouth of the alley, oozing ridiculousness. Who drives a Benz into the Barrens? An idiot, that's who.

Crouching again, I wait as they pull into the alley across from where I'm perched. The October wind picks up, whipping loose strands of hair from the braid I hastily put up after having left the hospital. With the humming highway half a mile away, I can still hear the engine purring, even after their lights are extinguished.

I glance at my phone, angling it toward the streetlight a block away. Ten minutes is all I'm willing to wait to see what they're up to, then I'm going home. I'm cold, hungry, and emotionally exhausted. It's harder than I expected trying to find out who ambushed us and put my brother in a coma. Plus, being at the hospital for hours is more draining than I'd ever expected.

I roll my neck, trying to work out the tension headache creeping up, when a silhouette catches my eye. Someone is doing a horrible job of sneaking between the dark patches between the buildings, heading straight for my building. They obviously aren't used to being here. I smirk, watching them crouch and roll, like they're in a spy movie or something.

My grin slides from my face as a soft click from a car door echoes through the still night. A man in black is peering around the building to track the figure on the opposite sidewalk. So, this is what they're doing. Could be a runaway or an initiate who wanted out.

The closer the figure comes, though, the less convinced I am. They cross in front of my building, glancing back, their features lit up by the flickering street lamp. Her pale, young face glows and disappears as the light diffuses, plunging everything into shadows. The man detaches from his hiding spot and hustles across the road, pudgy legs working hard.

I can't leave this girl to get beaten and raped or kidnapped for ransom. Either way, she'll come home in pieces, if she comes home at all. I slide down the fire escape, praying the small clank won't alert anyone to my presence as I reach the bottom. A small cry rings out in the night, abruptly cut off. A scuffling of feet follows. I quicken my pace, hoping we are out of the car's sight so I can hustle her away.

I slow as I approach the alley's opening and hum a tune stuck in my head I heard in the elevator at the hospital earlier. Hands stuffed in my pockets, I swing around to the sidewalk as they are about halfway to the corner.

"Well, hello there. Nice night for a stroll, hmm?" I grin at the greasy man decked out in an ill-fitting suit. I wish I could wink. This would be the perfect situation for it. I try not to glance at the girl, keeping my focus on the man with one hand over her mouth, and the other looped around her waist.

"Fuck off. You don't want any of this." His lip curls, sneering his wide-set mouth, narrowing his beady eyes that are way too close together. His peripheral vision must be terrible. Excellent.

"Oh, I don't know. Seems like a fun time. Is it fun, sweetie?" I look into her bright blue eyes, terror radiating from them. Frantically, she shakes her head as her feet try to find purchase on the pavement.

"I said fuck off, cunt!" He struggles to adjust the tiny slip of a girl as he drags her backward again with his pudgy arms. He's taller than me, yet he's still struggling to control her. The girl is doing her best to flail, trying to kick him in the balls, but her legs are too short. We're still shadowed in darkness, but the car is only halfway out of sight as I follow them into the street.

"You know, I never did like being called a cunt. So unoriginal."

When he glances back to his friends, I skip several steps forward and pull out my knife, then slip it up my sleeve. The girl's eyes are fixed on me, filled with horror and what I can only hope is awareness. I'm confident I can save her and kill her kidnapper before the others find out, but not if she steps in my sharp blade's path.

Unfortunately, she's an idiot and goes completely limp before I'm close enough to stab him. The man whips back, almost dropping her, while I run, knife falling into my open palm. When he sees me coming, he dumps her and reaches for what I'm assuming is a gun, but I'm there first, stabbing him in the throat, yanking it sideways as I pull it out.

Blood spurts with each heartbeat, covering me from collarbone to toe. This is not going the way I'd planned. The girl retreats behind me as the would-be kidnapper drops to his knees, hands falling away from his neck.

"Don't scream," I say, futile advice as a car door slams shut. The other kidnapper rounds the mouth of the alley. I'm already screwed and desperately hope he's the last one. I pull out my handgun and squeeze the trigger, popping him in the forehead. His head leads the way of his body falling to the ground. Tires squeal as the Benz takes off out of the alley.

"Shit," I mutter, looking down at my blood-soaked clothes, then at the girl.

Behind me, she whimpers, her eyes fixed on the bodies. At least she didn't scream.

"You okay?" No way she's okay.

"Yeah," she squeaks.

Definitely not okay.

"You get any blood on you?"

"I don't think so."

"Good. Where you live, sweetie?" I ask, pasting an innocent smile on my face, like I didn't drop two corpses at her feet a minute ago, but she's not buying it.

"That way." She nods toward the river.

Either she lives in King territory, or she doesn't want to tell me. Smart of her, a lot smarter than sneaking along a dark street at midnight or going limp when someone is coming at her with a knife.

"You want me to walk with you?"

"What do you do with the . . . the . . ." Her eyes flit back to the dearly departed.

"The bodies? Nothing," I wipe my knife on my leg, but it doesn't do much.

Great, now I need a shower. Hopefully, I can sneak inside my house without good ol' Uncle Victor seeing me.

"Nothing? But won't someone come for them? Don't you need a cleanup?"

Her eyes grow wide, probably realizing she's said too much. She knows about cleanup crews but not how to move in the Barrens. She's well dressed, so not from the lower gangs, either. Who the hell is this girl?

"No one cares in the Barrens. Either whoever they belong to will come fetch them or someone will drag them to the river. You sure you don't want me to walk home with you? The Barrens isn't exactly a nice neighborhood." I gesture to the guys behind me.

"I . . . I'm not supposed to be out." She tucks her chin to her chest and folds her arms over her stomach.

Growing up in my family, seeing someone shot is pretty common. Do regular kids understand this stuff at her age? Clearly, she's wise to some of it, but maybe I just scarred her for life. The therapy bills will be astronomical.

"I gathered as much. Let's get out of here. Scavengers will be showing up soon, and we don't want to be caught in that mess. They're vicious when trying to take a dead man's shoes." I hold out my hand, hoping there's not too much blood on it to help her up, but she doesn't hesitate.

"I'm Sam, by the way."

"Emma." She tucks her arms around herself again, whipping her head left, then right.

"Well, Emma, let's get you home. We crossing the bridge or staying on the east side?"

"Crossing. Long walk, though. You don't have to take me all the way there." Her eyes scream vulnerability, and I can't leave her to deal with this shit alone. What would be the point of saving her to throw her to the scavengers of the Barrens straight after?

"No biggy. I can walk with you. We could take an Uber, but I doubt they'll let me in with this mess." Our steps echo through the night as we walk toward the nearest footbridge that spans the river, away from the mess I created.

Emma isn't kidding when she says it's a long walk. I'm starting to suspect she hitched a ride close to the river and walked the rest of the way into no-man's-land. My feet are aching, and the blood on my neck is flaking and making my neck itch. Emma offered me her hoodie to wipe it off, but the temperature drop is enough for me to stop her. Dealing with blood is annoying, but I've survived worse.

The houses grow larger and fancier the further we travel. With my extracurricular activities, I tend to go all over the city but never this far into King territory. Déjà vu hits me hard when I notice the street names. The whole neighborhood is a mirror image of the Byrns' side of Synd. We turn up Park Street West when my steps falter. Emma glances back in confusion and stops.

"Emma, I know you don't trust me, and that's cool. But I need you to tell me your last name. Now."

I stare at the house capping off the end of the block. All the lights are on, blazing out the windows. More beams illuminate the circle drive, the double front doors winged on either side, and the massive yards encircling the mansion. I recognize this house, though I've never been here. It's a replica of the house I'll be going to after I drop Emma off all the way on the other side of the river.

"Um, I'm not supposed to tell people from the east side my last name." She shuffles her feet, swaying from side to side, and dropping her chin to her chest.

I sigh. "How old are you, Emma?"

A commotion on the side lawn by the tree line south of the house draws my eye. Several figures' raised voices carry on the wind, throwing arms in the air. Heated arguments erupt before two of them stomp away, and the rest set off into the trees.

"Thirteen," she answers, pulling my attention back to her.

Fan-fucking-tastic.

"Well, let's get this over with, Emma King. I'm sure they're worried about where you are." This is great, the perfect situation to meet Shane King officially.

"Do you think they know?" she whispers as more shouts ring out.

Oh, to be young and naïve again. I was her age when Dad died, throwing our whole existence into chaos, and Mason trained me to be nothing like Emma King. He never wanted me to have to be saved by someone else. He never wanted me to owe anyone, especially for my life. That's a debt that can never be paid. I don't think I was ever as innocent as this girl in front of me.

"I'm pretty sure they've figured it out," I chuckle, trudging along again, hoping they aren't in a "shoot first, ask questions later" type of mood. I pull my hood over my hair, trying to hide my face. The cold, damp patches from half-dried blood send a shiver through me.

We make it past the ridiculously large fountain that houses a mermaid bubbling water out of her mouth, just as absurd as the one in my own driveway. The massive doors swing open, light bracketing around an intimidating frame, casting him mostly in shadow.

"Emma Caroline King. In, now." The authority in his voice is unmistakable. It's the same tone Mason used on me when I was young and disappointing.

Emma's shoulders slump as she trudges toward the steps. Warily, I trail her to the stairs and halt at the bottom. I can almost make out his features: sharp jaw, clenched tight, strong arms crossed over his chest, dark hair, disheveled and sticking up everywhere, as if he's run his fingers through it all night.

My stomach clenches when Emma reaches the top step, head dropping. She says something I can't make out, but she's gesturing back to me. He nods, and his eyes follow her as she slips through the doors. The full weight of his gaze swings around, with dark eyes like pools of night. What little I can see of his face morphs from a disgruntled caregiver to a ruthless leader.

"Where did you find her?" Steel laces his question, and I straighten my spine.

I contemplate walking away, but Mason's face flashes in my mind. I should have stayed at the end of the driveway. Hell, I should have stopped at the street. I could have watched her from there.

"Bad part of town. She isn't hurt," I reply, breaking eye contact to check my surroundings subtly. The last thing I need is an ambush so far from my territory. I shouldn't be here.

"She said you saved her. Saved her from what."

"Couple guys tried to grab her. They won't bother her again."

"Oh? And how could you possibly know that, Byrns?"

Shit. My eyes whip back to him, wheels turning in my mind. Shit, shit, shit. I was banking on him not recognizing me, not with the hood. I certainly can't afford this excursion getting back to Victor. He'll eviscerate me. I'll take my chances living in the Barrens rather than deal with my uncle finding out I've saved Emma King. This is possibly the stupidest thing I've ever done. Walked straight up to the Kings' house, practically bowed at their feet. Pretty sure he's not going to buy my airhead act anymore. Better to make him wonder than giving away the whole game.

"Dead men can't kidnap errant teenagers." I pray he'll leave it at that, but disbelief fills his face as if he can't imagine I'm deadly enough to take out two grown men.

"Why didn't you send her home in a car?"

My eyebrows shoot up. "You'd rather I send her in a car alone than walk her home?"

His face darkens. "I'd prefer her to be as far away from you as possible, Princess."

"That's a shame, since, without me, she wouldn't be tucked snugly in bed right now. She'd be a statistic. You're welcome, King." I gather an invisible skirt and curtsy, keeping eye contact as he scowls at me.

A commotion behind catches his attention, and I spin, then slip into the dark where the trees line the driveway. As I blend in between two trunks, Shane's curses, and heavy footfalls echo after me. I take off, weaving through the dense brush toward the safety of the east side of the river.

Shane King can chase me all he wants. No one has caught me yet, and I'll be damned if he'll be the first.

ELEVEN

SHANE

The sidewalk is dark and empty, devoid of life. I breathe out another curse, stomping back to the house. How the hell did she slip away? My back was turned for maybe ten seconds. There's no way she just disappeared. Her appearance, coupled with the anxiety of finding Emma's bedroom empty, sent me into overdrive. I don't have enough energy to confront Emma at this point. Her sneaking out and apparently miles from home . . . I suck in a deep breath, what-ifs running through my mind. The knowledge I have Byrns little sister to thank for Emma not being lost or dead is too much at this point. I bound up the front steps, texting Freddy to call off the search, almost running into Alex at the top.

"Did I just see Emma slamming her bedroom door? Where the hell was she?" he demands, frustration warring with panic painted across his face. It isn't often he gets worked up, but finding Emma gone sends him spiraling. Pissed doesn't even begin to describe what he was when I told him he couldn't go scouring the city for her.

"A bad part of town, apparently, whatever the fuck that means," I bite out, stomping past him and up the stairs to my office. I collapse in my chair, exhaustion weighing me down. Alex, of course, follows, running his hands over his face.

"Who found her? One of ours?"

"Oh, no, because that would be too easy." I laugh ruefully, seeing Samantha's face tucked under her hood in my mind's eye. She was trying to hide her face, though we haven't ever actually met formally. I wonder if she thought I wouldn't recognize her, despite the internet plastering her face everywhere.

Ren stalks in, head buried in his tablet. He sits before saying, "Can't find anything on the cameras."

I'm not surprised he already knew Emma was back. I'm sure he has alerts set up for every boundary surrounding this place. Him not finding Byrns is surprising, though. He can find anyone.

"Shane, who found her?" Alex yells.

I scowl, looking out the window. "Samantha fucking Byrns."

A beat of silence follows, then Alex laughs. I whip my head back, glaring at him, but he doesn't even notice. Ren has finally pulled his eyes away from his tablet. Alex wipes away tears, and I consider throwing his ass out.

"Glad to see someone sees the hilarity of this situation," Ren quips, glancing down again.

"Seriously?" Alex chuckles, barely able to get the words out. "Samantha Byrns dropped her off at home? Like they were out for a girl's night?"

"I wish. According to her, Emma was in trouble. She said they tried to kidnap her, and Samantha, good Samaritan that she is, saved her," I scoff.

Alex's laughter dies. "Wait, someone tried to snatch Emma?"

"That's what Samantha said. I'm not convinced that's how it went down. She also 'took care of it.'"

Ren's head pops up. "As in, she killed them?"

"I believe her exact words were 'dead men can't kidnap errant teenagers.'" I shake my head, wondering what really happened.

A soft knock at the door has Alex up. He pulls Emma into his arms. I shoot to my feet, trying to see her face. Hopefully, this little adventure will curb her need to run off. She pushes him away and takes his chair, refusing to look at me as she twists her hands in her lap.

"Emma, are you okay?" I ask, my tone softer than my rolling emotions.

"I'm okay. I mean, it wasn't . . ." She takes a deep breath. "I'm sorry."

"I need you to tell me what happened," I say gently, wishing she would look at me.

"I just wanted to go out, and you never let me. Some of my friends from school said there was a party, so I left."

"Snuck out," I correct, glaring at her.

She nods, still not looking at me. "I got a car, but when I got to the house, it was dark. But I was already out, so I had them take me closer to the river."

"Not exactly a safe place, Emma," Alex chimes.

"I know, but you never let me go anywhere! You always tell me it's too dangerous or there's too many people or whatever. I just wanted to see what the fuss was about. So, I started walking but then it got dark. I didn't really know where I was. I was having . . ."

Don't say it, I think.

"Fun. It was nice to be out and not have fourteen people following me. Then it wasn't so much fun." She sniffs, wiping her eyes with her sleeve.

"Tell us what you remember, every detail, no matter how small or insignificant," Ren tells her.

"I was on a street, but there wasn't much light, and no cars and then a man grabbed me. He was trying to pull me somewhere, but I couldn't see where. I tried to get away, but he was stronger than me"—she sobs— "and then she showed up. She was so badass. She was talking back to him, and she didn't seem like she was scared at all."

She finally meets my eyes, awe swimming in hers. Fuck. The last thing I need is for her to develop a hero complex with Samantha Byrns. I can't imagine how it would look for someone who clearly isn't who we thought she was to save someone sweet and innocent like Emma. I'm still not convinced she didn't have help, though. Someone else must have come, or they both were extremely fucking lucky. Maybe they just didn't want to kill someone who had such a high profile as Byrns's sister.

"Who else was there?" Ren asks when I don't say anything.

"The guy trying to grab me and then another guy. She took care of them," Emma whispers.

I sigh. "Samantha was covered in blood."

Emma's head pops up, eyes wide. "You know who she is?"

"Yes. Do you?" I raise an eyebrow and watch her face morph into her lying one. She opens her mouth, but I cut her off. "Don't lie."

"Maybe." She gives me a small smile.

"Go to bed, Emma, you'll feel better tomorrow. No more sneaking out, especially right now."

The last thing I need is her breaking down. I wonder for the millionth time if I should get her a therapist, but honestly, who the hell would be able to help her when her brother runs illicit businesses and runs half the city? They'd either not help, saying she's fine because they'd be afraid of pissing me off, or they'd tell us what we already know: abandonment, isolation, corruption, questionable moral values . . . the list would go on and on. Five years. I only need to make it five more years, and I can send Emma to college, and she can finally have a normal life beyond the blood and corruption of the world we live in here.

Emma waves, Alex squeezing her arm as she passes, and the door clicks behind her, leaving a silence in her wake.

"It would have been helpful to ask about the men," Ren comments.

"I'd rather her not have to relive it so soon. Later, when she's had a little time, maybe. I still don't believe Princess Byrns was able to take out two men by herself while saving Emma. It's too far-fetched." I lean back, crossing my legs, contemplating how she could have accomplished it.

Alex settles back in the chair. "Well, she is the sister of Mason Byrns. I mean, they're a part of the same world we are. It's not *that* surprising he would have taught her how to take care of herself."

"True, we've been telling you for years to train Emma in at least basic self-defense, Shane."

"We aren't having this conversation again. She's too young. Plus, if she would stop sneaking out, we wouldn't have this problem anyway. You'd think with all the resources we have, we'd be able to keep an eye on her," I scowl.

They exchange a look I refuse to respond to. Keeping Emma safe is my first priority, above everything else. If I could get away with not sending her to school, I would, but everyone revolted when I brought up homeschooling. My mouth tips up as I remember the horror on Alex's face when he thought we'd be teaching her math.

"Fine, but I'm going on record as saying I think you're being dumb. And I think you're underestimating Samantha Byrns. Way back at the gala, I told you there was more to her than we thought. Clearly, you're wrong. I'm not saying she's some secret badass, but she's not an airhead," Alex states.

"I agree," Ren says, surprising the hell out of me. "There's more to her than meets the eye."

"What do you mean?" I ask, wondering what the hell he's seeing I'm not.

He sighs, shaking his head. "You have an image of her that's been cultivated by the media. It makes sense she would be more than who they portray. I'm not sure how much is an act, but . . ."

"What do we do about it?" I ask as he stares out the window, clearly not going to finish his thought.

"I could find her, have a little chat. Obviously, a friendly one— wouldn't want to scare her off." Alex grins.

I roll my eyes. "The last thing we need is you trying to score with the Byrns princess. Mason would wake up from the coma just to cut your dick off for even trying."

"I can take Ren with, if it's that big of a deal, geesh. I mean, unless she's down for a . . ."

"Stop." I hold my hand up. "We're not going there. Yes, go talk to her but discreetly. Ren, you go with him, make sure he doesn't hit on her."

"What are we going to do about Victor Smith?" Ren asks.

"Nothing. We know why Ashford didn't take over yet?"

"Seems Victor pulled familial connections, and Colin went along with it. Not a lot is coming from the Byrns' side, obviously, but that's what I've heard so far."

"Alex?" I eye him, but his face is buried in his phone.

"What?" He still doesn't look up.

"Anything about Colin stepping back? Victor taking over?"

"What?" He glances up. "Oh, people are pissed. No one wants to work with him, he's an asshole. Mayor said we should take over, but I told him to keep that shit to himself."

"For fuck's sake. This whole thing is a shit show. Do we have an update on Mason, at least?"

"No," Ren says, dismissing me.

"Thanks a lot, motherfucker. Alex, fix this."

"What, you want me to go give him mouth-to-mouth?"

"I don't give a fuck what you do, but we can't keep going like this. The east side needs a leader, or we'll be forced to step up, and we all know how that will go down. If Victor can't pull it off, we'll have to take him out," I state, a knot forming in my stomach.

We've never crossed the line when dealing with the other side of the city. The Byrns and Kings have always stayed out of each other's business. To start now would throw the whole city into turmoil. A complete shake-up would shut things down in a way we can't predict.

"We can't go through another overhaul," Ren says.

"We will if we have to—if we're forced to. We rebuilt once before; we can do it again."

"When the coup happened, there was already a framework in place. This would be catastrophic, just like the Wraith said. Trying to start over, while taking over the east side? Impossible." He shakes his head.

"Then, we'll work with Victor as much as we can. I refuse to roll over for him, though. He's an asshole. Fuck him if he thinks he's anything other than a figurehead."

Alex eyes me. "What about Sam?"

"What about her?"

"Well, we're going to get more info, but maybe she could give us a little more insight on what's going on inside the Byrns' territory."

"You're reaching. Even if she did help Emma, there's no reason she'd have any insider's information. She's a pretty face, used to distract the masses from what they're actually doing, much like we use you for." I grin.

Ren laughs. "Take that pretty face of yours and get shit done."

TWELVE

SAMANTHA

"I met Shane King the other night," I whisper to Mason. Maybe he'll wake up if I piss him off enough. I don't believe he can hear me; otherwise, I'd never tell him about my run-in with the head of the Kings. He'd be ranting and raving if he could, threatening me with an asinine task that would last the rest of my days.

Every day he fails to wake up, the doctor's faces grow grimmer. The fact he's alive with brain function after getting shot in the head is a miracle. They put him in a coma to help with brain swelling, but two days ago, they took him off the meds, and he's still laying there, bandages long gone, eyes still shut tight. The machines beep, signaling Mason is still breathing, his heart still beating.

"I saved his little sister from being kidnapped in the Barrens. It was weird. They drove a Benz but couldn't snatch a teenage girl quietly. I'm worried, Mason. First, the ambush, now the King's inner circle is being targeted. I think something's coming. I need you to wake up and take care of everything. I can't do this alone."

I swipe at the tears on my face angrily. I am not a pretty crier, and this place is crawling with guys, hoping to carry dirt on me back to Victor. I trust very few of them.

"Victor took over operations, walked in, and took charge until you're back, or so he says. Colin tried to object, but Victor claimed family status. Byrns' blood doesn't run through that bastard's veins. I think Colin's afraid of ruffling too many feathers since we can't figure out who Victor has in his pocket. Colin is trying to protect me too much. Wake up, Mason. Don't leave me with this shitshow."

Colin sticks his head in the room. "Samantha?"

"Yeah?" I croak out.

"Time to go. Docs are coming in to assess him." He gestures behind.

He won't let them in until I'm gone. At least there's one person I can trust in this crazy crisis. Ever since the attack, Colin's been extra vigilant, protecting me instead of taking his rightful place. As second, he should be leading, carrying out my brother's orders, but here he is, ferrying me to and from the hospital.

We walk to Colin's car, and I wait by the curb as he checks for trackers and bombs.

"You find any more details on what happened?" he asks as he turns out of the lot.

"No. No one is willing to talk. I'm not sure they know anything. I'm tempted to go to Helms in the Reapers' territory, since he's ignoring my calls and texts."

The houses fly by as Colin weaves through the neighborhood. I've done all I can to figure out who set up an ambush on us. Not many people know about the meeting, which should narrow the pool of suspects, but it's only making it more difficult to find information. I'm getting more about Emma's attempted kidnapping than the hit on us. At this point, I've exhausted all I can do in the light of day. It's time to start looking in the dark crevices of the city.

"I think Helms is suspicious of our involvement." Colin's voice snaps me away from my scheming.

"You think he blames us? We were getting shot at, too. Besides, why would he save me if he thought we set him up?" Shock seeps into my voice.

"I don't know. They're in lock down now. Helms was paranoid before, wouldn't discuss what the meeting was about or where it would be. Mason tried to get him to come to the Depot, but Helms wouldn't listen. He even sent a messenger the day before. An actual person. Now, after all that, he skips out? Ghosts our asses? He might have been the one to set the ambush up. I don't know." Colin sighs, the tires crunching on the gravel.

The hideous fountain looms ahead, giving me flashbacks of the Kings' house. I glance at him, wondering if I should mention the whole fiasco. I open my mouth but snap it shut when he starts up again.

"Listen, Sammy, I need you to be careful. I don't blame you for wanting answers. I do, too, but others are watching. Mason will go insane if he wakes up and finds out I let you get yourself killed trying to find answers. He'll burn the whole city down."

The concern on Colin's face is the only thing keeping me from stabbing him. I remind myself he doesn't know what I do in the dark, long after he's tucked into bed. The message is clear: keep looking but stop being a dumbass about it. In that case, I'll keep my encounter with the Kings to myself for now.

"Got it." I nod, shoving my door open and bounding up the stairs, hoping I can make it to my room without having to talk to anyone else, particularly my uncle.

Dodging Victor and his creepy half smile is exhausting. Visiting Mason is exhausting. Searching for answers is exhausting.

"How is my nephew doing today, Samantha?" Victor's voice skitters across my skin, and I cringe, stopping halfway up the grand staircase.

"You mean how is the head of the Byrns' mafia doing?" I shoot a scathing look over my shoulder. Evading questions about Mason's condition is exhausting. I should start a list of all the things that exhaust me these days. When all this madness is over, I'm taking a vacation with a private beach, where no one bugs me.

"Mafia? I hardly think we're illustrious enough for that title. A glorified gang perhaps. Although, I might be able to help raise our status." Victor examines his fingernails, missing the hatred burning in my eyes.

"I wouldn't get too comfortable, Uncle. Circumstances change quite quickly around here, if you haven't noticed."

"Oh, I certainly have." The grin he shoots me borders on insanity. Cold settles in my bones as I stare at his retreating back. I need answers—and for Mason to wake the hell up. I need a shower and some help and that fucking vacation. I can't fight these battles on my own.

I cannot fucking believe it. I'm perched on another roof, hands stuffed in my black hoodie, trying not to freeze my ass off, when I spot her draped in all black, complete with a stocking cap over her blonde hair. At least she's not trying to ninja roll around the streets. This area is marginally better than the last time I saw her, at least. In fact, the street we're on is downright jolly compared to when we met. Still, not the place for a thirteen-year-old girl, who happens to be the head of a mafia family's little sister.

She glances in every shop, most of which are closed or boarded up, down every alley, and checks every face she passes. I don't want to babysit this girl again, but evidently, Shane didn't teach his sister what Mason taught me. Someone needs to step up so she doesn't become a statistic.

I take the inside stairs this time, nodding to Rocco, the head chef, as I make my way through the kitchen, swiping a basket of bread sticks on the way out. He waves his butcher knife over his head before his booming laugh echoes over the shouts of the other workers. I grin, pushing open the back door.

I jog to catch up to Emma and sidle up next to her, waving the still-warm garlic laced dough in front of her. She jolts back, almost stepping into the street, but I grab her elbow and pull her back.

"Fancy some of the best Italian food this side of the Barrens?" I ask, waving the basket in front of her.

"Sam! Oh, I've been looking for you forever!" Emma shoves the food into her mouth, mumbling something I can't make out.

"Slow down, girl, you'll choke. You know you're not supposed to be on this side of the river, right? This place isn't much better than the Barrens. You have anything to defend yourself with this time?" Doubtful.

"Yep! I have a switchblade. I think I know how to close it now. I practiced in my room this morning." My eyebrows shoot up. "I watched a video. I'm sure I got it down." Emma reaches in her pocket to show me all the skills she's picked up from some asinine doomsday prepper online, but I grab her wrist before she can pull the knife out.

"Nope, I believe you. Don't want to go flashing that around here. Someone might get the wrong idea."

"I didn't think of that." Her crestfallen face tugs at my heart, all while I try to steel it against her. I cannot feel sorry for this girl. The last thing I need is Emma thinking we can be friends, but she seems lonely.

Bars with lights, music, and drunks spilling out of them surround us as we walk. More than a few men catcall us, Emma wincing at the more vulgar ones.

"For being the little sister of a mafia boss, you're a bit . . ."

"Sheltered," she finishes, dejectedly. "Shane doesn't let me see these parts of things. I mean, I understand some stuff and been trying to learn. But he thinks I'm a little kid."

I sigh. I don't know how to talk to teenagers. She isn't like me at thirteen. At her age, I knew how to handle a gun. I knew where to stab a man so he wouldn't move again. Dad was barely cold in the ground when Mason kicked my training into overdrive, never wanting me to be vulnerable. Shane pretends he can keep Emma safe by controlling her instead of giving her any skills, and it's going to get her killed—or worse.

"Emma, do you know who I am?"

"You're Sam." She beams, grabbing another bread stick from the basket.

"Do you know my last name, though?" Shivers crawl up my back as we cross to a quieter street, and I glance over my shoulder, searching the dark. I can't shake the uneasiness that someone is out there, watching.

"Oh, you're a Byrns," she replies, oblivious to the changes swirling around us.

"Okay, so you know we're not supposed to be talking. Especially like this," I prompt with a grimace.

"I thought you could help me. Shane won't listen when I tell him I want to be trained. I thought you could talk to him or train me yourself."

Hope and embarrassment gathers in her eyes, and I pull my lip between my teeth, trying to work out how to let her down easily. Better to just rip off the bandaid.

"I can't train you. Even if I had the time, I'm not the best choice. You could ask one of your brother's men? Like his second, maybe?" Colin would have trained me if Mason hadn't been willing.

"Ren and Alex won't do it. They'll never go behind Shane's back." Misery is clear in her voice. I want to help, but protocols or not, there is no way I can. I have so many other things going on, starting with finding those responsible for shooting Mason and exacting my revenge. Throwing secret training lessons with sweet little Emma isn't on the table.

"I'm sorry, Emma, I wish I could help. I've just got a lot on my plate. We should get you home before your brother finds out you're gallivanting around again." I fish my phone out of my hoodie and order a car. With someone out there watching us, the sooner she's out of here, the better.

"Is it because your brother got shot?" My head whips up at her words. We've tried to keep Mason's hospital stay quiet, but with so many people around, the news is bound to get around, particularly with Victor making so much noise about taking over. It hasn't hit the media yet, but it's only a matter of time. We fed them the line he took a vacation so they won't go snooping.

"What have you heard?" My harsh tone startles her. Shit, this girl is sensitive.

"Not much. I heard he got shot and that someone else is running things over here for now. I'm sure he'll be fine, right?"

I nod, my eyes trailing past the dark alleys and blackened storefronts. I'm about to reassure her when my eyes catch on a shadow down the block, tucked away far enough into the alley. I can't make out the details. Person or trash? I turn, and the shadow shifts—definitely a person. Someone is following us.

My phone dings, an alert for Emma's ride. A car pulls around the corner, gliding smoothly next to us. I check the plates and driver. The last thing I want to do is stuff her in a car that'll drive her to a bloody death. Not after all the work I've done to keep her alive. Emma opens the door and I glare at her, making her freeze. I make my way to tap on the driver's side window.

"Hello, David. You recognize me?" I lean in, up close and personal, and slip my knife out of my sleeve holster, examining the blade flashing in the lights from his dash. His eyes widen, and his throat bobs. I don't usually use this tactic, but being a part of the Byrns' family has its advantages.

"Yes, ma'am." His eyes never leave the knife.

"Good. Then you know I mean it when I say that if you don't take my friend here straight home, do not pass go, do not collect $200, that I will hold you personally responsible, right?"

He nods, trembling, sweat dotting his receding hairline.

"Perfect. And you understand a quick death won't be in the cards for you if anything goes wrong." I lift his chin with the knife's tip to lock eyes with him. "Say you understand, David."

"I understand," he whispers.

"Perfect. Emma, close the door. David is going to bring you home," I say, my eyes never leaving his. "Make sure you text me when you get there so I can give David the tip he deserves."

"But I don't have your number," she says, searching her pockets for her phone. I hold it out to her through the back window. I swiped it when she was distracted with the doughy goodness earlier.

"Keep your phone closer than your weapon, sweetie. Backup is always a phone call away."

I step back, watching David execute a perfect turn at the next block, complete with a signal, like he's afraid I'll chase him down if he doesn't follow every traffic law known to man. I sigh in relief when they're out of sight before searching for whoever is trying to tail me, but the night is quiet, the shadows nothing more than darkness.

Time to go hunting.

I make it five blocks before I'm pissed. Not only is there two of them, but they're not even trying to hide the fact they're trailing me. The audacity of some men. For some reason, they think I'm weaker merely because I have a vagina. I mean, I can't throw a man through a window, but I can suffocate him with my thighs at the very least.

I pop around a corner and scramble on a dumpster, using the extra height to reach the stone awning over the door to the apartment building. Most of the rooms are empty, this being one of the places we use to house initiates before they're sworn into our ranks. The few initiates we have, we moved to the Depot when Mason went down. Victor said it was to protect them, but that explanation is flimsy.

I use the sills of the windows to scale my way up the building. Climbing is slow, but it's still faster than picking the lock. I have to remind myself to not look down to see whether the two have rounded the corner. I find the window I want half open on the third floor, shove it up the rest of the way to slip inside, and close it behind me.

Several minutes pass as I wait for them. After what feels like half the night, they appear. I hold my breath as they pause in front of the door to the apartments, praying they keep going. Their hesitation lasts long enough for them to check the locked door before they're moving again, toward the trap I set. I run to the apartment door as soon as they clear the dumpster, flying down the stairs and around corners. I'm almost to the bottom when I miss a step, and I land on my knee hard. I grit my teeth, hobbling the rest of the way, then pausing to inch the main door open. It swings out, allowing me to squeeze through the gap.

I doubt these two are here to take me out. Based on the leisurely pace they've set, they don't seem to care whether I notice them. I peek around the dumpster as they reach the point where they'll have to turn back. The alley is a dead-end, so I lean against the building and wait, rubbing my knee in a futile attempt to stop the throbbing.

"Where the hell did she go?" A man's voice hisses into the night, his partner murmuring an unintelligible response. Their rapid footsteps approach my hiding spot, and I pull out my switchblade. I might not think they're here to hurt me, but I'm not about to be caught off guard. They're still arguing as they pass me in frustrated whispers.

"What's up, buttercup? Or is it buttercups?" I call out.

They both swing around, one reaching behind for his gun, but when he spots me, his tattooed hand falls to his side. I'm momentarily speechless because—hot damn—this man is gorgeous. My gaze travels over his close-cropped ebony hair to his stormy gray eyes. He could rival Ryker for the most striking eyes. Scruff covers his strong jaw, accented by his full, round lips.

You cannot ogle this man, I scold myself, forcing my gaze away and am met with another ridiculously stunning guy. Holy shit, they're everywhere. Where Mr. Tall Dark and Handsome is glowering, this guy is grinning like a loon, *and* I fucking know him.

I realize why he looked so familiar when I met him weeks ago. Alex King. I stopped looking for pictures of the Kings years ago. The few the media does manage are blurry when it comes to Shane and Ren. Alex's picture, though, is splashed across sites, the public face of the King family. I couldn't make out a lot of Shane's features the other night, but I'm sure he's as gorgeous as these two. They probably swagger around, not a care in the world, knowing where their status doesn't reach, their looks will fill in the gaps.

Alex King, who accosted me at the gala—who, according to the media, I followed to a restaurant—is running his fingers through his short-cropped dirty blond waves before settling his hand on his hip. The street lamp beyond us catches the stud in his ear as he winks at me. His green eyes dance while he bites his lip. I swear I can see the outline of abs clearly through their dark, long-sleeve shirts. Pity I didn't see those through Alex's tux a few weeks ago.

Ten seconds. That's what I'm taking to gawk at them, then we'll get down to business. I tell myself it's because I'm surprised to see him again, but honestly, they're hot, and they clearly know it.

"That was a merry little chase you sent us on, Bug. We haven't had that much fun in weeks." His grin widens.

"If you thought that was fun, you must be pretty bored," I reply, trying to settle my rapidly beating heart. I try for nonchalance, but one glance at the other guy, and I don't think I'm pulling it off. I'm assuming this elusive, rarely seen gumdrop of a man is Ren King. Something tickles the back of my brain, trying to remind me where I've seen him, but it's just out of reach.

"Oh, we're bored. We could use a little more fun in our lives, couldn't we?" He nudges his friend, who doesn't move an inch. It must be like hitting a brick wall. His muscles probably have muscles.

"Sorry, boys. I don't play that way. I'm sure you could find a little entertainment a couple blocks up, though. Rita's always has a varied selection."

I'm kicking myself for not playing the part I've carefully cultivated over the years, but I don't have the energy anymore. Shane already saw me dressed down, claiming to have killed two men without any help. Pile on the shit with Mason, and I can't find it in me to pretend I'm lost or something. Plus, they've been following me for a while. Who knows what they've seen me do. At least I can have a little fun while they harass me.

"What?" Alex's smile falls from his lips, his eyes clouding with confusion, then frustration. His nostrils flare as he sucks in a deep breath.

"We don't pay for sex." His friend's smoky voice is edged with irritation, but his face is blank, like he doesn't care either way.

"Well, bully for you, then. You're not going to be getting it from me either way." I push upright, hoping to distract them enough to slip away.

Maybe I can play it off as having an off night. I can convince them I'm trying to fly under the radar, just enjoying a night out, without someone following me. The thought makes me snicker.

"I think there's been a misunderstanding. I'm Alex. We met at the gala a couple weeks ago. This is Ren. We just wanted to have a little chat."

That's not ominous being spoken in a dark, dead-end alley at almost midnight by someone who's quite often portrayed as our rivals. Not to mention their exploits on the west side of Synd are glaringly obvious, since I know how to read between the lines. I mean, the media reports the same over here. The fact that he's willing to give me his name now, when he didn't bother before, is telling. He was the distraction to keep me from interrupting the big bad mafia boss's little tête-à-tête. This night just keeps getting better and better.

"Sorry, boys. I'm not in a chatty mood. Got places to be." I shift my feet, testing the waters of how far they'll go to keep me here. Ren sways with me, eyes fixed on my body.

"All we need is a minute, Bug. Then you can be on your way. Surely, you can give us that, right?" Alex's grin is back, flashing straight, white teeth. I sigh, weighing the options of dodging them or their questions. I might stick him for spite if he keeps calling me bug, although that might expose me more than anything else. Decisions, decisions.

"What do you want."

"Why were you talking to that girl before? She didn't look old enough to be hanging out with the likes of you," Alex says.

I try not to be offended. I'm not sure if he is calling me old, a whore, or a mafia princess. I mean, they're part of a mafia, too, and older than me, so he definitely called me a whore. Dick.

"She needed directions."

His eyebrows shoot to his hairline, almost disappearing beneath the locks that have fallen forward.

"Directions?"

"Yup, least I could do was help a girl out, right? We gotta stick together. Never know who's lurking in the shadows," I reply, sarcasm dripping from my tone.

Ren leans to the side, eyes still on me, growling something to Alex, who nods carefully. Having both of them staring at me is making my skin itch.

"Listen, I think you know who we are by now. We plainly know who you are. We just want some more details on what happened to Emma the other night is all," Alex explains.

"Couple guys tried to grab her. I stopped them, dropped her at home. Not much else to tell." I shrug, looking off to the street. Now I'm annoyed I wasted this much time when I should be trying to find someone who can slip a message to Helms, which is my latest goal. Then I can convince him we had nothing to do with the ambush. We can team up and figure out what the hell happened. Victor clearly isn't going to do anything. Colin is too deep in the shit, trying to stay in Victor's good graces, and no one else seems to care.

"They're all dead? Who else was there? Did someone else step in? Did it look like they were targeting her specifically? What were they driving?" Alex fires off question after question, eyes intense. He's no longer the joking man before. He's in serious mode.

I hesitate, narrowing my eyes. I could tell them about the other guy, about the car, about my suspicions, but this is starting to feel more like an interrogation than a friendly little chat. This isn't how shit works in our world. My place in the family affords me with a lot, more than the Kings are giving, including respect. Am I not important enough to request a meeting? Shane can do things the right way, if he's so worried, instead of sending his two lackeys.

"Yeah, I'm going to have to decline any further questions, boys. Why don't you tell Shane King if he needs information to seek it out himself." I step sideways.

Ren reaches out, as if he's going to grab me, but Alex yanks him back, shaking his head.

"We don't want trouble between our families, Sammy," Alex says. I rear my head back like he slapped me. No one calls me Sammy except Mason, and lately, Colin.

"It's Sam," I snap, "and I don't give a flying fuck what you want. Do shit the right way next time, or I'll stab first and ask questions later."

I flip them off and turn, force my feet to move, tears gathering in my eyes. The shit going down in my life is enough, but now, I've completely blown my cover. Maybe I can pass it off as stress instead of a one-eighty personality shift. A tear slips over the edge, tracking down my face, but I won't run. No matter how much I want to.

THIRTEEN

REN

"Well, that was a bust. Do we follow her?" Alex asks, leaning around me to track Sam's disappearing form. "I doubt she'll appreciate that. She was clear she won't be talking to anyone other than Shane," I respond, walking out the alley and peering up and down the street. Sam faded into the darkness much faster than I imagined she would.

We make our way back, the streets getting gradually brighter the closer we get to club row. A line of them on each side of the river faces each other, bright lights flashing over the water, booming music echoing across. As the clubs fight to be heard, they create a cacophony of sounds, and my head pounds. I'm not a fan of the clubs, no matter which side they're on, but unfortunately, our business frequently takes us here. These businesses are the closest ones to the river, the Barrens only being a few blocks wide before the clubs take over.

Most of our contacts like to meet in the mass of people, innocently assuming we won't do anything if they double cross us. They forget we know where they live, where they hang out, who their friends are, and usually, I know before anyone else if they've crossed the line between being criminals and fucking us over. We've perfected our systems, so we rarely have to deal with moles these days, but there's always one, like Marco, who thinks they can push us.

"We didn't get much. Shane isn't going to be happy about that," Alex comments, gently pushing a woman who stumbles into him. He doesn't even look at her, too preoccupied with Sam, I'm sure.

"Well, it's not like we could force her. Wouldn't be a good look if we kidnapped her." I tip my head at the bouncer at one of the clubs.

He hooks his thumb over his shoulder, inviting us in, but I ignore him. Alex is lost in thought, barely paying attention to where we're going until we slip into the car parked in a random alley.

"You really think she would have stabbed me?" He's energized by the thought. Idiot.

I roll my eyes. "Doubt it. You're too pretty for her to cut," I scoff.

"Weird, though, how she reacted at the end, right?"

I suck in a breath, trying not to snap at him. "Perhaps you shouldn't have called her Sammy. In fact, you might need to lay off the pet names altogether."

"Nah, she's like a cute little ladybug, flitting around and looking all adorable." He smirks.

I don't mention the tear I saw trickling down her cheek. I doubt Alex noticed. I can't figure out why calling her Sammy would affect her so much. She tried to hide behind her ire, but when Alex called her Sammy, pain flooded her eyes. I didn't recognize it at first, but looking back, that was exactly what it was: deep-seated pain. The only source I can fathom it stems from is Mason. I hate deciphering feelings. They change so suddenly; I can't track them. I can't analyze them. It would be much easier if everyone just said what they meant instead of hiding behind propriety or whatever the fuck they're running from.

"I doubt she'd think it was adorable, you comparing her to a ladybug," I say, driving farther away from the lights, crossing the bridge to our side, the tension easing from my shoulders. I'd rather be in King territory, especially if shit goes down.

"Ah, well, I just won't tell her, then. How do you think she slipped us? I mean, we checked the door."

"She clearly used the apartment. She could have locked the door behind her."

He doesn't look convinced. "But it was a deadbolt. Unless she has a key, which, then begs the question, why would she? And why was she in the Barrens when Emma was there? And why was she dressed like that?"

"You have questions I don't have answers to, Alex. You know as much as I do." I concede, although it hurts to admit it.

The closer we look at Samantha Byrns, the more of a puzzle she becomes. She's starting to become like the Wraith: impossible to track, a riddle I can't decipher. I hate every minute of it.

"You think she knows about the article?" He turns wide eyes to me, easily skipping past the things he doesn't understand. I wish I had his ability to turn off the need-to-know, to understand everything. Most of the time, I don't bother paying attention to what's going on around me if it won't affect me, but when something smacks me in the face, I can't turn away like he does.

"I'm sure she's seen it. I doubt she cares. Every week, the media has some speculation on who she's dating, who she's meeting, how it will affect her brother. It's probably why she's cultivated such a careful persona in front of them. Have you spoken with Victor yet?" I ask.

"No, he's still not returning any calls. I told Shane to text Colin instead. You think she's got a persona? I knew there was more than meets the eye with her. At the gala, there were times . . ."

"Your fascination with Samantha Byrns is starting to rival Shane's," I comment, pulling into the drive, nodding to the guards stationed out front.

When Sam dropped Emma off, Shane raged, putting a guard shack at the end of the drive, as if that'll keep her out. "There's just something about her . . ."

I hate when he doesn't finish his sentences, trailing off into nothing, never spelling out his thoughts.

"Get out." I grab a water bottle from the back seat, gesturing toward the door, before taking a sip.

"Do you think she thought I was calling her a whore?"

I choke, water dribbling down my chin. I swipe it off with my sleeve, gaping at him. "What?"

"Well, there was that whole paying-for-sex thing, but I think she was fucking with us. Then I said it didn't seem like Emma would hang out with someone like her. Her whole body changed. I wonder if she thought I was calling her a whore or a streetwalker or something. I wasn't. You think she thought I was?"

I rub my face, wishing he would just get the fuck out and leave me alone. This is a conversation for Shane, although I doubt he would appreciate Alex's confession, for a very different reason.

"I'm sure you'll charm her the next time we cross paths, and she'll forget all about the time you insinuated she was a hooker." Exhaustion seeps into my bones.

"You think we'll see her again? I mean, not at some swanky party where she's all dolled up and looking like a blue-ringed octopus?" Hope blooms across his face.

"What the fuck is that?"

"A blue-ringed octopus. You know, they look all pretty, but they're super poisonous. They release a toxin; makes it so you can't breathe or move and then you have a heart attack and die, like in minutes. I think they live in Australia, like on the reefs and stuff."

"The random shit you remember, I swear. To answer your question, yes, I think we'll be seeing a lot more of Sam than we ever have before.

Be careful, Alex, I have a feeling you'll get sucked into her orbit, and the ending might not be what you imagine."

He crosses his arms, staring out the window. "Now you sound like Shane. It's not like I'm going to slip and stick my dick in her or something. I have some class, you know."

A knock on the window startles me, and I curse, rolling it down for Shane to lean in.

"What the hell are you two doing?"

"We were talking," Alex grumbles, still pouting.

"Well, how did it go?"

I hesitate, wondering how to word things so he doesn't freak out when we tell him Emma was out on her own again, but Alex doesn't have the same qualms, always leaping into shit before thinking things through.

"Emma was down on club row just now, with Sam. We saw her get in a car, think Sam sent her home. Then we had a chat. You're not going to like it, though," he says, leaning over the console, both of them boxing me in. I swipe my clammy palms on my pants.

"Basically, she reiterated what she told you before. She said you should request a meeting if you had questions," I blurt, hoping he'll drop it, and they'll both leave me the fuck alone.

"A meeting? Like she's someone who can even do that? She probably doesn't even know the protocols of requesting a meeting." He scoffs.

"You really think she's just an airhead? I mean, she's grown up in the life," Alex says, leaning in more.

"I choose to believe what she presents, which is someone who doesn't give a damn about anything other than the status her brother affords her."

I eye him, wondering if he actually believes what he's saying or merely hiding to save face. Instead of the confident leader he usually presents, though, indecision and confusion fill his eyes. He doesn't understand what we're up against any more than the rest of us, which I'm not sure is comforting or horrifying.

"Hold on to that line of thinking too long, and you'll miss the signs when something else comes along," I mutter.

"Okay, Confucius." He scoffs, pulling back. Alex pushes his door open, finally vacating my space, and I sigh in relief, the tingling in my fingers fading.

"You coming?" he calls, halfway out of the car.

"Shut the door, Alex."

He slams it shut, and I wait until they're clear before gunning it around the fountain and back out into the dark streets. This time of night, our area of the city is quiet, all the rich and ridiculous tucked into their beds. There aren't any fancy parties or stupid balls to attend tonight for them to gossip at and spend all their money. I ignore the fact we're among those elite, even though, on the surface, we're the same. Under the clothes and mansions and money, we're a family taking care of those under us, running the city for them, instead of corrupt cops and dirty politicians taking advantage of them. Most people would say we're no better, bringing in the corruption with drugs and guns and god knows what else, but it's all about control. We hold it so others can't. Our control allows for those who usually are ignored to be taken care of.

I slow when I hit the edge of the Barrens, taking the bridge closest to the Byrns estate, then speeding up when I clear the other side. I doubt I'll find her, but something is driving me to try anyway. Likely, she called a car or had one stashed away, like we did. She's probably already home, locked up tight. I wonder if she would have given us more if we would have asked about her brother instead of focusing on Emma. I shake my head, scanning the suburbs' dark streets.

My phone rings, and I hit the button on my steering wheel. "What?"

"Where the hell did you go? Shane's reading Emma the riot act, and I have nothing to do now."

I roll my eyes. "Why don't you try to solve one of the many problems cropping up? Like the lower gang in the ninth isn't tithing. Or the shit with Marco. You could let off some steam, sending him down the river. Or—crazy thought—you could go to bed."

I kill the lights, the closer I get to the Byrns' estate. There, security isn't as visible as ours, but I'd rather not be accosted, especially since I have no reason to actually be here. I turn the corner and catch a shadow detaching from the tree line a block away, headed straight for the mansion. Our place has lights strategically placed, lighting up the corners of the backyard, but the Byrns' place is dark, unless you count the few windows spilling light from the upper level. I almost miss Alex's retort. I'm so focused on the figure slipping in and out of the dark.

"You know I won't sleep. Maybe I will deal with Marco. You said Junior wants to be there? You think he'll try to interfere, or is he wanting to participate?"

"It's James, and participate," I mumble, leaning over the wheel, trying to get a closer look. Right when I think they'll disappear, they glance behind, their face glowing from the streetlight a block down, and there she is: Samantha Byrns. She's sneaking across the lawn now, headed for a side door. She checks the windows as she passes, and a shiver runs down my spine.

"Ren, you still there?"

"Yeah," I mutter.

"What are you doing? Did you find something?"

"Yeah." I watch as she slides the door closed behind her, none the wiser I was watching.

"Well, what is it?"

"Something interesting."

FOURTEEN

SAMANTHA

I'm still annoyed when I slide the side door closed. It took me forever to walk home. The creeping prickles along my back when Alex and Ren were following me, tagged along, itching between my shoulder blades all the way home. I took the long way to the estate, hoping to lose them, but apprehension stalked me right to the door.

The library is dark and silent, the only light glowing from the moon, filtering through the open curtains. I love this room, but tonight, it feels intimidating and lonely. I listen for any movement from the hall. It's after two in the morning, with only the guards awake at this point. I've done all I can to avoid being here during the day, to avoid the suffocating absence of Mason and men's leering eyes that have slunk to Victor's side. The men I thought who would never abandon my brother, who would stand by Colin's side as the rightful person to take over, are curiously quiet. Everyone is holding their breath, with the fate of our family and organization so uncertain.

I check the hallway, breathing a sigh of relief when I find it empty. The house is a maze, designed to disorient anyone who breaks in . . . or out. Built by my many-greats grandfather when he settled here. He established the city and set up how it should be run with our family at the center. Synd has evolved since then, but the underbelly of it all is still rooted in my family's history.

I turn the corner and rush up the stairs, intent on a shower and my bed. I may be used to operating at night, but lately, I've been up before dawn, too, which is taking a toll on me. I'm almost there when Victor steps out of a room three doors down from mine: Mason's room.

"Ah, Samantha. You're coming in late, are you not? I hope you weren't tarnishing our good name." Victor's lip curls, the insinuation clear.

"Just a little stroll."

I wouldn't answer if I didn't have to. At this point, I'm afraid of what he'll do if I openly defy him. I'd like to think others would back me up, but I'm not convinced enough to do it yet.

"Oh? And who were you seeing this evening? Anyone I would happen to know?"

I study his long face, avoiding his empty, watery eyes, trying to determine whether he's fishing or knows I was meeting with someone.

"Why would you think I was meeting anyone? Having me tailed, Uncle?" I try to keep my tone even, as if I don't think that's a possibility, but I'm not sure I pull it off.

"Of course not, Samantha. Why ever would I need to have you followed? It's not like you're a threat, are you?"

"I'm quite loyal, Victor. Never fear that." Loyal to Mason, to the Byrns, not to him, never to him.

"Oh, I don't have much to fear from you, dear." He chuckles, wheezing. "I would caution you to be careful, though. There are many out there that would like to hit us while we're transitioning. You wouldn't want to give the impression that we aren't able to stand on our own, would you?"

I shake my head slowly, trying to decipher his warnings.

"I didn't think so. Appearances can be so deceiving. You happen upon an innocent conversation with someone, and others interpret it as nefarious. Step in a situation, and suddenly, you're on a radar. One meeting can turn into a disaster. I thought you'd be better at navigating these situations, seeing as how you've grown up with it. Perhaps Mason didn't teach you as well as he thought he did. I won't judge you too harshly, though, given what you are." Victor shakes his head in mock disappointment.

"And what is that?"

"A woman, of course. Don't worry, dear, we'll find a way for you to be useful. Never fear." He strides past me to the stairs, leaving me to drown in a pool of obvious accusations and threats he's flung me into.

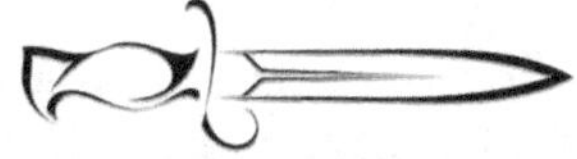

"Mason, I won't be able to come back for a while. Victor is probably having me tailed. I think he knows about my saving Emma and those two jackasses cornering me. I'm sure it looked like we were meeting instead of them accosting me. I'm sure he suspects I'm trying to reach Helms. Colin is picking guys we trust to guard your room, but I need you to wake up. Love you."

I kiss his forehead, something he'd never let me do if he were awake, pushing his black hair back. He looks like he's sleeping. I'd jump on his bed if I thought it would help, forcing his eyes open, like we did when we were kids. He'd glare at me and try to pelt me with pillows, and everything would go back to normal. Him running our section of the city and me working behind the scenes, with no one the wiser.

I think back to Shane calling me princess. He bought the persona I carefully cultivate to the world. Usually, it makes me giddy knowing I'm able to play the part so well, but with him, it's annoying. I hate to admit I've thought about our short interaction much more than is strictly necessary. Between my mind wandering back on my encounter with him, plus the run-in with Alex and Ren . . . they're taking up too much of my daydreams.

I need to focus on other things: what Victor is planning, the ambush—who's apparently snatching our people off the street, rather than those three. The more I think about it, though, the more I wonder if I'll be seeking them out for information sooner rather than later.

I pull my hand away from Mason, shaking my head, set off on my mission: catching my tail. What I do with him—well, I'm not sure yet, but it won't be pretty.

I end up walking for hours. I left the hospital long after sunset, hoping I'd be able to be home early, but it's after one in the morning, and I still haven't trapped my prey. Whoever it is, they aren't a newbie. I hope it isn't someone I know. I walk to the club's entrance, the bass making the concrete shudder, past a line of girls in way-too-short dresses for this late in the year freezing their asses off. I'm in dark jeans and an off-the-shoulder sweater, my feet tucked into my ballet flats.

I flash a smile at the bouncer, one of ours, and leave the groans behind as I slip through the door.

Step one: a drink.

Step two: bathroom.

Step three: slip out the back.

Step four: catch whoever follows.

I make it to step three and wait. And wait. And wait some more. I'm about to give up when a figure lumbers out the back door I had exited fifteen minutes before, and another appears at the narrow opening by the front of the club.

"Oh, goody, there's two of you," I quip from the darkness, making the thin man spin. His friend hems me in, forcing me back to keep both in my line of sight. They're both mid-30s, lanky. Everything about them seems long. They are nothing alike, yet the same: unforgettable, perfect to be tailing someone. They could work for the Byrns, and I wouldn't recognize them.

"Vicky send you guys to tail me?" They look at each other, probably trying to figure out who Vicky is. These kinds of guys aren't that bright, so I hope I can get them to talk without using more persuasive methods.

"We don't know a Vicky," Thing One says.

"Sure you don't. Listen, I'm going to cut to the chase here. I need you two to move on. No more following me. No more reporting back to Victor. You go your way, and I'll go mine."

"Can't do that," Thing Two replies.

I knew they couldn't. Victor would kill them, but I had to try.

"Yeah, I figured that. How about I stab you both now, get it over, real fast and easy." I reach behind and pull my knife out from under my sweater. Thing One jumps back, hands in front, warding me off.

"We don't want any of that," he exclaims, voice squeaking, trying to placate me as I advance on him.

"Well, why don't you tell me what you've been passing along to my illustrious Uncle, huh?"

"He wanted to see where . . ." His eyes shift over my shoulder toward his partner.

Thing Two wraps his arms around my upper body like I anticipated, trying to pull me away. Neither of them reach for their weapons, which is telling.

I'm about to flip Thing Two when he grunts and releases me, doubling over, which causes me to stumble forward. Thing One rushes me, and I straighten for his attack. It never comes. He speeds past, flipping a knife out.

Confused, I turn, taking in the scene. Thing Two is pummeling someone, not noticing his friend approaching from behind. I watch in shock as he is violently thrown back, straight on to Thing One's blade. I can't help but wince as chaos ensues.

Thing One is gaping at his blade, slick with blood. Thing Two is howling, clutching his back, and there stands my would-be rescuer.

Alex King.

Chest heaving, a black eye already darkening his face, he's nothing like the happy-go-lucky man I met the other night. Blood is flecked across his fists and running from his nose along with a cut across his strong jaw.

"What in the ever-loving hell are you doing?!" I yell, finding my voice.

Alex zeros in on the two men bouncing around. They've forgotten all about us. Thing Two, who is now cussing out his partner, stumbles closer. Alex grabs his arm, wrenching it behind and forcing him to his knees. I lunge, trying to grab Thing One, but he takes off for the road, his footsteps lost in the bass flowing from the club.

Alex growls, baring his teeth at Thing Two, who squirms, blood seeping from his wound. He's sputtering and whimpering now that his partner has abandoned him. Obviously, they never thought they'd be in this situation. I wasn't even going to kill them. I can't question dead men.

"I need to get him to the hospital," I say, putting my knife away.

"He's not going anywhere." Alex glares down at his captive, face fierce.

"He's going to die if he's not patched up."

"Good." He grins manically. I swear Thing Two is about to piss his pants.

"Are you going to tell your keeper what happened?" I ask the man trembling at my feet. He shakes his head, like an obedient puppy, eager to please.

"See? He's going to be stitched up, say he got jumped, and talk Thing One into keeping his mouth shut. Right?" He nods, swaying from the blood loss.

"Who the hell is Thing One?" Alex's bright green eyes find mine, stuck between bafflement and rage.

"The other guy who ran off. This is Thing Two. We didn't exchange names before you decided to step in white-knighting it everywhere." I scowl. The audacity of some men.

"He grabbed you," he says, like that's enough of a reason.

"Yes, like I wanted him to. A lot easier to get answers when one person is unconscious."

"But he grabbed you."

I swear it's like talking to a toddler.

"Listen, I'm going to need you to see yourself out of this situation. Now. I don't need your help. I don't want your help, and I'm getting a little annoyed that you keep following me around."

"I wasn't following you."

I scoff, rolling my eyes. Maybe if I ignore him, he'll wander away. Doubtful, but I'm willing to give anything a try at this point.

"You ready for a little stroll, Thing Two?" His eyes flick between Alex and me, doubt and pain clouding his face.

"I'm not letting him go. He'll just try to kill you again," Alex growls, twisting the man's arm.

I throw up my hands, beyond done with this.

"He wasn't trying to kill me!" The bleeding man nods, still swinging his panicked eyes between us.

"Of course he's going to say that! Please tell me you're not that naïve, Bug."

"Would you stop calling me bug! I have a fucking name, you know!"

"Is that really what you want to focus on here? A pet name?" he yells. Thank god the music drowns out our spat from people milling about the front of the club.

"I am not a pet! I don't even know you. Can't you leave me the hell alone?"

"I never said you were a pet. For fuck's sake, Sam. You could say 'thank you.'"

"Thank you? Thank you?! Why the hell would I say thank you for sticking your nose into my business? What would possibly possess me to thank you for screwing things up so royally that I'll be spending the rest of the night tracking some asshole down before he gets back to whomever is paying him? Are you so thick that it's inconceivable that a woman could handle shit on her own? You have to step in, you stubborn ass."

"I'm stubborn?!" Alex throws his hands in the air before planting them on his hips.

"Yes, you are stubborn. And an ass." I cross my arms, ready to battle it out with this ridiculously sexy man.

Movement from the corner of my eye has me pausing whatever vitriol I'm going to throw at him next. Thing Two limps as fast as his bleeding kidney will allow toward the lights and freedom from the two crazy people screaming at each other in a back alley.

"Oh, for fuck's sake," I sigh as Alex whips around. He's about to take off after the dead-man-walking when I grab his arm, pulling him back. Calmly, I unsheathe my knife, cock my arm back, and let it fly. The blade sinks cleanly into the base of Thing Two's neck, and he drops, dead before he hits the ground.

FIFTEEN

ALEX

I hurry up the steps of Shane's house, my house, but old habits die hard. I've never felt like I belonged, even though I was raised here alongside Shane and Ren. They had fathers—shitty fathers, but they were still there. It's a miracle I survived past age five after my own dad died.

I hustle down the hall, intent on Shane's office. My blood is still pumping from the fight and watching Sam take that guy out. The scene replayed in my head the whole ride. She's more skilled than we thought, and I got hard reliving it. Even her screaming at me after was ridiculously hot.

Taking a deep breath, I push open the door, finding both Shane and Ren inside. I amble over to the chair and listen to them bicker about some lower gang that hasn't been tithing.

"We should take care of them ourselves," Ren states, knowing his tone will piss Shane off.

"Why the hell would we do that when we pay other people to do it for us? Let the initiates take care of it or Jason's group. He's been itchin' for a fight ever since he found out his girl got knocked up by some other dude," Shane replies, eyes fixed on his computer.

"More and more of the gangs are stepping out of line. They're worried about their people going missing. A show of force from us will set a precedent."

Ren looks at me, confusion coloring his eyes as he examines my damaged face, courtesy of Thing One. Great, now I'm calling him by Sam's stupid nickname. I fight a grin when I remember our argument over my pet name for her.

"What the hell happened to you?" Shane glares, which would intimidate me if I didn't know him.

"Got in a little fight." This time, I grin.

"You look like you ran into a fist about seventeen times," Ren comments.

"Sounds about right." I rub my knuckles on my pants to erase the blood there.

"Cut the bullshit, Alex. I thought you were going to talk to Denise about the disappearances," Shane demands.

"Well, I was, and I did, but she didn't know anything. She did hear about someone who might shed some light on our predicament, so I went to have a chat with him, but he was bouncing down at NightStorm—"

"The new nightclub? The one in Byrns' territory?" Ren says.

"One and the same."

"Wait"—Shane pinches the bridge of his nose—"you're telling me you went into Byrns' territory, without backup and then got the shit kicked out of you?"

"When you put it that way, it sounds bad." I grin at him again, unfazed.

"Maybe next time a text, dumbass," Ren says dryly.

I shrug, my shoulder twinging a little.

"So, did you at least get something out of it?" Shane groans.

I don't think he means getting to see Sam again or watching her kill Thing Two or getting a raging hard-on over the whole thing.

"Uhh, sort of." I try to discreetly adjust myself, but of course, they notice. Ren scowls, probably thinking I got my dick wet.

"I swear if you went east side to find some random fuck, I'm going to make you run an initiate group for a fucking month," Shane growls.

"Nope, but it was just as hot. I got to the club and happened to glance down the alley, and what do I see but our little friend in a bit of trouble?"

"Our little friend?"

"The one and only Samantha Byrns. Getting jumped. So, I, like the good Samaritan I am, went to help."

"Help?" Shane asks.

"You can't leave well enough alone, can you? We have a plan to figure out how she connects to all this." Ren shakes his head, looking disgusted.

"Would you get to the point already?"

"I would if you two would quit interrupting. Geesh." I pause, and Shane's face turns red. "So, two guys, one grabbed her. I pulled him off, and he got a couple hits in. I may have been a little distracted, making sure the other guy wasn't going to take Sam but then Thing One ended up stabbing Thing Two when I threw him off me."

"Who is Thing One and Thing Two?" Ren questions.

"Sam named them Thing One and Thing Two. So, Thing One took off, and Thing Two ended up no longer among the living." I'm dying to tell them how he died, practically bouncing in my seat with anticipation.

"Did you at least question him before you killed him?" Shane's asks, muffling his words as he rubs his hands over his face.

"Well, not exactly."

"What do you mean, 'not exactly?'"

"Sam started yelling at me for helping her! It wasn't my fault he got away." I wince, wishing I could stuff that revelation back in my mouth.

"I thought you said you killed him? So, is he alive or dead?" Ren chimes in.

"Oh, he's most certainly dead, but I didn't kill him. He tried to limp away, and Sam whipped a knife out and chucked it at him, like a fucking ninja, and the blade sunk into his neck. It was hot as fuck." I sigh, imagining it all again.

"There's something wrong with you. You're telling me she got a lucky shot, and that's what got your dick hard?" Shane rolls his eyes.

"That was not a lucky shot. Thing Two was at least thirty feet away when she threw it. This woman knows how to handle her knives. I wonder what else she's exceptional at handling?" I sigh again. "I think I'm in love."

"Oh, for fuck's sake. I can't deal with him." Ren throws his hands up and slams the door on his way out. Such a sensitive baby.

"Alex, I need you to focus and not on her tits. Why were they after her?"

"According to Sam, they weren't. She said they were tailing her. I don't think she knew for sure who sent them. There was a fair bit of yelling on her part. She also thinks we're still following her."

"Well, of course she thinks we're following her when you're literally showing up right when you think she's in trouble. Were you?"

"Course not. You said we should lay off, so I did." I'm insulted he thinks I'd disobey direct orders. I may go off the grid every once in a while, but I'm not about to disrespect him. I owe him too much.

"Wouldn't blame you if you did," Shane mutters, eyes wandering back to his computer.

"Oh ho! Is someone smitten by the forbidden Samantha Byrns?" I smirk, waiting for him to rise to the bait.

"The last thing I am is 'smitten' by Princess Byrns. I had a two-minute conversation with her, and it was the most infuriating experience I've ever been through. And then she disappeared. You can't be smitten with someone after one encounter."

"Doth protest too much, methinks. We're just going to ignore the fact that you've been obsessed with any information you come across about her for years, then?"

"I think it's obvious why I need to keep an on eye the other side of the river," he states dryly, leveling me with a look.

"Sure, we can keep pretending that's why, but if you ask me . . ."

"Which I didn't."

"I think you're salty because the only details you can dig up on her is that she's an airhead, which she definitely is not," I reply, picking dried blood from my fingers.

"And your three short interactions have given you such an insight on her to deduce she's not an airhead?" The skepticism comes through loud and clear.

"Yup. Plus watching her for an entire night. I mean, she set up a trap both Ren and I fell for. She cornered us, Shane. She disappeared and reappeared behind us. I still can't wrap my head around how she did it unless she hopped in the dumpster, but I'm sure we'd have heard her."

"Ren thinks she hid in the apartment building until you passed."

"I checked the door. Locked. So, unless she's real handy with a lock pick, as in, extraordinary levels of handy, which is entirely possible, she didn't use the building."

"Whatever. I don't care how she did it. I care about why she's meeting with Emma. We've got problems if they're intentionally meeting. I don't want Samantha anywhere near my sister. The whole thing is a disaster waiting to happen." Shane drums his fingers on his desk, staring off.

"Sam. I don't think she likes to be called Samantha. Or Sammy."

"Why the hell do I care?"

"Thought I'd mention it, in case you ever have an actual conversation with her. She bit my head off when I called her Sammy." I keep the sight of her shimmering tears to myself.

"I think I'm going to send Emma to Aunt Marge's," he says, ignoring my insight.

"She's going to hate you."

"Better she hates me than be dead or caught in whatever scheme Byrns is starting."

"You really think she's trying to use Emma? If she wanted to do that, she wouldn't have helped her not be kidnapped," I point out.

It's obvious Sam is on our side in this scenario, but Shane is hell-bent on her being the villain. Ren, too, but that's not surprising. There are few people Ren trusts and considers only two of them friends, who are both in this house. She might not actually be on our side, but she's not the enemy. I'm certain.

"I wouldn't put it past her uncle. I can't figure out if she's working with him or fighting against him. Every report I receive contradicts itself. I don't trust Victor farther than I can throw him. Whatever he's doing over there is shady as shit. He isn't even supposed to be running things. Do we have an update on Mason Byrns?"

"I don't keep track of that shit. Ask Ren." I push myself to my feet. I need a shower and some pain meds. Maybe I'll be able to find sleep tonight instead of staring at my ceiling until 4 a.m., like usual.

"Alex"—I swivel, meetings Shane's concerned gaze—"don't get too attached to her. We can't afford the distraction."

"Aw, Shane, didn't you know? I'm always up for a good distraction."

SIXTEEN

SAMANTHA

"Colin!"

I race down the estate's stairs. Colin pauses at his car, glancing back at me. A look flashes across his face too fast for me to decipher before his usual soft smile takes over.

"What's up, Sam?" he huffs, hand still on the car door.

"Where are you going? I thought we were going to the Depot together?" I'm a little hurt he didn't remember he planned on driving me.

"Yeah, about that . . ." He rubs his neck, avoiding my eyes.

"Spit it out, Ashford."

"Maybe you should stay here," he suggests sheepishly.

"I need to be there, Colin. I need to figure out what Victor is planning. People are disappearing, right off the street, and no one is saying anything. I have to be at this meeting." I sound like I'm pleading, but I don't care. I'll never solve Mason's ambush if I'm shut out.

"You think you need to be there, Sam, but you don't. I can tell you everything when I come back. I'm worried about you. I don't want you on Victor's radar. Leave the disappearances to us. We'll get to the bottom of whatever is going on." He squeezes my shoulder and gets in, dismissing me completely.

I can't believe he's going to leave me behind. I'm not a child in need of coddling. He's been like a brother to me, helping train and raise me alongside Mason. He's stressed, but I have to fight the feeling he just patted me on the head and told me to behave.

I rap my knuckles on the window. He sighs as he rolls it down. I bite back the retort I want to hurl at him.

"You'll tell me everything?"

"Yes, Sam. I know what I'm doing."

"Okay, but make sure you ask about questioning the lower gangs on who they're losing and if anyone has any leads. And ask about the ambush. Ask if anyone else can get a hold of Helms. He's our best bet at anything we haven't been able to dig up. Don't forget to ask Shake about the missing shipments, too." I rattle off instructions, even as Colin's knuckles turn white on his steering wheel.

"I have done this sort of thing before, Sam. I told you I know what I'm doing. Besides, I'm pretty sure we know who's snatching people."

"What? Who? How come you didn't tell me?"

"Victor thinks it's the Kings, and for once, I agree with him," Colin answers.

What utter bullshit. I didn't tell anyone about Emma or her attempted kidnapping. Victor suspects something, but the last thing I need is him breathing down my neck. I wouldn't put it past him to use the Kings for whatever plans he has and be damned protocols our families have had in place for years. We stay here, they stay there. No harm, no foul. The thought of the Kings being behind this, even without knowing about Emma, is laughable. They wouldn't be that stupid.

"That's bullshit, Colin. Why would they be taking people?"

"Flesh trade, Sam. There's a lot of money in it. Shane King, he's not like us. He doesn't have morals."

I scoff. "Oh, yes, because we're filled with morals running a criminal organization."

"You know what I mean. They don't care about selling girls. They don't care if a new drug is laced with arsenic. They don't care about anything other than money and amassing more power. I assume they'll be coming for us next."

"They're not orchestrating the disappearances," I snap.

Colin's face tightens, lips pressed into a thin line. "I know them better than you, Samantha."

"A few weeks ago, Emma King was almost kidnapped. Why would they try to kidnap their own family?"

Colin's forehead furrows in thought. I want to keep the whole thing to myself, but I can't have Colin thinking the Kings are at fault. That slows down finding any tangible information on the real villains.

"Are you sure?"

I bristle at the skepticism in his voice. He's never asked me if I'm sure about information. Hurt blossoms in my chest that he no longer trusts my abilities, my judgment. Granted, I usually go to Mason for this sort of thing, but Colin should know me better.

Mason wouldn't doubt me, I think, the pain doubling.

"Yeah, I'm sure," I mutter.

"It doesn't matter. What matters is that you're safe. Don't do something stupid, Sammy. Mason's going to need you when he wakes up."

With that final punch to the gut, his car rolls away. I thought Mason was open with me about things, but what if he didn't tell me about the Kings? What if Colin is right, and these guys are into more shady shit than we are? It doesn't add up with what I've seen, though. Nothing is adding up anymore. The deeper I fall into the shadows, the more questions than answers I find.

Alex's smirking face and twinkling green eyes flash through my mind. I can't meld that picture with someone who deals in flesh. They couldn't keep it quiet if they were dabbling in the trade. I've never heard of dirty drugs, sex trafficking, or even dirty deals from the west side. I deal in information; that's my bread and butter. I would have picked up on the whispers if they were.

Unless this is their big move. I dismiss the thought, though. The Kings aren't our rivals, not really. They're not our allies, either, but either way, the possibility of them running an underground operation is ridiculous. Regardless, maybe it's time to have a little chat with Shane King. He's clearly not going to come to me. Colin is cutting me out; I've gathered all I can from the streets, and Helms is hiding up north. The Kings are the next logical option—maybe the only option left, actually. I would prefer to wait for this little mission until I have a plan, but the meeting at the Depot is the best opportunity to not be tailed. I take off, hoping I'll finally get answers.

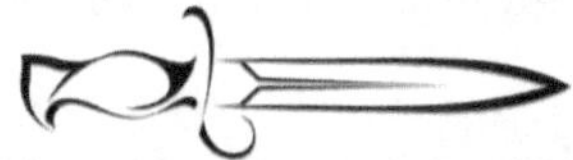

I sit in Shane's office, spinning in his chair. I can barely make out objects in the dark, but I sit, taking in a glimpse of someone who is an enigma to me. I haven't seen him in ten years, other than our brief encounter a few weeks ago. I had watched him from my window when he'd met with my brother after the attempted coup, which put most of the leaders in our city in the ground. Mason said they were merely reestablishing protocols with the west when I asked who he was. I was thirteen, my world thrown into chaos, but I still remember thinking he was the most intimidating person ever.

Then the rules were handed down. I was not to go to the west side. I couldn't talk to anyone under King control. I was to train and learn and would never be a victim like so many women in our past. I was never to seek out Shane King or those closest to him. Under no circumstances should they ever be informed I'm the Wraith. Mason made it clear: death would be preferable if they found out.

Once I proved I could handle my shit, some of those rules were relaxed. Sometimes, I'd go into King territory but never too far, at least not until I'd walked Emma home. Sometimes, I'd meet with someone under King control, but it was always on Mason's say-so.

I learned. I trained. I became stronger.

Every once in a while, Mason would warn me away from them, fear and guilt in his eyes. Now I'm breaking those rules. One by one, they're falling by the wayside. I hope my brother understands I have no choice.

Soft footfalls approach from the hall. I tense, then relax my muscles, trying to appear calm and in control, my heart threatening to beat out of my chest. I don't think he'll try to hurt me, but between Mason's warnings and taking the final step of shattering my carefully crafted persona, I'm scared to fucking death. The handle jiggles before the door swings open silently. In steps all six-foot-three inches of the head of the King family. He flips on the lights and startles at the sight of me, still spinning in his chair. Quickly, his face morphs into a scowl.

"How the hell did you get in here?" he growls, stalking toward me.

"Ah, ah, ah," I caution, pulling the gun from under the desk.

He pulls up short, staring at it, then back at me. I'm sure he's contemplating whether he can get to me before I shoot him.

Newsflash: he can't.

He might be wondering if I have the stomach to shoot him.

Another newsflash: I don't, but what he doesn't know won't hurt him.

I gesture to the chair opposite, and he sinks down, icy blue eyes burning with hatred. My nose crinkles as I take in his features. Bastard has those long eyelashes, the kind every girl is secretly envious of. They're dark, too, and his eyebrows perfectly frame his face. I mentally shake myself.

"Easy, cupcake. I think it's time for you and I to have a little chat."

I pull an apple out of my front pocket of my black hoodie. It's a little bruised from all the climbing, but it's edible.

"That's my gun." He eyes my fruit like it kicked his puppy before meeting my gaze. I take a giant bite, buying time to pull my shit together.

His jaw ticks, looking like it was chiseled out of marble, along with his abs, I'm sure.

I don't know what they're putting in the water on this side of town, but these men are gorgeous. It makes me irrationally mad. Why can't they be dumpy or have pimples? Would it kill them to eat a cheeseburger every once in a while, pack on a few pounds? Would help when trying to concentrate in their presence. I might be able to keep my drool in my mouth if they didn't look like they were stepping out of an underwear ad. No, Shane has to have an entirely symmetrical face, unruly hair that is begging to have fingers run through, grabbed on, pulled . . . I shake my head, blinking rapidly. This is getting out of hand.

Maybe, if I keep staring at him, I'll become desensitized to his good looks, or he'll piss me off enough that I'll forget, like with Alex. With the way he's looking at me, getting more annoyed with every bite I take, I might test that theory sooner rather than later.

Once I've eaten around the bruised parts, I chuck the rest in his trash. Shane presses his lips into a thin line, and his jaw twitches again. I want to laugh, but I'm too worried whether I can pull this off and come out the other side unscathed. When I'm the Wraith, I can shut off my emotions, knowing I'm helping my family. This time, though, doubt is clouding my ability to think. I'm half expecting Mason to bust through the door and ream me out for being here. Those fears, coupled with Colin's suspicions, and Shane's hooded gaze, are derailing my abilities.

"You going to tell me why you're here, or do you have another snack tucked away somewhere?" he spits out.

Note to self: don't tell him about the cashews stashed in my pocket.

"Can't blame a girl for eating"—I shrug—"I believe you have information for me."

"And you thought breaking into my office and holding me at gunpoint was a good way to procure that information?"

"I only have this for my safety, and I can't exactly enact protocols."

"You're right, you can't. So, why do you think I'll tell you anything?" Shane raises an eyebrow.

"'Cause I have the gun?" It wasn't meant to be a question. I tried to plan beforehand, but this was as far as I got. I was more concerned with getting in and out without being caught.

"You don't sound so sure about that, Princess."

I roll my eyes. What is up with these guys and their pet names? I have a fucking name, and no one wants to use it. I debate whether it's worth bitching about, but he'll most likely ignore me, like Alex did.

"A lot of rumors are floating around, some of them pertaining to you. You want more on what happened to Emma, I want to know . . ." I scrounge for the words.

Shane frowns, hands clenching, before gripping the arms of his chair. "You want to know about the ambush on your brother."

"Actually, you're not behind the disappearances, are you?" I study his face, looking for a tell, but his expression hardens, confirming my suspicions.

"I'd think that much was obvious. We're not going to continue this conversation."

"I hardly see the issue in sharing information. You need something from me; I need something from you. We go our separate ways and live happily ever after." I try to not hold my breath as he studies my face, contemplating my words. I pray he has something on the hit against my brother.

Shane pushes himself up slowly, making my gun waver. His eyes dart to it and back to my face. I swivel the chair to keep the gun on him as he saunters around the desk before he plants his hands on the arms of my chair, boxing me in. He leans in, lips brushing my ear, and my breath hitches, pinpricks running through my body as he invades my space.

"I think you'll find, Princess, I don't need anything from you. There's not a fucking thing you could give me that I would find value in. You're worthless to me. A silly little girl, playing at being indispensable. Do not think for one second that your little display here intimidates me. The only thing you are is a problem. And I take care of problems very thoroughly, so they never come back."

His nose grazes my cheek as he pulls back before stepping several paces away and crosses his arms over his muscled chest, the scowl firmly back in place. I inhale, trying to find my mask, the one that allows me to face living in a world with so much blood and death, but the remnants are scattered at my feet, stomped on by this man.

Without realizing, he's punched through all the walls I've surrounded my heart with, and hit me right where it hurts: my worth. I'm constantly playing catch up. No one will notice if I disappear. I want to think I'm indispensable, but I'm not.

I'm important to Mason but only as a sister. He's ferocious in making sure I'm independent, capable, strong. I wonder if he made me that way to keep me from asking for more. My brother loves me but only as a sibling, not as an integral part of the Byrns' gang. Within the organization I am expendable. Always replaceable. With someone wiser and smarter and better in the wings to fill my place. I'm needed by no one.

I nod once, gathering all the strength left in me to rise, hoping I can leave with as much dignity as possible. I avoid his eyes as I put the desk between us, setting the gun down carefully. I didn't take the safety off, not that he can tell. I only wanted help, but maybe I wanted more, something I'm not willing to admit to myself.

A door opening and shutting down the hall has Shane breaking our connection. I take the opportunity to sidle to the window I'd left open. I can be out and gone before any of his goons find me.

"Going to throw yourself out the window, Princess?" He's staring at me again, still as a statue.

"As good of an escape route as any," I reply, trying to give him a cheeky grin, but it falls flat.

He sighs, pinching the bridge of his nose, then strides toward the door, grabbing the gun off the desk on the way. He pops his head out and calls for someone whose footsteps pound closer. Shane murmurs to them before pinning me in place with his gaze.

"Do not go out the window. There are guards below now. Titus will be on the other side of this door. You'll stay here until I come back. Am I clear?"

My eyes narrow before I say, "Crystal."

He clicks the door behind him, and his footsteps fall away. I shiver at the feelings he stirs in me at his orders. I can't figure out if it's a turn on or annoying. I'm going with annoying so I can sleep tonight. Whatever he has planned for me, though, I'm not sticking around for it. I'm not good at following orders, anyway. I check the window, and sure enough, two guards are loitering below, faces turned upward. I slide it closed, hoping they'll wander away after thinking I've given up, but they stay put. I'll take my chances with Titus, then.

To lure him in or surprise him in the hall . . . decisions, decisions.

Lure him in it is.

I look around, trying to figure out how to bait him. My usual routine is to start breaking shit, but if Shane comes back . . . nope, better to go the sobbing route. I start sniffling, add in a few hiccups, cracking the door just a little.

"Please stay inside, Miss." Titus, who can't be more than seventeen, doesn't turn around.

"I just, I need . . . I'm sorry." I break down, covering my face with my hands, whimpering pathetically.

"Shit. Okay. I'm sure Mr. Shane will be right back." Titus awkwardly pats my shoulder, trying to comfort me.

"I'm sorry"—I blubber—"I'm so scared and alone." I fling myself into his arms, forcing him to grab me to stop us both from falling. I sway us from side to side, spinning and still wailing. Finally, I straighten, pretending to gather myself once more.

"Are you okay, Miss?"

I feel bad for this kid. I hope Shane doesn't do anything drastic for my antics. "Great!" I slap on a cheeky grin and shove him into the office. The surprise on his face right before I fling the door shut makes me almost regret what I've done, but I still jam one of my knives into the frame, hoping it will hold him long enough for me to make my escape.

I dust off my hands, glancing left and right, hoping I can navigate this massive house without running into anyone. I dash to the right, looking for the stairs, finding them right where they should be. I stop and listen, then skip down before pausing to see if anyone else is around. The way is clear, but déjà vu hits me.

Like the streets surrounding us, the layout of the house is identical to mine. To anyone else, it wouldn't be noticeable. It could be a coincidence. My ancestors built our house. They could've had the same architect or something, but the more I see, the less it feels like a coincidence.

I'm banking on this estate having the same secrets as my own. The front door is just down the stairs and around the corner, but I'm not confident enough in my door-jamming skills to count on no one to be waiting for me. I push next to a painting, and the wall pops out with a faint click. Home sweet home. I grin and pull it to duck into the secret passage.

"Sam?" Alex's voice floats from the opposite end, startling me.

Clearly, Shane didn't tell him about my little visit. Hopefully, that also means Shane doesn't realize I'm nearly gone.

I shoot him a smirk, a wink, then slip into the dark, pulling the door closed. Finding the sliding bolt, I slam it home. Inside, it's pitch black, but adrenaline pumps through my body, convincing me I can navigate every step flawlessly. I fly around corners, barely slowing when I come to a set of stairs, then another and another. Hooking to the left at a split in directions, I slow as the tunnel inclines again. A door ahead should put me at the back of the property, right near the trees. I almost run into the ladder but catch myself before my shins crash into the metal.

The hinges squeak when I push the trap door up, and I pause, trying to quiet my heavy breaths. I strain to catch any sound over my pounding heart. I open it more, peeking out. I'm met with only darkness, the lights of the mansion behind me scarcely illuminating a small shack, a shed for guards in another lifetime. Dust motes swirl up when I exit, and my nose itches. Our tunnel at home comes out to a shed, filled with rakes and shovels. I think the gardener still uses it, unlike this place.

I glance back at the house and see shadowy figures running back and forth. Part of me wishes Alex hadn't seen me. I'm more of a threat than I was before now, which means they might be hunting me. I vow to stay on my side of the river as I steal into the trees. I should have never come here. I should have known a King would never help a Byrns. And a Byrns can never trust a King.

SEVENTEEN

REN

"Sam is gone. Must have gone out through the tunnels," Alex heaves out, flopping down.

Shane leans back in his chair, rolling his neck. "This is fucking ridiculous. How the hell did she find out about the tunnels?"

"You said her house is the same layout. Probably has the same tunnels. Wouldn't be hard to navigate for her if they are," I answer, staring at my tablet again. I'm checking the cameras, but I can feel the frustration burning out of him.

"What are you going to do with Titus?" Alex asks.

What a disaster. Shane should have known better than to put such a young kid guarding her. He's fresh out of initiation. His emotions run a little close to the surface for me, but he's a good one. We stick newbies in the city, but Titus showed promise, so Shane brought him on as a guard instead. I wonder if he's rethinking that decision now. As long as he doesn't make me fix his fuck up. I hate having to rework shit.

"He said she was crying or faking it, more than likely. I don't blame him for not knowing what to do. We should put him on outside duty, so it doesn't look like we're playing favorites or some bullshit," Shane mutters, tipping his head back.

Alex nods and pulls out his phone.

"Sorry about earlier," Shane says, looking at his computer instead of Alex. I found Alex in the downstairs hallway, trying to open the hidden panel after Shane discovered Sam gone. Shane went ballistic when Alex said she disappeared into them.

"No biggy, man." He doesn't look up from his phone.

Alex is never good at being on the receiving end of apologies. He thinks it's okay for Shane and me to treat him like shit, like he deserves it or something. He laughs it off, but the hint of shame is always present in his eyes.

"I'm serious, Alex. Not your fault she got away," Shane insists, looking at him.

They meet eyes, and Alex nods, relief warring with grief flashing across Shane's face.

"What were you going to do, anyway? I mean, she broke in and shit, but why not let her go? You're not going to start a war over her, are you?"

"Honestly, I was going to find Emma."

I can't help but chime in. "Why would you willingly put them in the same place at the same time? That would be disastrous for what you're trying to accomplish with Emma."

"I thought if I could show Emma that Sam isn't the 'awesome and amazing' person Emma keeps going on about, she'll stop seeking out the Byrns princess. She treats Samantha like an idol or something. I caught her playing with a switchblade yesterday. Said she was practicing, so she could be like Sam when she grows up. The whole thing is getting out of hand."

"I think showing her Sam can sneak in to the house without anyone the wiser will only elevate her in Emma's eyes." I set my tablet down, giving them my full attention. "I think you should send her away for now. If you're set on her not training, and you don't want her sneaking out to find Sam, then sending her to Marge's is the easiest way to deal with things."

"But that would only be a temp solution. You know that, right?" Alex tilts his head, eyeing Shane.

"I know, but at this point, I don't see any other options," he admits.

I hold up a hand to stop Alex from arguing. "You could train her. Alex and I would do it. Or send her to initiation. I mean, she's thirteen. You think she's still a kid, but when we were her age, we were already deep into the process."

"She *is* still a kid. She deserves to have an actual childhood, unlike us. I'm not going to put my baby sister through the shit we went through. We can teach her the basics when she's a little older. She'll never need them if we're lucky. She can go off to college and move away and do whatever she wants."

I barely contain my eyeroll. We've had this conversation before. Somehow, he has this dream for Emma to run away to another world far away from ours, as if he can save her from who her family is. It's not a terrible dream. He never wants her to have to worry about looking over her shoulder, wondering who she can trust, living with the fear of someone taking everything from her. Unfortunately, it's unrealistic. No one can escape our world. Shane will have to accept that if he wants a relationship with her when she's grown. I don't want her to live in fear, either, but it's fanciful to think she'll survive without training. We can't protect her forever. We can't protect her from herself.

"What if she disagrees?" I scroll through the cameras again.

"She doesn't know what she wants." I catch his glare out of the corner of my eye.

The door bursts open, Emma's heavy breathing behind me. I don't have to look to know her hands are in fists. Alex jumped when she blasted in, but I knew she was eavesdropping. She does it more than either of them realizes, but I keep my mouth shut. I don't particularly agree with keeping her in the dark, and this is one way I can work around Shane's feelings, without him blowing a gasket.

"I do, too, know what I want!" she yells.

Shane explodes to his feet. "What the hell, Emma? You should be in bed."

"I'm not a . . . a fucking child!"

I wince, peeking at Alex, and he ducks his head, turning away.

"Watch your language," Shane snarls. "If you don't want to be treated like a child, then don't act like one."

"I don't!"

"Sneaking out, hiding things, no regard for your safety, and lying are just a few ways you're acting like a child. We have rules for a reason, and while you're living in our house, you'll follow those rules."

Emma's scream of frustration is ear-piercing, making us all wince as she storms out, slamming the door behind her.

"Gee, Dad, take it down a notch," Alex quips.

Shane collapses in his chair, the fight slipping away. Trying to keep everything together, raising his sister, and with all the shit going down in Synd, he looks exhausted. Add in dealing with Samantha Byrns and her antics, and he might fall apart before we're done with this shit show. The last thing we need is for me to take over while he has a mental breakdown.

"I have something we need to discuss, if we're done talking about Shane's morphing into a sitcom dad." I smirk, flipping my tablet around.

Alex leans forward. "What are we looking at?"

"Nothing yet. I haven't pressed play."

"I'm going to smother you in your sleep."

I start the video without answering. Sometimes, I wonder if they know I'm joking or if they think I'm really this literal. None of us had a normal upbringing, being raised in a mafia family, but my father was more intense than Shane's. Alex's had been dead long before we reached the age to understand. I'm thankful my father mostly ignored Alex. It might have made things easier for me, but I don't think Alex would have survived. My father might have fucked me up more in some ways with his tactics, but at least I saved Alex from a worse fate.

"Where is this?" Shane demands.

"Angelo's."

"How did you get this?"

"I have my ways, but this one was particularly hard to procure. You probably forgot about it, but I didn't. It's the night Mason Byrns was shot."

They squint at the screen. I've reviewed it so many times I can close my eyes and watch it play out behind my lids.

Several cars pull up outside the restaurant. Two dozen guys pile out, weapons drawn. There isn't any sound, but the chaos is clear as they open fire. The attackers go down, one by one. Whenever one falters, someone drags them to the cars and shoves them inside, cleaning up the scene in the crossfire, leaving no witnesses behind. Alex grunts, probably at the flash of something sailing through the air, and the gunmen pause. Several of them start for the shattered window but then most drop before grabbing their fallen comrades and dashing for the getaway cars before tearing off screen. I glance down, the video cuts out, and I turn the tablet back around.

"Holy shit," Alex breathes. "That didn't look like a random hit. That looked like—"

"An ambush," I finish. Shane taps his fingers against his lips, deep in thought. "What did Sam want, Shane?"

"Does anyone else have access to this footage?" Shane asks as I bite back my response.

"Not as far as I can tell. The video is heavily encrypted, so I asked Nemesis to hack it. This is what she sent. Now, why did Sam break into your office?"

Alex clears his throat. "What do we actually know about this Nemesis chick? Are we sure we trust her?"

I sigh. "Why do you do this every time, Alex? I've been working with her for years. Regardless, she gets us the information and doesn't rat us out."

"Yeah, but what do we know about her? Other than she's a her?"

I throw my hands in the air. "Nothing! She's a fucking hacker! She's reliable and excellent at what she does."

"How do we stop her from hacking us? What if she's watching us right now?" Alex checks the corners of the room, like she'll pop out from behind the goddamn potted plant or something.

"We don't stop her. She knows everything about us. You can't hide from her, but we don't need to because she makes very good money off us. If you trust me, then you trust her."

"Fine, but I'm going on record as saying I don't like it. I don't understand it, so I don't like it."

"What would you like me to do with the video, Shane?" I grit my teeth. That's the ultimate question, beyond what Sam wanted.

He eyes me, then glances at Alex before saying, "Let's hold back for now. See how this plays out."

"Wait, we're not showing Sam?" Alex spins to him. Dammit, he is way too interested in this woman. Shane is being pulled further into the intrigue of who she actually is as well. Throw in Emma's obsession, and we might have a problem on our hands. Alex is his own person, but his life belongs to the Kings. We can't afford to divide our stance with it comes to Sam or the Byrns clan as a whole. Shane is the head, though, so he'll make the decision best for the family, regardless of how Alex feels about things. Alex will fall in line, for the most part.

"No. We're not. I'm meeting with Helms tomorrow. Hopefully, he'll shed some light into what the hell is going on around here. I'll ask him about the ambush, and we'll figure out from there if there's anything we need to share. I'm not about to hand over something for nothing. Besides, we're not supposed to be dealing with Samantha. Victor is the temporary head—he's who we're dealing with." He sighs, as if it's not what he actually wants to do.

"I don't like Victor," Alex grumbles.

"No one likes Victor, but I'd take that asshole over Colin," I mumble. I haven't made it clear how little I trust Mason's second, but he always rubbed me the wrong way. He's the type to tell someone he's a nice guy, then stab them in the back. I've never seen evidence of it, but I can't shake the feelings in my gut I have when we meet.

"This is the way things stand; the way it's been for decades. We may not like Victor, but with Mason in a coma, we might have to deal with Victor for a lot more years than we'd like. The last thing we need is to give him a reason to start a war. The entire city will suffer with no guarantee of a winner. Bringing Sam into this situation will only exacerbate the whole thing. Victor would retaliate if he knows we handed this over to her without informing him."

"I don't like this. Why didn't Colin take over? He's the second. You'd think he would be first in line to shut that shit down. He rolled over and offered up the whole Byrns mafia on a silver platter to that asshat," Alex states, like it's a personal affront.

"We can't all have raging hard-ons for violence like you, Alex. Maybe there was an actual reason why Colin decided to step away instead of fighting for his place." The words turn to ash in my mouth. I can't seem to turn off the devil's advocate in me. The need to continually see all sides and point them out isn't pleasant, especially when they take it personally.

"No, Alex is right. Colin should have taken over. I'd much rather be working with him if we need to solve this issue of disappearances together. The only reason I can think is he stepped back to protect Samantha, unless she's in league with Victor as well, but from what we've seen, she's working on her own."

I'm not convinced Sam has the Byrns' organization's best interest in mind, rather than solely her brother. She might have gone rogue, which could get her killed. There's no way she'll survive if her family isn't behind her. A twinge in my chest has me rubbing the spot. Sam has never been a player in our world before now. I don't understand why she suddenly feels she's qualified to find answers, with the sudden shift in her demeanor when we met her in the alley, along with what Alex told us happened at the club. Plus, the fact she broke into our house. Not being able to track her on any of the cameras is annoying as hell. There's something more to her than meets the eye, but I can't put my finger on it. The more we cross paths with her, the more intriguing she becomes, and I don't know if I can afford to be sucked in her orbit. The mystery of Samantha Byrns might be too much for me to resist, though.

"I doubt she'd break in here to exchange information if she was working with Victor. Unless that was the plan all along, but it's a poorly laid one. Did you figure out how she got in?" I hold my breath, wondering if he'll confirm my guess she was here for help, instead of nefarious reasons.

He waves away my words. "I assume the tunnels."

I nod, then frown at the screen in my hands. "I don't think so. I think she climbed." I swing the tablet around again, showing them a still of the backyard. The ten-second clip plays, repeating on a loop, but both of their faces are blank.

Shane crooks his eyebrow at me, waiting for an explanation.

"Right there"—I point—"the darkening. I think she skirted the cameras, but this one caught her shadow."

He shakes his head. "I don't see it, but if you say so. We're still locking down the tunnels."

Alex's eyes are still fixed on the screen. "You think she'll come back?"

"No, I don't."

I stare at him. "What did you say to her that would prevent her from seeking us out again?"

"Nothing that wasn't true. She had a gun on me, so regardless, I'm going to take every precaution we need to. It will be safer for Emma, anyway."

"I doubt this is the last time she'll be walking these halls," I predict, even as he scowls. "From what you told us, it's unlikely she would have shot you. I would be surprised if the gun was even loaded."

"After our little encounter, I wouldn't be so sure. Next time, she might pull the trigger, and I'm not sure I'd blame her."

EIGHTEEN

SAMANTHA

My phone buzzing in my hand startles me enough I almost drop it. I glance around, though no one is in my room at the Depot. I had to fight tooth and nail for a spot here, but Mason eventually relented, giving me a virtual closet-sized space far from the initiates. He'd tried to discourage me from using the space by only having a bed and small desk in here, but that doesn't stop me. I'm thankful I fought so hard now that going home is like dodging landmines.

I pull up the text, reading the message three times before I absorb what it says. An address, time, and signature. Ryker Helms finally responded. I only have four hours before the meeting, so I need to hustle. The last thing I'm going to do is show up somewhere without scoping it out first. I rise, mind racing with all I have to do and what front I need to present to Helms, when Shane's words come back to me.

Worthless. A problem.

I shake my head, as if I can erase the words from my memories. I want to chalk them up to some misogynistic male ego trip, but his words cut deeper each time I recall them. He has no idea what I'm capable of. He doesn't know what I do as the Wraith. He doesn't know anything about me. The real me. The one I can't afford to show. Reminding myself doesn't prevent his words from weaving into my own self-doubts until I can't distinguish his cutting remarks from my own anxieties.

I understand my place in the family, and I'm fine with it. I will never take over for my brother, and I never wanted to. I thought I had convinced myself I was okay with where I am and what I'm doing. When Mason was shot, though, it threw not only our organization into a frenzy but my own place within the world. My security is gone. The thought that I'm only important because of who I am to Mason hit me like a ton of bricks. I need to get my shit together and hit back twice as hard.

I straighten and steel myself to do what needs to be done for me and my family. My clothes are now my armor, makeup my mask. I wield them as well as I can, pulling my dark-brown hair back into a ponytail, and give myself one last look in the mirror over my desk. I'm not good at pep talks, so I stick out my tongue at the woman staring back, hoping she'll match the energy her smoky eyes are projecting.

By this point in the year, it's normally cold enough for a coat, but we're getting a few balmy days. The sun is starting to set when I step out and sling my leather jacket on, since it'll turn cooler before long.

I arrive at the club an hour early. This is one of the more established hot spots, but I've only been here once or twice, with the club being in King territory. I go around back, checking the alleys and exits. I find one propped open for employees and slide inside, acting like I belong in my jeans and leather.

No one is in the hallway. I can familiarize myself with all the ways in and out of this space. I have to dodge one or two people around corners, but no one pays me any mind. I make my way back, set on waiting outside for Helms to appear. I wish I knew specifically where in the club he's planning on meeting, but beggars can't be choosers.

I step out when a large body blocks my way, forcing me to stumble back. A hand shoots out, wrapping around my upper arm, stopping me from falling on my ass. I curse myself for not noticing them. I pop my head up as I am either about to thank them or cuss them out, but my mouth falls open, every thought fleeing my head.

"Well, well, well. We meet again, Princess. I must admit, I'm surprised you're stupid enough to come over the river so soon, but, then again, you don't seem to have much self-preservation."

Shane. Fucking. King.

Nowhere in my speculations about how this night would go did I ever think I'd see him. Stabbed? Maybe. Random drive-by? Likely. Another ambush? Hopefully not. But literally running into Shane King? Nope.

"I have immunity."

The words are the first thing to pop in my head. I hope I can stretch the truth enough to convince him I have permission to be in his realm. Immunity means he can't touch me. He can't kill me. He can't hold me. I hold immunity when I work most of my jobs for Mason. A random meeting with Helms? Murky at best.

Shane's eyebrows shoot up, then he snorts, a half sneer on his full lips. It isn't something any random member claims. Calling on immunity when I don't have it allows the other side to do whatever the hell they want.

"What could you be doing to garner immunity, hmm?"

"I'm attending a neutral meeting with a third party not associated with either of our families." I mentally pat myself on the back for being so vague.

"Who?" he demands.

I roll my eyes. "Like I'll tell you, and you can't make me. I know how this works. So, if you could remove your hand and let me be on my way, we'll pretend we didn't run into each other." Literally.

"If you know how this works, then you'll remember I have the right to question who the other party is to verify it truly is a neutral meeting." His hand flexes, squeezing my bicep. I'm not afraid with as much as he wants to intimidate me, which is disconcerting. I'm used to men throwing their weight around, using fear to get their way. Shane doesn't need to throw it around. Power exudes from him like a pheromone, warning his prey he's the deadliest thing in the area.

"Try again. I do have to if there are more than just little ol' me. Since I'm the only one here . . ." I peer around him. Is he alone, too, or are his shadows with him? The alley is dark and empty.

"No Tweedledee and Tweedledum?" I ask sweetly.

Shane opens his mouth, but a voice cuts down the side street.

"Good. You're both here. Let's get this over with, unless you two need another minute to figure out whether you're going to fuck or fight." Ryker Helms stalks over, gesturing us inside.

"The last thing I would do is fuck a Byrns," Shane mutters, pushing past me into the club.

I follow Shane. I would prefer to meet with Helms alone, but I'll take anything at this point. I'm drained trying to find info without giving it away that I'm working alone.

My phone buzzes in my pocket, and I stop to read the text from Colin. He's putting more guys on Mason's room. I want to ask what happened, but I have no energy to deal with more than one crisis at a time. This meeting could give me what I need, what *we* need.

"Coming, Princess?" Shane calls from the top of the stairs where Ryker had disappeared.

I hustle up, brushing past him. I'm determined to be the confident woman I usually am in this meeting; that means being indifferent to King. I don't make it far before I realize I have no idea where Ryker went. At least half a dozen doors line the hall.

Shane settles his hand on my lower back, under my jacket, guiding me gently toward the one at the end. I want to step away, but his warmth seeps through the shirt. I don't want to rely on this man, but I let myself imagine he's here for me. To support me instead of tearing me down. I hold on to the sensation for the ten seconds it takes to reach the door, then slough him off. It's a comforting dream, but dreams rarely become reality.

"Sit. I didn't want to do this anyway, but I'm sick of my phone blowing up from the two of you."

I shoot a quizzical look to Shane, who sits across the table from me instead of the open chair to my right. So, Shane's been trying to reach him, too. Curiouser and curiouser.

"I'd rather do this without her," Shane announces, settling in.

"That makes two of us," I mutter, earning a glare.

"I don't give a flying fuck what you want. I'm doing this out of professional courtesy," Ryker grumbles.

"Then, why is she here and not Victor?" Shane asks.

"'She' has a name, and it's Sam. You should learn it," I snap, my shoulders bunching. He's a gigantic asshole who's used to dominating and getting his way.

"You say that like I care, Princess." Shane curls his lip, narrowing his eyes at me.

Ryker's slams his hand on the table, making Shane and me twitch. He's glaring, baring his teeth.

"Would you two shut the fuck up? Get the fuck out if you don't like it. We have bigger issues to deal with than your bickering. She's here because she fucking owes me. You're here because you're the head of the Kings. Now, both of you are going to keep your mouths shut and listen, got it?"

We nod, properly chastised. I'm not about to piss Helms off; he looks like he could squeeze my head like a melon, and he's got information I desperately need. I'm not sure why Shane agrees, though. I doubt Helms has any more info about the disappearances or Emma's attempted kidnapping.

"Good." He fixes his eyes on me. "I don't know what went down that night. I didn't have anything to do with it, which you know, or I'm sure you'd slip in my window and slit my throat. I took care of the men who executed the hit. They were junior-level guys out of Harris. I did find out they were working for someone else, but they were so low in the pecking order none of them knew who is in charge. I'm trying to work my way up the chain, but it's slow going. I have my suspicions, but until I have concrete proof, you'll settle for that."

Disappointment wells in me. I wanted to take care of them myself. One of them shot my brother, and I can't let it go. Letting Helms run down any leads chafes against everything I am. I want to be in control of this, but allowing someone else help may be the best way to exact my revenge.

"Why?" What does Helms have invested in this? Why is he willing to help us? He doesn't acknowledge the Byrns or King clans unless it suits him. He never stirs up trouble. He never asks for help. He runs his territory and ignores everything south most of the time.

"I lost men that night, too. It shouldn't have gone down the way it did. I'm doing what should be done," he relents.

"Payment?" I ask, not because I want to but because nothing in our world is free.

Helms's eyes bore into mine. I can practically see the gears turning in his head, probably thinking of how I could ever repay him for the revenge, the information, finding the answers, and last but not least, saving my life. It is something I've been pushing from my mind, not wanting to remember how close I came to being a blood splatter on the wall. Mason's injury consumes me enough not to fall apart from the memories haunting my sleep.

Helms's mouth quirks, a knowing look in his eyes. "Nothing . . . yet. I might need your particular . . . skill set later."

Does he know? The twinkle in his eye tells me he knows I'm the Wraith. How in the hell does Ryker fucking Helms know what I do? No one has that knowledge, not even Colin. My jobs are secrets wrapped in suspicions, carried out in the darkest parts of the night, with only the stars left as witnesses. I should be wary of the leader of the Reapers, but I can't help but trust him. I have to assume he'll keep it a little bit longer.

Helms turns to Shane. "You're here about the disappearances."

"Anything you know about them," Shane answers, all business now, turning away from me.

"Again, I don't have much. There isn't much of a profile on who they're grabbing other than people under the age of about thirty-five."

"That's it? Women under thirty-five? What am I supposed to do with that?"

"Not women. People. They don't discriminate against gender. Everyone's fair game if they're under thirty-five. At this point, whoever they are, they're doing things quietly. I've reached out to some other Chapters to see if they've had similar things go down in their cities, but I haven't heard back. Whatever this is, we don't want a repeat of ten years ago."

"Is that what you were going to talk to Mason about?" I ask.

"No, but they might be related. There's been an influx of a new drug. It's like cocaine and heroin wrapped in ecstasy. It's potent, it's lethal, and it's spreading.

"Name?" Shane asks.

"Oracle. Stupid name if you ask me, but I don't name drugs, so what do I know? I wanted to know if Mason heard of it and if his guys were slanging it. I was going to meet with you next, Shane, but then shit went sideways, and we went into lockdown. You heard anything?"

"I haven't, but we let the lower gangs handle shit. I'll do some digging." Shane glances at his phone but slips it back in his pocket when he catches me watching.

"I wasn't actually asking you." Helms chuckles, eyes on me again. He isn't asking me as Sam, the sister of the head of a mafia. He's asking the Wraith. Confusion colors Shane's face. The deference Helms shows me clashes with Shane's image of me, I'm sure.

"There's been more bodies dumped in the Barrens lately. A couple of them told me they're worried the police will come in and try to clean the place up. I talked to my contact at the station, and he assured me they're focused on their section of the city—they won't be interfering with our business. Nothing about Oracle, but that's not uncommon. I'd bet it was in the rich crowd for now, if the drug hasn't spread yet. I can put out some feelers, see what comes up. You think the disappearances are connected to this?"

"Maybe. I can't find one, but I don't believe in coincidences. People being kidnapped and a deadly drug coming in at the same time? That'd be a pretty big coincidence, don't you think?"

"Kidnappings in the Barrens and a new drug in the rich circles? Seems like a squeeze to me. They'll meet in the middle before long. This isn't going to peter out. We're going to have to step in sooner rather than later. Which means we're going to have to work together, which I know everyone is super excited about, but it's a necessity," I say, shooting a bemused smile at Helms. Shane needs me, contrary to what he'd said last night.

"If anyone is working together, it's going to be Helms and I. You're not needed. We're capable of keeping this city from going to shit," Shane announces. Cocky asshole.

Ryker snickers, sizing up Shane. I let a giggle slip before I smother it. Yup, I am totally okay with Helms knowing who I am. Taunting Shane is an added bonus.

"I'll let you deal with him, Sam. I'll be in touch. And stop fucking texting me every day. That goes for both of you."

Helms strides for the door and lets it click closed, leaving me alone with Shane for the second time in two days. I brace myself for questions, yelling, orders, but Shane just sits there, staring at Ryker's empty chair. I open my mouth, then snap it shut, pursing my lips, not knowing what to say.

I wait for him to figure out his questions, leg jiggling. I'm tempted to pull out the granola bar I stashed in my coat pocket, but based on his reaction last time, I figure his head might explode.

I'm about to say fuck it and ask him what the hell he wants to do when he lurches to his feet, makes his way around the table, then steps out the door, slamming it shut as he goes.

What. The. Fuck.

NINETEEN

SHANE

Who the hell is Samantha Byrns?

The question bounces around my head the entire walk through the club. Employees are rushing around, setting up in anticipation for the night crowd that will descend in a couple of hours. I hook around a corner, intent on getting home.

Helms treated her like a mafia boss. He deferred to her, asked for information, and expected that whatever she said would be accurate. He didn't once question whether what she said was true. How did she get all that information, anyway? Alex and Ren said she skulks around, popping into places here and there, but never staying long. She spends a lot of her time on the streets—because she doesn't have anything better to do or because she doesn't have anywhere else to go? Whatever she's into is a helluva lot more involved, though. I can't reconcile the different versions of Samantha in my head. Is she the airhead she presents at parties? Is she a ninja, breaking into places? Is she whoever the hell Helms thinks she is? After I shot her down last night, she was vulnerable. Something nags at me, but I can't put my finger on.

Regardless, I don't need her help to deal with all the shit going on in Synd. Between Alex, Ren, and me, we'll deal with whoever thinks they can come in and fuck with our side of the city. I did this ten years ago, and I'll do it again. Whatever happens, I need to get Emma out of here. I won't have her caught in the crossfire if the city blows.

"Hey!"

I ignore Samantha calling after me. It isn't my fault she can't take a hint. I was clear last night—and again today—I'm not going to bother with her. It's not worth it. She'll be more of a distraction than anything, especially to Alex.

"Seriously? I know you can hear me!"

I push open the door that leads to the club's office hallway. Ahead is a seldom-used back door I can slip out before Samantha catches up. I have to give her credit for being tenacious, at least.

"Shane King!" She yells as something hits the back of my head. My hand flies up, and I swing around, gaping at her.

"What the hell was that?"

"A granola bar. Now that I have your attention, we need to discuss some things." She folds her arms over her chest, thinking it's intimidating, but all it does is push her tits together.

I focus on her face. I can't afford the distraction any more than Alex. "I told you last night . . . and again, five minutes ago, I have no intention of discussing anything with you. I don't want your help. I don't need your help. I will deal with this myself." I go to leave, but of course, she isn't done.

"Are you really that fucking stubborn? Or are you so puffed up on your own goddamn male ego that you can't believe a woman could add something of value?"

I explode. This fucking woman is going to be the death of me. I pivot, backing her against the wall and plant my hand above her head.

I expect to glimpse fear in her eyes, but they're blazing. I can't tell if she thinks I'm a misogynist or if she's trying to get a reaction from me. Either way, she's got my full attention.

"Listen carefully, Princess. I don't care if you're a woman or a potted fucking plant. The truth is, between the plant and you, I'll take the plant. Every. Fucking. Time. Do whatever you want. Wear your black leather and pretend you're a bad bitch. Flirt your ass into a drug den. Fuck whatever junkie is currently feeding you info. Burn your half of the city to the ground for all I care. Just stay the hell out of my way."

"Yes, because the only way a pretty little princess like me would be able to accomplish anything is by flaunting my body or fucking some lowlife, right? There's absolutely no possibility that maybe I have actual skills, that I'm more capable than you at something. You've got an ideal box in your head I'm supposed to fit in, and anything that contradicts that must be an act on my part. God, I hope you're not passing all that toxicity on to Emma," Sam sneers.

"You leave my little sister out of this. You know nothing about her. You will keep your ass as far away from her as possible. The last thing I want is her to be influenced by someone like you."

"Oh, heaven forbid she learns how to be strong and independent and capable of taking care of herself without the aid of a man! It would be truly tragic if she figured out how to navigate this life on her own instead of hiding behind your skirts. She'd be a failure, then, huh?"

"Of course I want her to be those things! I'm not a fucking idiot, but she's only thirteen. She shouldn't have to worry about those things yet," I growl.

Why can no one understand I'm trying to protect my little sister?

"A lot of girls have to worry about it long before they should. Maybe you should listen to what she wants instead of trying to control her," Samantha says quietly.

"I'm not controlling her." I feel myself leaning in, even as I try to keep the small space between us. How we've gone from yelling at each other to her giving me advice about how to raise my sister, I don't know, but I need to jump off this train before we derail.

"Are you serious? You're the most stubborn, controlling man I've ever met! The lengths you will go to not have to lean on another person is astounding."

Good. We're back to yelling.

"I have plenty of people to lean on. You're upset none of them is you. No matter how much you poke and prod and act like you're one of us, that will never change. You will never be one of us. Why are you even here? Why are you trying? Whatever you do isn't going to change anything. If you were actually strong and independent, you wouldn't be chasing after me, begging for scraps. If you were so capable of taking care of yourself, you wouldn't need Alex to step in and save your ass. And without a man? Please, Princess, enlighten me to how you got here without your brother? You would be a nobody, a whore on the street, without him. Now that he's not here to elevate your status, I doubt you'll last long."

Samantha is nearly hyperventilating by the time I'm done. She looks like she's having a panic attack. She's trying to hide her reaction but failing. I thought confronting her would make me feel better. More in control, but all I've done is show how much this woman keeps getting under my skin. She's burrowing into my core, and I need to stop before she sinks her claws into me and never lets go.

"Fuck." I breathe, watching her try to pull the pieces of herself back together. "Sam, I . . ."

I lean farther into her, hesitating a second before I slam my mouth on hers. She stiffens, and I'm about to pull back when her body loosens the smallest bit. I drag the band holding her hair up and twist my hand in her locks. I yank her head back and angle my lips over hers, plunging my tongue into her mouth, owning her completely. A voice in my head screams for me to stop, but my body won't listen. Finally, I rip my mouth from hers, pulling back sharply. Her eyes flutter open, shock, alarm, and something else in them. I yank my hand from her hair, trying to distance myself from her in every way possible.

"Goddammit!" I slam my hand against the wall, making her flinch.

I stride away, certain she won't follow me now. I push the door open and step into the ever-darkening night, breathing in the crisp air, convinced it will clear my head of whatever the hell just happened. I need to get as far away from Samantha Byrns as possible.

"What did Helms want?" Ren demands as I duck into the passenger seat. Alex pulls up to the mouth of the alley, waiting for traffic to clear. My leg bounces, still riding the high of my stand-off with Samantha and that damn kiss. I want to blame her, but this whole fiasco is my fucking fault.

"He wanted to talk about the disappearances. You guys ever hear of Oracle?" I need to get my mind straight, focus on the problems I can fix.

"Nope. Is that a new fortune teller? 'Cause I swear there was a psychic who came through a couple years ago, and she told me things that blew my mind. Like, shit that happened. Crazy shit, man," Alex says, glancing back and forth, trying to find a spot to edge in.

"Of course you saw a psychic. They're frauds, Alex. No way she knew anything. They say something vague, and you fill in the blanks—" Ren replies.

"It's a new drug, potent and addicting," I add.

"I'll check with the others, see if they've heard anything about it. Probably up in the richie-rich neighborhoods if it's shiny and new."

Alex is repeating what Samantha said. I don't want to put my faith in her, but some things she mentioned held truth. Sifting through her words to find the truth is harder, though.

I glance toward the front of the club and spot her. Of course, she can't slip away into the night like every other time we cross paths these days. She's standing on the sidewalk, staring at the dense traffic, cell phone in hand. She glances at the device, shaking her head, and turns toward us. She hasn't spotted us yet, but she soon will if she keeps walking this way. Shit.

"Would you hurry the fuck up and get us the hell out of here? For fuck's sake, Alex," I bark.

"Geez, you do see the other cars bumper-to-bumper, right? Not like I can squeeze between them like the Nightbus. Why are you in such a hurry anyhow? Got a hot date?"

"Of course you'd make some geek reference," Ren mutters.

"Go right. I want to get home and put things in motion to move Emma out of the city. Something's coming, and I don't like it. The sooner she's away, the easier I'll sleep at night."

Alex laughs. "Oh, shit. I get it now. You don't want to offer her a ride home? She looks a little lost."

"Who?" Ren leans forward, looking around. He grunts and leans back when he spots Samantha, ignoring what's happening. I wish I could ignore her, too.

Alex starts to roll down the window, and I smack him on the back of the head, which doesn't faze him.

"Hey there, Bug! Fancy seeing you here. You out for a night of clubbing in our neck of the woods? I'm hurt I didn't get an invite." He cackles.

Samantha stops a good four feet from the car, planting a hand on her hip. She glances in the back, then at me, glaring before she turns back to Alex.

"Doesn't surprise me Shane didn't tell you," Samantha calls out over the blaring stereos and honking horns.

"Wait, tell us what? Come here, Bug, I can barely hear you." Alex turns to me. "You knew she was here?"

"She was in the meeting," I mutter, fixing my eyes on the windshield.

Alex's eyebrows shoot up, but I ignore him. I'm sure Ren's are raised as well. I went ten years without seeing her, and I will gladly go ten more, but she's everywhere now. Like fate has intervened, challenging me.

"Yup." She pops the *p* obnoxiously, taking a step closer, but still keeping her distance.

"Well, isn't that a pleasant surprise. How was it?" Alex murmurs.

"Oh, the middle was fine. It was the beginning and end where things went a little sideways. Wouldn't you agree, boss?"

I refuse to rise to the bait. I'm not going to tell them anything. It's embarrassing enough that I let her rile me up enough to react. I'm not about to add fuel to the fire by telling my two best friends about our spat . . . or the kiss.

The back window rolls down. I think about telling Ren not to engage with her. He generally doesn't, preferring to sit back and let Alex and me do the talking, but he won't listen to me if I speak up now. I may be the head of the Kings, but they're my best friends, my brothers. We've grown up together. They're content to let me lead, but I depend on them. They are the only ones I trust with my life. Plus, they do whatever the hell they want most of the time, anyway.

Ren calls out, "Tell me, Samantha, where is your uncle tonight?"

I glimpse her out of the corner of my eye as she shrugs, looking a bit stunned.

"What's wrong there, Bug?"

"Name"—she points to herself—"Sam. And I thought he didn't talk." She points to Ren.

"No. I simply don't care to talk to you." Ren rolls the window back up.

If she doesn't have useful information for him, she won't exist. At least, that's his usual way. I glance at the side mirror, though, and he's still watching her. We need to get the hell out of here.

I gesture to the road. "Let's go, Alex. You've missed like four openings."

"You got big plans for tonight, Sam? Planning any B and Es? Perhaps a little sleuthing?" Alex snickers, his body shaking as he holds back his laughter.

"I was thinking about hitting up the Barrens," she murmurs.

Sam glances at her phone again, face twisting into a scowl. Something is going on, but I convince myself I don't give a shit, even though it bugs me.

"You shouldn't go to the Barrens alone," I say gruffly, turning my face away.

"Well, if I wasn't going into the Barrens, then I wouldn't have been there for Emma, so I guess it's a good thing I don't listen to egotistical men, isn't it?"

I turn, glaring at her. "I didn't say 'don't go into the Barrens.' I said, 'you shouldn't go alone.'"

"Well, we can't all be blessed with friends now, can we?"

She's trying to be flippant, but her eyes give her away. A pang of something shoots through me. Unease? Sympathy? Concern? Pity? I don't want to feel anything for this woman, but seeing the loneliness in her eyes sparks a disquiet in me, I fear will lodge itself in my mind. I stare at her until she breaks eye contact. She whiteknuckles her phone, showing her inner turmoil.

"Well, this turned awkward . . ." Alex mutters, breaking the tension.

"Not as awkward as it's going to be if you don't start fucking driving," I mutter.

"Ooookay, we'll catch ya later, Bug. Have fun in the Barrens."

Sam halfheartedly waves, turning to dart across the gridlocked traffic. I lose track of her in the thickening crowd. Alex throws the car into reverse, glancing in the rearview, before flying down the alley and coming to the next street. He narrowly avoids hitting a car, laughing when they lay on their horn. His sense of self-preservation worries me sometimes.

Ren leans between the seats. "Shane, did something happen with Sam? You seem even more agitated than last night."

Leave it to Ren to notice my tenseness. I contemplate how much to share, which feels strange. I don't question whether to tell them things, but this is different. My leg bounces while I deliberate what to say.

Alex's mouth drops open. "Dude, are you blushing?"

"Shut the hell up."

"You totally are! Please tell me you didn't fuck her."

"What the hell, Alex. Of course I didn't fuck her!"

"Wouldn't blame you if you did," Ren quips from the back seat.

"I would!" Alex says, "You weren't in there nearly long enough for a meeting and a good dicking. Unless you didn't wait until she finished, which is fucked up, man."

"I didn't fuck her! She looked like she was about to freak the hell out, so I took care of it."

"How did you take care of it?" Ren asks.

"I calmed her down," I say, looking out the window, hoping they'll drop it.

"You're going to have to be more specific there, man. 'Cause I know how I'd calm her down . . ." Alex smirks, waggling his eyebrows.

"I kissed her," I mumble.

"Excuse me? Did you just say you kissed her? To calm her down from a panic attack? Am I getting that right?"

Shit, Alex will never let this go.

"It worked, so drop it."

"Oh, it worked, Ren! It worked. She started to freak out, and he kissed her to calm her down. But it's okay because it worked! Next time, I'm having a panic attack, I'm going to need you to—"

"You don't have panic attacks, Alex. I'm less concerned about your tactics than I am on why she was having a panic attack in the first place. What did you say to her?" Ren flicks me in the back of the head.

"I called her out on her bullshit."

"With your tongue?" Alex chimes in.

Ren groans. "What happened in the meeting, Shane?"

"Something isn't right. Helms took care of the guys who carried out the hit on Byrns. Some guys out of Harris, but it's a bigger operation. He's looking into things. She's got him convinced he needs her particular skill set, whatever that means. He kept deferring to her, asking her questions about this drug, and the Barrens. It was like a switch flipped halfway, though. She went from being concerned about Mason to all business. I don't trust her."

"Interesting." Ren taps his fingers on my seat.

I grit my teeth. "Spit it out, Ren. What are you thinking?"

"Not sure yet, but you're right. Something doesn't add up with Samantha Byrns. We shouldn't trust her, if only for the fact that her relationship with Victor is . . . vague. Did you know he is attending a gala tonight?"

"For who? Rude that we didn't get an invite," Alex exclaims.

"Some rich bitch. It didn't concern us, so I didn't mention it, but what is curious is Sam didn't know about it, either. I believe Mason was supposed to attend, with her as his date. So, why isn't she attending with her uncle instead? Or is she, and she was merely lying about what she was doing tonight?"

"I'd be happy to tail her again."

"Fuck off, Alex. This is one piece of ass you shouldn't chase. I highly doubt she's interested, and I'd rather not have to fight a war because you fucked Byrns's sister."

We turn on to our street, and the other houses fall away, trees replacing them. Usually, I'm grateful for the privacy. Tonight, they're shrouded in shadows, concealing an enemy I'm afraid I'll never see coming.

TWENTY

SAMANTHA

The house was quiet when I arrived home to change. I didn't run into Victor or deal with any nasty sneers from the men in his pocket. I slipped in and out, almost making a clean getaway when Colin ambushed me and insisted on coming along.

We're stuffed in the back of a car, heading for a club I have no intention of going into, that sits on the edge of the Barrens. I appreciate Colin coming with me, but I can't help but be pissed.

When he found out where I was going, he repeated Shane's words, *You're not going alone*, as if I haven't done this thousands of times before. They don't want trouble down here, and if someone aims for destruction, I'm sure I can handle them. I don't expect Shane to realize that, but Colin should.

"Tell me again why we're going down here?" Colin asks for the sixth time.

"I'll tell you when we get there," I answer, like every other time he's asked.

Colin sighs, his leg jiggling. Do I think the driver will snitch on us? No. Am I willing to take that chance? Also, no.

"I think we should go another night. I've got to be back by two," he says.

What is the point in insisting on coming with me if he is on a time limit? Fucking men.

"What is your issue tonight?" I demand, sick to death of all this bullshit.

"What are you talking about? I don't want you going down there alone, and I have other things to do. Some of us have actual responsibilities, you know."

I rear back, gaping at him.

"Shit, I'm sorry, Sam. I didn't mean it like that. I'm just stressed. Victor is trying to push through some shit, and I can't do it all." Colin squeezes my hand, eyes imploring.

"What sort of things is he doing?" I haven't exactly been around much, but if it is big, I thought Colin would tell me.

"I don't want you to worry about things. I have everything under control. What you're doing is important, Sam. This whole thing has us all on edge."

I look out my window, contemplating Colin's words. I want to push him on what Victor's been up to, but I don't want to put more stress on him. He's trying to fly under the radar as it is, and it won't do us any good if I come in, guns blazing, looking for a fight. I don't like being in the dark, though. I need to concentrate on what's going on at home more than on what's going on in the streets. At least Helms dealt with the Harris gang. My lungs burn with regret for not dealing with them personally. At least Helms will keep me in the loop, unlike Colin or Shane.

Shane King is so infuriating. One minute, he's yelling at me, the next . . . I can't think about the incident without blushing. I've been kissed before, but I've never been kissed like that, like he was trying to consume me from the inside out. The entire world fell away and left me trembling. Desire flows through my body, settling between my legs. I squeeze them together.

I shake my head, remembering the intensity in his eyes moments before he descended on me. He seemed like he was about to apologize. Trying to explain those emotions away feels like a lie. It felt like more, but I can't trust myself in this. There are too many other emotions in the way to be rational. When he talked about his sister, though, he was more than just another asshole.

The only explanation I can settle on without falling down a rabbit hole is that he did it to fuck with my head. It's a lame explanation, though. I sat in that hallway for a good five minutes after he stormed off, unwilling to shatter the illusion. Twice now, I've slipped into an alternate reality where Shane is there for me—only me.

I need to gather my insecurities and shove them deep in my mind. Most of the time, I pretend they don't exist. They'll eventually go away if I don't acknowledge them, right? Lately, they've been cropping up at the most inopportune times. I can't put my finger on why those three men make me question myself, when I'm perfectly capable of hiding them around everyone else.

The car slows, and we hop out. I try not to rush, but with Colin's new time limit, I'm worried I won't be able to find everything I need. His presence is chafing me. I almost wish I would have invited one of the Kings to come.

"Did something happen?" I ask him as we walk away from the bright lights and thumping club music.

"What do you mean?" His head swings around, searching the dark corners of buildings and streets.

"You didn't seem all that concerned about me going out alone before. I'm just wondering if something happened to warrant a tagalong."

"Oh, I don't know. Could it be your brother getting shot? Or Victor taking over? Or you apparently getting wrapped up with the Kings?"

"I'm not wrapped up with the Kings." I stumble over a crack in the sidewalk.

"Oh, so you haven't been meeting up with them? Honestly, Sam, you've made some dumb decisions in your life, but this one takes the cake," he scowls.

"You have got to be fucking kidding me. Is this why you insisted on coming? So you could lecture me? Tell me I'm a stupid little girl who fucks shit up and doesn't know how to take care of herself? Or maybe I don't have the families' best interests in mind. Oh! Maybe I'm a secret agent, working for the 'other side,' as if we're not all in the same damn boat."

The fucking nerve. I'm not a child who needs to be scolded. He has no right to berate me about anything, especially when he didn't step up when we needed him.

"I like how you didn't deny that you've been seeing them. Did they at least give you any info? Anything we can use? Of course you didn't find anything. If you don't want to be treated like a child, then don't act like one. I get that you want to assert your independence here and prove you have a place in the family, but going behind our backs? How am I supposed to explain this to Victor?"

Colin pushes past me, taking the lead, though he has no idea where we're going. Regardless of how shitty he's being, I still need info about Oracle. With or without Colin's approval, I'm going to do what I need to seek out answers. I owe it to my brother and our city. There are dozens of lower gangs under us. They'll suffer if we can't get shit sorted out. I'm not going to let us be Synd's downfall, but before I can do anything, I need to set a few things straight with my brother's best friend.

I speed up and catch his arm. I swing myself around him, blocking his way. His eyes flash, nostrils flaring. He plants his feet, anger radiating from him, but I'm beyond caring. I'm done catering to other people's feelings at the expense of myself.

"Let's get a few things straight. I am not a child, nor am I acting like one, and I haven't for quite some time. I also have no need to 'assert my independence' or prove I have a place anywhere. I think you forgot who you're talking to. My name is Samantha fucking Byrns, and I don't need to have a place in this organization because my last fucking name proves everything for me. I also don't need to explain myself to you. I love and respect you, Colin, but if you don't pull your head out of your ass and start treating me with respect, I'm going to . . ."

"Going to what, Sam? Tell your brother? Oh, you can't. I'm sorry, but you have no power anymore. The only power you had was what your brother gave you. With him out of the picture, you're a sitting duck, but you keep acting like your precious last name is going to protect you."

"I was going to say 'smother you in your sleep,' but now I might engage in a little light stabbing. Seriously, what the hell is your problem?! You're supposed to be on my side," I cry out, exasperated.

Colin opens his mouth, eyes still burning with disapproval, then he snaps it shut. His face smooths out as I watch him process everything, until his eyes close, and he inhales deeply.

"I'm sorry. I told you I'm stressed, but something did happen, and I'm worried about you. I think someone is trying to eliminate us. Specifically, you and Mason. I can't say much, but there's been some suspicious shit going down at the hospital. You probably don't remember a lot of what happened ten years ago, but this is eerily similar. I did it in a shitty way, but I need you to care more about keeping yourself safe. I can't be there to protect you all the time." Colin sets his hands on my shoulders, squeezing gently while his eyes plead with me.

"I don't need you to protect me, Colin. I can take care of myself."

"Sure, you can, Sam. Let's just get this over. I'm ready for this night to be over." His hands tighten again, but instead of being reassuring, they feel like a weight pulling me down. He steps around me, and they fall away, and I can breathe again. This entire encounter is putting me on edge, but I follow after him.

The descent into the Barrens is gradual. Streetlights wink in and out next to a liquor store, and apartments light up the night. Block by block, the lamps fizzle out. The businesses are farther apart. Apartments turn into abandoned blocks filled with squatters.

The regular people, with regular lives and regular families, filling their days with regular jobs, pretend this place doesn't exist. They go about their lives as if they live in a normal city, ignoring the underbelly. They don't fight against it, because it never creeps into their lives. Out of sight, out of mind. What they fail to recognize, though, is that, without the Barrens, their normal lives would cease. Without us, their lives would be a chaotic mess. Most think this place is the worst, the most dangerous they'll ever know. They'll never know how wrong they are.

I try to fill Colin in on what Helms found. I keep my encounter with Shane to myself, if only to avoid him going off the rails about being in league with them. I thought Colin could fill in as my confidante, but I have to keep so much from him; I realize he's nothing like Mason.

Colin is my brother's best friend, which doesn't make him my best friend. I can't use him as a surrogate brother. I shudder, thinking about the betrayal he'd feel finding out I'm the Wraith, and we never told him. He'd be crushed. Add in all the shit with the Kings, and I realize we're drifting apart.

I knock on the ramshackle house, which is more of a shed than anything else. Other gangs come to the Barrens, guns blazing, literally and figuratively, expecting the residents here to bend and give them what they want. They see them as weak and easily manipulated. They're always in for a rude awakening when the people fight back. They have to be strong to live like this. They don't let other people take care of their shit for them.

"Mack! It's Sam. Want to spread the word. I got Colin with me. He's learning how to be a bodyguard. Got any tips for him?"

I grin at Colin's scowl. Hopefully, he'll keep his mouth shut. Mack doesn't like people in general, but he particularly hates pretty boys.

"Six feet," says a gruff voice from inside. I motion Colin to step back, and he reaches for me, but I wave him away.

"Open up, Mack," I say, planting my hands on my hips as the door creaks, a soft light spilling out.

"Thought I said six feet?" Mack mirrors me, thick hands planting on his hips. His beard is out of control, almost taking over his ruddy face, a little scruffier every time I see him.

"When have I ever followed orders?" I smirk at him, making his mouth twitch. My ultimate goal is to coax a full-blown smile out of this guy. After three years, a twitch is all I've ever received.

"Well, what do you want? I got shit to do. I don't like the looks of that one." Mack mutters something under his breath, which sounds suspiciously like "pretty boy."

"Oracle."

"Oof. You go deep, don't you, girly? Nasty shit. Stay away. That tar would put me down. It'll take you right out."

"Any idea where it's coming from? Or going?"

"It started in the south, going everywhere." Mack crosses his arms, glaring over my shoulder at Colin, who is on his phone when I look, not paying attention.

"Seen any more shinies?"

"More and more every week. Don't know why they need to bring those fancy things down here. Couple from Murdocks tried to pinch one last week. Didn't go well for them."

"They snatching a lot, then?"

"Nah, moved beyond. Still comin' around, though. They're lookin', can't figure out what. Figure that's your deal. Going to cause any trouble?" Mack gestures behind me.

"Nope. You seen Nicki?" Mack is still eying Colin, waiting for him to make a move, but Colin is typing furiously on his phone. I doubt he notices the danger he's putting himself in. After the lecture he handed me not ten minutes before, I expected more from him.

"Working the Egg."

Well, shit. I have no desire to go to that part of the Barrens tonight. Anyone else I visit won't talk to me with a guard dog following along. They aren't stupid. Mack just doesn't give a shit. Half the time, I think he's hoping some idiot will try to take him out.

"Thanks Mack," I say, tossing him a bag of cookies from inside my jacket.

His eyes light up before he scowls, trying to act tough. "Why the hell would I want these?"

"'Cause they're butterscotch," I reply, winking at him before turning away.

I tried to pay him for his info when I first came to the Barrens, but most of them don't want cash. They want what they can't get otherwise. It took me years to figure out each one of my contact's vices and use them to pay for what I need. I like to think it makes them like me more, but that's wishful thinking.

"Let's go," I say, grabbing Colin's arm.

He didn't notice Mack slamming the door behind us. "Oh, we're done already?" He glances around, looking like he's forgotten where we are.

"What the hell is up with you, Colin? We're in the fucking Barrens, and you're not being even a little bit careful. You're going to get yourself killed. You just lectured me about this shit! What is so important?"

I march us down the road, still contemplating whether to go to the Egg. I could go if I ditch Colin.

"You were friends with that guy. Nothing happened. Settle down, Sam." He rips his arm from my grip, then stuffs his hands into his jean pockets and makes his way back toward the brighter lit streets.

Guess our little foray is over.

"What's so important you were texting the entire time?"

I've let him slide too many times on not giving me details about what's going on at home. I'm not going to let him brush me off again.

"You need to go anywhere else? I need to get going," he says.

"I thought you didn't need to be back until two? It's midnight. Why do you have a meeting this late? What's it for?"

"Got moved up. Let's go."

"You go. I got other places to hit and then I'll be home." I stop, swinging back toward the depths of the Barrens.

I am done catering to his attitude, especially if he isn't going to talk to me.

"For fuck's sake, Sam, I told you, you can't go alone. I don't have time to go anywhere else." Colin's voice floats back to me, so I whirl on him.

"Sorry, Colin, but again, I'm not a child. I don't need your permission. I let you come with me. Go if you've got somewhere else to be, but I'm not waiting around for an escort I didn't ask for in the first place. I'm sick of you keeping me out of the loop. I thought we were in this together, but you keep shutting me out. I'm going to figure this shit show out alone. I'd rather it be with you, but I can do it without you, too."

"Aw, hell, Sam. You know it's not like that. The less you know, the better. What if someone grabs you? Like they tried with the King girl?" Colin implores me, but it's a flimsy excuse.

"You think if I tell some kidnapper I don't have any dirt for them, they'll pat me on the head and let me go? That's not how shit works. Besides, the more info I have, the easier I can avoid the pitfalls. I'd rather have all the pieces. You shutting me out is putting me in danger, and that's shitty of you."

"I'm sorry, Sammy." Colin wraps his arm around my back, rubbing lightly. I stiffen, awkwardly, patting his side. I can't remember the last time Colin hugged me. We're close, but not the hugging-type. This one, though, feels different: forced. I pull back, stepping out from his embrace.

"If you're sorry, tell me what's so important. Who are you meeting? What is Victor trying to push through? Give me something."

He sighs, running his hand through his mussed hair as he scans the area. I have all night to stand here and wait for him to trust me with something—anything.

"A shipment is coming in. That's what I was texting about. I'm not going to a meeting; it's more of a reminder. We're going to clean house a little. Victor insists I lead this one, thinks showing my face will be a deterrent for others."

"Okay. I don't know why you thought you needed to keep it from me. Is there anything about who's kidnapping these people? Helms thinks it might be related to Mason's hit."

"I'm sure it's not." Colin glances at his watch. "Shit, I gotta go now. Promise me you'll go home, Sam. Please? I'll come back with you later. I don't want to worry about you when I'm dealing with this other shit."

I eye him, a pinch in my chest distracting me. He waves and takes off toward the brighter parts of the city, leaving me in the shadows, contemplating the chills traveling along my spine.

Long after he's disappeared, I stand, thinking about what Colin revealed, when it hits me: he's lying. Maybe not lying, but there are definitely things he's keeping to himself. He told me just enough to keep me from asking more questions. Why, though? Is it to keep me safe or something else?

Skittering echoes down the street, reminding me how long I've been in one place, which is never a good idea. I scan the shadows, searching for any movement, but nothing jumps out. I move down another alley, navigating the maze with ease. I don't want this entire trip to be a waste, no matter how much I don't want to visit Nicki while she's working, so off I go into the night, hoping to find answers instead of more questions.

TWENTY-ONE

REN

I watch Sam from the shadows, kicking myself for not being more careful with my feet. I thought she'd come investigate the noise, but she turns down another street, the darkness swallowing her. The last thing she needs to think is we're still tailing her, which is exactly what I'm doing, but I shove the thought aside.

My phone buzzes in my pocket, and I pull up Alex's text. He's asking where I am. I don't know how to respond, so I slip it back into my pocket. I haven't told either of them what I'm doing. Alex is harassing Shane about working with Sam, becoming more obsessed with the woman every day.

I just want to figure her out.

I don't like puzzles, and I don't like loose ends. Samantha Byrns is becoming both, and it chafes. If I need to give up a night of sleep to find out who she is and what she's up to, so be it. There's more to her than what Shane is seeing. She gets under his skin too easily for him to view her objectively. She is no princess. She isn't an airhead, blindly using her body to get what she wants. I need to find out how deep her secrets go.

I cross the bridge toward King territory. The Barrens are neutral but rough, and I'm not looking for trouble tonight. My worn-in boots whisper on the concrete. The streets are mostly dark, only the light from the rest of the surrounding city illuminating them. I avoid most of the drug dens and prostitutes, skirting a couple of scavengers tucked around the base of a bridge, waiting for the river to deliver them goods. When I approach my destination, I cross back over to the Byrns' side of the river.

The closer I come to the Egg, the brighter it gets. This place isn't like club row or the suburbs, but it's bright for the Barrens. Cars and motorcycles rumble, music reverberates, and the chatter of people grow louder. I slip between two buildings, keeping myself in the shadows. Peering around the corner of an abandoned shack, I see it.

The Egg.

This is where most of the people in the Barren do business. They have their own barter system, their own hierarchy, their own rules. It's fascinating to watch this community develop and flourish in its own right, with most others in the city none the wiser. They don't allow outsiders in the Egg, not even someone like me, who should hold more sway than most. We're all part of the underworld, but they don't care. They'll help us if we talk to the right person but never at the Egg. I can't figure out why Sam thinks she'll be let into this exclusive area.

Beyond my hiding spot is a chain-link fence. There's only one way in and out on each side of the wide bridge that spans at least a hundred feet, with rough-looking men guarding it thirty feet away from my hiding spot. It's less of a bridge and more of a canal, the river a mere foot down. Someone could probably gain access by swimming to the sides, but no one tests that theory.

A deeper pocket of black emerges in front of the gate, and I track Sam, who is striding up to the men like she's done this a thousand times before. She reaches into her jacket, and they perk up. She passes off a couple bags, and they let her walk right in, grins all around.

What. The. Fuck.

Every new layer I discover confuses me more when it comes to Samantha Byrns, and it's pissing me off. Most people are cut and dry. They aren't nearly as nuanced as they claim to be. Sure, most embrace their shades of gray, but everyone has limits. It isn't hard to find their cores, their hopes and ambitions, fears and doubts, wants and needs. Sam doesn't fit into any of the boxes, though, as much as the others want to shove her into them.

It makes her interesting to Alex, infuriating to Shane, and intriguing to me. Not that I'll ever admit it. She rattles me to the point of anger. If I can figure her out, I can banish her from my mind and focus on more important things. The last thing I want is for her to intrigue me.

Sam makes her way around the area, stopping to talk and laugh with several people. A couple times, I lose track of her in the crowd, but she always pops back up. She speaks with a woman for a while before passing another bag along and moves on. Another layer. She gave Mack a bag, too. Is she peddling drugs? It doesn't seem to fit what I know, but she has access, at the very least. Is it Oracle? Most likely not.

I think about the video of her brother's hit. I've watched it, frame by frame, analyzing every angle. There isn't much, and my hacker, Nemesis, hasn't found any other cameras yet. Whoever is blocking them has skills or money to hire well. Right at the end, a shadow appears at the top of the screen. Several small flashes, barely visible through the broken window, and the men outside drop one by one. It took me hours of watching it before determining someone was shooting from the ceiling. The longer I study Sam, the more I'm convinced she's the culprit, which goes against everything we've found about her.

We know she's trained, but I can't help but think she has more skills than we thought. I've seen the restaurant where the ambush took place. She had to have climbed on top of the beam and flipped upside down to shoot them. I haven't mentioned it to Shane yet, since he's having a hard time seeing her as any type of threat. Sooner or later, though, he'll have to give up on this thought that Samantha Byrns is a pretty little princess pampered with marginal training put on this earth to merely annoy him.

Sam saunters to the gate, waving at the others. She's comfortable here. They accept her. It makes more sense why she was able to save Emma from the kidnappers. She's clearly spent a lot of time in the Barrens, and they've made her one of their own. It also explains why Emma trusted Sam to bring her home. Sam knows how to connect with people.

When Shane turned her down, he said she acted upset. Why would she care if a virtual stranger didn't want to work with her? It makes sense now. She's a chameleon, adapting her personality to fit what others want to see. When Shane rejected her, she'd become unmoored, showing a little of the layers underneath. Shane's words hit a nerve in her, the true core of her, beneath those masks she wears so well.

I'm about to head to my next mission when I see Sam hesitate, glancing back at the crowd before her shadow is swallowed by the darkness. I switch directions, following. When I reach the side street, she's disappeared. I follow what I think is the most likely route, but she's vanished. Then I remember to look up. There, on the roof, is a silhouette, perched and facing my direction.

I can't make out any details, but I can feel her eyes on me. We stare at each other, waiting for the other to make a move, when she turns away, taking off into the night. I don't follow.

I breathe a little easier when I step on to club row on the Byrns' side of the river. I always feel hyper-aware when I'm in the Barrens, and I'm not entirely comfortable moving through their space. Checking my phone, I find texts from Shane and Alex, who are increasingly irritated. I should respond, but my night isn't done yet.

I slip into the black car, nodding to the driver, who pulls out into traffic, taking us to the gala. I close my eyes as we travel out of the illuminated streets toward the ritzy business area. The gala is at a botanical garden, which seems irresponsible in November. I never did understand why rich people want to huddle around heaters outside, pretending to care about butterflies, speaking in passive aggressive tones like they don't actually hate each other.

Getting out two blocks from the event, I wait until our man pulls away, taillights fading into the night. I track the cars lined around the circular drive, waiting for their occupants to fill them as the event ends. A few are leaving already, false laughter tinkling out and grating my nerves. A town car pulls up next to me, and I slip in the back, scarcely closing the door before we're pulling into the line. The driver's eyes meet mine, but dart away. It's slow going, but I have the time to wait.

I spot him before we arrive at the front, dressed to the nines and laughing with another asshole in a tux. A young woman is on his arm, sequins winking off her dress. She's not much older than Sam. He was always a bit creepy. The question is, is he merely a creep or someone intent on starting a war?

The car door opens, and the woman starts to slide in but stops when she spots me. Victor nudges her, but I shake my head slowly. She backs out, gaping at him with wide eyes, before she turns and walks off. Confusion clouds his face before he's getting in, spying me as he shuts the door, which locks behind him.

"Hello, Victor."

"What the hell do you think you're doing? Who the fuck are you?" He pats his pockets, but I banked on him not carrying while at a gala. Amateur. I think about fucking with him, since he hasn't done any research upon taking over the Byrns' territory. I wonder what else he's fucking up. I note to set Nemesis on his tail. My palms itch as I kick myself for not doing so earlier.

"I'm Ren King. I'm sure you've heard of me. I have a few questions you're going to answer for me."

"Why would I do that? The last time I checked, you're an auxiliary player. King isn't even your real name."

"And you're not a Byrns, so let's skip the posturing. What knowledge do you possess regarding Oracle?" I peer out the window, unconcerned at turning my back on him.

"I don't know what you're talking about," he says. I can feel his glare on the back of my head. I can also taste his lies.

"Anything on the kidnappings?" I ask, looking back at him.

"Kidnappings?" He laughs. "I'd hardly escalate the situation to that. A few hookers from the streets wander off, and we're classifying them as kidnapped?"

"I don't care how you classify them, but I'll take the information you've gathered."

I pull the cuffs of my jacket over my wrists, anticipating his response before he opens his mouth.

"I don't have any information, and even if I did, I wouldn't tell you. I don't know what King thinks this little scare tactic will accomplish. I'm not afraid of . . ."

"Oh, I think you're petrified of us, but if you think this is an example of our scare tactics, you're in for a rude awakening."

His wheezing laugh sets my teeth on edge. I only have, at best, twenty minutes before we reach the Byrns' estate, and I want to be far away by that point. I hoped this would go easier, but of course, when dealing with another person, nothing ever goes how I want. This is why I leave these things to Alex. I don't have enough patience for the banter.

"I think you'll find, Ren King"—he sneers out my name—"that I can be your worst nightmare. Truly, I'd like to see your best scare tactic."

I raise my eyebrow, contemplating if he's bluffing. Is he really so in the dark about the Kings that he hasn't heard of how we deal with enemies?

Although most of the stories are embellished, the truth is often enough to dissuade others from taunting us.

"Last chance to tell me what I want to know," I say, slipping my gloved hand in my pocket.

"Fuck off."

I nod once, pulling a syringe out and flipping the cap off with my thumb. I plunge the needle into his neck. I yank back and toss the remnants out the window. I wait for the drugs to take effect while he paws at his neck.

"What the hell did you stick me with!?" Victor yells, looking from me to the driver, as if they'll interfere.

"Scopolamine, also known as Devil's Breath. Plus a few other ingredients mixed in to speed up the process. Don't worry, though, it won't kill you. It will only loosen your tongue a bit. Interestingly enough, the doctor who discovered it was an obstetrician. I could tell you more about him, but we're running out of time." I lace my fingers in my lap, waiting for him to stop swearing. If only he knew the increased agitation distributes the drug faster through his bloodstream.

"I'll kill you for this!" Victor pants as dry mouth sets in.

"What do you know about Oracle?"

"I . . . I . . . it's a drug. I don't know what's in it. I tried to get my hands on some to sell, but I can't find any. Exclusive, nothing on the streets yet." His eyes dialate rapidly and sweat pops out on his forehead. If he pisses his pants, I might have to bail.

"Where is it coming from?"

"I don't know."

"Who's selling it?"

"I don't know."

"You're telling me you know people who are taking it, but they don't know where they're buying it from?"

"After they take it, they don't remember anything. It wipes their memories or something. I don't know. I don't know. I don't know." Victor shudders.

I'm sure it isn't a pleasant experience having to tell the truth. To feel like your words are not your own, that your brain's power to reason is wiped out. I have no desire to ever experience what Victor is currently going through. Thankfully, I don't have to employ this tactic often.

"And the kidnappings? Who's behind them?"

"I can't find them. They're hiding." A sob escapes him, making my lip curl in disgust. How in the world did the Byrns allow this man to lead them? Pathetic.

"What do you know about them?"

"One minute, they're there, and the next, poof! Gone. No one comes back, no one escapes. No one sees them. They're ghosts. You can't find ghosts who don't want to be found. They're everywhere and nowhere . . ." He rocks back and forth, hands twitching in his lap.

"What are your plans for Sam?" The question pops out before I can stop myself. I wasn't going to ask him, but hopefully, he's so far gone he won't remember my questions on her.

"The ghosts will take that bitch, too. I know it. The ghosts . . . the ghosts . . ." Victor's eyes lock with mine, exuding fear and paranoia.

We pull up in front of the estate, which is fan-fucking-tastic. I hate when my plans aren't executed properly. Thank god our driver has enough sense to not pull into the drive. I reach across Victor and pop open the door as it unlocks. As soon as I pull back, he launches himself out of the car, stumbling to keep his feet. He takes one step before he collapses on the concrete. Maybe I should have warned him about the blood rush.

Whoops.

I shut the door, and the driver pulls away, leaving the pathetic excuse for a gang leader in the dirt for his men to pick up. As we pass the trees lining the yard, I see Sam hiding within the shadows. Her gaze follows the car before turning and disappearing between the trees.

TWENTY-TWO

SHANE

"I'm sorry, you did what?" I gape at Ren, who is sitting across the kitchen counter.

He couldn't have actually drugged the Byrns' acting leader.

Ren bites into his sandwich he insisted on making before he told us where he went off to. I've never seen someone chew slower. I look to Alex, hoping for some support, but he's staring at his phone, tension lining his face.

"Victor didn't give me much before he descended into the hallucinations, but he's as worried about these kidnappings as we are. He's also tried to get his hands on Oracle but was unsuccessful. It's flowing in from the south. Only the elite can afford it at this point."

"How did he know it came from the south?" Alex asks, his fingers flying across the screen as he frowns.

"He didn't," Ren says before taking another bite.

Getting information out of him is infuriating. He either gives you way too much or not enough.

"Who told you that?" I ask.

"Overheard it from a source."

"You going to be more specific?"

He pauses, contemplating my question. I always trust Ren won't keep vital information we need from us, but something in his eyes is making me wary. He *is* keeping something from us. I can't imagine what it could be. Clearly, it's something he hasn't fully worked out yet.

"Fine. But then I'm going to bed."

"Okay, but you'll need to be ready for a meeting at ten. I set up one with Colin Ashford, Mason's second. I figure we might get more out of him than Victor, but that was before your little excursion tonight," I tell him.

"Pass."

"You can't pass, asshole," Alex blurts, throwing his phone on the counter.

"I can and will. The last thing I should do is willingly go into Byrns' territory, much less the estate so soon after drugging their supposed leader."

"Fine, I'll go alone while Alex drives Emma to Aunt Marge's. I'd rather they not think I'm afraid to go without one of you, anyway. Now, start talking Ren."

"I decided to see what our little pet was up to. I wasn't convinced she was going into the Barrens instead of the fancy gala, so I followed her."

"What the fuck? Why do I give you two orders? You never listen." I throw up my hands, turning to pour myself a drink. A very strong drink.

"I follow the ones that matter. Surprisingly, she did go to the Barrens, specifically the Egg."

"Let me guess, she went alone." Frustration flows through my veins. I take a deep breath, hoping to calm the rage. I shouldn't care. I don't care. I remind myself there's no reason for me to be upset, since she isn't mine to worry about, but it doesn't work.

"She went with Colin, but the tension is growing between them. He left before she went to the Egg. All this is besides the point. The interesting part is they let her in."

"Wait, in? Like *in* in?"

"Yes, Alex. Like *in* in. She handed them something, and they let her right on in. Spoke with a lot of them. Spent a long time with someone named Nicki and then left. I'm not sure, but I believe she might have spotted me. Oh, and again, when I dumped Victor in their driveway. I also surmised that Victor thinks Sam will be kidnapped, maybe at his request if he can find these ghosts, but he was too far gone for me to decipher his true intentions regarding her."

Ren goes back to eating, as if he hasn't dropped a bombshell on us. Alex cusses Ren out, both trying to coax more answers from him and railing at him for leaving Sam in danger. At least we know Victor and Sam aren't on the same side. Victor wanting to sell Oracle isn't surprising, but it's batshit crazy. From what we've gathered about the drug, it isn't something we want in the city. We run drugs, but we can't control something this unpredictable, and we need control.

"He didn't know anything about the kidnappings?" I ask.

"As I said, no, he did not." Ren brings his plate to the sink, annoyance crossing his face as he rinses it off.

"Victor could be lying."

"I injected him with Devil's Breath, Alex. No way he's lying. By that point, it was in his system long enough for paranoia to start setting in. Shane, you need to figure out what you're going to do about Sam."

"I vote we bring her here. She's not safe there if he's planning on feeding her to the wolves or ghosts or whatever," Alex pipes up.

"You think she'll come here voluntarily? She's not our concern. Besides, she's a distraction we can't afford. I don't have the time or patience to babysit her. And neither do you, Alex," I say before he can volunteer for the job. "Ren? What do you think?"

He's silent, staring at the counter. Rushing him won't do any good, but he sits for so long I want to shake him. I expect him to side with me. There's no way he wants that woman here. Imagining her being back in my house, arguing with me about every little thing, makes my chest spasm.

"You make a good point, Shane. She would be a distraction." He holds up a hand at Alex's protest. "However, I think we should keep our options open. Samantha Byrns might not be our enemy, but at this point, she's not an ally, either. I don't trust her yet, but I believe she's more than meets the eye. Perhaps you should try to see her as a source to be tapped instead of an obstacle to overcome, Shane."

"I'd tap that . . ." Alex snickers, breaking the tension.

Ren rolls his eyes and strides from the kitchen, done with both of us.

"Which is the exact reason she shouldn't be in this house. I don't trust her, Alex, and neither should you," I warn.

"Maybe you should listen to Ren for once, Shane. Stop seeing her as the enemy. She could surprise you." He sighs as I shake my head. "Just think about it." He waves and follows Ren out.

I blow out a breath. Serious Alex is always hard to argue with.

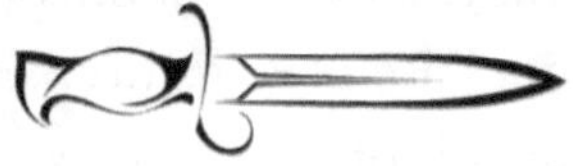

Déjà vu hits me as I pull up to the Byrns' estate. I feel like I'm eighteen again, newly minted leader of the Kings, trying not to puke before meeting with Mason Byrns. I didn't know how I was going to build my family again after the attempted coup and was sure Byrns was going to tell me we were going to be rivals or go to war.

I glance up at the same window, like I did ten years ago. The curtains fluttered back then, and a young Samantha had peeked out. The curtains stay still now, though. She's probably still sleeping after her late night, skipping around the Barrens.

The front door opens before I top the stairs, revealing an older man, heavily laden with weapons. I count five, but the way he moves suggests more are hidden under his clothes. He looks ready for an ambush. He eyes me warily, looking over my shoulder.

"I'm here for Colin."

He scowls and walks away, gesturing me to follow. Ten steps in, and he turns to the right, leading me into a weird sitting room. Leather couches and two wingback chairs crowded around a fireplace and built-ins with what appear to be fake books. Who fills bookshelves with fake books? The room is dark with heavy curtains covering the windows. In my house, this room is an actual library, with a desk for Emma to do her homework.

The room is empty, both of life and people. I turn to ask the one-man artillery crew where Colin is, but he's gone, the door ajar. I want to walk out and get away from this whole situation, especially since he's kept me waiting. I have no desire to work with Victor, but I'm hoping Colin will be my way in. These last couple of weeks have been insane, and I need answers on what's happening on this side of the river.

You could ask Sam, the voice in my head whispers, but I'm trying to ignore it. Colin is the better choice over all. He'll have an insider's look at things, and I won't be distracted talking to him.

I pass the bookshelves, confirming none of them have titles on the spines. I'm tempted to pick one up and see if the pages are blank, but before I can, Sam's angry voice filters in.

"How the hell should I know why Ren King was in your car? It's not like we're besties, braiding each other's hair at sleepovers!" Sam's voice cuts through clearly. I catch a muffled response and move toward the door.

"Oh my God, you have got to be fucking kidding me. I'm not conspiring with anyone. Fucking ridiculous. Besides, meeting up with the Kings and colluding with them would be totally different things. Are you really that paranoid?"

"Please lower your voice, my dear. You must know one in my position should always be paranoid. That's how you prevent getting shot." Victor pauses. "Maybe if your brother . . ."

"You leave my goddamn brother out of this. I haven't forgotten who was informed of that meeting, Uncle. The list is quite short if I recall."

The accusation is clear in her tone. I'm surprised she's threatening him, if her position in the house is as precarious as Ren thinks.

"That it was. However, if you're implying I had anything to do with the hit, you'll be sorely disappointed. I did hear an interesting story about *you*, though. Apparently, you let a little morsel slip through your fingers. You had an opportunity right in the palm of your hands and failed to act."

"I have no idea what you're talking about."

"Emma King. You were able to save her from a terrible fate, yes?"

"So, what? Are you telling me you wanted me to bring her here? How would that benefit us?" Sam's tone drops, a wariness seeping through.

I strain to make out Victor's response as I inch closer to the door. Is he honestly suggesting she should have kidnapped my sister? I stiffen, rage flowing through me. The wrath I would rain down on them would be endless. This whole conversation reaffirms my resolve to protect Emma. Thank god Alex is getting her out.

"The possibilities were endless. You failed this family," Victor sneers.

"This family? This family doesn't kidnap children. This family doesn't start needless wars. This family doesn't fuck over innocent people. And you, you are not my fucking family."

"Listen closely, my dear niece, I am the only family you have left, and even I would dispose of you in a heartbeat, if it benefited this family. You are quite literally useless to this empire. You could disappear tomorrow, and no one would mourn you, you stupid girl. Remember, you are only here because of my grace, and the off chance I might find use for you. I would tread very carefully, Samantha". He pauses. "Now, if you'll excuse me, I have a meeting to attend."

Sam mumbles something, and her footsteps thunder down the stairs. I pull back from behind the door quietly, trying to glimpse her. She stomps past, disgust and rage on her face, head swinging toward me, and our eyes lock. I nod once, hoping she won't interfere in this meeting. I want to walk away and forget her and what she stirs in me. It would be so much easier for me if I could.

She shakes her head, looking disappointed, before turning into the bowels of the house. My stomach turns as I think back to our conversations before. I said eerily similar words. It takes me a minute, but I'm able to pinpoint the feeling in my gut: shame. I didn't care while I was saying them, knowing they were a means to an end, but hearing from another's mouth makes them more personal, more shocking.

Her defense of Emma is both surprising and not. Alex's words from last night, urging me to stop seeing her as the enemy, resonated in the empty space around me. *She might surprise you.* That means owning up to my own shit, which I'm not sure I want to do. I slough off the thoughts. I'll cross that bridge when I come to it.

I'm seated in one of the chairs when Victor comes in. We've never been formally introduced. Up close, he's greasier than I thought he would be. He's dressed impeccably, not one piece of short graying hair out of place, but he possesses an oily quality to him. His conversation with Sam makes him more snakelike.

"Ah, King. I hope I didn't keep you waiting too long." Victor holds his hand out to me, as if we're business colleagues meeting about a merger or something.

"I'm not here for you, Victor." I don't rise or shake his hand. The last thing he deserves is my respect.

He stiffens, then settles himself in the other chair. "Yes, well, Colin is, unfortunately, unavailable. I told him I would attend in his place."

"Then, I'll be going." I rise, straightening my cuffs. I hate wearing suits, but for these meetings, it helps to keep up appearances. I'm grateful for the armor now.

"Excuse me?"

"What did you expect to happen here, Victor?" I pick lint from my sleeve, unfazed.

"You wanted a meeting, and you got one. I expected you to be grateful I made time in my schedule to do this," he scolds, as if I'm some kid he can kick around.

I smirk. Men like him are so predictable. The hint of insult sends them into a downward spiral. Now to trigger a full-on meltdown.

"I think you're mistaking me for someone else, Victor. I'm Shane King, and I don't bow to you. I don't recognize your leadership, or your supposed control over the Byrns' territory. Therefore, I will not be conducting any meetings with you—ever. Have Colin call me to reschedule." I make my way around the couch toward the door. I have to contain my gleefulness at his sound of protest.

"You think you can walk into my house and speak to me like this? You will respect me, boy, or I'll . . ."

"You'll what?" I swing around, slipping my hands in my pockets, a model of restraint.

"You don't want to find out," he says, trying to sound intimidating, but it comes out pathetic, just like him. I had considered working with him if it were to have come down to it, before I knew the plans he had for my little sister, but it's time for him to find out how lethal I can be.

"Are you threatening me, Victor?" I arch an eyebrow while he sputters, his face reddening.

"You don't decide who leads here. This is my domain, and I can do whatever I want. You think you can walk in here and start demanding things, you insignificant piece of shit? I don't give a fuck who you are! You're going to give me what I want."

"And what is it you want?"

"I want to know what the fuck your little lackey did to me! I know he was in the car with me! I know it was him. I demand retribution."

Victor's eyes are crazed, like the drugs aren't completely out of his system yet. My gun's weight rests on my back, reassuring me of its protection should he try to attack.

"Prove it."

"I don't have to prove shit to you!"

"This has been . . . illuminating, Victor. Thank you." I turn, heading for the door.

"We're not done here!"

"We most certainly are. I'll be seeing you, Victor," I say over my shoulder, strolling out the room, then the front door, leaving him screaming into an empty room.

My car is right where I parked it. As confident as I am Victor won't try to shoot me out in the open, I'm not going to take chances with how far I've pushed him. I spin out from the drive and head home. I check my rearview as I pull up to a stoplight several blocks away. I wouldn't put it past Victor to have me tailed. I jump, though, when there is a knock on my passenger window.

Sam's deep brown eyes, face set in a scowl, bore into me. She gestures to the door, and I roll my eyes, unlocking the door for her to slide in. As soon as the door shuts, I take off.

"What the hell, King! At least let me put my seatbelt on."

"Aren't you afraid of being seen with me, Princess? People might get the wrong idea." I smirk at her.

She scrunches her pert nose in irritation. If I'm going to try to work with Sam, I need to not be distracted, so I ignore the tightness in my chest and focus on the road.

"I'm guessing you heard my tiff with Victor, then?"

"I heard enough. You weren't exactly quiet. Question is, did you stick around to eavesdrop on my conversation, Princess?"

"So, you're admitting you were eavesdropping?" she clucks. "Not very professional, boss. I would think you'd know better than that."

"Don't call me that," I growl.

"Then, don't call me princess."

"God, you're fucking irritating. What do you want?" At least I can tell Alex I tried to get along with her. He can't blame me if she's a brat.

"What did Ren do to Victor?" she says, sarcasm oozing from her question.

"You'll have to ask Ren." I smirk again. At least I'll have fun riling her up while I put up with her.

"This isn't funny, Shane. I mean, it was funny watching Victor fall on his face in the driveway, but keeping shit from me isn't working anymore. We both know something has to change, so why don't you stop being such an asshole? I get it, you don't like me. You don't want help from me. You don't want to have anything to do with me. So, can we skip all the bullshit and get this over with?"

I glance at her as she stares out her window. Her tone doesn't match her face. She stuffs her hands in her hoodie, with slumped shoulders. The usual fire in her is smothered, although she's hiding it behind sarcasm and spite. I didn't notice before, but dark rings circle her dull eyes. Another pang shoots through my chest.

"Victor said whoever is kidnapping people are ghosts. And he can't find any Oracle, though he's tried," I say.

"Okay, they don't seem to be taking people from the Barrens anymore, but they still have all their fancy cars down there. Oracle is being shipped in from the south. Some MC from a different city is distributing it. I told Helms. He's going to look into it, see if he can figure out who they are."

I hum, waiting for her to continue. I clear my throat, trying to prompt her. She raises an eyebrow at me. Apparently, it's my turn.

"I'm sending Emma away," I mutter. It's the first thing to pop in my head.

She nods and purses her lips. "Probably for the best. You know she kept sneaking out, even after the incident, right?"

"I'm aware," I say through gritted teeth.

"You going to tell me your plan for dealing with this shit?" She waves, gesturing to the traffic in front of us.

"You going to tell me how the hell you . . ." I clamp my mouth shut. The last thing I want to do is confirm Ren was following her last night.

"Got all the juicy gossip? Maybe I picked it up at a drug den," she deadpans. "Or from a potted plant."

Guilt bleeds into my veins, and I contemplate apologizing. Some of the shit I've thrown at her wasn't warranted, but I don't want to give her too many ideas.

"Why isn't Colin running things?" I slow the car at another red light.

"You'd have to ask him. Good luck, though. He's been in a shitty mood lately," she says, opening her door and slamming it behind her.

I quickly roll down the window. "Sam!"

"Yeah?"

"Victor's planning something," I tell her, leaning over the console.

"Duh."

"No, he's planning something for you. Watch yourself."

"Aw, don't worry about me, boss. He can't catch a ghost."

I watch her walk away getting lost in the crowd of regular people out for lunch. Someone honks behind me, forcing me to move. My mind stays on Sam long after I drive away.

TWENTY-THREE

SAMANTHA

It's been years since I've been to this park surrounded by cafes, bookstores, and cute little boutiques. It's like the ones in some cutesy ass town where they decorate the street lamps for Christmas. I drive through at night sometimes, when everything is shut down and the residents are fast asleep. I remember this park. Our dad used to take Mason and me here when we were young. I never knew why he did, when we had such a large yard to play in, but I never complained. They have ducks here, and I am all about the ducks.

I sit on a bench overlooking the pond, which is, sadly, duck-free. They moved on for warmer parts, but still, I sit. When I got out of Shane's car, I recognized the area, and without thinking, my feet carried me here. For hours, I've watched the people go about their lives, shopping bags slung over their shoulders, coffee cups in their gloved hands.

I should leave. I'm hardly dressed for the weather, even with the sun up, but it's setting, and I'll be screwed. I've been here so long someone is bound to find me, but I can't force my legs to work, not yet.

A little longer, I think.

My phone buzzes again. It's been going off all day, but I haven't checked who is so insistent to reach me. I'm only a little worried it's the hospital. The hope Mason will wake up has dwindled in the face of everything else. I need some time. If I keep moving, I can ignore the doubts and fears that plague me, but I'm exhausted. I want . . . I don't know what I want anymore.

I want my brother to wake up. I want an answer on who is supplying Oracle. I want to know who is taking people. I want to know who's hitting the lower gangs. I want to know why the Kings hate me.

I should have mentioned the lower gang problems to Shane, but we were having a semi-productive conversation, and if I had stayed in his car any longer, it would have devolved into yelling, or I would have blurted the questions racing through my mind.

Why did he kiss me? Why aren't I good enough to work with? Why is he wanting to talk to Colin when I offered information freely? Why does he constantly make me doubt myself? Why can't I get him out of my head?

Between the three of them, they keep popping into my mind at the most inopportune times. I can't afford the distraction, and they're walking distractions. It's clear I'm a means to an end for them. I want to purge them from my thoughts, but no matter how much I try, they keep coming back. It's frustrating and annoying. I wonder if this was exactly what Mason was worried about when he warned me away from them, but it doesn't add up. He made it seem like me meeting the Kings would be a death sentence. Regardless of how much shit Shane has thrown at me, I've never felt threatened by him. He throws his weight around and spews bullshit, but he's never physically hurt me, and I doubt he will. There's something about him that pulls me in every time.

When I saw his car, I didn't hesitate to get in. I didn't expect a full-blown conversation and for him to treat me equally, but I wanted to know what he had overheard. I wanted to know what Ren did to Victor so I could replicate it if necessary. I don't understand the switch in him or why he told me Emma was sent away. I think he just needed to tell someone. I sigh, burrowing farther into my sweatshirt, when a gust of wind picks up. I should forget about Shane. I should forget about them all. Something changed in him, and I saw a little more of his layers. The same layers I glimpsed when he talked about Emma at the meeting. If there's more to me than they think, I shouldn't be surprised there's more to Shane than I see.

Leaves rustle, and suddenly, Ren appears before sitting next to me, bundled up like I should be. He doesn't acknowledge me but sits, watching the pond. I turn back, too. I'm exhausted down to my bones. I don't have it in me to ask why he's here. I'm resigned to this being my life for the foreseeable future. They'll keep coming around. I'll pretend they don't affect me. They'll disappear. I'll try to forget. The cycle will start again. Maybe I'll ruffle their feathers once in a while, just to even things up.

"It's cold," he says after ten minutes of silence.

"Huh?" I glance out of my peripheral.

"It's cold."

"Yeah. And?"

"Just an observation."

"Oh. You don't strike me as a small talker." I turn back to the pond, wishing there were ducks.

"I'm not. I'm also not one to sit for hours, staring at a pond, either, but here we are."

"Have you been here the whole time?" I sputter, stomach clenching, glancing over my shoulder. I doubt Shane or Alex would sit around in the cold like crazy people, just to watch me fixate on nothing.

He meets my gaze, gray eyes assessing me. I always feel like he sees more than I want to show him. He files it away, picking apart every minute detail. If anyone is able to figure out that I'm the Wraith, it'll be him. I should ask him about Victor, like I did Shane, but between my apathy and him actually being in front of me, I don't have the nerve or energy. With his full focus on me, my face flushes.

"Why are you here, Sam?" he asks, looking away again.

"This is my vacation spot. Hard to get away this time of year."

"I'm not going to sugarcoat things for you—"

I chuckle. "You guys have been sugarcoating things so far? Could've fooled me. Listen, I don't need you to hash it out again. I've heard you three loud and clear. You don't trust me. I'm a problem and distraction. I'm worthless. The list goes on. So, this little tête-à-tête doesn't need to continue. You can go home now. No more need to follow me. No more need to worry about what I'm doing. I'm just going to sit on my bench."

I hide the dejection from my voice. I'm not sure why I care so much. Maybe it's my insecurities thrown back in my face. Maybe it's my fear they're right about everything. Maybe it's jealousy; they have each other, and my someone is locked in a coma. It doesn't matter. I'm done fighting. Helms is taking care of the hit. Colin is taking care of Oracle. Shane will deal with the disappearances. He's right: I'm not needed, so I'll sit on my bench and wait until the world sinks or swims.

"Interesting," Ren murmurs.

"What's interesting?" I ask.

"You."

"Great. This has been lovely, but I'm sure you have places to be."

"Not really. I am curious, though, what were you handing out at the Egg?"

My phone buzzes again, drawing Ren's eyes to my pocket. Someone followed me last night, but I convinced myself it wasn't him. I shouldn't be surprised it was. I sigh, wondering how many secrets he's going to uncover before he's satisfied and moves on.

"You won't believe me, so why ask?" I eye him, waiting for a response, but his eyes are fixed on the water.

"Fine, it was baked goods." He wrinkles his nose in confusion, and it makes him kind of adorable, more human.

"Like pot cookies?"

I laugh. "No, like actual home-baked cookies. And brownies. And some lemon squares. They don't get a lot of that sort of stuff down there."

I'm about to tell him it's how I pay them, how I tried for years to figure out their system, how I kept coming back until they let me in their inner sanctum, but I stop myself.

I forgot.

I forgot Ren is not my friend. Everything I tell him goes straight to Shane and Alex. They don't trust me, and I shouldn't trust them. Another text chimes, reminding me of all I'm avoiding by sitting on this damn bench.

"What did you do to Victor?" I ask.

"Why? Want the recipe?" He wiggles his eyebrows at me, and I'm momentarily stunned.

"Did you just make a joke?" I tilt my head, trying to read his eyes, but his mask slams back into place.

"Are you done?" he asks nonchalantly.

"Done with what?"

"Sulking."

"I'm not sulking. I'm vacationing, remember?"

"Sure you are. You're aware Victor has nefarious plans for you, right?" he responds, getting up and stuffing his hands in his pockets.

Ren is always impeccably dressed, whether it's dark jeans and a gray shirt, like the first time I met him, or a suit and tie.

"I know. He told me. So did Shane. I'm good."

I squint at him, the nearby lamp silhouetting him. He hums, searching my face before nodding.

"Interesting."

My eyes track back to the water, not willing to watch him walk away. Something settles over my shoulders. Warmth seeps into me, sending a shiver down my spine. Glancing over my shoulder, I see Ren's retreating back, no longer encased in a jacket.

Interesting indeed.

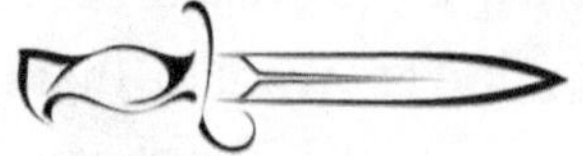

Standing outside my childhood home, I feel like a stranger. It always felt like a haven. Now, it feels like a deathtrap. I debate going to the Depot, lying low and hoping no one notices, but that's impossible. Without knowing who Victor has in his pocket, I can't trust anyone except Colin. With the way he's been acting lately, I don't know if I can rely on him to be there when I need him.

I've seen my brother's second less and less as the weeks pass, but last night's freak out left me more rattled than I want to admit. I expected him to slide into the space my brother left open, but the whole thought is unrealistic. It isn't fair to Colin. He has enough to worry about without me forcing him into a role he never signed up for. I got in late last night, but I caught a glimpse of him closeted away with Victor in the receiving room. I hope Colin is keeping his enemies close, instead of getting sucked into Victor's schemes. I need someone on the inside. So, if shit hits the fan, I'll get a heads up. I don't want to be in a hospital bed next to my brother—or worse: in an unmarked grave. I have a feeling if my uncle can't find a use for me, that's exactly where I'll end up.

My mind drifts to the place I'll be safe, but I shove the thought aside. It's only for extreme emergencies, and I'll probably think twice before I go. I'm not going to run unless I'm forced to.

I pull out my phone, glancing at the notifications. *Text messages: 27. Missed calls: 3.* Well, someone certainly wanted to talk to me. Two of the missed calls are from informants—they can wait. One from Colin. The text messages . . . all from Alex King. Of fucking course.

I flip through them. Not a fucking one is important. They are all flirty banter and then whining when I don't answer. I glare at the screen as if my phone betrayed me. My finger twitches as I go to block him, but I save him in my contacts. At least I'll be aware if he calls. As I press save, his brand-new contact pops up—incoming call. I answer and turn to walk deeper between the trees.

"What the hell, Alex! How did you get my number?"

"Finally! Where have you been? I've been texting you all day." His voice holds a hint of a smile as he scolds me.

"I was busy."

"Busy sitting on your ass. Wish I had a day I could sit around doing nothing."

"Of course Ren told you where I was. What do you want, Alex?" The sooner this conversation is done, the sooner I can continue moping. All I want is one day to sulk, and they've ruined it.

"All right, I get it. Bug's in a bad mood. Want to grab dinner?"

"Huh?"

"Dinner. You know, the meal that happens at the end of the day."

"I know what dinner is, you dolt. Why do you want to go to dinner with me?"

First, Shane is civil to me. Then Ren seeks me out. Now Alex is asking me to dinner? The turnaround is too sharp. Either they're fucking with me or trying to use me. I already told Shane a lot of info, so what do they want from me? I doubt anyone would appreciate another article linking Alex and me, so he must be asking me without Shane's say-so.

"Figure we both eat, so we could go together. Might be fun . . ."

"You're as bad as Ren is at trying to pull off small talk. What do you want, Alex?"

"Ren is bad at small talk, isn't he? Let me guess, he tried to talk about the weather? It's the only thing he thinks small talk is." Alex snickers.

"Why don't you tell me whatever it is you want, and we can skip this song and dance."

"We don't have to go dancing, but if you want to, we totally can. I'm a pretty good dancer, you know." His flirtatious banter is back.

"I don't want to go dancing! Just tell me what you want, Alex. You don't need to pretend to be nice to me to get information!"

"Oh, well . . ." Alex clears his throat. "Actually . . . you know what, never mind. You're obviously busy, so I'll see you around, Sam."

It isn't him hanging up that stuns me so much as it is the silence left in its wake. Staring at the black screen, I wonder if all he really wanted was someone to go to dinner with. The ache in my chest deepens, exhaustion settling deeper in my bones as I trudge to the house, feeling like, maybe this time, I'm the asshole.

TWENTY-FOUR

ALEX

"What's your problem?" Ren calls out as he strides in the kitchen. My eyes are fixed on my dark phone screen.

"Nothing," I mutter, slipping it in my pocket, walking to the fridge.

"I thought you were going out."

I grunt, hiding behind the door. Excitement coursed through me when Ren told us where he went. It does every time I think about Sam. I couldn't hide the smirk pulling at my mouth before I made my escape, intent on asking Sam to meet up. After our call, the energy drained out of me, leaving me in no mood for Ren's probing.

I slam the door, grumbling, "Well, now I'm not. Let's order food."

"I figured you'd be trying to track Sam down. What happened? She shoot you down?" I don't know why he's pushing me. Most of the time, he doesn't care, but every once in a while, he doubles down and keeps digging until I'm baring my soul. I hate it.

"Not exactly," I mumble, pulling out my phone again.

"Spill, Alex." Ren slides on to the stool, waiting for me to answer his questions.

"I'm sorry, are *you* trying to get me to talk about my feelings, Ren?" I ask, leaning on the counter.

"I'm not going to put up with your shitty attitude for the next week. So, let's get this over with."

"You two are dickholes, and you guys are mean, and I don't want to talk about it." I straighten, pulling the fridge open again. It's fully stocked with nothing to eat.

"What are you, seven? Tell me what happened, so we can get this shitshow done with."

I glance over my shoulder, and he's buried in his tablet. I bet the only reason Sam wouldn't meet up with me is because of the asshole currently scowling at his screen. The door swings open, and Shane, asshole number two, comes waltzing in.

"What are we doing for food? I'm starving." Shane slips onto the stool next to Ren, leaning over his shoulder, as if he can decipher Ren's work. He pushes Shane back, making him wobble, almost spilling on the floor. I can't muster up a smirk at their antics, though.

Sam's voice keeps ringing in my ears, asking me what I want from her, telling me I don't need to be nice to her, like she expected me to cave and tell her I needed her to do recon for me or kill a guy I didn't want to deal with. Ren's little meet-up with her probably didn't help her mood. Between him and Shane, I'll never get anywhere with her.

I keep staring at the fridge, hoping food will hop out and into my hands, as Ren and Shane snipe at each other. I block them out, replaying my interactions with Sam instead.

"Hey, dipshit, you going to make food or run up the electric bill?" Shane calls out, pulling me from my musings.

"Fuck you," I reply, but there isn't any heat in my words. I slam the door shut and load a menu on my phone. "I'm getting subs. You guys want any?"

"What crawled up your ass and died?" Shane eyes me.

"Sam shot him down for dinner," Ren answers.

"You asked her to dinner? Why?"

"Because some of us want to actually get to know her. I might get somewhere if you weren't shitting on her and Ren wasn't ambushing her all the time."

"And where are you wanting to get with her, Alex?" Ren presses.

"Tonight, it was dinner, asshole, but I can't even get her to do that without her thinking I have some ulterior motive, and I blame you two. If you guys weren't so . . ." I huff out a breath. This conversation is pointless. Shane will tell me to back off either way.

"Mean?" Ren quips, a half smile on his face. Bastard.

Shane tucks his chin to his chest. "Alex, we can't afford any missteps right now, and Samantha Byrns is a huge misstep."

"Like, perhaps you shouldn't kiss her?" Ren quips, a small smirk on his face.

Ren is in a rare form tonight. Maybe his meeting with Sam knocked something loose in his head.

"Fuck you. That was to fix a problem, nothing more," Shane scowls.

"Personally, if I pushed her against the wall to grind against her, it would only create more problems," Ren murmurs.

"Oh, for fuck's sake. Fine. Alex, if you wanna fuck her, go ahead, but don't let your feelings interfere with the shit we have going on here. We have enough on our plates without having to worry about the Byrns princess, too." Shane shoves away from the counter, toppling over the stool.

Shane is sucking in deep breaths, pacing across the kitchen.

"Uh, Shane . . ." I hesitate, not wanting to set him off.

"What?"

"What the hell is going on with you?" I ask.

I've never seen him this worked up over a woman before. Usually, he gets his kicks with some girl at the club, never bringing them home. Most of the time, he doesn't even remember their name. It makes sense for him, not being able to let anyone too close. The last thing you want to do is get caught up in some scheme when you're the head of a mafia family.

"She's driving me insane!" he explodes, throwing up his hands. "I can't figure her out, and you two don't fucking help, either."

"What the hell did we do?" Ren's head whips toward him.

"You"—he points to me—"won't stop trying to bring her into the fold. And you"—he points to Ren—"keep telling me she's not to be trusted. Then off you go to meet up with her to watch fucking ducks and chit chat, like you're besties or something."

"There weren't any ducks," Ren admits, eyes wide.

"Fuck the ducks!" he cries, picking up the stool and chucking it, then leaving a hole in the wall in the process. Shane stares at the hole and wraps his hands around the back of his head, blowing out a breath. Slowly, I walk around the island and pick it up, seeing a small crack running through the seat.

"Did you know ducks die after having sex?" I announce, setting the stool upright. "Well, the one I fucked did, anyway."

Shane huffs out a laugh, tipping his head to the ceiling. Ren's head is cocked to the side, watching Shane's breakdown with narrowed eyes.

"You know, Shane, this might be the time to start thinking about working with Sam instead of actively keeping her out of the loop. She's the only eyes we have on that side of the river at this point. Helms trusts her at any rate. It may be beneficial to us to use her as a resource," Ren suggests, still watching him.

"Maybe. Dealing with Victor is impossible, and Colin hardly returns my calls. The mayor is still pretending shit isn't happening. We'll need someone to at least tell us what's going on if this shit goes sideways. I hate having to rely on her, though. I'd rather get one of our guys in there, but Victor locked everything down. All their initiates got moved from the Depot. Did you know that?"

"I did. He's very paranoid, with good reason. However, Sam also has access to the Barrens. Perhaps we can use that to our advantage. Anything we ask her, though, is going to have to be done in a delicate manner."

"Are you two for fucking real? You're discussing her like she's an informant or weapon. She's a fucking human being. One you two have been pretty shitty to. Why would she want to help us? All she knows is you two are assholes. She's not an idiot."

These two are insane.

Shane glares at me. "Pick a side, Alex. You either want us to work with her, or you think we should back off. Which is it?"

"How about neither? You need to get your shit straight, Shane. You can't fuck her over one minute and then fuck her the next. All I did was ask her to get something to eat, and she was on high alert. You start coming at her, asking her to work with us, she's going to see right through you. She's going to wonder what the hell made you change your tune. I bet she freaked out on me because you two fucked with her head today. Driving her around and meeting her at parks, for fuck's sake."

Shane collapses on the broken stool, which creaks under his weight. The workaround they want to use on Sam isn't anything new for us, but not on this scale, and certainly not on someone like her. Sam understands our life. She lives it. She's also the wariest person I've come across other than Ren, who takes the cake in that department.

"You're right," Shane concedes, "but goddammit. Somethings gotta give."

Ren taps a rhythm onto the counter. "Perhaps you're both right. She'll be suspicious if we try to foster some sort of communication with her, but we also don't know how trustworthy she is. She's still a Byrns, regardless of who is in charge. She's hiding . . . well, that's neither here nor there. She's been clear on wanting to work with us. I also think she's . . ." Ren stares out the window.

Night has fallen, but the lights on the house make the side yard visible enough to the tree line that no one can sneak up on us. I follow his gaze, wondering if he sees something or if he's lost in thought.

"She's what, Ren?" I prompt.

"What?" He pulls his gaze away, shaking his head. "Oh, I believe she's lonely."

I nod, looking out the window. "Yeah, I see that."

"Well, Alex, you can have the job of trying to foster whatever with her, then. At least she'll answer your calls. Wait, how the hell did you get her number?" Shane pins Ren with a look.

"Oh, yes, I programmed our numbers into her phone. Hers is in both of yours as well. I anticipated we would need to be able to at least have the possibility to get in touch with her, if need be," Ren answers, checking out of the conversation and pulling up some weird code on his tablet.

"How did you do that?" Shane demands.

Ren shrugs his shoulder, refusing to answer.

I sigh. "Shane, if I'm going to do this, I'm doing it my way. I'm not going to bully her into anything. That's your deal, and you have to deal with the fallout from that."

He snorts, giving me a wry look. "I don't imagine we'll have much interaction with her. Do whatever you want, Alex, but I wouldn't hold your breath that she'll come crawling to your bed."

"Fucker. I actually like her. Not because she has a pussy. Maybe if you pulled your head out of your ass for two fucking seconds, you'd see the reason you're all twisted about her is because you kind of like her, too."

"I'm not twisted about her."

"The chair says otherwise," Ren mutters.

I laugh as Shane's face darkens. I check my messages, knowing she won't text me, but hoping for it anyway. I pull up her thread, scanning through the dozens of messages I had sent her over the last few hours. We knew she was at that park, Ren watching on, waiting. He thought she was meeting someone, but as the hours stretched on, and no one showed, Ren figured she was moping. I hesitate, my thumb hovering over the keyboard, but I lock it and slide the device back into my pocket.

"Alex," Shane calls out. "Do what you need to do, but if she gives you any info . . ."

"I won't keep it to myself. You don't have to worry about that."

My chest twinges; he's questioning my loyalty. I may be interested in Sam, but my allegiance is to the King family. As shitty as our childhoods were, I've only gotten this far because of Shane and Ren. Their dads were assholes, but they didn't kick my ass out when my own dad got killed. Shane, Ren, and I were inseparable by that point. I owe my life to them, many times over. They're my brothers, regardless of the blood running through our veins. The fact I carry a last name at all is due solely to Shane's dad.

"I know you won't. I wasn't questioning your loyalty," he says, squeezing my shoulder. "If she says something, make sure you don't read her wrong. She's a good actress, that's all."

Shane's concerned gaze meets mine before he walks out the door. I watch as it swings shut behind him, wondering if he's warning me or himself. He may say he's not caught up in Sam, but he's as messed up about her as I am, just in different ways. I wonder if Ren will join us in our misery of figuring this girl out. Looking at him, I grin, knowing he's already caught, but he won't admit it—not yet, maybe not ever.

"So, Ren, whatcha working on?" I plop next to him, taking Shane's stool.

"When is the food getting here?" he asks.

"Twenty minutes. Now, what are you doing?"

"Do you really care, or are you trying to distract yourself so you won't text Sam for the thirty-seventh time today?" He raises an eyebrow at me.

"Shit, man. Why can't you help me instead of calling me out like that?"

Ren shakes his head, turning back to the screen, tapping away until he pulls a report up.

"Something is tripping the alarm." I have no idea what the numbers mean, but I nod like they make perfect sense to me. I'm not dumb, but Ren's brain works differently. He thinks in numbers, instead of emotions, like me.

"Something? Don't you mean someone?"

"Not sure. I can't find anything on the cameras. They're very good if it is someone, instead of an animal or a glitch in the system."

"You think it's Sam, don't you?"

"No, I don't. She's not stupid enough to trip an alarm."

"Uh, what was that?" I ask, not quite comprehending Ren complimenting her.

"I'm not Shane, Alex. I'm not blinded by my emotions for her to not be able to notice she's more than meets the eye."

"So, you have emotions for her?" I grin, giddy. Lately, I've felt like there was no purpose in what we were doing. The same problems every fucking day. I'm not happy shit is going down, but meeting Sam is an unexpected perk. I need to force Shane and Ren past their crazy bullshit, and maybe we can shake things up, have some fun.

"I'm not going to answer that. Shane's right, Alex, you need to realize she's adaptable. If she thinks she can pull info from you, she'll use whatever means she can, including playing with your feelings for her." He pins me in place, his gray eyes lined with worry.

"Stop worrying so much. You'll get wrinkles." I laugh, punching his arm before I make my way to the door.

They're right. She could use me, but I'm convinced she won't. I may be stupid, but something about Sam calls to me. Beyond wanting her in my bed, a thread tugs at my heart, telling me I need her in my life. I rub my temples, giving up trying to figure it out. Whatever happens will happen, whether I think it to death or not. I'm going to enjoy the ride either way. I make it to the foyer before I pull my phone out and fire off a text to Sam, grinning as it switches from delivered to read.

TWENTY-FIVE

SHANE

"**G**et in," I yell out my window. Sam's nose scrunches in that distracting way, pulling my eyes down to her lips. Even if Alex wasn't bringing it up every seven seconds, I still can't get our kiss out of my head. She's like a drug I need another hit of, but I push it from my mind and concentrate on what we need to do tonight.

"Hello to you, too," Sam says, buckling her seatbelt.

"Helms called. He's got a lead for us. We're going to check it out," I tell her, pulling back out into traffic.

"Us? We?"

"Yes, a lead for *us*. *We* are going to check it out."

"I mean, I'm not complaining, but you going to tell me why you're suddenly so keen on working with me?"

I can feel her eyes on me, but I refuse to turn away from the road. "Don't know what you're talking about," I mutter.

She huffs, and we drive in silence for a good five minutes before she cracks. "How did you find me?"

"Suspicious much? You told Alex you were going to the Barrens."

She shakes her head, looking out her window. I'm all for driving in silence, but I actually *want* to talk to her. It's been a week of only getting updates from Alex on what little he can drag out of her, and I need answers on Victor's movements. She's still sleeping at the Byrns' estate, so I doubt he's acted on his threats, but her safety has been on my mind more than it should be. Every time I ask Alex, he says she dodges the question or stops responding.

"Anything happening on your end?" I ask, trying to be nonchalant.

"Not much. Oracle is trickling into the suburbs; it'll be in the lower gangs' hands soon, I'm sure. The news said more people are disappearing from there, too. So, whatever this is, they're escalating. The police aren't really doing much, but apparently, *someone* told them to lay off. You guys have any lower gangs getting hit?"

She finally looks at me, waiting. "Not really. Seems they're concentrating on your side of the river."

The traffic is thickening the closer we get to club row. I thought having a conversation with her would be hard, stilted. I thought I'd have to question everything coming from her mouth. After hearing her spat with Victor, the idea of her trying to double cross us isn't at the forefront in my mind.

"Not surprising. Victor hasn't been concentrating on protecting them like we're supposed to."

"How has it been with good ol' Victor? He giving you any trouble?"

"Why? You going to beat him up for me if he is?" Sarcasm laces her voice.

"I doubt you need me to beat him up. I'm sure you would be fine without my help."

"Oh my god, was that an actual compliment? From the great Shane King? I'm beside myself."

She fans herself, eyes rolling back. I try to hide my smile, but she catches it and snickers. It falls from my face when I imagine her in danger. Would she tell us if something went wrong? I'm not so sure, and I don't know how to feel about that.

"Tell me, Princess, is he still threatening you?"

"If I tell you, will you guys stop asking? Because I swear Alex blows up my phone about a hundred times a day since he got my number, and half of the time, he's asking me about this shit in particular. The answer is no, he's not, but I haven't seen him much this past week. I'm away from the house when I can help it."

I don't know how to respond. I turn into an alley next to the club and reach in the back to grab a bag Ren handed me earlier.

"Here, put this on," I say, shoving the bag at her. She doesn't take it, so I drop it in her lap.

"What's this?"

"Something to wear. We need to blend in." I pick up my phone to text Alex and Ren our status.

"I'm not wearing this."

"You're not dressed for clubbing. Wear it." I pull up the cameras around the estate, ensuring things are secure.

"If you gave me, oh, any warning at all, I would be dressed appropriately, but I'm not wearing this! Where did you even find this thing?"

"We don't have time for you to be a diva, Princess. Put on the damn dress!" I snap, slamming the door shut, then lean against it, trying to give her some privacy. Her muffled curses and yelps prompt me to almost turn around, but she yells at me, then cusses me out again.

"This is fucking ridiculous! You can't honestly expect me to wear this!" she says, getting out of the car and coming around. My mouth falls open before I snap it shut, frowning. I'm going to kill Ren.

He picked a short, black sheath dress with a deep vee, which would have been enough. My gaze travels up her toned legs. One side of the dress is intact, but the other side has cut-outs, thin strings of diamonds holding the sides together, all the way up to her hip. It's sleeveless, but there are two diamond straps linked to a wide choker, sparkling with more diamonds. As another 'fuck you' to my growing hard-on, another string of diamonds plunges between her breasts. Her hands are planted on her hips, glare fixed on me, tiny feet encased in silver heels tapping away in her annoyance.

"You look fine. Let's go." It's physically painful to pull my eyes away.

"And where the hell am I supposed to put these?!" she grumbles, waving a switchblade and a small gun in my general direction.

My lips tip up, and I snatch the switchblade from her, stepping close enough to feel her breath hitch. I'm definitely not the only one affected so much by our kiss. I slowly slide the knife down the front, brushing her skin lightly with my fingers. I tuck it neatly in, and withdraw my hand.

Reaching into my back pocket, I take out the thigh holster I brought, and I drop to my knees, watching her eyes go wide before I skim my palms up the back of her leg, nudging them a part as I push up the short hem of the dress. I strap on the holster and gently take the gun from her slackened hands, tucking it in before pulling the dress down, hiding it from others' eyes.

Her gaze is fixed on me, lips parted. I bow my head, closing my eyes and give us ten seconds, a little time to pull herself together. I stand, ghosting my fingertips along her hips, still wondering how the hell I got myself into the situation, when, a few short weeks ago, I couldn't stand the sight of this woman. Ren slams open the side door to the club, breaking the moment.

"You two coming, or are you planning on standing in the alley all night?" he calls, annoyance in his voice.

"Come on, Princess. Time to put on a show," I say gruffly, stepping around her, hoping she doesn't skip out on us when my back is turned. Ren's eyes are fixed over my shoulder, and I glance back and almost lose my composure again. The back of the dress is almost as stunning as the front, dipping deep and exposing her entire back with one glittering chain strung in the middle. My hand twitches before curling into a fist, and I force my eyes forward. Now I'm really going to kill Ren.

"Couldn't have picked up a plain black dress, could you?" I mutter as I pass him.

"What would be the fun in that?" He responds slyly, quirking a half smile at me.

It's early, but the music is already beating against my eardrums. I try to be subtle as I adjust myself, but Ren's huff of laughter tells me I failed, so I flip him off over my shoulder. We're on the King's side of the river, but after talking with Helms, I'm on edge. Combined with my own personal plans, nerves race through my veins. Those personal plans involve me giving in a little to my own desires, and I can't fucking wait.

Sam's heels click against the concrete floor as we make our way inside. The hallway we're in is dimly lit, but the flashing lights of the dance floor are ahead. I turn and reach past Ren, grabbing Sam's hand and pulling her to my side.

"Stay close," I say in her ear. She nods before she glances back at Ren. I tip my chin, and he makes his way past us, disappearing into the growing crowd. Usually, I bring Alex to this type of mission, but Ren has a way of blending in. Plus, his attention to detail will help more than Alex causing a disturbance, which is his usual go-to.

"Where's he going?" she asks, leaning up to my ear. Her breasts are pressed against my arm, and I suppress a shudder. My cock twitches as I peer down at her, and I'm caught in her eyes. They're such a dark-brown they seem black in the dim light. I need to focus, which will be a lot harder than I originally anticipated. Especially with her in that dress.

"He's the lookout you can't see. We're the distraction."

"Well, good thing you picked me then, huh?" she taunts, mouth pulling into a thin line.

"What do you mean?"

"Ironic that you said I'm a distraction, and now, I'm precisely what you need."

I rack my brain, trying to remember if I ever told her that. I've said a lot of things, but I'm sure I've never said those words to her. Fucking bastard.

"Alex has a big mouth" is all I say before I pull her out of the hallway, gripping her hand.

She's not exactly short, but in this crowd, I could lose her in a second. For once, I'm trying to keep her as close to me as possible. I make my way to the bar, flag the bartender, and order for us before turning to her. I take a deep breath before I wrap my arm around her waist, reeling her in to my chest.

"What are you doing?" Sam chokes out, body stiffening.

"Told you we have a part to play, Princess." I reach back and grab her drink and pass it to her before taking my own. I tip my head to the bartender, and he nods back.

"How did you know my drink?"

There goes her damn nose again.

"There's a lot I know about you."

I sip my whiskey, scanning the crowd subtly. Sam keeps shifting from side to side as her eyes bounce around the room.

I lean in, mouth close to her ear. "You should stop that, Princess, before you make me any harder than I already am after seeing you in this dress."

I cover my smile at her huff behind my glass before spotting Ren up on the balcony, leaning casually against the rail, his own glass in hand. A woman walks up to him, but he ignores her until she wanders away.

Grabbing Sam's hand again, I lead us to my table, which is roped off. I slide in the booth, tugging Sam's hand to sit down. She aims for the seat, but I pull her on to my lap instead.

"Seriously, you're going to have to give me more. Tugging me around everywhere is getting old," she fumes, setting her drink down and wrapping an arm around my neck.

"I would have thought it was obvious, but I can absolutely give you more if that's what you're wanting, Sam."

Ren tried to warn me it would be hard to go from hating this woman to working with her, but he was wrong. Bantering with her is so much easier than tearing her down. It's certainly more fun. I still don't know if I can trust her, but she's more than I thought she was. Playing with her will be exciting, if nothing else.

"Did you hit your head? Is that what this is?" she retorts.

"Maybe I decided to stop fighting. Ever think of that?"

"Listen, boss, I don't know what game you're playing, but I'm not falling for it. I'll do what we need to but then we can go back to normal." She moves her arm, spinning in my lap and grabbing her drink.

My hands settle on her hips, my left thumb rubbing small circles on the exposed skin, and she tenses again. I'm suddenly very grateful for Ren's choice. I lean in, closing the small distance between us and brushing her dark hair over her shoulder before settling my hand again.

"I'll let you in on a little secret, Princess. I love games. We can play this one as long as you'd like." She trembles, sucking in a deep breath, which pushes her back into me.

"Who are we looking for, anyway?" She squirms in my lap, and I grip her hips harder, digging my fingers in. She can pretend she isn't affected by me all she wants, but her body betrays her every time.

I use the excuse of answering her to lean in again. "See those guys by the bar?"

She nods. I don't have to point out which ones. Anyone who lives like us will spot who I'm talking about. She murmurs something, but the music drowns out her words. I tip her face toward me until our eyes meet, and I raise my eyebrow in question.

"What are we expecting them to do?" Sam leans back, scrutinizing them.

"Helms thinks they're doing recon. They're a part of the group who's been kidnapping people. If they lure anyone out, we can have some more fun," I purr, skimming my nose down the arch of her neck, nipping at the juncture of her shoulder.

Sam digs her elbow into my stomach, dark eyes flashing. I grunt, then grin. I wonder how far I can push her before she snaps. Out of my peripheral, I see one of the men weave his way toward the bathroom. The other, though, is watching someone on the balcony . . . Ren. He's got at least three woman around him that he's actively ignoring, not that they mind. They're content to ogle him from not quite afar. His eyes are on us, though.

I fish my phone out of my pocket and text him. I tap it against my thigh, waiting for a reply, which catches Sam's attention.

"Problem, boss?" she asks, ducking her head.

"I think they've made Ren."

My phone buzzes, and I curse at his response. Sam wiggles on me, twisting herself around and slinging her arm around my neck again. Instinctively, I wrap my arm around her waist as she tucks her face into my neck.

"What'd he say?" she mumbles. I suppress a shudder of my own.

"Ren doesn't always follow orders well. He likes to pick and choose which ones he follows. He needs to stop watching us and start blending in, but he's refusing."

"Is he an exhibitionist?" Her tone rings with curiosity, but I jerk back to look at her face.

"Why would you ask that?"

She shrugs in response, looking out into the crowd. Bathroom guy isn't back yet, which worries me. Plus, Ren is making his way down to the dance floor. Shit, this whole night feels like a waste of time. I'd rather forget why we are here and play with Sam instead, but I can't go back to Helms without something.

I nudge Sam's hip, slipping her on to the seat before handing her phone over. "I'm going to check on bathroom guy. Wait here for Ren. I'm sure they suspect we're here together, so we'll have to switch tactics.

You've got our numbers if we're separated, but if something goes down, try to keep them alive."

"Trusting me not to run out on you guys?" she teases, a smile playing on her lips.

"Run if you want, Princess. Chasing you would be the highlight of our night."

TWENTY-SIX

SAMANTHA

My eyes are glued to Shane's ass encased in those dark jeans as he walks away from me. His complete one-eighty is messing with my head, but I'm done complaining. He wants to play? Fine, I can get on board with that. I won't think of the fallout. I won't worry about tomorrow. I'll let tonight unfold and deal with everything else later.

Ren slides into the booth next to me, sipping a glass of amber liquid. I haven't spoken to him since he'd tracked me down at the lake. I imagine we'll sit in silence, pretending the other doesn't exist, but his gray eyes fix on me.

"What's up, buttercup?" I ask before sipping my drink.

"I hate the club," he says, scanning the crowd.

"I could take it or leave it."

"You seem like the kind of girl that likes to dance."

"Not in this dress, I don't," I scoff. I can't ignore the fact that the little number is an insanely hot dress, but there is so much skin showing

I can't move in it. I usually opt for more leg, something that better conceals my weapons.

"You don't like the dress? I thought it was perfect for you."

"You picked this?" I gape at him as he tips his glass in my direction.

His lips pull up, hinting at a smile. "A dress like that can only be worn by a woman like you," he murmurs.

Thumping music almost drowns out his voice. I don't know how to respond, so I look away, trying to find the man by the bar. The faintest whisper of sensation travels up my arm. Ren's light touch moves to the strap, following it up to the choker. I hold my breath, split between pulling away and leaning closer. These men are messing with my head.

His breath hits my neck, and his gaze follows the path of his hand. I didn't even hear him move, I'm so focused on his touch . He hooks a finger under the choker and pulls gently, making me sway toward him.

"Do you like them all looking at you? Knowing they all want to fuck you? Does it make you feel powerful to know they'll go home and pleasure themselves, thinking about you in and out of this dress?" he purrs in my ear.

"Does that include you?" I ask, afraid of his answer.

"Wouldn't you like to know." He chuckles, releasing me.

When I peek, he's calmly watching the crowd, as if he didn't leave me in a puddle with mere words. Between Shane and Ren, I'll be wobbling out of here. Throw Alex and his flirting in, and I'm officially fucked.

Even if I am going to enjoy tonight, I still remind myself this isn't real. Shane's earlier words, thrown at me in such contempt, roll through my mind. These men change directions so abruptly I'm getting whiplash. They are definitely playing games with me, but to what end? I turn to Ren to demand answers, when he clutches my hand, yanking me out of the booth.

"Little warning would be nice," I say, tugging my hem down, hoping no one saw the holster peeking out. I grab at my phone, but Ren snatches it up and slips it in his pocket.

His hand settles on my bare lower back, and a delicious heat shoots straight between my legs. Gentle pressure has him guiding me toward the dance floor. I try to glance back, but he blocks my view with his broad shoulders, hand drifting under the fabric and gripping my side. An ache spreads through my body. Between the club's heat and Ren's hands on me, my skin is flushed. I hope he doesn't notice.

On the dance floor, his hand falls away, leaving me bereft. He pulls my hips back to him and rests my back to his chest, moving to the beat, letting the crowd swallow us up. It feels like we're in a bubble in the middle of a throng of people. I close my eyes, letting the music flow through me, trying to make myself trust Ren won't let anything happen to me. It's surprising how quickly my body relaxes, letting him lead. I'm sure it makes me stupid or gullible. Probably both.

My eyes fly open when another body steps to my front, hand sliding up my hip. Shane's cocky smirk is there as he presses in closer, sandwiching my body between them. He's saying something to Ren, but I don't catch it. They move in unison, and I'm just along for the ride. I can't concentrate on whose hands are where as they converse over my head, as if I'm not here.

I don't have time to process what's happening when Shane whisks me through the dancers, away from Ren. I glance back, but the crowd's already swallowed him. We head to a closed door, slipping through and stepping in to a brightly lit hallway. Shane spins and pins me to the wall with his body. My hands fly to his chest. Whether to push him away or pull him close, I can't decide.

"They're splitting up. There's a car in the alley outside." He nods to the door at the end of the hall. "Ren is following one. We're going after the car. They've got a girl with them," he mutters into my ear, squeezing my side before pulling back as swiftly as he pinned me. It takes a moment to switch gears, to reign in my libido and remember why we're here.

I snake my hand up my dress to grab my gun. I shake out my limbs as we hurry past doors, mentally trying to slip from one role to the other.

241

Adrenaline courses through my veins, sloughing off the last webs of desire pulsing through me. I need to focus on the girl and not the feel of Shane's hands on my body.

Shane creeps forward, inching open the door. Then we're out, the cold night air blasting me after the heat from the club. We hide behind a dumpster, peering over the top to reveal a car. The Benz is parked twenty feet away, but I can make out the silhouette of a man in the driver's seat. I press my back to the wall, emulating Shane's stance. His gun out, lose in his hand, he catches my eye while we wait in silence.

A strangled cry echoes through the night, and two men come around the corner down the alley, dragging a young girl with them. Her scream is cut off by a meaty hand. I glance behind, hoping to see Ren, but he's nowhere to be found.

There isn't time to formulate a plan, but I assume Shane wants me to stay behind him, like a good little girl. I'm not going to let an opportunity pass me by to get information because it might hurt his feelings though.

As the men stomp forward, Shane raises his gun, bracing on the dumpster and shoots the driver in the back of the head. Everyone scatters, one hauling the girl to hide behind the car's hood. She's shrieking, which only adds to the chaos. Shane fires another couple of shots and ducks while they return fire.

I crouch, peering around, and watch as the girl breaks free of her captors, running back up the alley. Ren appears from the shadows, scoops her up, and throws her over his shoulder. They're gone before the men can raise their guns. Her shouts fade, leaving us to take out the remaining two.

"You got a plan here, boss? Or are we flying by the seat of our pants?" I ask, trying to keep an eye on the men as they argue behind the car. One tries to creep to the driver's side, and I pop off a shot, making him scurry back and swear loudly. Shane glares over his shoulder, like shooting next to his head was too much for him.

"If you've got any ideas, I'm all ears," he barks.

Well, then. I'm about to suggest we split up when the kidnappers take off toward the opposite end of the alley. Shane swears violently and runs off after them. Well, shit, guess we're just winging it.

I take off after him, but when Shane goes left, I go right, following the second gunman. For such a pudgy man, he's certainly speedy. I'm cursing the heels Ren picked out by the end of the first block. I contemplate kicking them off but barefoot would be worse. The kidnapper is busting his ass up alleys, flinging himself around buildings.

I swing around a corner, expecting to spot him ahead, but I'm jerked to the side, my gun clattering across the concrete. His fat arm wraps around my throat, cutting off my breath. I slam my elbow into his stomach, and he grunts, but the pressure doesn't subside. Stomping my foot on his instep causes him to stumble enough for me to pull his arm away a little and suck in air. I rear my head back and connect with his nose. That's enough for him to let go, howling.

I spin, plunging my hand in my dress for my knife, but he's raising his gun to my face, so I drop to the ground, landing on my ass. I kick out, connecting with his kneecap, and he collapses, a bullet sinking into the asphalt inches from my hand. Somehow, he kept hold of his gun, so I kick again, knocking it away.

"You fucking bitch!" he yells, struggling to rise on his shattered knee.

"Newsflash, big guy, you're not going to be able to stand on that," I say, hoisting up, brushing my hands on my tattered dress. I grab my knife, wincing at my scraped palms.

A string of curses are hurled at me, but I ignore them while I try to spot where our guns flew off to without taking my eyes off him. He lunges at me but one slash of my knife to his arm, and he rears back, clutching the wound.

"You're fucking dead. Just like your brother," he sneers.

"Who do you work for?" I ask, ignoring the ache and rage his words elicit. I pull in a deep breath, calming my racing heart. I'm used to this type of thing. I'm trained to deal in these situations. I just need to get my shit together.

"Like I'd tell you, cunt." He throws himself to the side this time, reaching for his gun, but I kick it away, slashing at him again.

I hate I can't kill him. I hate I don't have my phone. I hate this whole damn thing. Fucking Kings getting me into this mess.

"Listen, you can tell me who you're working for, or . . . I can kill you."

He spits at me. I look down to see if he hit me—'cause gross—and find half of the chains are broken on my dress. As much as I pitched a fit about wearing this outfit, I liked it. Now it's fucking ruined. Bastard.

"You made me ruin my dress. This was a gift, you know." I glare at him, but he sneers, blood still seeping between his sausage fingers from the gash in his arm.

"Waiting around for your little friends to come save you? Worthless whore. I can't wait to see you put up. Cunty little bitches like you always break so easily." He leers at me, making my skin crawl. I have no idea what he's talking about, but it doesn't sound good for me.

"Who are you working for?"

"Fuck you. You'll catch a pretty penny for sure. Maybe they'll let me play beforehand. Bet you'll scream and fight, but you'll like it, won't you? Whores like you always act so high and mighty until we catch you."

"Who are you working for?"

This is bad. Really fucking bad. Colin mentioned the flesh trade, but this disgusting piece of shit is confirming everything. Someone is grabbing people to sell. We're so totally fucked. These aren't little operations run out of a rundown warehouse. They're huge affairs. With so many layers, getting to the top of the food chain is almost impossible. I need to get back to the guys and tell them.

I'm so caught up in what he revealed I don't notice him reach for the chunk of asphalt until the rock is flying at me. Thankfully, it hits my shoulder instead of my head, but it gives him enough of an opening to lunge again for the gun. I jump, stabbing toward his neck, hoping I can reach him while throbbing in pain. Shit, I hate making mistakes.

His gurgling tells me I hit my mark as I roll off him, leaving my knife stuck in his flesh. He brings his hands up to claw at the handle and then he rips it out. Dumb, since now, he'll bleed out faster. He throws the knife, and it grazes my hurt shoulder. Pain radiates from the wound as hatred burns from his eyes as he slumps on his side. They go blank.

Fuck. Shane is going to be pissed.

TWENTY-SEVEN

REN

This girl is pissing me off. Most people piss me off, but this one is annoying as hell. I snatched her when she ran from her would-be captors, but getting any information out of her is impossible. She keeps sobbing, then miraculously feeling better enough to rub my thigh in the back of the car. For the seventh time, I encircle her wrist and place her hand back in her own lap, gritting my teeth when she giggles.

"You want me to wait, boss?" the driver calls out.

I planned on sending him on his way, but now I'm rethinking with the way this girl is acting.

"Yes, I won't be long."

The girl lets out a giggling shriek as I push out the car, nostrils flaring. I wish I could have gone with Sam instead. At least I wouldn't have to listen to this girl's inane chatter. She can't be much older than eighteen. I take a deep breath, holding it until my lungs constrict, before blowing out and opening her door. Of course, she couldn't open it on her own because she couldn't pretend to trip and try to fall into my arms, which is exactly what she does. For a split-second I think about letting her crash to the concrete, but I snap my hand out and grab her upper arm, steadying her before stepping away. She sways toward me, but I spin around, marching her up to the door.

I haven't spoken to her other than to tell her to stop struggling. When the tittering started, I clammed up, unwilling to give her more ammo. As I knock, I pray there's someone home. I could stash her at a safe house, but I doubt the men who grabbed her know where she lives. They most likely marked her at the club, seeing her as an easy target.

"So, are you going to come in?" she probes suggestively, rubbing her tits along my arm.

"No." I don't bother looking at her but shuffle to the side, trying to keep distance between us.

"Seriously? Isn't that why you got me away from those guys?" she snarls. She's dropped the breathy tone, a nasally pitch bleeding through.

"No."

The door opens, and a beefy man, faded tattoos covering most of his body, including his bald head, stands there, shotgun in hand. I suppress the urge to roll my eyes when she squeaks, stepping closer to me. The man glares before narrowing his eyes at me. I can tell the exact moment he places who I am. This isn't the best part of town, and I'm not surprised he recognizes me.

"Sir," he says, tucking the gun behind him, like I'll forget he has it. I raise an eyebrow, and his face flushes.

"Daddy?" the girl yelps, hiding behind me.

"Get in the house, May," he grumbles, giving me an apologetic look. May scrambles to obey but doesn't miss the opportunity to peek back, shooting me what I'm sure she thinks passes for seduction. He knocks the butt of the gun on the ground, making her jump and scurry away.

"I'm sorry, Sir. May is . . ." He grapples for the words.

Deciding to put him out of his misery, I interject. "She was down on club row. Couple guys grabbed her. Might want to keep a closer eye on her."

I turn, intent on getting as far away from this whole shit show before May comes back, making some asinine claim to trap me into staying when he speaks.

"Getting bad out here. Lots of people going missin'."

I frown over my shoulder, nodding. I'm not discussing what's going on with this man, much less King business, but if the problem is seeping into these areas . . .

He closes the door as I climb back in the car, telling our man to take me back to the club. I pull out my phone. Alex has called me fourteen times in less than twenty minutes. He never could handle being left out of the loop. I thought his head would explode when Shane told him we needed him at the drop off for the shipment tonight. It got worse when he found out we were bringing Sam.

"Alex, I don't have time to give you updates every minute. What the fuck do you want?" I snap when he picks up.

"We got a problem down here," Alex replies gruffly, his usual smile missing from his voice.

"Deal with it. I have to get back to Shane and Sam."

"You're not with them? What happened?" Alarm fills his voice, the noises in the background growing muffled.

"We'll fill you in when we're home. Deal with your shit," I say, exasperated.

"Uh, I don't know how to do that. It's missing."

"What do you mean 'missing?' What's missing?"

"The shipment, it's gone. We found the truck, but it's empty. Driver's gone, too."

I curse under my breath. This is the last thing we need. It's not unusual for someone to snatch a load from us, but it's happening more often lately. I grab my tablet to find out what the fuck happened.

"Where?"

"East side, by Hampshire." Alex answers before bellowing something at the men he's with.

"Why the fuck was the truck all the way down there? It wasn't supposed to be anywhere close to Byrns' territory."

"I know, but that's where we found it. I'm going to see what I can find here, but it looks pretty . . ."

A boom rattles in my ear, and the line crackles out. It clicks back, and another explosion rings out. I yell Alex's name, though he can't answer. Snapping and popping erupts, then men shout.

"Ren?"

"Alex, what the fuck just happened?" My panic seeps into my voice, but I steady myself.

"Truck blew up. Someone rigged it to go as soon as the door popped. Fuck, this is going to be a helluva clean up," Alex sighs, like that's the worst of our problems.

I close my eyes, the anxiety bleeding out of me, then relief fills me. I hate splitting up for this exact reason. If I had been there, I could have . . . done nothing. I wouldn't have done anything differently than Alex. My presence doesn't mean we'll never get hurt, but not having control . . . I clench my fists and pop one knuckle after another before shaking my hands out.

"Ren? You good?"

I suck in a breath, counting, before letting it out in a whoosh. "Call Graves. How many did we lose?"

The trembling in my hands subsides as he gives me the numbers, assuring me he'll call our man for the cleanup before hanging up. I contemplate texting Shane, but the last time I saw him was in the middle of a firefight, so I'd rather not distract him.

"Everything okay, boss?" our man inquires, keeping his eyes on the road.

"Everything is fine," I respond, looking out the window at the dark buildings passing by.

Whoever is coming into our city isn't fucking around. The more we learn about them, the more it pisses me off that I can't figure out who they are. It's a large operation, with a lot of money, with the way they've been able to override the cameras, encrypting videos left and right. Nemesis is costing us an arm and a leg trying to find everything she can on them, yet even she's having trouble. To my knowledge, she's never failed, and it's pissing her off, too. At this point, I think she'd work for free to beat these people at their own game.

A text comes through, Shane's name flashing on the screen before the screen goes dark.

Lost my man, going to find Sam. Where the fuck are you?

"Shane, are you telling me you lost our pet?" I grumble down the line when he picks up.

"Fuck you, she took off. I'm looking for her now."

"Maybe she took advantage of your distraction and dipped again," I suggest, though I don't believe it.

"No, the two split up. I went after one, she followed the other. I'll find her. She's probably back at the club, waiting," he retorts, an edge in his voice.

"I'm sure she's fine."

"Of course she's fine," he snaps.

"Well, Alex had some troubles. Someone took the shipment and dumped the truck in Byrns' territory. Then blew up the truck, while he was standing next to it. Alex is going to call Graves down there to deal with everything, hopefully before we have to deal with the cops. I'll deal with the commissioner if it comes to that."

"Who the fuck took our shit?!" Shane yells.

"I'm sure we'll find out. Get Sam and go home. We'll deal with things there," I order. Shane chuckles on the other end.

"Whatever you say, boss man." Sarcasm drips from his voice.

"Go to hell," I mutter, hanging up before he can give me more shit.

"We still going to the club?" the driver asks.

"Yes."

Tapping my fingers on my leg, I itch to grab my tablet again. I want to start investigating who stole our latest gun shipment and tried to blow Alex up. I want to search the cameras around the club, see if I can find out where Sam went. That realization pulls me up short. I shouldn't care what happened to her. It wouldn't affect my life whatsoever if she somehow disappeared.

I don't entirely trust her, even if I've encouraged Shane to work with her. I close my eyes, leaning my head back against the seat, the image of Sam in the dress I chose for her clear in my mind. She looked exactly like I knew she would: fucking delicious. As soon as I saw it, I knew the dress was made for her and only her. I shouldn't have touched her, told her the things I did at the club, but I couldn't help it. She was a walking temptation for me in that dress. Sam wants us to think she's unaffected by our presence, but her body gives her away in the slight gasps of breath, the minute trembling of her body, the flush of her skin.

My eyes fly open, and I squeeze myself through my pants, trying to relieve the pressure and gain control of my body. I curse, knowing I need to stop thinking about her, fantasizing about what it would be like to have her under me, on top of me, in front of me. Nothing good will come from that line of thinking. Sam is nothing but an intriguing puzzle wrapped in a beautiful package. I can't afford to dabble in anything she would offer, not that she's offering anything to me anyway. No, Samantha Byrns doesn't belong on my mind—or my cock.

SAMANTHA

I'm bemoaning the state of my dress when Shane finally finds me. I collected my gun and knife and cleaned them as best I could before sitting opposite of the corpse, waiting for someone to come. My shoulder is fucking killing me, the slice stinging every time I move. I'm pissed by the time he decides to show up, so I glare at him as his footsteps echo around the corner.

"Sam? What the fuck!" he hollers, crouching and grabbing my arms, making me wince from the pain in my shoulder.

"Watch it, asshole!" I shriek, flinching backward.

"Fuck. Where else are you hurt?" he demands, his hands running up and down my body, searching for more injuries.

"I took a rock to the shoulder. Sliced it a little. Knock it off." I push his hands away, scowling.

"Fuck." He pulls at his hair, leaning back.

"You said that already. Did you catch your guy?"

"No, I lost him in the crowd. I tried to track him, that's why it took me so long to come for you." I search his face while he pulls out his phone and taps at the screen. He looks . . . relieved. Like he was worried about me.

"Well, I got some shit from my man before he died."

"You mean before you killed him?" He cocks his eyebrow at me.

"He may have fallen on my knife . . . and shattered his kneecap on my foot . . . but honestly it was his own fault," I grin wickedly.

"I'm sure it was. Let's get out of here. I'll call for a cleanup."

Shane helps me up gingerly, as if I'll break, and I roll my eyes. He shrugs off his jacket and drapes it over my shoulders. He tucks me under his arm, heading back to the car. I don't need the coddling, but he seems to need it, so I let him. I have to admit, it's kind of nice to have someone take care of me for once.

I don't want to burst the bubble we're in, but I need to tell him what I learned. His phone buzzes, and he drops his arm before grabbing my hand to pull me along. Guess I should have expected the gentleness wouldn't last long.

"What the fuck, I can't leave you alone for five fucking minutes," he gripes, then pauses to listen to whoever is on the line. "I don't see how that's going to fucking help a goddamn thing." Another pause follows. I think I catch Alex's laugh, but I can't be sure. "Fuck off," Shane grumbles before hanging up.

I tug my hand, trying to pull free, but he tightens his grip and strides on.

"You know, these shoes aren't easy to walk in . . ." I pull my hand back again, but Shane growls. Before I can snap back at him, he flings me over his shoulder like a sack of potatoes.

"What the hell, Shane! Put me down!" I shriek, pounding my fists on his back. I feel a sharp sting. "Did you just smack my ass?!"

"Stop squirming," he tells me, his arm tight around my thighs.

I hit him with my good arm a few more times for good measure, but I'm too tired to keep fighting. My dress is riding up with every step he takes, and after a few attempts to awkwardly pull the hem down, I give up on that, too. I shouldn't be surprised by his actions with how they pulled me around like a ragdoll in the club. And I'll never admit it, but not having to walk back to the car is the best thing to happen tonight 'cause my feet are killing me.

I breathe a sigh of relief as we round the final corner, the car waiting ahead. I twist around, but Shane smacks my ass again. Huffing, I ride out the last block. He sets me on my feet more gently than I expect and reaches around to open the passenger door for me to climb in. I immediately kick off my shoes, stretching my toes out and groaning. Never again. I officially fucking hate heels.

I expect Shane to climb in, too, but he stands outside, making phone calls, so I peel off his jacket. Pawing through the clothes I threw in the back of the car, I search for my hoodie. I half crawl into the back, my ass hanging out between the seats. I'm fucking freezing, and I'm not going to walk home in this dress from wherever Shane drops me off. I find my shirt and pants but still no hoodie.

"What the hell are you doing?" Shane asks, dropping into the driver's seat.

"I can't find my hoodie. And I need to change. Get out," I respond, my voice muffled as I throw other clothes aside.

"Sam, sit down."

"Why do you have so many fucking clothes back here?! It's like a goddamn boutique!"

I grab hold of what I think is my hoodie, crying out in triumph and wiggle myself back, plopping down in my seat. It's too big. I don't even fucking care anymore, so I yank the sweatshirt over my head, then reach for my pants in the backseat, but they're lost in the mess I made.

"Are you done? Can we go now that you've stolen my sweatshirt?" He eyes me with appreciation in his eyes.

"Well, once you find mine, you can have yours back. I need my pants, though, so you can dive in and find them." I wave toward the back, resting my head back and closing my eyes. This rollercoaster of a night can be done now.

"We'll find them later. I want to be out of here before Jax shows up," he says, starting the car and turning down another alley.

"Who's Jax?"

"Our cleanup guy."

"Ahh," I say, closing my eyes again. It's still early, but between the fight, the running, and the guys messing with my head, I'm exhausted.

Regardless of everything, something has obviously changed between us. Even if I wanted to exchange info before, I knew not to trust the Kings. But now? I don't know what to think, but I trust him enough to keep me safe while he drives.

"Princess," Shane whispers, nudging me.

"What?" I whisper back, eyes still closed.

I hear him sigh, then he cradles me, waking me up fully. I hadn't registered we weren't moving anymore. For a second, I panic, my fight-or-flight taking over. I arch upward and shoot my hand toward him and smack him in the face, which only makes him clutch me tighter while he curses.

"Sorry! Oh my god. I'm sorry," I cry, covering my face with my hands. I feel bad, but I can't help the giggles from erupting out of me. I try to smother them, since he's still swearing. His jaw turns red.

"It's not fucking funny." He glares at me, stepping forward again.

"Seriously," I gasp, "put me down. I can walk. Wait, where are we?" My house but not my house. Goddammit, he took me to the King estate.

"You don't have any shoes. At least, this time, you can use the front door instead of slipping in through the tunnels," he quips, shaking his head as we climb the stairs.

"I got out using the tunnels. I got in through a window. Didn't know about your tunnels until after," I inform him, crossing my arms. I contemplate putting my arm around his neck, but that would be weird.

"Good to know I should secure my windows, then."

"Shane, put me down. I can walk from here," I say as we reach the top of the stairs.

He pauses, gazing at me before setting me on my feet again and opening the door, gesturing me in first. I knew the house would be like mine, but it's . . . homey, like actual people live here. My house doesn't have the same warmth. Or maybe it did, but now it's cold and blank without my brother in it.

"This way." He gestures, leading me up the stairs.

"Where are we going?" I ask when he turns the opposite way of his study.

"To clean you up."

"Uhh, I'm fine. I can tell you what I learned and then I can go . . ." I glance behind me, expecting to see other people, but no one is around. A bunch of guys always loiter at my house, especially now that Victor is taking over.

"We're not talking until you're cleaned up and I've looked at your shoulder."

The farther I fall with these guys, the more confused I become. I don't understand why Shane is suddenly so concerned, but warning bells ring in my head. There has to be more to it than making sure I'm okay. They either want to keep me here until I spill all my secrets or they want to keep an eye on me. Maybe both.

Instead of a bathroom, Shane leads me to a bedroom with a king-sized four-post bed. It's massive, but hardly dwarfs the space. The attached bathroom is almost as large, and I realize this is the master suite. Mason stays in this room at home, but I haven't been inside in years.

Standing in the doorway, staring at the huge enclosed shower, I wait for Shane to leave, but he putters around, turning on the shower, grabbing towels and a first aid kit. I could run now, but I do want get clean. Rolling around in a dirty alley isn't exactly how I wanted to spend my night, but here we are.

"Take the hoodie off," Shane says, breaking into my thoughts.

"Yeah, I'm good, boss. I can clean myself up," I answer, avoiding his eyes.

He steps in front of me, hands on his hips, blue eyes blazing. I cross my arms, ready for a fight. He's about to find out how stubborn I can actually be.

"Take it off, Sam. Now."

I shake my head, matching his energy. He sighs deeply, and before I can react, the hoodie is halfway over my head, the thick fabric muffling my shouts. I try to pull away, but he seizes my hip and whips the sweatshirt the rest of the way off, leaving me standing in a ripped dress, half gaping open from thigh to hip on one side.

"Seriously? This is ridiculous." I attempt to step out of his grip, but he latches on to my other side and swings me up on the counter, standing in front of me, glaring.

"This would be a lot easier if you'd listen."

"So, I don't do what you want, and you think you can manhandle me?" I retort, pushing against his chest, which does absolutely nothing. He's like a brick wall—feels like one, too.

"You can make this easy or hard, but either way, I'm going to win, so choose carefully." He smirks, as if this is all a joke.

"Fine, do your worst," I say sarcastically, crossing my arms again and staring over his shoulder.

He pokes and prods my shoulder, but I barely feel the pain anymore, only wincing slightly when he stabs at a particularly sore spot. It's bruised, so I don't know what he thinks he's accomplishing. I can't deny having him this close is disorienting. His dark hair brushes against my jaw as he bends to examine my flesh, forcing me to suppress a shudder.

When he straightens, he plants both hands on the counter, boxing me in, staring into my eyes. I try to glance away, to not be captivated, but I'm caught in his orbit. His eyes bore into mine, searching for something. My muscles relax, and I purse my lips. I'm tired of fighting. Apparently, he finds whatever he's looking for because he tucks his hands under my ass and picks me up before walking us toward the shower.

I open my mouth to argue, but I'm done protesting. He steps right in, clothes and all, and slams me against the wall, his mouth descending on mine. He devours me as the water sluices down our bodies and plasters my hair to my face. My tongue duels with his, the adrenaline from earlier coming back full force, right along with the desire.

Heat is flowing through my body and pooling between my legs as his body pins me to the wall while his hands explore my flesh, taking care to avoid my injured shoulder. He pushes the flaps of the dress aside, reaching around to grab my ass, fingering the strap of my thong. A thought flashes through my mind that I should stop this, but I push it aside. This whole night has been leading to this moment, and no matter what happens tomorrow, I'm going to let go and enjoy it. I've been dreaming about our last kiss too often to give up on the chance to do it again.

I moan as his lips leave mine to trail down my neck and find the sensitive juncture he nipped at earlier. He latches on, leaving a mark, but I'm beyond caring. He snakes his hand up, cups my tit, and squeezes almost too hard. Tipping my head back against the tiles, I moan.

Shane growls when the dress won't move any further, and he steps back, sliding my trembling legs to the floor. He rips his shirt over his head. A wet smack echoes through the space as it hits the floor, and he reaches for his pants. I'm mesmerized as he pushes them down, my eyes following, soaking in every groove on his stomach and ripple of muscles until his cock springs free. I freeze, wondering if this is a dream. Then his hands are on me again, gathering the hem of my dress and peeling the ripped fabric off my body.

He pauses, taking in every inch of me, then his mouth is on mine again, his hands everywhere, yet it's not enough. Hands gripping my hips, he lifts me again, and I wrap my legs around him, the delicious friction of his cock pushing and rubbing in all the right places. I grip his shoulders and dig my nails in when he leaves my mouth, blazing a path down my neck and pulling a taut nipple in his mouth. I cry out as he moves to the other one, swirling and sucking.

"I swear if you're not on birth control . . ." he snaps, nipping at the bud.

"Implant," I gasp out, my hips jerking toward him.

"Thank fuck." Shane presses his chest into mine, burying his head back into my neck.

My pussy clenches when he hooks a finger on the strap of my thong to pull them off, but between our position and the water, they won't slide down. He growls again, unhooking my legs and dropping to his knees. As soon as he yanks them off, his tongue finds my clit, and I'm forced to grab his hair and hold on, legs shaking. He slides them further apart, and pushes a finger inside me swiftly, almost brutally, but the move only makes me tremble harder.

I chant his name, so close to the edge, when he stops, and I cry out in frustration. He peers up, intensity burning in his eyes. I wonder if he's going to leave me here, empty and wanting.

"When you come, Princess, I want it to be around my cock."

A whimper escaped me at his words. He nips my thigh before rising, hooking a hand under my knee, and without warning, impales me, filling me up completely. I gasp, grabbing his arms. He doesn't give me any time to recover before he's thrusting, whispering words I can't make out over the roar in my ears. My pussy quivers around him as his cock drives into me over and over.

I squirm, trying to find purchase, so I can take him deeper, but the wet floor makes it nearly impossible. Shane wraps his arms around me and hauls me up, my other leg folding instinctively around his waist. I bury my face into his neck, biting and sucking until his hand encircles my throat, my head thumping back against the tiles. Then he's sucking a nipple between his lips. His thrusts become more erratic while I tremble in his arms.

"Come for me, Princess," he groans.

I spasm. My hand falls, finding my clit while he watches, thrusting harder into me. My climax hits me sharply, and I let out a groan, shivering as the sensation flows through me. He plunges in two more times and grunts, tensing and holding deep inside.

He collapses against me, both of us breathing hard while lingering pulses shoot through me. When another shot of lightning hits me, my pussy spasms around him, making him jerk with a grunt. He's holding me up, which is perfect because I'm pretty sure I'd be a puddle on the floor by now.

"Fuck," Shane breathes into my neck. I don't know if that's the satisfied kind or the mistake kind, so I concentrate on slowing my thundering heart, untangling my legs from him as he pulls out. I can feel the remnants of us sliding down my thighs.

I have no idea what to say. I'm not usually fucking men on the fly. I go in with both parties knowing exactly what it is, which is release. This, though, this is different, if only because he's someone I definitely shouldn't be fucking but also because I really want to fuck his friends, too. That's a conversation we are never going to have, though. It certainly isn't something I can ever see happening.

I step closer to the spray, letting the water fall over my face so I can avoid his gaze. I can feel his eyes on me, tracking my every move. I have no idea what he's expecting from me—a thank you? A slap on the ass and an atta boy? Whatever it is, I'm going to pretend to be normal, like this is nothing, even though it might be everything. It's the only recourse I can see to get out of this with an ounce of dignity.

I can't believe I just let Shane King fuck me. And I loved every goddamn minute of it.

ALEX

I can hear Shane's pounding footsteps all the way in the kitchen. He's in a mood this morning, and I'm pretty sure it has everything to do with the woman I saw sneaking out the front door earlier. Sam thought she snuck out with us none the wiser, but I watched from my bedroom window until she crawled into the car, skirting the guard shack Shane installed.

"Alex," Shane mutters, making a beeline for the coffee.

"Good morning! How did everything go last night?" I ask, hiding my grin by shoving another spoonful of cereal into my mouth.

"Fine."

"Oh? Nothing exciting happened? Perhaps something stimulating? No big climax we need to talk about?"

"Fuck you," he spits, glowering.

"Come on, Shane, give me all the dirty details. I'm dying to know if she—"

"Do not finish that sentence." He slams the cupboard closed.

Ren walks in, looking like he barely slept himself. Great, they're both grumpy. Makes it more fun to tease them when they are all tied up over a woman.

"What about you, Ren? Have a good night?" I wink at Shane, who is still shooting daggers at me.

"It was fine," he says, getting his own coffee.

"Probably not as fine as Shane's."

"I'm sure not. He was practically balls deep in her when I saw them last." Ren smirks, making me choke on my spoon.

"Oh, for fuck's sake. The last time I saw you, you were carting that girl off to safety, and we were in the middle of a gunfight," Shane hisses.

"Actually, I saw you hauling Sam over your shoulder and smacking her ass on the way back to your car. I figured I should find my own ride home after that."

Ren is always stating things so matter-of-factly I never know if he's joking or not. Either way, Shane's face turns red, which is always a sure sign he got laid.

"You're blushing, Shane." I smirk at him, and he flips me off.

"You going to call her?" Ren asks.

"What? No. She bolted at dawn, I'm sure. Didn't even wake me up."

"It was more around seven," I murmur, finishing up my breakfast.

Shane's gaze swings to me. "You saw her? Why didn't you stop her?"

"Uh, because she was climbing into a car? Did you want me to yell out the window?" I go to the sink and rinse out my bowl.

Shane mumbles curses under his breath, striding out, probably to go sulk more. You'd think getting laid would relax him, but he is wound tighter than a nun's asshole.

"Alex, you need to call Sam," Ren states before sipping his coffee.

"Why? You think I'm going to play matchmaker with those two? Fuck that. Maybe I'll have a shot with her if Shane is acting all butt hurt."

"I don't care if you fuck her, but I'm assuming Shane didn't take the time to find out if she got any intel from the man she killed. We need to know what he said. Helms will be asking as well. He wasn't pleased when I told him we didn't have anyone to question."

"Fine, but Shane can suck my dick if he thinks I'm going to be his little informant on her. He's going to have to deal with shit on his own," I snap.

"I'm sure he'll throw his little temper tantrum and go back to pretending he hates her. Shane can't keep his head around Samantha Byrns," Ren quips.

"Oh, and you can?" Shane says, stepping back into the room.

"I don't know what you're talking about."

Shane shakes his head. "Sure you don't. Listen, Alex, I need you to call her and figure out what she got from the guy she stabbed. Ren, figure out where the hell she learned to fight. Jax said the guy had a shattered kneecap, three broken fingers, a broken nose, and a knife wound clean through the jugular, from the side. Either she's got more skills than we thought or someone helped her."

"Already on it," I tell them, pulling up my messages with her.

My phone pings, and I grin, making plans. When I glance up, both Ren and Shane are glaring at me.

"What?" I ask innocently.

"Alex, I'm not going to tell you to watch yourself around her . . ."

"Because you already got there first?"

"Goddammit, Alex! For once, can you be fucking serious?" Shane bursts out.

"Whoa, boss, I'm just havin' fun. If you want me to back off, say so." I backtrack, hands raised in defense. I'll stand down if Shane is truly interested in Sam, even if it's the last thing I want to do.

"Not to get caught up in your drama, but it seems as if Shane is averse to sharing," Ren says.

"Sharing would be fine if I was going to fuck her again, which I'm not. Last night was to get her out of my system. Go right ahead and run your game. But that woman has secrets wrapped in more secrets. Don't get caught in her web, Alex. She's hiding something. We can't trust her. Remember that if you decide to try to get your dick wet."

"We've had this conversation, Shane. I don't know why you think having it again will change how I feel about her or what I plan to do. But I think you've got blinders on if you think Sam is out of your system," I remind him. Leave it to Shane to fuck everything up with someone I actually like.

He waves away my accusations. "Whatever. Don't let her get away with not telling you anything." With those parting words of wisdom, Shane stalks away again.

"Interesting," Ren murmurs, sipping his coffee before walking out as well, leaving me to deal with Sam.

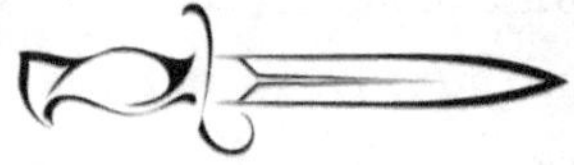

The hospital is an imposing building, taking up several blocks. Gazing around, I spot them: a couple of men here and there, loitering. I recognize a few as the Byrns' hires, protecting their boss, who is apparently still deep in a coma. I wait across the street at a small park, keeping my eye out for Sam.

When she appears, I almost don't recognize her. Her hair is blowing in the crisp wind coming off the river, but she doesn't bother to pull it back. She's usually in all black, leggings and hoodie. Today, she looks like she came from a job interview. I'm almost certain she's wearing a blouse under her leather jacket.

"What did you need to talk about, Alex?" Sam calls, avoiding my eyes when she reaches me.

"You okay, Bug?"

"I'm fine. What's so important we need to do this face-to-face?" She still isn't looking at me. I don't know if she's avoiding my gaze or trying to find who's watching us, but either way, I don't like it.

"Let's go. A lot of prying eyes out here," I say, gesturing back to my car.

"I can't. I-I have to get going, so let's get this over," she stutters, lifting her eyes to mine. There's a bruise on her forehead, almost hidden by her hair.

"What the fuck happened to your face?" I growl.

Shock fills her face before she blurts, "Nothing."

"Bullshit. Did that happen last night? I thought your shoulder was the only thing hurt?"

"Yeah, last night. It's nothing." She's back to avoiding my eyes, as if I'll drop it if she ignores me long enough. An uneasy feeling settles in my stomach.

"Did someone hurt you?" With the way she's acting, someone's fucked with her head.

"What? God, no. It was an accident. I tripped. Drop it, Alex."

Her eyes fill with the fire I'm used to. I know she's lying, but I can't make her tell me, so I'll wait it out, see if she'll trust me with the truth, eventually. Victor has to be behind her injuries. If that fucker puts his hands on her, he's a dead man. I don't care if it breaks the truce between our families and starts a war. I'll burn his entire fucking world down to get to him.

"Fine, but if you 'trip' again," I say sarcastically, "let me know."

"I really gotta go, so text me whatever you wanted to talk about."

I grab her arm to stop her, but she winces, and I yank my hand back. This woman is a walking ball of hurt, and she won't even tell me what the hell happened.

"Sam, we need to know what the guy you killed last night said. Did he tell you anything?"

"That's what you wanted to talk about?" she blurts, disappointment in her eyes before she blinks it away. "Of course. Sorry."

"Why did you think I wanted to meet? We can't text about this type of shit." I have a feeling she thought I was here for Shane, which, I guess, technically, I am. This whole situation is becoming more complicated now that they've hooked up. I stuff the jealousy churning in my gut down deep, ignoring the queasiness in my stomach.

"Doesn't matter. I need to go. I'll text you later." Sam tries to take off again, still looking around.

It hits me she doesn't want Victor's men to see us together. It makes sense if he's accusing her of working with us. I still need the information, so I jog after her.

"Alex! What are you doing? You can't just follow me around."

"Well, you're not telling me what I need to know. You're obviously in trouble, and you're lying to me, Bug. Seems like the only way to get answers is to follow you around until you're ready to give them. So, where we headed?" I ask, falling into step with her.

"I am going to see someone. *You* are going home."

"That why you're all dressed up? Who's the guy?" More jealousy whips through me, clipping my words.

Sam stops, jabbing her finger at my chest. "Do not interfere with my shit, Alex King. I am in no mood to deal with your guys' bullshit."

She huffs and keeps marching along. God, she's sexy when she's all fired up. I grin, catching up to her quickly.

"That was hot. We're going to have so much fun today if you keep that up, Bug."

She mutters under her breath, but I'm pretty sure she's cursing me out. We pass the hospital, and I wave cheerfully at one of the guys eyeing us.

"Stop that," she demands.

"But it's so fun to fuck with them. So, who are we going to see again?"

"Just go home, Alex. I'm sure Shane has better things for you to do than follow me around."

"Not really. He said to take care of you, so that's what I'm doing."

Sam rolls her eyes. "Bullshit. He told you to find out what I know. Then stomped around and puffed out his chest."

Laughing, I sling my arm around her shoulder, which she immediately shoves off. She's in as bad a mood as Shane and Ren.

"Maybe he needs a little more sexual healing." I wink at her while her cheeks turn red. "Aw, you're blushing!"

"We are not talking about this."

"Why not? Is it weird talking about fucking Shane when you want to fuck me, too?" I joke, grinning, but she stays silent. Holy shit. My grin falls from my face, and I clear my throat, buying time to figure out how to open that door a little wider. Shane said he was cool with sharing . . . if I can get her on board, this whole thing will get real fun real fast.

"I don't know what you're talking about," she says, clearly lying, picking up her speed.

It's cute she thinks she can run away from this conversation. I'll let her think she can, because chasing her is the kind of thrill I live for. I wait until we come to the end of the street before I hook her elbow and herd her toward the parking garage, her squawking the whole way.

"Settle down, Bug. I'd rather not walk the whole way to god knows where when my car is right here."

As we approach my vehicle, Sam scoffs. I'm not surprised. It's flashy as hell, but I didn't buy it. Shane decided Ren and I needed rides, and they showed up in the drive one day. I'm not complaining.

"A fucking Maserati? Seriously? You guys are absurd. Who drives this shit?"

I crowd behind her, trapping her between my body and the door. Bringing my hands up to rest on the frame, I pen her in, my chest close to her back. I expect a snarky remark, a sassy comeback, but she waits, body quivering.

"Now we're going to finish that conversation, Bug," I drawl into her ear, wisps of her auburn hair tickling my cheek.

"I don't know what you're talking about," she whispers, but the breathlessness in her voice makes me chuckle.

"Oh? Well, let me refresh your memory. You said you wanted to fuck me." I trail my nose along the shell of her ear, then capture her lobe and nibble. She tilts her head, giving me more access, without even realizing.

"I didn't say that," she breathes out, her eyes falling closed. I press a light kiss behind her ear and pull back.

"My bad." I grin as she sways back, but I lean more, keeping that small distance between us. If she wants this, she's going to have to enthusiastically agree. I want her ready and willing. I drop my hands and shove them in my pockets.

She sucks in a breath. "Wait."

"Yes, Bug? Something you wanted to add?" I rock back on my heels, waiting for her to admit she wants this as much as I do.

"I . . . I shouldn't." Her chin dips, hair falling forward and blocking any hope of seeing her face.

"Shouldn't what?" This was not how I anticipated this going.

"We shouldn't . . . I can't . . ."

"Ah, Sam, are you worried about Shane? Worried about what we'll think of you? Because you should know that won't be a problem." The last thing she needs is to be embarrassed about who she wants to fuck.

"What's that supposed to mean?" She's still hiding, but if this whole thing is easier behind a shield, so be it. I want to know what she's thinking, but I'm not going to force her because it'll make me feel better. She'll pull away again, hide behind her walls. I step in again, boxing her in enough to feel me there.

"We don't mind sharing, Sam. So, whatever you want, say the word. You wanna fuck one of us? All of us? I mean, I can't speak for Ren, but I don't give two shits if you want us all, as long as I get to taste you, too."

Caressing her arm from shoulder to fingertip, I feel her tremble. Her whole body is wound tight. She nods her head, almost imperceptibly.

"I'm going to need words, Sam. Tell me what you want."

"You," she whimpers, "I want you."

I move my hand, dusting it along the hem of her shirt, ducking my fingers underneath to her flushed skin. She shudders, pressing into me while my hand continues its path along her stomach. Every so often, her breath hitches, and I file it away, learning all the ways her body responds to me. I pop the button of her pants and explore further, skimming the sensitive places, each pass bringing me closer to where I want to be.

I duck my head into her neck, growling when I reach her thong and follow the seam down one side and up the other. I can feel the heat from her pussy begging me to put us both out of our misery.

"Need something, Bug? You want me to make you come?"

She mewls in response, her hips jerking forward, trying to chase my fingers. I want to draw this out as long as possible, but the longer I wait, the more likely I am to fuck her right here in the open.

I push the fabric aside and swipe along her slit, finding her dripping, and I groan, my chest pushing her into metal. I grip her hip with my other hand, keeping her still as I explore, swirling to her clit and back to her core. I push a finger in while she whimpers, whispering my name over and over. I go slow, bringing her close to the edge, then backing off, drawing out every shiver and noise.

"I can't wait to hear those sounds when I'm deep inside you. Your pussy squeezing my cock instead of my fingers."

I bite her neck, soothing away the pain with my tongue while my fingers keep up their assault.

"Alex," she moans, "please."

"Please, what? You want me to make you come, Sam?" I speed up my pace, holding her tighter as her body shudders, her pussy quivering for me.

"Please . . ." she sobs, hips matching my rhythm.

My thumb finds her clit, and she explodes, her cries echoing out across the empty space. I wrap my free arm around her waist, holding her up as she crashes through her orgasm while my fingers linger, curling inside her, prolonging her pleasure. Watching her come is almost my undoing, and I clench my jaw, holding her tight. As her bones become jelly, I sweep her hair aside, planting kisses along her neck, murmuring nonsense into her skin.

When she recovers, I pull my hand from her, licking her arousal from my fingers and groaning again. Of course she tastes amazing. All it makes me want to do is bury my face between her thighs and live there for days. Her astonished gaze watches me over her shoulder, so I smirk, twisting her body around and capture her mouth with my own, letting her taste herself on me.

I pull back, still cupping her face. "So, about your meeting?" I quirk an eyebrow.

"Goddammit, fine. There is no meeting," she says, dropping her head to my chest.

I laugh, gathering her in my arms, grateful I won't have to let her go any time soon.

THIRTY

SAMANTHA

Alex drops me at the Depot. He wanted to take me back to King territory, but I was adamant that wouldn't be happening. I can't imagine Shane would appreciate Alex bringing me home for lunch. Plus, there's the whole sharing thing. Alex says Shane won't care, but I snuck out early this morning from his bed, then hours later, let Alex make me come in a goddamn parking garage. I'm not against it, but I don't know if I trust Shane to be on board. I'm still not sure how I feel about sleeping with Shane to begin with—and to throw Alex in the mix? It's too much to think about right now.

A shudder runs through me, remembering Alex's hands on me, inside of me, which leads me straight into flashes of my night with Shane. Heat rushes to my core, and I shake my head, making my way to the room set aside for me. I'm pretty sure Shane and I are a one-night-stand type of thing.

Alex hinted at future "adventures" on the drive over.

Ren . . . figuring out that man would take years, but I can't see him ever wanting me.

I don't know why I'm muddling my way through this, since I should be running as far away from them as I can. It isn't like we have a future. I need to get my head into reality. We have bigger fish to fry, whether we're fucking. Plus, they've all been dicks to me at some point or another, so I can't allow myself to be blindsided because they can make my body flood with desire.

I'm about to unlock my door when a shuffling comes from the other side. I freeze and listen. Someone is in my room. No one has the code to this room, not even Mason. It's supposed to be impenetrable. The heating system switches off, and I can make out someone breathing behind the wood. I back away silently, glancing down the hall.

Someone thinks they can ambush me. It's almost comical, but with everything happening, I'm not laughing. Goddammit, just when I find one safe place, it's compromised. The Depot is no longer safe. The estate is getting more and more treacherous. Soon, I'll only have one place to go to: the safehouse.

We have dozens of safehouses scattered around the city, but only one Mason and I keep secret. We've never used it. The house is buried under shell companies, is listed as a rental, and always has tenants. Everything is handled through anonymous businesses. It's also in King territory, snuggled in with the other houses, tucked away in the suburbs. I'd bet my life the Kings have no idea.

I don't want to run, but it's looking like things are escalating to a point where I can't handle it myself if I don't have a safe place to go to rest. I make it to the back stairwell, jumping when my phone buzzes. I silence it without checking. I creep down the stairs, picking up echoing voices across the building's warehouse section. A dozen or so men are talking and laughing, oblivious as I slip out a side door, only a soft click marking my escape.

Walking away swiftly, I don't dare check if anyone is following me, at least not yet. Nothing gives away a person more than their neck craning around. I breathe deep, thanking my various trainers over the years. I've made a habit of being silent, living in the shadows. I had to reteach myself how to walk like a normal person when I got home from the mountain training cabin when I was fifteen.

Once I'm far enough away, I detour into a coffee shop, busy with the lunch rush. I sweep to a table near the back, plopping down with eyes fixed on the front windows. I ignore the others' glares, who are waiting for an empty table to open up. Sorry, my needs trump yours.

I grab my phone, pulling up my contacts, but stall out. My thumb hovers over Mason's name, grief filling me, threatening to spill out. Glancing up, I struggle to lock down my emotions. I can't afford to fall apart. I could call Colin, but he's been more and more distant as the days drag on, holing up with Victor.

Alex's face flashes in my mind, followed closely by Shane's, then Ren's, but I dismiss them. I almost laugh out loud, thinking of their reactions if I called to tell them someone was in my room, and I didn't have a plan. Alex would laugh while loading a magazine. Shane would cuss me out. Maybe tell me to deal with them myself. That thought sobers me, reminding me that I can't rely on them.

They're not my friends, allies, anything, but if I were to call one of them in this situation, I would opt for Ren. He seems to be able to keep his shit together. He wouldn't help, but at least I would keep some dignity. I jolt when my phone buzzes again, Helms's name popping up. I hesitate but answer.

"Byrns."

"Helms. What can I do for you?" I try to sound unaffected, but I'm struggling.

"You can pick up the first time I call. I don't have all day to track your ass down for answers." Ryker's deep voice growls with annoyance.

"Oh, I'm so sorry I wasn't available the minute you needed me. Someone else wanted to talk to me enough to try to ambush me, so I decided evading them was more important than a chat with you at the moment. Please accept my deepest apologies." I let the sarcasm seep into my tone.

Fucking men.

"Sure you are," he says, his tone equally sarcastic. "Wait, someone ambushed you?"

I curse myself for not thinking my shit through. The fewer people who know about what's going on with me personally, the safer I am. I may trust Ryker, but I also don't know what he'll inadvertently pass on to the Kings.

"I'm sure it's nothing. Forget I said anything. What did you need?" I ask in a futile attempt to steer the conversation back.

"Who was it?" He moved right past, asking questions to demanding answers. Honestly, he sounds like Shane, which makes my chest twinge.

"Don't know. Like I said, I evaded them."

"Tell me what happened," he demands.

I duck my head, and lower my voice, relating what happened at the Depot, which isn't a lot. As much as I don't want to admit it, telling someone eases the tension in my shoulders. I'm not going to make this a habit, but for once, I can ease my anxiety I carry around like a weight on my shoulders. If it makes it back to the Kings, so be it. I'll deal with the fallout later. Seems like I'm pushing out the consequences a lot these days when it comes to the Kings. Future me is not going to be a happy camper.

"What happened last night?" he demands. No speculation, no questions, comments, or concerns. He moves on to the next thing. Then his question registers, and for a split-second, I assume he's talking about Shane and I hooking up. My brain clicks over before I respond and sound like a complete idiot. Thank god, I remember there was a whole night before I ended up fucking Shane in his shower . . . and twice more in his bed. I never got around to telling Shane what I learned last night—or Alex earlier when he met me outside the hospital.

"We've got problems. Big ones."

"Why didn't you tell the Kings'?" he asks.

"Uh, you know, just didn't get around to it," I hedge. No way am I going to admit I was distracted by Shane's cock.

"You trust them?"

"I mean, with this? Or in general?" I'm buying time to figure out my answer. I'm supposed to say no, but the more I cross paths with them, the less I understand my brother's rules to stay away. The less I understand Colin's assessment of them. I feel like I'm missing something, like something is being hidden from me—from my own family, not the Kings.

"Better figure out how much you trust them because, if you're right about it being traffickers, we're going to need all the allies we can gather." He drops that bomb and hangs up.

Staring at Alex's message thread, I contemplate texting him to get ahead of whatever bullshit's coming from Shane. I scan the headlines instead, trying to read between the lines, but they're all speculation about where I've disappeared to, whether I'm holed up with Alex King, or if I'm merely lying low because Mason is in the hospital. As if they have nothing else to write about other than the stupid dresses I wear.

I curse under my breath, earning dirty looks from all the socialites gossiping over their lattes. I stick my tongue out at them, slipping my phone in my pocket, and casually stroll to the back. An employee yelps when I come down the hall. Putting my finger to my lips, I smile while I slip out the back door. I scan the alley and head home, praying the surprises are over for now.

A couple hour's sleep at the estate is all I fit in before footsteps pounding toward my door jolt me awake, darkness filtering in through my window. I snatch my gun off the nightstand instinctively, flipping off the safety before my feet hit the floor. I tug my shoes on and snatch the backpack from under my bed, trying to figure out what the hell is going on. So many people are yelling I can't distinguish one from another or what they're saying. My body is instantly on alert, muscles tensing for action.

I move to the window, praying they'll pass by my door, but seconds later, the wood shudders as if someone is hammering it with a battering ram. The handle rattles, and they pound again, screaming at me to open up. Victor is bellowing on the other side, trying to force his way into my room. Colin's telling Victor to calm down. I'm not fucking stupid—there's no way I'm subjecting myself to that. I'm pretty sure I'll kill him if I open the door. I held back before, but like I told Colin, I'm not stopping myself next time. That man will never lay a hand on me again.

I hesitate for a second before I throw open the window, wriggling out on the thin ledge built into the bricks. A guard is rushing around the house, so up I go. I've made this climb so many times, the lack of moonlight doesn't bother me; if anything, it helps me make my escape. After pulling myself onto the flat roof, I hurry across, trying to find the door cleverly sunken behind an AC unit. I really hope Colin didn't tell Victor about the tunnels because, judging by the shouts in the yard, they've surrounded the house.

Catching the edge with my fingertips, I lift the metal before I shimmy down the ladder. Shutting the door behind me, I pull out my phone to light the way. It takes a lot longer to figure out where I am, since I rarely use this entrance, but I'm able to navigate to the same tunnel I took to get out of the Kings' house. I have a sense of déjà vu as I listen at the trap door I crack open. Like before, the way is clear, and I throw my phone in my backpack, gripping my gun before making my way into the woods.

I'm used to walking, but after two miles, weaving in and out of yards, avoiding cars and people alike, I'm getting tired. I find a quiet playground and pull myself on the bridge, which is shrouded in shadows, hoping for a bit of a reprieve, so I can figure out what to do next.

Colin called at least a dozen times, texting when I didn't answer. Apparently, Victor heard about my little outing with the Kings and didn't take too kindly to my foray. Colin scolds me for being irresponsible when I don't respond. Fuck them both.

I roll my eyes when my phone lights up, expecting to see Colin's name, only to be met with Shane's flashing with an incoming call. Shock rolls through me, and I answer.

"What the fuck, Byrns!" Shane shouts down the line before I say anything.

"What can I do for you, King?"

"Why the hell didn't you tell me you had a full-on fucking conversation with your victim?!" Ooh, he's pissed. Exactly what I need, another man thinking I owe them something. First Helms, then Victor and Colin, and now, Shane King.

"I was a little preoccupied at the time." By him . . .

"No fucking excuse! You think you're so fucking important that we have to bring you along? Cause you might want to rethink that," he thunders.

"Well, I think I'm the one who got information when you didn't get anything, so yeah, I guess I was important enough to bring along, wasn't I?" I have a split-second of satisfaction when he bursts my bubble, snorting out a derisive laugh.

"Try again, Princess. You're not nearly as important as you think you are. You're replaceable and forgettable."

"Too bad you weren't saying that last night, huh?"

I can't help but lash out as his words punch through my defenses. I thought we had become . . . not friends but something other than at each other's throats. I shouldn't be surprised he's lashing out again, but I am.

"You were a distraction. A warm, willing body. Keeping you never even crossed my mind. I can't imagine it has for anyone else, either. But thanks for the fuck."

The silence is the only indication he's hung up. I thought I was prepared for the fallout of sleeping with Shane King, but I didn't think it would hurt so much when he turned on me again. It isn't even the words, it's the way he said them—vicious, cold, unfeeling. I can't understand why he hates me so much, or maybe now, he hates that he fucked me. He gave in to his desires, and that's unacceptable to him. It isn't like I thought we'd ride off into the sunset, living happily ever after, but still.

Seeing no other options, I resign myself to the safehouse. I shiver as I jump down, telling myself it's from the wind and not from the numbness seeping into my body.

THIRTY-ONE

REN

"It's been a fucking week, Shane! Something isn't right. What the fuck did you say to her?" Alex bellows. Making my way closer to Shane's office door, I'm not able to catch his reply, but it's most likely more of the same. They've been having this argument since Sam fell off the grid.

Alex keeps texting her, but they go unread. I could let slip that Shane took a little midnight run to the Byrns' estate to see if he could find her, but I'm not going to put myself in the middle of their spat. Shane will have to eventually tell us what happened. The way he won't meet Alex's eyes makes me think he's ashamed of whatever he did. I'll keep it to myself that I did my own journey to the other side of the river. The similarities between our two houses is remarkable, but they don't need to know what I was doing or what I accomplished. It wouldn't make a difference in the outcome, anyway.

The study door bursts open, and Alex storms out, slamming the door behind him. He stops short when he sees me, still seething.

"You'd better have a fucking answer, Ren, or I swear to fucking god..."

The door swings open before I can respond, and Shane starts cussing Alex out. How one woman can make them lose their minds is beyond me. Maybe her pussy is magical or something. Alex won't confirm whether he's slept with Sam, but it's pretty obvious by the way he's acting something happened between them. I let them tear into each other a little more before I turn my tablet around, pressing play. It takes a bit, but they fall silent, zoning in on the video. I've watched it a dozen times, but I still can't identify the players in this game.

"What am I looking at here, Ren?" Shane asks, eyes fixed on the screen as it loops to the beginning.

"It's a meeting. Or at least the end of a meeting. I don't recognize the men leaving, but they're driving the same cars we've spotted in the Barrens. This man"—I point to another one exiting after them—"I have no clue who that is." There's a brief exchange, and the man walks off, rounding a corner as the group gets into their cars and leaves.

"That's not much to go on . . ." Shane murmurs, squinting at the screen. "Wait, what is that?"

"That is a trunk full of drugs. Most likely Oracle."

"So, they've got a contact in the city," Alex sighs.

"Looks like it. Someone high up somewhere, I think. I'm still trying to find witnesses, but this was in the Byrns' territory, so it's slow going, as you can imagine."

"I'll give Colin a call." Shane turns toward his study, but I stop him.

"I wouldn't."

"Why not? Maybe he knows where Sam is, too," Alex says, of course, with his one-track mind focused on a woman.

"Regardless if he knows where she is, which I doubt he does, the fewer people we bring in to this, the better. We assume we can trust Colin, but I'm not convinced."

He failed to protect Sam, which is why I don't trust him. Alex will assume I feel the same way he does, and Shane will think I'm taking sides.

Neither of them will understand what Sam's disappearance actually shows, which is a weakness within the Byrns' empire. As much as Victor is a shit leader, his misstep is rooted in not seeing how important and valuable the Byrns princess is to their operations. If they pull their heads out of their asses long enough, they'll find who she really is beneath the masks.

Shane sighs. "Fine, but we need eyes in there now. Ren, call Helms and see if he has anyone."

I raise my eyebrows, while Alex scowls at him, but he ignores us striding back into his office.

"So, you didn't find where Sam went?"

"No, Alex, I didn't. The last I have is the video from the playground. I'm sure she'll pop up somewhere."

I follow Shane, closing the door behind me. Alex is too volatile at the moment, and I don't have the patience to deal with his tantrums. Shane glances up from his desk, giving me a questioning look.

"Why is it I'm calling Helms, and you're not?" I lean against the door.

"He's not happy with me right now."

"Would that have anything to do with our little pet?"

Shane scoffs. "I may have informed him I talked to her after he spilled their conversation. He might blame me for her running. Do you really not know where she is, Ren?"

"I wouldn't keep something like that to myself. It does no good at this point."

"Do you think she's . . ." He gazes out the window.

"No. I don't think she's dead." He flinches at my words. "Whatever you said to her, I don't believe she's hiding because of you."

"I told her she was . . ." he murmurs.

I sigh, nodding, though he's lost in thought. I can't absolve him of whatever guilt he's holding on to. He's intent on punishing himself, even if he isn't at fault. Sam bewitched them somehow. I can't pretend I'm immune to her, though. The night at the club only reinforced I need to keep my distance. Sam is someone who will blindside me, trapping me before I realize what's happening. Someone has to keep a level head in this place.

I go to my own office, which is twice the size of Shane's, filled with screens and gadgets on one side, the other lined with books. No one else is allowed in here. I like having one space no one else will fill with nonsense. I call Helms while typing out a quick message to Nemesis. It goes exactly how I thought it would. He grumbles about Shane's cock getting in the way of dealing with our other issues, commands me to figure out where Sam is. Informing him I don't work for him does little to dissuade him, though.

"We need eyes on the east side of the river," I say, trying to cut off his tirade.

"I had eyes. Unfortunately, you lost her," he growls.

"I thought the first time you met Sam was when her brother was shot . . ."

"It was the first time I met her in person."

Interesting.

"Hmm. Well, is there anyone else, until we can find your informant?"

"She wasn't an informant." His annoyance rings through. "Everyone I send in turns up dead. I'm done sending my men into a death trap. Figure this shit out, Ren, or we're fucked," he demands before hanging up.

Very interesting.

Phone in hand, I fiddle with it, contemplating. Alex has been texting and calling Sam. Though he'll never admit it, Shane has tried, too. I imagine Helms made some calls as well. No one can seem to get a hold of our elusive little pet. She's capable of disappearing, fading into the shadows, then popping up when we least expect it. Sam has much more extensive training than any of us realized. Shane's assessment of her before is laughable. She's the furthest thing from an airhead. I haven't shared with Shane or Alex my theories, but I believe she's hiding in plain sight. Tucked away somewhere, traveling through the dark, gathering whatever information she can.

Making up my mind, I slip my phone back in my pocket and set the code on my door. I don't bother to change, but I grab an extra gun and slip out the side door silently. Alex tried to find her, combing club row and the coffee shops on the east side, and Shane has staked out the Byrns estate. They searched the places they've encountered her, but they forgot where Sam is the most comfortable. I remember, though. I climb into my car and take off for the Barrens.

I'm halfway across the city before I'm cursing myself. I forgot the brownies in the kitchen, although they probably won't accept them from me. Sam built up some type of rapport with them, allowing her into their community. A few baked goods aren't going to help me achieve the same results. I try not to think too hard about why I'm going through all this trouble for one woman, one I don't particularly like.

After I park in a forgotten alley, I sit, contemplating whether to go straight to the Egg. The chances of Sam being there are slim, but it's the only place I can come up with other than Mack's place. The Barrens may make up a thin strip in the grand scheme of our city, but it spans the whole river from the southern edge, butting all the way up to the Reapers' territory in the north. I can't search it all alone, especially at night. I shove open the door, resigning myself to the Egg, hoping I'm lucky.

The walk is silent, no buzzing lights, devoid of people. A shoe scuffles on concrete, but when I backtrack and wait, no one is there. I'm almost to the Egg when I realize I'm hoping someone is following me, hoping Sam is out there wondering what the hell I'm doing. I hate the feeling I get whenever I try to figure out why I care. My emotions don't make sense, they're not logical. She's just a woman, an interesting puzzle to put together, nothing more. At least that's all she should be, but she's sucked me in to her orbit. Trying to keep my distance and keep emotions and feelings out of it is getting harder and harder the more we're forced to interact with her.

I told Shane I didn't trust her, but I didn't share all my concerns. Admitting to myself I'm afraid of trusting her makes me feel exposed, vulnerable. Knowing she's hiding secrets, keeping things from us, makes her a liability, a threat, but the irrational part of my brain doesn't care. I need to focus on figuring out what she's hiding instead of deciphering who she is as a person because I can't care. I don't know if I have it in me to try.

The Egg is muted, though it's Friday night. It should be teeming with people, trading goods and making deals, but only a handful of people are milling about. The men at the gates are armed, as usual, but with more of everything: more men, more guns, more defenses. They've locked shit up, striving to keep out whoever is terrorizing our city. The Barrens don't fuck around with security. The normal people don't realize how protective these people are of their own. In the suburbs, I could blow a fucking house up, and the curtains would flutter, but that's all. Here, they'd form a mob, and the arsonist would be floating in the river by the end of the night.

I don't spot Sam, which isn't surprising. I could sit and wait, see if she shows up. But, knowing her, she'll find me first and hide until I leave. Nothing I do will change anything if she doesn't want to be found. I won't pretend my skills exceed hers. Alex may think she needs safe keeping, as if our protection will make any difference, but discounting her abilities only does her a disservice. My lip pulls up a bit, remembering how he tried to save her from the two men tailing her. Alex's methods may have changed, but he's still trying to save her. The only thing she needs saving from is from her own mind.

Frustration runs through me as I back away into the darkened alley, away from the Egg. I knew this was a long shot, but knowing I can't find her grates on me. I've poured over the cameras, enlisted Nemesis's help, driven to all the places I can imagine she could be, but nothing.

She's disappeared, like a ghost. That thought pulls me up short, reminding me of Victor's words. *You can't find ghosts who don't want to be found. The ghosts will take that bitch, too.*

I may have told Alex she will come around when she wants to, when she gets whatever she's after, but knowing the dangers infiltrating our city are adept at being unseen worries me. The implications Victor is working for them grows more every day, and with the threats he's leveled at Sam, there's a likely chance he's sent them after her.

Ghosts. Capable of disappearing into the night without a whisper at their passing, taking Sam with them. I shake my head, moving again. She wouldn't be easy to grab, less likely to keep. At least now I have a direction, a theory to pursue: to find Sam. It doesn't hit me until I'm driving home that I'm no longer doing this for Shane or Alex. I'm doing it for me, too.

Fuck.

THIRTY-TWO

SAMANTHA

My phone vibrates as I hop over the back fence, trying to avoid crunching the strewn leaves. I silence it without looking and listen to the deadened air. After almost two weeks, I still don't feel safe.

The house is modest, blending in with the others on the street. I expected the place to be rundown, but it's well-kept and appears lived in. I have no idea who's taking care of the outside; the inside had a layer of dust on everything. It took me most of the first couple of days to clean everything to keep from sneezing with every step.

When I'm sure I'm still alone, I creep to the back door and slide inside the kitchen. The lights are on timers, thick curtains covering every window. At least no one will be peeking in. Down the hallway, I scan each bedroom. I don't know if they're considered bedrooms, since they don't have closets, but there are mattresses in them, with nowhere for someone to hide. I drop my bag in the living room, heading for the bathroom.

It's harder than I thought to travel to the Barrens now that I'm trying to avoid cameras as much as possible. My three sets of clothes, all black, give me a sense that, if someone spots me, I'll be difficult to identify.

My phone goes off again, and I sigh. I should turn it off, but I'm hoping the hospital will miraculously call and tell me Mason is awake and that he can deal with all the bullshit at our doorstep. They never do. Alex, Helms, Colin, and even Shane calls, but I ignore them. I can't afford any more drama than I currently have in my life.

None of them are calling now, though. Ren's name flashes across the screen, and I watch until my phone goes dark. Immediately, it rings again, his name coming up. Over and over, he calls. I didn't know I had his number. Pure curiosity has me hovering over the accept button, but I can't make myself swipe. It has to be Alex using Ren's phone. There's absolutely no reason Ren would call me. I'm pretty sure he doesn't know I exist half of the time, whether I'm standing in front of him or not.

Except at the club . . .

I push the thought away as my phone stops. I wait, thinking he'll call again, but nothing happens. I exhale sharply, relief warring with disappointment. Then the silence is broken with the purr of engines.

They don't sound like any of the usual cars on this street, and a sense of foreboding runs through my body when they stop, right outside the safehouse.

My backpack is across the living room. I have at least a dozen escape routes in place for a getaway, so I'm not as worried as I should be. I dash for my bag but switch directions mid-step when I hear the *pop pop pop* of bullets.

The picture window shatters, shards tinkling to the ground behind the thick curtains. I bolt for the stairs to the finished attic, cursing myself for thinking I could relax even a little. If they shoot up the house, so be it, but I have to get out *now*. I make it to the bottom of the stairs, and a hail of bullets fly around me. A burning pain races through my side, but I don't stop, stumbling upward before ultimately gaining my feet at the top.

The area is technically finished, but nothing fills the room, just an empty space echoing the sounds of gunfire and shouts. It sounds like they've surrounded the house. I press a hand to my side and wince. I pull my hand away, eyeing the red coating my palm.

"Shit."

My side feels hot, like something is burning through my skin. I have my gun, but there aren't enough rounds to take them all out. My best hope is to bottleneck them on the stairs, and hope for the best. All my escape plans, a complete waste.

For some reason, a barrage of men trying to take me out never crossed my mind. I figured anyone would ambush me coming home, or it'd be one guy sneaking in. These guys are evidently not worried about the neighbors. Someone is sure to call the cops, which makes figuring out their identity harder.

Victor, the Kings, Helms—none of them would do something this drastic, and whoever is trying to set up shop in our city is working in the shadows, using subtle methods rather than this blaze of announcing their presence. The only likely person is Victor, but I can't imagine he'd go to these lengths to get rid of me.

Who wants me dead this badly? Victor's face flashes through my mind again. I want to believe the men loyal to my brother would intervene if he tried. Colin would stop him if he knew. I don't think I have any other enemies, but I've clearly pissed someone off. My mind flashes back to the man in the alley, the one I stabbed in the neck. He said I was dead, like Mason. I thought he was spouting empty threats, but maybe I should have taken him more seriously.

Could this be their big move? Why they want to take me out is beyond me. I'm a nobody in the grand scheme of things. Ambushing Mason makes sense. Helms will be harder to hit, with his protocols in place for lock down. No one is getting in or out of his area without his permission.

Helms has it easy with the Reapers' territory only being a couple dozen blocks of the city. The next logical hit would be Shane or the Kings as a whole. Colin's warnings they're behind everything comes back, but regardless of whether there's an attempt on them doesn't mean they're working with these guys. As shitty as they've been to me, I can't help but trust we're all fighting to take back one thing: our city. I could be blinded by them, not willing to see what's in front of me, but nothing points to them.

Still no reason someone would try to take me out. I'm just Sam. To the outside world, I'm an airhead, a mafia boss's sister, a socialite who cares more about dresses and parties than getting my hands dirty. I have no official title, no claim to anything other than my last name.

So, why are they trying to kill me? I've got some info, tried to figure things out, killed a few guys, but no more or less than what other people have done. They couldn't have figured out what I do at night. No one would know I'm the Wraith. I'm sure it took Helms years to unravel that secret, unless Mason told him, which I doubt.

The sudden silence is jarring. I pad back to the stairs quietly, wiping my bloody hand on my pants and gripping my gun. I wait, coiled tight, expecting them to rush the house, but nothing happens. Then a whoosh shatters the silence, and the night explodes, literally.

Breaking glass, a hiss and bright flames burst into view from my perch. Fucking bastards have Molotovs. They aren't going to rush in, risking one of them get shot. No, they're going to burn the house down, with me inside. If there was a doubt before on whether they want to take me alive, here's the answer. Already, the curtains and sparse furniture are engulfed in flames, the mist from the alcohol splashing along the carpet and igniting.

I wait as long as I can before bolting, skipping half the stairs on my way down. I grab the post at the bottom, using the momentum to swing around and skid down the hall to the one door I didn't bother checking. The rest of the house has basic locks, but this one has a code, like the ones at the Depot. I smash the keys, my bloody fingers smearing red on it. I have to input the numbers twice before I get them right, and it finally pops open. The smoke, contrasting the blaze, floats lazily along the ceiling toward me. Before I fling myself inside, I pull the door shut as the flames lick at my heels. The door is fireproof, at least. It's explosion-proof, too, but I don't know what will happen if the whole house burns down above the reinforced door and the block frame encasing the stairs. I could be trapped for days with no one knowing.

I stumble down and collapse on the raggedy couch pushed against one wall, sucking in deep breaths of air. My side is still bleeding, but the adrenaline keeps the pain at bay for now. I have to do something about my wound—and soon. The last thing I need is for shock to set in. I stand as soon as I can, intent on making it to the sink across the small space, and my vision blurs.

"Shit, shit, shit," I mutter. I'm slurring my words. With how much blood I've lost, along with the Molotov fumes, I'm failing fast. My side vibrates as I focus on putting one foot in front of the other, holding as much pressure on my bullet wound as I can handle. It happens again before my sluggish thoughts remind me of my phone. Somehow, I've kept it with me through the entire ordeal.

It almost slips from my bloody fingers, but I catch the case right before it falls. I can't concentrate on who it is, I can only pray someone who will help is on the other end. I swipe it with my nose, the only thing not covered in blood now, and I almost sob when it connects.

"SAM!" Ren's voice roars down the phone.

Relief floods my body. Hearing his voice. I wobble, almost losing my grip on the only lifeline I have left. I close my eyes, hoping it will help, but the move only makes it feel like my head is encased in a bubble floating above my head. I won't make it like this. I'm fading fast, and I don't have the strength to hold back my tears. I can't feel them fall, though, as my body starts to tremble.

"Help," I whimper, my throat tightening.

He shouts something else, but I can't make it out, and my knees give out. A coldness seeps through me as I tumble. Alex is begging on the line, and Shane is cursing over and over.

The last thought before I lose consciousness: even if they get here in time, they'll never get through the door.

ALEX

"Fucking hell, Ren! She better be able to get us in!" Shane yells, tires squealing as we speed around the corner. Ren found the safehouse Sam is staying in ten minutes ago, and now it's in flames. Sirens are echoing in the distance, but they'll never be here in time to save the house, to save her.

Shane curses, spotting tail lights racing away down the block. Our car jumps forward, like he's going to follow them, before he slams on the brakes in front of the inferno. I'm out before we've come to a full stop, trying to find any way in. Flames dance out of the shattered windows, lighting up the night.

"The back!" Ren yells, throwing himself out of the car, phone pressed to his ear. I've never heard him so frantic before. He's the calm one. While Shane yells, and I freak out, Ren is unflappable—until now. Fifteen minutes ago, he burst in the kitchen, bellowing to get our asses in the car. How he found where she is, I don't know, and I don't care.

Racing around the back, I smash through the door, which easily gives way. I have no idea where she is, but I start checking every room frantically. Smoke curls along the walls, making it harder to see clearly, and with each empty space, I become more desperate. The heat is suffocating the farther down the hall we go.

"Guys!" Ren's voice cuts through the hissing flames. "Get me in here, Nemesis!"

By the thunderous look on Ren's face, she isn't understanding the seriousness of the situation. In my haste, I ran past the door he's standing at. In the wall is an innocuous keypad smeared with blood. I throw myself at it, impatience getting the best of me. I rear back a second time, but Shane grabs me, hauling me away.

I twist, trying to pull free, but his grip is firm. The pad glows green, and the door pops open. How it's still working with the fire, I don't know. I race down the rickety stairs. It's blessedly cool in the basement after the heat from upstairs. The smoke flows down with me, making me cough, but I forge ahead.

Passed out in the middle of the floor, phone inches from her fingertips, is Sam, with blood pooled around her side. Seeing her so still, I freeze, not registering the other two plowing into the room. Shane shoves into me to get to Sam, jolting me out of whatever trance I'm in. I start to rush forward, but Ren pulls me back as Shane rolls her over and gathers her in his arms, shouting at us to get out.

The fire has spread even more when we climb upstairs. The inferno is rolling along the ceiling now, eating up the walls. Soon, our escape route will be cut off if we don't hurry. Ren leads the way, with Shane carrying Sam close behind. We're almost to the kitchen when the crackling starts. Glancing up, I lunge forward, pushing them through the doorway seconds before the ceiling collapses right where we were standing. Cinders float, landing on my arm, soot covering my hair. It's a miracle I made it through before it collapsed.

Outside, the cool winter air is heaven for my lungs. Sucking in deep breaths, we make our way to the car. The sirens are blocks away now, their lights flashing off the houses. We need to get out of here before they arrive. The last thing we want to handle is needless questioning.

I skid around the front of the car to the driver's seat. As soon as the doors shut behind my friends, I slam on the gas and get the hell away, praying we're quick enough to save her. Flying around corners, Shane is shouting at me to slow down. Ren is on the phone again, with god knows who. My only thought is to bring her home, to safety. I can't ask if she's breathing, if she's gone. I'm not ready for the answer. Somehow, in such a short amount of time, I can't imagine the world without her.

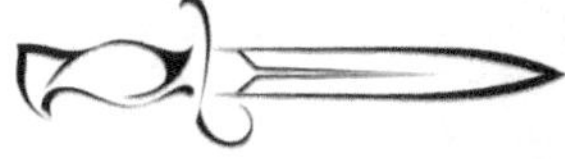

"What do you mean I'm not allowed in there?!" I can't believe Ren thinks he can stop me.

"Doc is fixing her up, and he can't do that with you yelling at him. He's doing what needs to be done. Be patient." He's retreated behind his mask of indifference. Gone is the Ren who ranted and raved, who showed emotion when we were racing into an inferno. Ren called the doctor and threatened him so thoroughly the man beat us home, waiting patiently on our front steps. Now, though, Ren is calm, as if it doesn't matter if Sam is alive or dead. I don't understand it. I feed off emotions, but they don't compute for him.

"You want me to be patient? Are you fucking serious? At least tell me what the hell he's doing to her," I demand, collapsing in a chair Shane had dragged over to sit outside her door.

"He's stitching up her bullet wound. Looks like it went clean through and didn't hit anything vital, but she bled a lot. He's also looking at her head."

Glaring, I whip my head up. "What's wrong with her head?"

"There's a bruise from when she passed out. She doesn't have any smoke in her lungs—or burns, so she was probably downstairs before the fire started or shortly after. We won't know until after she wakes up," he tells me, dropping in a chair across from me.

Finally, I find a crack in his armor, and exhaustion fills his face before he drops his head in his hands. It's after two in the morning, the adrenaline slowly fading while we sit and wait for answers. When Doc comes out with Shane, he nods to us before striding away down the hall. We watch him until he's out of sight.

"Well?" I ask.

"She'll be okay. Needs to rest." Shane sighs, leaning against the wall.

"What the fuck happened? How did she get shot? Do we at least know how the damn house was on fire with her inside?" I demand, looking to Ren.

He's the one who found her, after all.

Ren clears his throat, glancing down at his dead tablet that's almost always in his hands.

"It seems whoever they are shot at the house and then threw Molotov cocktails in. I don't know how they found her. They were driving a Mercedes-Benz, though."

"The same ones from the video?" Shane asks, eyes blazing.

"The exact same. The plates match, but following them is a dead-end, as we suspected." He yawns, settling more in his seat.

"You two should get some sleep. There's nothing more we can do now, anyway. We'll figure things out in the morning," Shane says, turning back to Sam's door.

"Yeah, I'm going to stay right here. I want to be here when she wakes up," I tell him. I'm expecting a fight, but Shane nods, staring at his feet before turning to slide down to the floor.

We sit for a while, waiting, fighting exhaustion. Ren seems to forget his tablet is dead every ten minutes and tries to wake it up. Shane dozes, twitching awake every now and then.

I almost laugh, thinking back to a couple of weeks ago, when we only had a vague understanding of who Samantha Byrns was. She swept into our lives and turned everything upside down. I felt like I was only existing before, waiting for the next meeting, the next shipment, the next assignment. I was comfortable, but Sam made it exciting. Every text, every encounter, felt like we were building toward something more. I wanted to see where this thing between us could have gone.

Looking at Ren and Shane, I hope we're on the same page that we need to protect her. That she belongs with us. It feels like we've been building up to this night for weeks, maybe months. I knew the minute she evaded Ren and me in the alley that she would end up being entwined in our lives. Shane fought it, Ren ignored it, but I knew. There was no other option for me.

Sam is exactly what we need. She woke us up, showing us what we were missing. I don't think the others notice yet. I think they're still locked in their mistrust to see the truth.

I'll follow Shane's lead, but I'll fight for her place here as much as I can. He's a stubborn bastard, so I don't expect him to give in right away, but maybe her getting shot will make him realize how important she is to us, to our lives.

My eyes find Ren resting his head against the wall, face smoothed out in sleep. I don't always understand him, but he sees more than Shane or I ever could. He's done more the last couple weeks to try to find Sam than he'll ever admit. He went to the Byrns' estate and brought back a duffel bag, though I'm sure he thinks no one saw. I also know he's slipped out the house long after he thinks everyone is sleeping, driving around, going to the Barrens, looking for Sam. He tries to play at being emotionless, uncaring, but he couldn't sit around, hoping she would pop up, even if that's what he told me. It's why I stopped bugging him about doing more.

"What?" Ren grunts at me, eyes still closed.

"Nothing."

"You're thinking very loudly for it to be nothing, Alex. Spill."

"You think this changes things?" I ask, glancing at Shane, who's fallen asleep against the wall with his hands still gripping Sam's bloody hoodie.

Ren opens his eyes, staring at Shane, too, before peering at me. He narrows his gaze at whatever emotion he catches on my face.

"I think that will depend on what Sam tells us when she wakes up. She was out there for two weeks, and we have no idea what she's discovered. I'm more concerned with how those men found out where she was." Frustration turns his mouth down.

"That's not what I was talking about, but you knew that. Let me know when you're ready to face the truth, brother," I chuckle, resting my head back.

"She might not want to be kept, Alex. You need to brace yourself for the possibility."

I close my eyes, not wanting to hear the truth in his words. Even if she doesn't see it, she's ours. I can't accept she might walk away, not after the pain and anxiety—the fear of almost losing her. If I have to beat the truth into Shane and Ren's skulls, I will.

THIRTY-FOUR

SAMANTHA

My eyes have sunken into my skull. That's the first thought I have when I wake up. Even closed, they feel like weights are sitting on my lids. Next comes the ache, like a stitch in my side after running for miles. I try to shift, but something is preventing me from moving. I should be panicking, but I'm detached, floating along in the space between waking and sleeping.

I peel my eyes open, and I'm in a bed, a heavy blanket draped over me. I don't know where I am, but the room is familiar. I can't put my finger on why, though. My thoughts are wisps, gathering in the corners of my brain and drifting away, out of reach. I suck in a breath, but there's a pulling sensation from the ache. The memories come rushing back: bullets flying, blood coating my hand, the safehouse going up in flames, finding my way to the bunker.

Ren's voice yelling my name.

The room—it's a bedroom in Shane's house, the layout the same as home, though the items inside are different from my own. I can't make out the whole of it, the small bedside lamp casting a glow, which doesn't quite reach the corners, but I'm alone. I don't know if I'm relieved or not. Low voices murmur from the hall through the cracked door. I close my eyes, concentrating on who's speaking.

"She's still sleeping, so we can't ask her," Shane gripes.

"I can't figure out how they found her."

Ren. His voice is strained, frustration bleeding through.

"Probably the same way we did, don't you think?"

There's Alex.

The gang's all here. Waiting outside for me to wake up. Heat crawls up my body, making me shiver. Their vigil is equal parts embarrassing and heartwarming.

"Maybe," Ren answers. "But Nemesis kept an eye on most of the city. They have a lot of capital if they found her through the cameras. She wasn't easy to find."

Who is Nemesis? I dismiss the question, trying to focus on their conversation before sleep drags me down into the dark again. My chest squeezes, and I try to remember how to breathe.

". . . same page. When do we show her the video?" Alex asks.

"Which one?"

Wait, videos? I have no clue what they're talking about, but they've evidently been keeping shit from me. No surprise there. I'm keeping shit from them, too.

"Either? Both? I mean, I think we should show her the one with her brother. She deserves to see it."

Mason? They have video of him? Bastards. All this time, I've been begging Shane to give me something, anything, and he's had this video up his sleeve the whole time. I want to be angry, to rage at him, but all I feel is a stabbing hurt radiating within my chest. At least Alex is on my side, but I hold my breath, waiting for Shane's response. Maybe he's changed his mind, decided I'm worth taking a chance on. He'll be the one to ultimately decide. The other two will follow his orders, no matter how much they agree with him.

"No . . ."

That one word cuts through me, and my eyes fill with tears, but I choke them back. He murmurs something else, but I can't hear anything over the roar in my ears. It shouldn't hit me so hard, his refusal to let me in, to trust me. I understood before, but after our last conversation, I still held out hope he would calm down and see I'm not his enemy. I thought the fact they came and found me, saved me, would have shifted something. It appears there's no redemption left for me. I'm enough to keep alive but nothing more.

Struggling, I wipe my eyes, fighting the groan, trying to escape when my side protests. I need to get myself under control before they realize I'm awake. The last thing I need is to be caught blubbering.

I'm the Wraith. I need to be stronger than this. I can't allow mere words to shatter my resolve. How these men are experts at punching through my barriers is beyond me, but I need to wall off my heart, stop chasing something that will clearly never be there. Ever since the gala months ago, I've dealt with one punch after another. I'll just pick myself up and deal with this one, too.

"Do we keep her here, then?" Alex's tone gives me hope. I've missed whatever they were saying with my pity party.

"Whatever you decide, there are people intent on killing her. There's an inherent risk with keeping her or letting her go," Ren states coldly.

"We're not keeping her . . ." Shane mutters. Alex curses them both, footsteps pounding away down the hall. One of them sighs in the wake of his tantrum.

Ren shatters the silence. "I think it would be best if I were the one to talk to her when she wakes. Alex is obviously . . . not a good choice. And you . . ."

"I'd end up yelling at her. I know. Let me know what she says. We need answers only she can give. See if you can find out what she's been up to since she dropped off the radar. I doubt she was holed up in the house learning to knit and watching trash TV. Sam isn't one to sit idly by, unfortunately."

Shane's footsteps follow Alex's, leaving Ren behind. I keep my eyes closed and smooth out my breathing, which is easier said than done after hearing them discuss me so callously. The door creaks and shuts soon after. I stay still, listening for any sign he's in the room, but after several minutes, I crack an eye. The door is closed, and I'm alone.

The initial hurt subsides to a dull ache, manageable if nothing else. They don't owe me anything. It doesn't matter I've slept with Shane. It doesn't matter we've worked together once or twice. It doesn't matter; they don't trust me. It doesn't matter they've pulled me from a burning building. I will deal with this the same way I deal with everything else, by pretending it doesn't exist. Eventually, the pain will go away. What matters now is my brother, our family, the organization. I need to focus on the threats and not my feelings for three men I shouldn't want in the first place.

I fall asleep after still trying to formulate a plan, deciding how much I should share with them. I contemplate whether to use Helms as the go-between, but I trash the thought. Ryker isn't one to pass notes between us. He'll tell me to pull my head out of my ass, be a big girl, and deal with my own shit. So, that's exactly what I'll do.

I don't know how long I sleep, but the sun is coming up when I open my eyes again. I flinch, grunting when my movement shoots pain through the right side of my body. Ren is sitting in a chair facing the bed, as if he's been here for a while. His eyes are closed, face softened while he rests. He doesn't look quite as intimidating now. Ren normally has an emotionless mask over his features, unless he's glaring at me, so to see him so peaceful is jarring.

I blow out a breath, my eyes not nearly as heavy as the last time, and find a glass of water with pills on the nightstand. I don't dwell on which one left the pain meds. It doesn't matter. I hiss as I scoot to sit against the headboard. Lifting my shirt, I see a neat line of stitches. Whoever sewed me up has done it before. I hope they called an actual doctor instead of sticking a needle in me themselves.

I'm not wearing my own shirt, which seems like something I should have known. The fact I'm not wearing my own clothes shouldn't surprise me, but it hits me I don't have *any* clothes anymore. I don't have anything at all. It's either locked up in the estate or burned up with the safehouse. Unless I'm willing to go back to the house, to Victor, I have nowhere to go. I have nothing.

Mechanically, I pick up the glass and throw back the pills, shutting down everything. But the next step, I can plan later, when I'm alone. Hopefully, they'll let me stay a day or two to recover, and I can come up with something in the meantime. Maybe Colin will know a place. He'll know whether Victor was behind the attempt on my life at any rate.

Ren clears his throat, making me jump again, and let out a curse under my breath. I was hoping I could be as emotionless as him, but I'm already flinching. Looking up, I meet his eyes, which, of course, tells me nothing. The ability of this man to shut off everything is ridiculous.

"How are you feeling?" he asks, which throws me. I expected an immediate interrogation.

"Fine."

What else am I going to say? My side feels like it's on fire? That I'm drowning? I'm so utterly exhausted from pretending like I'm not a failure? My entire life is falling apart at the seams, and I don't know if I care anymore? I'm so ridiculously alone, and being around them makes it harder to go back to my lonely existence every time they walk away?

"Liar," he whispers, eyes narrowing.

Usually, I wouldn't be able to back down from the challenge in his eyes, but I am completely out of fucks at this point, so I shrug, waiting for him to continue.

"What happened, Sam?"

"The usual. Ambush, bullets, fire. Not much to tell," I respond, looking away. His gray eyes have a way of capturing me, pulling me in until I don't register anything else. Best to avoid them.

"Who knew about the safehouse?"

"Does it matter?" I glance at him as his eyebrow raises.

I want to get this over with. It doesn't matter to them. It's something I'll add to my own list of shit to figure out. I'm not going to burden them with more.

"If you aren't up for this discussion, then perhaps I should let you rest," he suggests, shifting to stand.

"Why don't you just ask what you want to know?" I can hear the bitterness in my own voice, but he doesn't mention it, of course, but merely settles back in his chair.

"All right. Have you found anything else since you last spoke with Shane?"

My mind whirls with everything I've discovered while holed up in King territory, separating what they need to know versus what only matters to me.

"As a matter of fact, I have." I pause, resigning myself to telling them everything, even if they won't do the same for me.

I can break free if I don't hold any more secrets. I can cut myself off and get back to my life before they push me away. Before they turn it upside down . . . again.

"Well?" he prompts.

I sit there, staring into space. "The Guild," I murmur, causing him to curse.

I don't know why we haven't considered them before. It's so obvious they're trying to bring us down and take over Synd.

"Are you sure?" I'm not sure whether to be offended, but he's as blindsided as I was when I found out.

"Yes. It fits their pattern. Quietly taking out leaders. Snatching people in the dead of night. Taking over the drug trade. They'll bring in guns next. Convince the lower gangs they can take care of them better. You know what their real moneymaker is, though, right?"

"The Auction," he spits out, like it's a dirty word, which I suppose is.

"And the Trade. I imagine they'll try to take the Depot next, if they don't already have a warehouse holding their human assets. I don't know if they hold the Auction in the same city, though."

"They do." Ren drums his fingers on his legs, as if he's itching to throw something, or more than likely, he wishes his tablet was in his hands.

"Well, Ryker was right, then. You'll need all the allies you can gather. I don't know if you'll be able to convince Victor, but if you can get him to pull his head out of his ass long enough, I'm sure he'll work with you. Colin can help with him. Ryker doesn't want human traffickers in the city, and he might have some other clubs he can call for backup."

Ren is eyeing me, but I still can't figure out what he's thinking. "What about you?"

"What about me?"

"You're saying these things as if you won't be involved." Suspicion clouds his face.

"I'm only one person."

He sighs, dropping his elbows to his knees, his head hanging. It's the most relaxed I've ever seen him. He's always wound tight, like the need to be in complete control is vital or he'll break a part. Watching him deflate before me is unsettling but also mesmerizing. He breathes out my name, like a prayer or a curse, before shaking his head.

"I would hardly say you're only one person." He gazes at me from under his lashes.

I freeze, trying not to give anything away. If anyone can find out I'm the Wraith, it's this man before me. A mere glance at him tells me he sees things others don't, connecting what others miss.

Mason's voice echoes in my ear, telling me no one can know, but I desperately want to spill everything. I wouldn't consider it if Alex and Shane were here. Alex would feel betrayed, Shane would deny the truth, but Ren . . . maybe he would understand, but my brother's words are ringing through the silence, that they'll kill me. I never knew why, but I trust Mason. I have to because, if I don't, my world will no longer make sense.

"I don't have any allies to offer. Besides, it's been made pretty clear I'm not an asset to the Kings," I say, as if I have nothing to hide.

"Interesting" is all he says, hiding his eyes again.

"Anything I should know?"

I have to ask. I hold my breath, though I'm sure he won't tell me. Shane made his wishes clear on where I stand with them.

"You know more than we do at this point," he states, his gaze still glued to the floor.

"Do you know who tried to kill me?"

He twitches, which has me cocking my head, trying to figure out what he's thinking. Outright lying to me is apparently harder than making vague statements.

"I think you can hazard a guess at who it was."

My nose flares at his lack of response, my only outward sign of frustration. I'm never going to drag anything out of him. I shouldn't have tried. It only hurts me more in the end.

I'm about to make some excuse of tiredness to get him to leave when he sits back suddenly. He's done playing at being relaxed. It's a smart ploy on his part, to act like he's drained to have me to open up, and it works, though I've made up my mind to tell them what I knew before he thought to trick me.

"So, what's your plan, Sam?"

"Uh, survive?"

He can't think I'll tell him my plans, if I had any to begin with. He rolls his eyes, the most mundane thing I've seen him do so far.

"I think we're all aiming for survival. I meant with your housing situation."

I knew it was coming, but it still hits me like a ton of bricks. He's out of his mind if he thinks I'm going to ask to stay here. I still wouldn't ask whether I overheard them earlier or not. It's bad enough I owe them a debt for saving my life. To have them put a roof over my head? Clothes on my back? I'll never be able to repay them. A debt like that isn't something a Byrns can owe a King. Not without paying with their life in the end. I'm afraid I'm already going to have to, since a life debt hangs between us. I could use saving Emma as a trade, but I doubt Shane would accept, since I saved her without knowing who she was.

"Don't worry, I'll be out by today," I hedge, hoping he'll drop it.

"Not what I asked. Where are you going to go?"

"Not your business. I can leave now if you bring me my pants."

I don't want to ask who took them off in the first place. At least the shirt is long enough to cover the important parts.

He huffs out what sounds like a laugh, leaning forward again, saying, "I think we both know you don't have anywhere else to go, Sam."

"Not your concern. Again, pants?"

I don't want to admit to him he's right. I avoid his eyes and look around for my phone. I can call Colin, ask him where he thinks I should stay. I need to figure out if it was Victor or the Guild aiming to kill me. Maybe someone's finally figured out I'm the Wraith, and revenge is on the table. I could ask Helms for help, but I reject the idea again, suppressing a shudder.

The answer comes to me then: the Barrens. I have plenty of contacts there. I've taken care of them more than anyone else. Surely, someone will take me in, if only for a little while.

Throwing back the blankets, I swing my legs out to get up when I spot the blood streaks traveling up my right leg. The sheets are splotched. The white shirt I'm wearing has blood seeping through, blotting and spreading the more I move. I want to look at the stitches, but I'm not going to lift my shirt with Ren in the room.

He doesn't have the same qualms, appearing by my side and ripping the shirt up, practically tearing it off. I expect him to poke and prod, but his touch is gentle, pressing around the wound where blood is trickling down my flesh. It doesn't look infected, thank God. There's no way I'll be able to survive in the Barrens with an infection. I'll be dead in days. The next step is to find a way to the there. I don't have any money for a ride, and I'm not walking with this wound seeping blood the whole way there. Alex . . . no. I won't beg for charity.

"It's fine," I snap, trying to pull my clothing from his fingers, but he swats my hand away. I'm barely clothed, bleeding in the King's house. I shouldn't be having any reaction, but I can feel his eyes following the lines of my body. My black thong covers almost nothing, but at least I have something on, so he can't spot the wetness gathering between my legs.

"One would think you would pack more practical clothing if you were fleeing . . ." is all he says, lowering the shirt again and stepping back.

I was practical packing my bag before, but when they got dirty, I'd been forced to go back to the underwear I was wearing when I fled my house. I make a mental note to pack extra pairs in my next bag . . . if I live long enough to have one. I think about explaining myself, but he won't care.

"Do you have some bandages at least? And my pants? I can be on my way, then." I flip the blanket back over my lap, giving the illusion of modesty.

"Your pants were cut off you. Bandages are there." He points to the nightstand. "Don't leave until we've spoken again."

Ren strides out of the room, and I flip him off. I'll patch myself up, raid one of their rooms, and be on my way. I'll be long gone before they realize I've left. The snap of the lock thunders in his wake as I reach into the drawer on the side table for the first aid kit.

"Hey!" I yell out.

"Not stupid, Pet. Don't try to go out the window, or you'll rip your stitches. I'll be back soon," Ren answers, a hint of laughter in his voice still coming through, though his words are muffled. Bastard

SHANE

"**W**e're not having this discussion again, Alex. Just fucking drop it," I say when Ren comes in my study. I thought I could find answers, but I've been staring at the wall, thinking about the woman sleeping down the hall. I've called all my contacts, from the commissioner down to Ren's guy in the Barrens, and no one knows anything. I gave up after that.

"This is bullshit, and you fucking know it," he spits, slamming the door on his way out to sulk.

"Trouble in paradise?"

"Oh, fuck off, Ren. He's being completely irrational over a woman."

Ren's eyebrows dance up, making me want to break his goddamn nose. There is no way I'm going to force Sam to stay here or offer it in the first place. She'll have to come out and ask if she wants to stay. She probably has dozens of places she can run off to, anyway. She'll laugh in my face if I give her the option of staying here. I don't blame her at this point.

"She found out quite a bit while she was hiding out. We're in for a fucking fight if she's right." Ren breaks through my musings.

"What'd she find? Wait, you think she's lying?"

"No. I think she's right, but you seem to question everything that comes out of her mouth." Ren gives me a look I can't decipher. "It's the Guild. They're trying to take the city. Starting with the hit on Byrns, up to the attempt on Sam's life."

I rock back, shocked I didn't see it before. Of course it's the fucking Guild. They've been working their way across the state, taking out the local gangs, mafia, or police, and running their operation for a few months. Then, when the feds close in, they disappear, like shadows running from the dawn. Arrogantly, I thought we had a tight enough grip on the city that they wouldn't dare come here. Now I'm paying for my hubris.

"Do we know what their next move is?" I ask, already making plans in my head. We can hit them where it hurts if we can find their base.

"Sam seems to think they'll try to take the Depot," he comments, looking at his fingernails, as if this isn't something to worry about.

"Well, she's just a wealth of information, isn't she?" I retort.

Ren stares at me, waiting. I shake my head and glance out the window at the sun tracking across the sky

"We'll need to inform Helms. Sam thought we could convince Victor, with Colin's help. We're going to need something more, though."

"Okay, I get what she wants, but what do *you* think, Ren?"

"That's not what she wants"—he pauses—"we need to inform Helms. I trust him, and he's not going to run his mouth. I'm not convinced it was coincidental Victor took over instead of Colin . . ." He taps his fingers on his leg.

"You think Victor is working with the Guild?" I don't like the idea of someone in our city working with sex traffickers.

"Maybe. No. I don't think he's smart enough to pull it off, no matter how much of a dick I think he is, but I could be wrong. You know what we need, though."

At my questioning look, he drops a bomb. "The Wraith."

"No. Asking that psycho to help us? They'd turn on us whenever they felt like it."

"I'm sure she wouldn't do that . . ."

Ren's words filter through my brain. *She?*

"Are you telling me you know who the fucking Wraith is?" I demand.

"I have my suspicions. They're unconfirmed at this point, but we don't really have the time to do this the way I'd like. I think it would help in the end, but only if we can convince her to work with us. Having someone who will be able to slip in undetected? It would be invaluable at taking down the Guild."

I stare at my laptop, contemplating his explanation, trying to wrap my head around the fact Ren may have solved the puzzle of who the psychopathic hitman is. She—if it is a she—isn't someone many people realize is out there. She never fucks with the lower gangs, only taking high-risk jobs on high-profile people. The aftermath always gets ruled a home invasion or suicide. I gave up figuring out who she was a long time ago. Ren couldn't possibly think Sam is the Wraith. She might have more training and skill than we originally thought, but the idea she's as deadly as the Wraith is almost laughable.

"Did Nemesis find her?"

The only form of communication is an encrypted phone number, so it's likely the hacker would be able to discover the Wraith's identity, but Ren is shaking his head.

"Just leave it. I'll see if I can get her on board if we need to. We have more pressing issues," he says.

"More pressing than the Guild?"

"Time sensitive, then," he says, seeming annoyed. "What do you want to do about Sam?"

"Do whatever the hell you want." I wave him away, hoping he'll take the hint.

Ren rises, making his way to the door before pausing, then turns back to me. I try to keep my concentration on the screen, but my muscles bunch in anticipation.

"She doesn't have anywhere else to go. If you let her leave, she's dead."

"And I'm supposed to care, why?" I ask as my stomach turns.

"Just thought I'd remind you," he says, making his way out, closing the door behind him.

I curse, spinning in my chair, wondering what the hell I'm supposed to do now.

The sun is setting, momentarily blinding me as I gaze out my bedroom window overlooking the driveway. Sam gingerly makes her way down the front steps, nodding to Titus, who looks away, cheeks flushing. Her small frame is swallowed in my sweatshirt and the black leggings Ren procured from god knows where. She buries her hands in the front pocket, after pulling the hood up, hiding her face. I'm surprised Alex isn't there offering her a ride to wherever she's off to, but I haven't seen him since he blew up at me. I let him stew. If he can't understand why I'm letting her go, then so be it.

I watch as she goes around the monstrosity of a fountain, glancing back when she thinks she's hidden enough to not be noticed, but I do. I can't make out her face with the fading light and distance, though I wish I could. Ren's words keep rolling around in my head. I tried all afternoon to dismiss them, to convince myself she'll be fine left to her own devices, that she wants it this way, but they keep coming back.

I expect a car to be waiting at the drive, but there isn't. She turns right, and when she thinks she's out of sight, plops down on the sidewalk and burrows into herself. I resign to being stuck here, waiting with her, a hidden witness, but as minutes turn into an hour, I sigh, making my way downstairs and out the door.

I don't try to hide my footsteps as I approach, but she stays hunched over. She doesn't even have her phone out. I stop several feet away, looking up and down the road, but there's no sign of a car and no movement from her. She has to be freezing.

"What are you doing, Sam?"

"Waiting," she mumbles, scarcely above a whisper.

"For what?"

"Don't know yet. Something will come."

I have no idea what she's saying, but I can't leave her out here in the cold, especially with the sun setting. What would be the point of saving her ass from a burning building if I let her freeze to death?

"Do you need a ride somewhere?"

"Nope." She pops the *p*, some of her sass coming back.

"Sam, admit it, you don't have anywhere to go."

"Like I told Ren, not your concern." Her shoulders droop.

I'm sure she doesn't think I'll notice, but I see everything when it comes to her.

"Just come inside. It's fucking cold out."

"I'm fine."

"Why do you have to be so goddamn stubborn? Don't be fucking stupid, Princess, and get your ass in the house. Now."

Crossing my arms, I count silently. I'll give her thirty seconds to get over her pride before I'm throwing her over my shoulder and dragging her back. If she doesn't like it, too bad. The irony of the situation isn't lost on me—fighting with Alex earlier and hours later, planning on doing exactly what he wants.

I hit ten seconds before she's up and spinning around, eyes blazing, ready to give me a piece of her mind. I can't hide my grin. The last twenty-four hours have been a rollercoaster. I don't want to admit it, but I panicked last night. When we found her, laying on the floor not moving . . . thinking she was dead. Fear almost engulfed me. To see her standing in front of me, itching for a fight, soothes the terror a little.

"What the hell are you smiling at? You think you can come out here and tell me what to do? Sorry to break it to you, boss, but I don't answer to you."

I smirk just to piss her off some more. "Oh, Princess, I don't think you listen to anyone, do you? But you're going to listen to me, because if you don't, I'll be carrying your ass inside instead, and we both know how that ended last time."

Her mouth drops as I wink. I shouldn't be egging her on, but honestly, I can't help myself. There's plenty of shit we need to discuss, but I have to get her in the damn house first. I step toward her to follow through, when she stops me with a hand in the air.

Chin shooting up and walking with all the haughtiness she can muster, she marches past me, back toward the house. I turn to follow, making sure she doesn't try to slip away from me like she has so many times before. She twitches and wraps her arm around her waist. I scoop her up, cradling her in my arms while she shrieks.

"Don't be stupid, Sam. You're obviously in pain," I say, striding up the stairs again, nodding to a grinning Titus.

Her withering glare is lost on him as I hurry into the warmth and find Ren standing at the top of the stairs. Nodding to him, he shakes his head before disappearing into the depths of the house while I take her to the kitchen.

"You can put me down now."

"Not quite," I respond, pushing open the door and setting her on the counter. I stop her with a hand on her knee when she goes to slide down. I pull up her clothes, finding a fresh bandage over her wound. No blood has seeped through, so I leave it before looking at her.

"Are you satisfied?" she asks brusquely, raising an eyebrow.

"Not nearly enough," I quip, "but I'll settle for feeding you."

I move over to get leftovers from the fridge, then heat them up while she watches me. Once done, I step in front of her, handing her a bowl, waiting until she takes a bite before I drop onto the stool next to her. We eat in silence, but I can feel her eyes sliding to me. I ignore it, methodically eating my food. It's coming: the confrontation. We need to set things straight, and I'm sure we'll end up yelling at each other, no matter how I approach it.

I take our empty bowls, put them in the sink, and rinse them out before going back to her and scooping her up. She doesn't protest this time, which tells me how tired she really is. Maybe our conversation will need to wait until tomorrow. Her eyes flutter, almost closing as I carry her upstairs. When I reach the room she stayed in last night, I hesitate before continuing on to my own. I push away why I want her in my bed instead of a spare room.

After kicking the door shut, I set her in the middle of my bed. She's wobbling, eyes closed, which makes getting her sweatshirt off harder than it should be with how it drowns her frame, but she's in my stained red T-shirt. Her breathing evens out as I pull the comforter up, and she's fast asleep. I should go and get work done, come up with a plan of how we're going to attack the Guild, call Helms. Instead, I watch her sleep, trying to convince myself Sam Byrns is a means to an end, nothing more.

I'm fighting a losing battle. The last thing I'll do is admit it, but I know I am. I crawl under the covers, pulling them over us both, and count her breaths as the light fades.

THIRTY-SIX

SAMANTHA

I wake up in a cold sweat, gasping for breath. I'm panicking, trying to place where I am and why I can't move. The nightmare that woke me drifts away, flashes of blood and bullets, fading to blackness, only terror left in its wake.

I start to struggle, the stitches in my side tugging. My body is overheated, the covers boiling me from the inside out. I'm gasping, trying to kick the comforter down, swiveling my head from side to side, but it's dark. Rationally, I understand I should calm down, but my hysteria builds anyway, overriding my senses.

"Sam. Sam! Stop."

A voice cuts through my panic, but now, hands are everywhere, holding me down, pulling at my body. Tears slipping down my cheeks, then the suffocating weight is gone and a soft light clicks on, flooding the bedroom: a bedroom I recognize. I whip my head around, still gasping for breath, and Shane's concerned face fills the voids in my mind. He reaches out, gathering me to his chest, his hand stroking my hair. He's whispering something I can't quite make out over the pounding of my heart.

Muffled against him, a sob heaves out of me. "I'm sorry."

"Shh, I've got you," he murmurs, pressing a kiss to my hair.

I want to explain, maybe pull out of his arms. I should, but I wrap my arms around him instead. Borrowing his strength, if only for a moment. Our relationship is a constant push-pull, a battle neither can win, but I'm tired of fighting, at least for tonight.

I cling to him, my lifeline through the shadows.

We lay with my face buried in his chest before his hand twitches, skating down my body. It should be comforting, but instead, it heats my blood, making me tremble in his hold. Up and down, his hand skims along my back, ducking under my shirt to splay his hand on my bare skin. My fingers curl with the sensation, nails burrowing into him before skating down. He shudders, a low groan reverberating in his chest under my cheek.

The next pass of his hand has him fingering the waistline of my leggings. I don't know how far this will go, but I'm committed to not fighting him, myself, my feelings right now, in the dark of the night. I want him, and I'm sick of denying I do.

Dipping his hand, he squeezes my ass before he's pulling away, but I bury my protest. The rejection hurts, though. I don't expect anything from him, but it would be nice if, for once, someone would choose me. Just me. I won't go begging for it. It's not in me to beg.

When I think he'll roll over and ignore me for the rest of the night, he crawls over me and settles on my other side. He pulls my back into his chest and tucks his arm under my head. Confusion rides me until I remember I was shot. His hands are stroking my body again, and I forget the aches and pain.

I squirm, trying to pull my leg free so I can turn to him, but he grips my hip, wedging me into him, his cock lining up with my ass. I tremble when he skims up to my breast, pinching a nipple before moving to the other and repeating the move back and forth, over and over. A whimper escapes me, and Shane nuzzles my neck, pressing his lips right behind my ear, making me arch into him.

"Are you wet for me, Princess?" he breathes, but I have no response as his hands continue their exploration. I twitch as he brushes down my body, hooking his thumb in my pants, exposing my ass. I lift my hip as best I can, but the wound in my side throbs, and I let out a soft yelp. Shane freezes, wrapping his arm around my shoulders, holding me close.

"Sorry," he whispers, so softly I almost don't catch the words.

"Don't stop."

"Sam . . ." he warns.

I shake my head. I swear if he leaves me all hot and bothered, I'll have to take care of it myself, and it won't be nearly as satisfying.

"Please," I moan, grinding my ass on his cock. I know I'll win. He wants this as much as I do, regardless of the wound in my side.

"Don't worry, Princess, I'll be gentle. You going to tell me how wet you are, or are you going to make me see for myself?" The hoarseness in his voice tells me how much he's holding back, and I stutter out a grunt, punching my hips forward into his waiting hand. He's gentler getting my leggings off, revealing each inch of skin, but I grab the fabric and push it down, using my toes to peel them off. My thong goes with them, and I'm in nothing but his shirt. His boxers follow, and he draws my waist back, careful of my stitches.

My leg wraps over his, opening me up to his explorations. He circles light touches, skipping over all the places I'm desperate for him to touch. Fucking adrenaline-fueled Shane was a wild ride, but this borders on torture. I'm aching, body flushed as he keeps up his gentle torment. I don't know how much longer I can last before I push him down and take what I need when he swipes his finger along my opening, making me jerk, chasing his hand for more, always more.

"Look how your pussy is weeping for my cock," he groans, his chin brushing my hair as he tips his head back.

His hand leaves me aching, and he's gripping himself, guiding his cock into me. I heave back, trying to take him all in, but he holds me, easing in, inch by torturous inch. I'm practically purring when he's fully seated, light thrusts keeping me from throwing caution to the wind and thrashing against him.

"Shane," I whine when I can't take it anymore.

"Hmm? What do you need, Princess?" He's trying to sound nonchalant, but I can hear the strain in his voice.

"Fuck me. Now."

"You didn't say 'please,'" he growls.

I cry out in frustration. "Please, please, please," I chant, trying to rock on him to create any friction possible. I'm beyond caring. So much for my quest to never beg.

He hisses when I clench around him, snatching my hip to keep me still, burying himself deeper, plunging into me more with every thrust. My muscles bunch, my body winding tighter until I'm writhing in his arms, begging with each exhale of breath for release.

Shane's fingers find my clit, rubbing as his movements become more erratic. My climax builds higher, racing toward the edge of bliss. There's a spark, and I'm weightless, riding the high he's brought me to. Shane's rasping breath and a sound vibrating deep in his chest is all the warning I get when he jerks, clinging to me and sinking his teeth into my shoulder as he flies over the edge of ecstasy.

We're panting, still fused together. I bask in the feelings floating through my body as my heart slows. Shane swoops down, planting kisses along my neck, murmuring unintelligible words. I whine when he slips free of my body, unable to keep my eyes open. I want to hold on to this moment longer. I jolt when he swipes a warm washcloth over me. Every time he passes over my clit, my whole body spasms, sending lightning throughout. I swear he's taking longer on purpose, to see me quiver.

The comforter settles over me, Shane tucking himself behind me and pulling me close. It's not until I'm on the edge of sleep before I figure out what he'd been saying over and over into my skin: stay.

A lifetime later, the door to the bedroom slams open, making my body jackknife up. The sudden movement sends a stabbing pain through my wound, but at least it's eased some. A shirtless Ren is barreling in the room, throwing clothes at Shane, demanding he get up. He isn't fazed by my presence, barely sparing me a glance before throwing several shopping bags toward me.

"Where's the fucking fire, Ren? It's nine in the morning," Shane grumbles, even as he's pulling pants on.

I'm momentarily distracted by the two bare-chested men glaring at each other. My mind stutters, throwing images of being sandwiched between them, but I shake my head.

"When was the last time you saw Alex?"

"I don't know, right before lunch? He went off to sulk, so I let him. What's the big deal? You know what he's like when he's got something up his ass," Shane says, shrugging on a shirt.

"He didn't come home last night."

"He was probably blowing off steam. I'm not his mommy. He doesn't have a curfew, Ren. Is that seriously why you woke me up?"

Shane goes to pull off his shirt to crawl back under the sheets, but Ren shoves the tablet he's holding in Shane's face. Lips pursed, Shane studies it, then scowls. Glancing at me, he grabs his phone and starts tapping away.

"Umm, someone want to let me know what's going on?"

The look on Shane's face is accusatory, but I haven't seen Alex for days. Unless you count when I was passed out. I don't know how it could possibly be my fault whatever shit Alex got himself into.

"Get dressed" is all I get in return before they're striding out of the room.

As annoyed as I am, I dig through the bags quickly, finding everything I could need—all in my size. Apparently, Ren went shopping again. How he accomplished that in less than a day is beyond me, but I really don't care as I pull on a black hoodie and hustle out of the room.

I can hear their voices long before I make it to Shane's office. Obviously, Alex didn't go for a midnight stroll. Shane is barking orders down the phone, and Ren is typing on his laptop when I slip inside. Everything is a jumble. I plant myself in a chair, pulling out my phone to see if I can find my own answers. I skim through my messages, finding Alex's thread and seeing an unread message from after one in the morning.

Don't leave. Stay.

Then three minutes later.

I'm sorry.

I stare at those two words. They seem ominous now, knowing he's not here. I start to type, asking him where he is, when the phone is ripped from my hands, despite my cry of outrage. Ren glances down, reading the messages, then looks back to me. He holds it out for Shane, who curses and goes back to shouting down the line at someone.

"Was this the plan, Sam?" Ren asks quietly.

"I have no idea what's going on, so I'm going to say no."

He stares at me, searching my face for something, then nods before reaching for his tablet, my phone still clutched in his hands.

"Do you know where this is?"

Ren hands me the screen and starts tapping away at my phone. I think about protesting him using it, but I doubt he'll listen. A map is pulled up, a red pin marking a spot in the Byrns' territory.

"The Depot."

"You're sure?"

I roll my eyes. I've spent half my life at the Depot, but he doesn't know that. I nod instead of snarling back. Their reactions are starting to freak me out.

"Is Alex at the Depot?" I ask.

"His phone is. Has been since right after he texted you."

Ren is still studying me, as if I'll have some great insight or start spilling secrets of a master kidnapping plan. I meet his eyes, knowing I have nothing to do with this, but my mind is whirling. Why would Alex go there? What was he looking for? Is Victor keeping him there? It doesn't make sense. The Kings aren't our enemy, no matter what accusations Colin's thrown out. I told Colin they weren't behind anything, and I assume he passed my revelations on to Victor.

"Well, let's go get him," I say, standing.

Shane scoffs. "Sit down, Princess. You're not going anywhere."

"You can't honestly think I had anything to do with this!"

Push and pull. Back and forth. Trusting and questioning. I can never catch a break with these guys.

"You're injured."

I wave away Ren's words, rolling my eyes.

"You got fucking shot, Sam. You really think we're going to let you run off just to get yourself shot again? I've seen enough of your blood to last me a goddamn lifetime." Shane barks.

His words stop my retort, and his phone rings. He turns away, breaking the connection between us.

"Ren, there's no way you're going to sneak in without me."

"I'm pretty good at getting into places I shouldn't be able to."

"So, you've got some fancy computer skills . . ." I roll my eyes again. "This is different."

"Why is that?"

"Because even if you do somehow override the system, if you encounter anyone, they'll shoot first and ask questions later. That place is crawling with guys in the Byrns' gang. You won't be able to crawl in and out of a window. You need me."

I tap down the surge of panic Victor ordered my safehouse burned. A shiver rolls through me. No matter what happens, I need to get Alex out of this mess, since I'm sure I'm the reason he's there in the first place.

"You think you'll be able to actually convince anyone we come across they should let us pass? You realize we might have to harm them to get Alex back, right?"

"As long as they're not the ones who shot me, I say we have a good chance at them listening to me."

"They didn't. It was the Guild," he states matter-of-factly, leaving me stunned as he turns away.

How many other secrets are they keeping from me? I'm about to demand answers when I remember the larger crisis at hand. I'm not worried Alex is in danger. Even Victor knows if he makes a move against the Kings, he'll start a war. He's not that stupid . . . I hope.

I march over to them, huddled over the computer. "We'll be talking about all the shit you guys have been keeping from me later, but we're wasting time here. The sooner we get over there, the sooner Alex is home. Can I have a gun?"

"You're not going, Princess. Ren can handle this on his own." He spins in his chair, shutting me down—again.

"Okay."

I reach under his desk and find his hidden weapon. I check it, finding a full magazine, and slip it into my waistline, walking out the door before they've noticed. I make it halfway down the hall before Shane is bellowing after me. I ignore him, grabbing my shoes from his room, but he's blocking the door when I turn back.

"Why can't you just listen?!"

"Because you're being stupid. I'm fine. I know my own limits, and this isn't one of them. So, I can go with Ren, or we can meet there, and I'll end up saving them both when his ass gets caught, too. Choice is yours, boss."

He curses, glancing at Ren over his shoulder. At his second nod, he swears again and moves out of the way. He snatches the weapon from my pants as I pass him, despite my protest.

Shane eyes me and hands me a smaller gun before striding to his office without a backward glance. I follow Ren the opposite way. I hope I'm not going to regret insisting on going along, because walking back into the Byrns' territory could very well be my downfall.

THIRTY-SEVEN

ALEX

The walls are mocking me. The chair I'm sitting in is the only piece of furniture in this white box of walls. It's my own stupidity that landed me here, but I'm still going to cuss out every fucking person who walks through the door as if this is their fault. I'm not worried about being in here. It isn't like they'll kill me. The last thing Victor needs is to start a war with the Kings. Killing me will definitely accomplish that. They might rough me up a little, try to force info from me, but nothing too severe.

Glancing at the camera in the corner of the room, I wave to give them a little entertainment. They stuck me in here hours ago, taking my phone, but didn't bother to take my weapons. They didn't even check for any. I contemplate shooting the handle, but resign myself to waiting instead. I wonder if they know how crazy I can be. Probably not, based on my public persona. Victor doesn't seem to understand the nuances of running a criminal operation.

I've just started daydreaming, with Sam front and center, when the handle jiggles, swinging open to reveal Victor and Colin. I expected the wannabe leader to be immaculately dressed, like Shane described, but his suit is rumpled, eyes dull. It looks like taking over for Mason has taken its toll on him. It isn't an easy job; some people aren't up for it. Victor is apparently one of those people.

"What's up, Colin?" I ask, meeting his tired eyes. It looks like he hasn't slept in weeks.

"Alex King. I must confess, when Colin told me you were here, I didn't believe him. I mean, why in the world would Shane's right-hand man be spying on our operations?"

He's trying to be intimidating, but it only comes across as contrived, as if he's playing a part he can't quite pull off. It's like he's never had to be someone's worst nightmare before. Weird.

"Seals only sleep for a minute and a half at a time," I answer, plastering a bored look on my face.

He rears back but waves away my words, pacing around the room while Colin leans against the wall. Hopefully, we can get this little song and dance over soon, and I'll be back home before Shane and Ren realize I'm gone. I'll catch hell for sure. I can only hope they were able to keep Sam home safe. If she's out there, I'll track her down and bring her ass back, make them see she needs to be with us. It's the only reason I care about being locked up here.

"You know, it's amazing to me what a person will put on their phone. Didn't used to be a problem in my day, but alas, everything is right there at your fingertips if you know where to look."

He avoids my eyes, but it doesn't matter. I smother my grin, tasting the lies in the air.

Ren put more security on our phones than I can wrap my head around. I hated it at first, since I've locked myself out more times than I can count, but I'm glad he didn't give in when I demanded he remove it. I smile at Victor, though. He operates on bluffing. Unfortunately, he isn't very good at it. He's not a good leader, he's not a good bluffer, and he's not very intimidating. Three strikes and all that. It really makes me wonder what the hell Colin is playing at by allowing Victor to take over.

"I'm sorry you're old."

His glare is worth it, plus the snort Colin covers with a cough.

"What are your plans, boy?"

Rolling my eyes at his attempt to insult me, I fiddle with the peeling leather on the arm of my chair.

"Did you know humans are the only species whose brains shrink?"

The confusion filling his face is priceless. I think he'll hit me, but he continues pacing back and forth.

"Who is supplying Oracle in the city?"

"You know, a bag of weed was the first thing ever sold on the internet . . ." Victor's face is getting redder by the minute.

"Who are you selling the people you kidnap to?" It takes everything I have to not react to his question. He can't think we have anything to do with the kidnappings, unless he's trying to throw the heat off himself, but the intensity in his eyes tells me he's not behind this.

"Jellyfish are biologically immortal. They don't age and won't die unless they are killed. But since they have no brains, I doubt they appreciate how amazing they are."

He throws up his hands, thoroughly frustrated with me, which is the goal. He'll either let something slip or let me go if I can piss him off enough. Then, maybe this trip won't be a waste of time after all. Victor spins around, charges toward me, and grabs the front of my jacket to haul me up. I let him to see what he'll do.

I expect him to throw a punch, but he shakes me a little. Nostrils flaring and teeth clenched, I catch the vein bulging in his temple, threatening to burst under the stress he's buried under. I almost feel bad for the man.

"Where is she?" he spits out through gritted teeth, shaking me again.

I stare at him, keeping my mask in place. The last thing I'm going to do is give away Sam's location to this deranged man. Victor lets out an anguished cry and shoves me back in the chair. He spins back, trying to get himself under control, while Colin sits there, giving nothing away. I can't tell if he doesn't care or is successfully hiding his worry. Maybe this is typical for Victor, and he's used to this erratic behavior.

We sit in silence while Victor gets a grip on what little sanity he has left. As much as I want to piss him off, I don't want to tip him over the edge completely. Facing me again, he smooths down his wrinkled suit, opening his mouth to probably continue his interrogation—if you can call it that—when a knock at the door cuts him off.

Neither of them move. The look between Victor and Colin is telling. Victor presses his lips into a thin line, and I hold back another grin. They didn't tell anyone else I'm being kept here.

"Come in!" I call in a sing-song voice.

Victor glares at me; Colin pulls out a gun. The door rattles on its hinges, undoubtedly locked, then everything goes quiet again. I'm about to call out again, when a barrel is pointed at me, Colin's blank face on the other end.

"Put that away! We're not here to start a war," Victor hisses, flapping his hands in Colin's direction.

The gun is tucked away as Colin backs away. I let out a sigh, relaxing back in the chair, as a beep sounds from outside, and the door clicks open.

My mouth drops open when Ren and Sam stroll in. I bite back a curse, seeing Ren's glare as his eyes sweep up and down, searching for injuries. So much for the plan of getting out of here before they found out where I am. I skim my gaze over Sam, hope blooming in my chest. Thank god she didn't leave. I'd rather her be anywhere but here, but relief floods through me at the sight of her.

Her snarky smile she's shooting at Victor makes me want to grab her and do all sorts of dirty things to her.

"Hello, Uncle. We're here for that one," she quips, gesturing in my direction.

I stand, grinning at her. Ren is muttering under his breath, but I ignore him. Victor is still gaping like a fish, while Colin's stare is boring a hole in her head.

He's pissed, like being with us is an affront to him personally. Too fucking bad. I don't care what Shane or Ren says now. I'm keeping her. Colin will catch a bullet before I let her go back to the Byrns' estate. She'd be dead before she walked through the door, I'm convinced.

"Sam, what are you doing?" Colin sneers, eyes fixed on Ren now.

"More than you're currently accomplishing," she says coldly. "Victor, get your head out of your ass and start leading. You want everyone to think you're not completely useless. Stop making the Kings the enemy. We're going. I suggest you set up a meeting with Shane. Alex?"

Finally, she meets my eyes, her face a mask, but concern and relief flood her eyes. I can't help beaming at her, watching her cheeks heat as I study her. I start toward her, and her eyebrow pops up when I wrap my arm around her waist, planting a kiss on her cheek. Victor's choking is an added bonus.

"Hey, Bug, good to see you."

"Start walking, dumbass," she mutters out the corner of her mouth. I pout, catching the small twitch of her lips.

We're almost to the door when Victor recovers and calls out, "Well, I can't say I'm surprised you deserted your family. You were always one to be taken in by a pretty face."

I try to pivot, but Sam's nails dig into my leg, warning me to keep walking. Ren pauses, a look of contemplation on his face while he peers at Sam. She subtly shakes her head.

But Victor isn't done as he sneers at her. "I always knew you were a disgrace. A useless whore. With Mason no longer able to share his power, I knew you would run to whomever would take you. Is it just this one? Or are you fucking all three?"

I'm moving before I've fully registered what I'm doing, but the shit he's heaping on Sam, I can't stand for. My fist flies and connects with his face. Blood flies from his nose. I'm sure I broke it, and a grim satisfaction flows through me. I'll take my pound of flesh from him and lay it at her feet. She can do it herself, but she won't. She'll never attack him, for fear of what the retaliation would be. At this moment, I'll take whatever the repercussions are, if only to make him regret everything he's ever said to her.

Sam's voice cuts through the blood pounding in my ears. She's shouting at Ren, telling him to stop me, but Ren is letting me do this for the both of us. He may play his cards close to the chest, but I've seen him. He watches her in a way he's never watched a woman before. He might never admit it, but he wants her as badly as the rest of us. I grin, hitting Victor once more as he cowers. How this excuse of a human being was ever able to take over for Mason is beyond me. A click of a hammer snaps me out of my haze, and I freeze, still panting, Victor's blood trickling from my knuckles.

I ignore the weapon Colin is pointing at me, crouching down where Victor is recoiling. "If you so much as breathe her name again, your life will be forfeit."

Slowly rising, I nod to Colin before heading for the door, grabbing Sam along the way. We're out, and Sam tries to pull from my grasp, but I grip her tighter, needing to keep her close to absorb she's okay. We make it to the car before Ren starts in on me, but I don't care because she stayed. She's here. She came for me.

THIRTY-EIGHT

SAMANTHA

Alex prattles in the backseat, but I doubt Ren is paying attention. I'm certainly not. Last I checked, he was lamenting about the lack of leg room in Ren's car. I, on the other hand, am reliving Victor's words, but they don't phase me anymore. He's said it all before, and I'm sure he'll say them again. Although, with Alex's threat hanging in the air, he might think twice next time. Probably not, though; Victor isn't the brightest, but it doesn't matter.

My emotions are a jumbled mess, so I keep quiet, content to gaze out the window. I can hardly remember what vileness Victor threw at me. The only thing they do is remind me of Shane. When he told me I was worthless, I believed him. I thought I pushed them aside, brushed them off as easily as I do Victor's, but that's a lie. They've burrowed deep and made me feel less than. Trying to reconcile the man who can cut me down so effortlessly, with the one who held me last night, is impossible. Alex's defense of me to my uncle only worsens things, confusing me more.

At least I understand Alex. Between our encounters and the many conversations over texts, I know what I'm getting when it comes to him. Alex doesn't have many secrets. Then again, what do I know? He could be hiding his darker side beneath layers of flirting and sarcasm.

Alex is still talking when we pull into the King estate. He pops out as soon as we've stopped, but I stay put. Ren sighs, watching his friend bound up the steps as Shane opens the door, scowl firmly set in place. His face will freeze like that if he keeps it up.

"Well, that was unexpected," Ren comments in a low tone.

"What did you expect? Victor saw an opportunity; he was going to take it."

"I wasn't talking about that, but I'm sure you were aware of that," he murmurs, eyeing me.

I ignore him. The last thing I'm going to do is discuss what Victor said or the aftermath. I'm sure Shane will have enough to say about everything when they tell him. Glancing at Alex, I watch him reenact how he handed Victor his ass beating, while Shane's face turns to me, eyes narrowing, as if it's my fault Alex decided to take matters into his own hands. I didn't ask him to defend me. In fact, I actively tried to stop him. Admittedly, I didn't try hard, but neither did Ren. I'll be blamed regardless. It's the way things work around here.

I sigh, pushing out of the seat, ready to face whatever bullshit Shane is about to throw at me. I'm sure he's reconsidering offering me a place to stay. In fact, I'm not sure how long that offer is available. Maybe it was only for last night. I haven't had time to come up with an alternative. Hopefully, he'll give me more than a few minutes to get my shit and get the hell out. Come to think of it, I don't have any shit to pack. He could just toss my ass to the curb and shut the door in my face.

My footsteps are heavy as I plod up the stairs. Alex is pushing inside, talking about a shower. Ren hasn't followed, throwing me to the wolves to deal with this all on my own. Not surprising, but it still stings. I stop and wait in front of Shane, meeting his gaze. He's going to have to start the conversation if he wants to be rid of me. He shakes his head and turns to make his way in the house.

I peer back at Ren still sitting in his car, trying to figure out what just happened, but Ren gives me a half smirk and pulls out again. I think about running after him and begging him to take me, too. I don't care where he's going at this point. Anywhere is better than sitting in the Kings' house, having no idea what I'm supposed to be doing. Through the open door, Alex and Shane have disappeared. By the time I decide pleading with Ren is the better option, he's turning out the driveway.

I wander around, poking my head into various rooms to catalog the differences between my house and theirs. I'm still confused why they're a complete mirror of each other. I'm too tired to solve another mystery today. Shane's back is to me when I walk into the kitchen. I think about turning around and getting lost in the halls, but at some point, we'll need to get this over, so I plop myself on to a stool and wait.

After several minutes I'm antsy, shifting back and forth. I wish I had a snack, but getting up to dig through his cupboards seems a little too . . . something. I'm about to start messing around on my phone when he turns and leans against the counter. He watches me over the rim of his mug. I gather my armor when he sets the cup down, hoping my walls stay intact this time. It's failed me at every turn with this man, but maybe this time, I'll come out unscathed. He doesn't say a word, though, setting a plate with a sandwich on it in front of me, picking up his coffee again.

Eyeing the food, then him, I purse my lips. "Is it poisoned?"

"It's ham."

I crinkle my nose before I catch myself and mutter a 'thank you.' I try to sneak a glimpse of him from under my lashes, but he catches me and scowls.

"What?" I ask, not touching the food.

"Nothing. Eat, Sam."

I brace myself, taking a small bite, humming and using the sandwich to gesture at him. I barely chew before swallowing, almost making myself choke.

"For fuck's sake, it's not poisoned," he growls, setting a glass of water in front of me, which I grab like a lifeline before gulping down half of it in one go.

"I didn't think it was." I take another bite, getting mostly bread this time. Maybe I can eat the crust and convince him I'm full.

"Then, why the hell are you nibbling at it like a baby bird?"

"I'm not that hungry." I scrunch my nose as I look at the food.

"You haven't eaten since yesterday. What's wrong with it?" he says, leaning on the counter, demanding I meet his eye.

"Nothing! I appreciate you making me food."

His eyes narrow on my face. "You're lying. What's wrong with it?"

I roll my eyes, mumbling out, "I don't like ham."

His eyebrows shoot up in shock, and he takes a step back.

"Why didn't you just say so?"

"Uh, because you made me a sandwich. It's probably the nicest thing you've done for me. I wasn't going to complain. I mean, I'm a bitch, but I'm not an asshole."

"You're not a bitch. A spoiled little princess, but not a bitch. Give me that." He snatches the plate.

"So, I'm spoiled because I don't like ham? That's ridiculous."

My stomach rumbles. I am hungry, and I would have eaten it, even if I didn't like ham.

"*You're* ridiculous," he mutters.

"Great comeback."

I hop up to find something to eat myself.

"Sit your ass back down," he says, flinging the fridge open and pulling out another plate. As he unwraps and sets the food down, I slink back to the seat.

Tentatively, I pick up the sandwich, thanking my stars it's turkey. I don't register Shane's presence after my first bite, too focused on eating. When I'm licking the mayo from my finger, an apple, cut into slices appears on my plate. I look up while munching on them and find Shane is still watching me.

"What?" I say around a mouthful.

"What happened at the Depot?"

"Thought Alex would have filled you in by now."

We stare at each other, waiting for the other to break first. He shakes his head as I crunch into another slice. He's got questions, but I'm not going to hand out info willy-nilly. I tried more than once before with him, and it was a disaster. I'm not going to put myself in that position again. I don't know if I can make it through another one of his tirades.

"Listen, Princess, I'm only going to say this once . . ." His gaze skips away.

I slip another apple into my mouth, giving him time. It doesn't sound like he's kicking me out, so I can be patient.

He takes a deep breath. "I'm sorry."

"What exactly are we talking about?" My eyebrows shoot up, trying to decipher the look on his face.

"All that shit before."

He still won't meet my eyes.

"What shit?"

"You're really going to make me say it? Fuck, Sam," Shane snaps, running his hand through his hair.

My eyes go wide. "Shane, I am not fucking with you here. I have no idea what you're talking about. So, yeah, you're going to have to be more specific."

He focuses on me, frowning, but it quickly morphs to resignation. He scrubs his face, teeth clenched, before taking another deep breath. He looks like he's hyping himself up for battle.

"I'm sorry I was an asshole to you before. It's an excuse, but I thought you were some airhead who was trying to weasel her way into shit here for whatever reason because of what happened to your brother. Obviously, shit has changed now, but I thought I should say something."

"Hmm" is all I give him.

This is the last thing I expected. He's right, things have changed, but can I trust his words? He's still keeping things from me. It feels like he's only apologizing to use me or pull more information from me, something I'd do if I were in his position.

"Well?" He bites his lip, anticipation shining in his eyes.

But how do I trust myself to read him?

After a beat, I say, "Thank you" and stuff the last apple slice in my mouth.

"Seriously? That's it? You don't want to, I don't know, yell at me or something?"

"Nope," I pop the p because it makes the vein in his forehead pulse.

"We're going to have to work together, you know. So, if you've got something to say, now is the time." He narrows his eyes at me.

"Oh, that's not how this works. See, if I want to yell at you later, I can. Like if I find out you kept something crucial from me, then I reserve the right to go batshit crazy," I warn.

"Fine." He pauses, scanning my face. "Talk to Ren when he gets back."

"About what?" I swivel on the stool, tracking his retreating form.

"Everything."

I sigh, dropping the plate in the sink, and wander through the house again, finding myself in front of Alex's door.

"Alex?" I tap on the door, not wanting to wake him. It's the middle of the afternoon, but he was out all night. Personally, I need a nap, but I have to check on him first. I'm hiding it as best I can, but the ache in my side is getting worse the longer I'm on my feet. I may have pushed myself a little too far going to the Depot, but I won't admit anything to Shane.

"Come in."

His muffled reply comes, so I crack the door, finding the room dark. Shit, he is sleeping. I go to pull it shut again quietly, but him calling my name stops me.

"Sorry, I didn't mean to wake you. I'll come back later," I say, trying to leave again.

"Get in here, Bug." He calls out when I hesitate. "Don't make me get up and drag you in."

His room is smaller than Shane's, but not by much. I glimpse a walk-in closet with clothes strewn all over the floor, the bathroom next to it, but it's dark, and on every table, books. They're stacked everywhere. I spy the book he wanted to bid on at the gala all those months ago on his bedside table. I can't imagine how much he ultimately paid for it, but he just threw it on the table like a heathen.

The light peeking around the edges of the curtains is enough to find him propped up on an elbow in the middle of a king-sized bed, gazing owlishly at me. I stop inside the door, no longer sure what I'm doing. I should have texted him instead, but after my conversation with Shane, I didn't know where to go. I wandered around the house, but settling anywhere seemed . . . awkward. I went back to the spare room I stayed in before, but the bed had been stripped. I don't belong anywhere.

"I wanted to make sure you were okay," I murmur, wringing my hands. I forced myself to stop when his gaze dips to them, and I drop them limply by my sides instead. It's a nervous habit I thought I did away with long ago, but around these guys, it reappears, without me noticing. It's why I wear a hoodie most of the time. It gives me something to do with my hands—plus, they hold a lot of snacks.

"Feelin' a bit nervous there, Bug?" he grins.

"No." I give him a withering look, which doesn't faze him in the slightest. "I didn't think you'd answer if you were out. I'll let you get back to sleep." I wave lamely at the bed, intent on getting as far away from this room as possible.

"Wait!" He hops up, or at least tries to, but his legs are tangled in the bed sheets, and he stumbles to the floor with an *oomph*.

I try, I really do, but the giggle is past my lips before I can stuff it back in. His head snaps up, grouchy face in place and snarls at me, but that only makes me laugh harder. Watching him try to disentangle himself is even better, since he still can't stand. I sober a bit when I find he's only in his boxer briefs, but I still can't stop giggling.

"Sure, laugh at me instead of helping," he mutters, getting himself free and standing.

"Whoops." I grin, not one bit ashamed. "Well, see you later!"

I wave and spin, but he catches me before I can slip away. As he wraps his arms around my waist, I gasp at the pinch of pain. He swings me up, concern filling his eyes.

"Sorry, I forgot," he says, bringing me over to the bed and laying me down almost in the middle before trying to lift my shirt.

"It's fine—pinched a little, is all. Don't worry about it."

He glares at me until I drop the hem of my shirt and let him look. His touch is gentle as he peels off the bandages and examines the wound, brushing his fingers back and forth, then presses a kiss next to the stitches before pulling my shirt down.

I expect questions or a lecture, but he fixes the sheets. Usually, he doesn't stop talking, even while we text. He'll send fourteen rapid-fire messages, then asks why I'm not responding. He's tired, but it feels like more, as if he's content to just be. He slides next to me, covering us up, then gingerly wraps an arm around my waist, pulling me close. I freeze, worrying about what this all means.

"Relax, Sam," he breathes.

"I should go," I whisper back.

"Why?"

I contemplate lying, making some excuse, but his bed is comfortable, and all I want is to sink into him, but I don't know how to tell him I spent last night in Shane's bed.

"Uh, well . . . I kind of spent last night . . ."

"Yeah, I know. Is it weird for you?"

"No. Yes. I don't know." I puff out a breath, trying to find the words to explain. "It feels like I *should* feel weird about it."

"But it doesn't actually bother you, right?"

"I guess not . . ."

"Don't worry about what you *should* feel. Just . . . be. You good being here with me?" His chest pushes into my back as he holds his breath, waiting for my response.

"Yeah," I exhale, relaxing a little.

"Good."

The smile in his voice evident. He kisses my head and cuddles closer. I drift off, feeling safer than I have in a long time.

I wake with a moan in my throat. My body heated in all the right places, my bones like jelly. I snap fully awake when something nips my inner thigh. I flip the covers up, meeting Alex's glittering emerald gaze from between my legs. The cheeky bastard shimmied my leggings and panties off while I slept and is pressing kisses against my flesh.

I attempt to speak, but he takes the opportunity to put his tongue to use, licking from slit to clit, making me shudder and moan again. Leisurely, he swirls around my clit, taking his time to explore, and I whimper when he pulls back, spreading my legs farther to gaze at the wetness gathering there. My pussy clenches, silently begging him.

Alex's head swoops down, devouring me, humming when sounds escape my throat. I want it to be done and to never end all at the same time. He brings me to the brink, then eases back, never letting me crash over the edge. My hands move of their own accord, tugging at his hair to urge him on. My hips follow every time he swoops down to circle me until, at last, he slips a finger in and sucks on the sensitive bud. My eyes slam shut, and a million stars burst behind my lids. My sanity pinwheels away, leaving a quivering mess in its wake.

He keeps pumping his finger in and out steadily while I sink back into my body, my breaths coming out heavily. His body covers mine.

Bit by bit, he runs kisses up my skin the whole way. I run my fingers down his sides, tracing his abs, following the tattoos outlined on his chest. My hips chase his fingers again, but he keeps his pace steady. A slow-building ecstasy is replacing the explosiveness of before.

"Hi there, Bug," he chuckles, burying his face into my neck, biting and kissing up to my jaw before taking my lips. I can taste myself on him, which I never thought would turn me on, but a heady feeling comes over me. I try to reach down to take him in hand, force him to slip inside me, but he captures my wrists and holds them above my head.

"Ah, ah . . . not yet," he whispers against my lips. "I'm going to take my time with you. If you touch my cock right now, I won't be able to stop myself from devouring you . . . again."

He runs his hand down my arm along my side all the way to my hip, carefully avoiding my wound. He pulls his fingers from me and licks them clean, eyes smoldering. His cock is nestled between my thighs when he lowers his hips. I wiggle enough for him to slip in, but his hand holds me still, rubbing his length against me. With every stroke, he hits my clit, and my body spasms.

"Alex . . ." I babble.

"Hmm?"

"Please . . ." I breathe out, trying to pull him closer.

He shifts, gliding into me. I'm so wet he doesn't have to work for it at all. I gasp when he's fully seated, tilting my head back, and letting my eyes fall closed. His groan echoes through the bedroom when he stops, his cock twitching inside of me. I squirm when I can't stand it anymore, trying to create friction. My pussy tenses around him, and he grunts, resting his forehead on mine.

He's working to draw this out, to give us both an experience, but he's wound me too tight to wait. He drags his cock out before delving in again. I bring my leg up to wrap around his waist, but he grabs my ankle and pushes my knee to my chest instead, his thrusts becoming faster, harder. Our pants fill the room as he slams into me over and over. My orgasm is coiling tighter, making my legs shake. Alex guides my hand between us, using my fingers to rub my clit. His mouth latches on to my nipple and bites hard enough to send a shock of pleasure mixed with pain, straight to my core.

"Eyes on me, Sam. I want your eyes on me when you come around my cock," he grinds out.

His words tip me beyond reason, and I'm spasming around him. I hear him stutter out a groan over the pounding in my head, my body quivering and stalling. The aftershocks as he shallowly thrusts in and out are bolts of ecstasy, electrifying my nerves as he lowers my leg gently.

Alex rests his head on my chest, panting and saying nonsense words into my skin. His hands run up and down my side, sparking shivers along the way. I hold on to the feeling of complete serenity of this moment as tightly as I can, but it ebbs away.

"Wow," I sigh out, blinking at the ceiling.

"You're welcome," he says into my flesh. I shoot my hand out, smacking his side, while his body shakes with suppressed laughter.

THIRTY-NINE

REN

I glance at my watch for the fifth time in ten minutes. I don't like sitting in the open for this long, but Ryker Helms insisted this meeting happen in public. The bookstore I'm in has a little cafe stuffed in the back. I take advantage by grabbing a coffee while I wait for him to show his face. I have a book to blend in. Apparently, that's a waste, as most others around me are buried in their phones.

A man in his late twenties approaches, clearly part of Helms's MC. Their tattoo peeks out from his shirt and curls up his neck.

I nod, peering casually around to spot Helms or anyone else, but all I see are giggling kids pulling their parents along and older people rumbling about.

"King?" he asks gruffly when he reaches me.

I nod, trying to not show my annoyance Helms isn't here himself.

"Prez will be here in a minute. We ran into a little trouble before we got here." He settles into the seat across from me.

"Nothing too serious, I hope."

"Nah, just the dickhead running the Byrns' clan."

Helms appears, preventing me from asking anything more. Victor is making more than one enemy in the city. I contemplate again whether he could be in league with the Guild, but it doesn't add up. Unless he's getting something more than leading the Byrns' empire. From what I've gathered, he isn't. It would be plausible if Victor thinks he can control the Guild and is now reaping the consequences of those actions.

"Ren, we need to make this quick. Victor is demanding an audience with me and causing a ruckus at one of my bars. You wouldn't happen to know why, would you?" Helms's eyes pierce into me, but I'm not phased.

"Might have something to do with Samantha Byrns staying with us at the moment," I drawl.

"No shit. She good?"

I quirk an eyebrow at him. He seems . . . concerned. I still don't understand their relationship.

"She's fine. Ran into some trouble, but we were able to get out."

"Anything to do with that house burning to the ground the other night? Heard there was a gunfight right before it went up in flames."

Of course he knows what happened. Shane told me to share everything, but I'm still hesitant to give him information on Sam. The last thing we need is someone else going after her. Watching Helms, knowing Sam and Shane trust him, I should to let go of my wariness.

"It was a safehouse she was staying in. Like I said, she's fine."

"You know who's behind it? Same guys bringing this shit in to our city and snatching people?"

"The Guild," I reply, watching his reaction intently. He scowls, cursing before whipping out his phone to shoot off a text before meeting my gaze again.

"We're in the shit, then. Got some connections south of us who dealt with them a while ago. I'll reach out to find out how they pushed them out. They might be able to send some guys to help. I got another group up near Harris who might be able to step up as well."

He's lumping us together as a team. Shane assured me Helms would work with us, but even after the attempted coup a decade ago, I'm still not convinced. Sure, we've run our sections of the city peacefully since then, but that can change in an instant. Exhibit A: Victor Smith.

"I'm sure we'd all appreciate any additional information we can get our hands on. We're sending out the word to the lower gangs on both sides. The Guild tries to sway them to overthrow the larger gangs in whatever city they're trying to take, so assuring them we're handling things will go a long way," I tell him, checking the time again.

"We know where they're trying to set up the Trade?" Helms asks.

His companion, who's been silent for most of the conversation, chimes in before I can answer. "What's the Trade?"

I look to Helms to answer, but he's absorbed with his phone.

"The Guild is primarily a sex trafficking outfit. They come into cities, slowly trying to take more ground, until they can take out whomever is in charge-gangs, police, mafia, MCs. Once they do, they establish the Trade, and the Auction. The Auction is for the elite. Ultra-rich VIPs who are looking to purchase someone whom they can, then do whatever they want to. The Trade is for everyone they don't feel lives up to the Auction's standards. They sell flesh, and they do it well. Obviously, they also dabble in drugs and guns as well, mostly to supplement their real money-maker," I tell him matter-of-factly.

I have to shut off my emotions even more when thinking about the Guild. We might run on the wrong side of the law most of the time, but we draw the line at stealing away people's lives.

"It's vile is what it is," Helms says. "So, we got a location?"

"Sam thinks they'll try to take the Depot. It might be to our benefit to meet with Victor. We'd rather not step in and direct their lower gangs if we can help it, but we won't ignore them at the expense of the city. He's not exactly keen on working with us at the moment," I add. Better to get everything out in the open now rather than when Victor spews some bullshit.

"Can't imagine why . . ." he answers knowingly.

"Give us a minute," I tell his man, keeping my gaze on Helms as the other moves far enough away so he can't overhear.

"I trust Blue, you know," Helms says, looking both affronted and intrigued.

"I doubt he knows what I'm about to ask you. I'm fairly certain I discovered a potential ally for us. Someone with a particular skill set that would help in this instance, and I believe she's currently residing in my house."

Ryker sits back, breathing heavily. His reaction is all I need to confirm what I'd suspected since I followed Sam into the Barrens weeks ago. From what Shane shared about his meeting with Sam and Helms, I'm sure he knows as well.

"How'd you find out?" he asks, gazing around the space.

"I looked."

He sighs, shaking his head. "She know?"

"I haven't discussed things with her yet. From what I hear, neither have you. How long have you known?"

"Years. But that's a story for another time, and not one I'll share with you. I'll meet with Victor, see what his dumb ass wants. Make it clear he needs to make the right decision. I'm sure he'll try to say we go after the Kings, seeing as how you stole their princess."

I nod, I suspecting as much.

"As long as we're on the same page with where we sit. I'll be in touch." He disappears into the crowd, his man following behind.

I check my phone; it's after five. Cursing under my breath, I make my way home, strangely charged and subdued at Shane's order to give Sam everything I possess on both her and her family.

Twenty minutes later, I stroll into Alex's room, not caring one way or another whether they're dressed. Judging by the clothes strewn across the floor and Sam's squeak of protest, I gather they're naked. I make my way to the chair set up by a small table nestled next to the window and pick up one of the books, flipping it over to read the back.

"Please get dressed, Sam. I have some information for you," I say, ignoring Alex's snort of laughter.

"Seriously, Ren?! You couldn't have knocked?" Her voice is muffled by the comforter she's hiding underneath.

"I did knock, but I doubt you heard me over the panting and moaning."

She lets out another squawk, which is followed by a grunt from Alex. He rolls, leaving Sam to continue hiding while rubbing his side where she clearly elbowed him.

"Thanks a lot," he grumbles, pulling on underwear.

"You're welcome." I set the book down. "We need to sit down with Shane later and discuss my meeting."

He's nodding along, searching for pants, when Sam's head pokes out of the sheets covering everything but her head. My mouth twitches, but I hold back my smile. Her auburn hair is mussed, cheeks deliciously red.

No matter how adorably sexed up she looks right now, it isn't from me. Soon enough, she'll be cursing my name, so I hold my smirk back, looking out the window instead.

"What meeting?" she questions.

"I met with Helms this afternoon, among other things. I'd rather only go through everything once, so we'll wait until Shane is here. Are you getting dressed or not?"

I observe her from the corner of my eye, but she still doesn't move. Her eyes dip to Alex, who shrugs and walks to the bathroom, shutting the door behind him. Soon after, the shower starts up, but she stays tucked in his bed.

"I don't have all day, Sam."

"Well, you'll just wait a little longer, Ren. I'm a little busy, if you didn't notice."

I suppress whatever emotion shoots through me when she says my name. I can't even identify what it is. It's there whenever she's near, stronger when she speaks to me. I had hoped ignoring it would lessen her potency, her allure, but it only makes it more difficult to remember all the reasons why being intrigued by this woman is disastrous for me.

She was always bound to ensnare Alex. She killed a man in front of him, and that was the beginning of the end for him. He needs someone to protect, someone who doesn't actually need the protection. Alex fills a bleakness within Sam. The fact she's never annoyed by his incessant rambling is a miracle.

Shane's slow descent into her isn't surprising, either, if one knows him well enough. Sam is a challenge perfectly tailored for him. Finding someone who understands our world, who can stand and live through it, is rare. As soon as Shane is able to move past her last name, he will be lost in her, if he isn't already. Neither Shane nor Sam trust easily, but once it's gained, they will be fiercely loyal.

Sam clears her throat, snapping me out of my musings. She shoos me toward the door. I think about ignoring her and see if she'll drop the covers, but my resolve isn't strong enough to withstand the sight. I walk out, finding Shane coming out of his own room. I shut the door quietly behind me. Alex calls out something, and Sam's soft reply follows. I pause, trying to imagine how this will affect my carefully crafted world, but I can't anticipate the outcome, which pisses me off.

"Hey, How'd it go?" he asks, stopping next to me.

"Fine."

He nods, his eyes fixed on Alex's closed door. "She in there?"

"Are you sure you want to know the answer?"

"I don't care, I just want to make sure she's not sneaking out," he says, still fixated on the wood.

"Sure, you don't," I remark, moving away toward the kitchen.

"Ren," he calls, waiting until I turn back. "If we make it through this, we need to figure out if she fits."

I wait for him to continue, but he just sits there, staring at me.

"Do you want her to fit?"

He sucks in a breath, not answering, his gaze returning to Alex's bedroom.

"Shane, you should be having this conversation with Alex, not me. I'll deal with whatever you decide."

He lets out a short laugh. "Sure, Ren. Let me know when you fall down the rabbit hole."

"Don't hold your breath, brother," I call over my shoulder.

Shane's chuckle follows me, calling my bluff.

FORTY

SAMANTHA

I slip from Alex's room before he's out of the shower. I'm not running away from facing him, but after Ren had walked in, an awkwardness followed. It's one thing for them all to know I've slept with Alex, too, and something different to have it smack them in the face. Alex's advice to do what feels right is all well and good when it only affects me but rubbing in I've fucked Shane and Alex? That affects them all, even Ren. Plus, I've never talked to Shane about what I did with Alex before, and I don't know if I want to have the conversation now, either.

Useless whore.

Victor's words echo through my head, making me stop in my tracks. Is he right? I don't think I'm a whore, but then again, I have no idea how this works. Alex made it clear he doesn't care one way or the other, but maybe that's only to get laid. I don't know where I stand with them, and it freaks me out. I never know what they're thinking

What will Shane think?

What will Ren think?

I shake the words away and start back down the hall. Ren is locked up tighter than Fort Knox. I want him, but I doubt he will ever make a move on me. On some level, I understand him, though I shouldn't be able to. I remember our conversation by the pond. The simple interaction stuck in my mind. With everything coming down around me, he'd been there. He didn't need to sit with me. Ren pulled me away from the brink of giving up completely. He confuses me, but I still feel like I understand him.

I stand between two doors across the hall from one another, contemplating which one Ren went to. One is his bedroom, the other his office. Alex told me to knock and wait, but I'm not about to sit around in the hallway biding my time. Knowing my luck, Shane will come along and ask questions I don't know the answers to.

I try the office first, but he doesn't answer. I turn to the bedroom and knock, listening. I try the door, but it's locked. I smile, knowing how to sneak into this particular room. Then I push open a false panel in his room, grinning. Some doors in the tunnels are locked from my side, but I took the ones connecting the interior. Seems after my little escape, Shane was a tiny bit paranoid.

Ren's room is exactly how I pictured it. The same layout as Alex's, but everything is in its place. It's lived in, but there are no clothes on the floor, no books whatsoever, no messy bed. I glance into his bathroom, seeing more of the same.

I think about unlocking the door to fuck with him, but I'm not looking to get shot again, so I settle in a chair and wait. The sun sinks lower as an hour passes, casting shadows throughout the room while I doze, wondering if he'll ever come. My neck and my side aches.

I'm about to give up and go find him when the lock clicks. I suppress a grin when he walks in, his face buried in his tablet, so he doesn't notice me. I run through all the ways I can scare him, but I settle for a classic, and I click on the lamp next to me.

"Leave the gun . . ."

I don't get the rest out when Ren has his .45 pointed at me. To my credit, I don't flinch.

"Take the cannoli," I say, smiling, which he doesn't notice.

I watch him as he stalks to his walk-in closet, disappearing from my view, but I can hear him slamming things closed. My smile disappears. Sneaking in his bedroom wasn't as funny as I thought it would be based on his reaction. Ren is obviously a private person. I waltzed in, regardless of his privacy.

I start for the door, reaching for the handle before calling out, "Sorry, I'll be in the . . ."

"How did you get in here, Samantha?" he asks, crossing his arms and leaning against the door frame.

"False panel by your bathroom." I glance over my shoulder. "I'll wait downstairs. Sorry."

"Wait . . ." he says. I freeze, staring at the whorls on the wood in front of me. "Let's just get this over."

I drop my hand and spin around, leaning back on the door instead. No way am I going back to the chair. I've embarrassed myself enough. Ren stares at his feet, brows pulled down, hiding his eyes. I'm cursing myself, knowing I've let myself become too comfortable. It's easy with Alex, with his smile and quickness to laugh, but I still shouldn't have forgotten. These men aren't my friends. They're tentative allies at best. At worst, they still think I'm useless, replaceable, a liability.

After a minute of sitting in silence, I murmur, "I can go. I didn't—"

"What do you want to start with? The videos or you." His gaze is still fixed on his feet.

"What the hell is that supposed to mean?"

My heart pounds. I know what he's going to say, though. I've been waiting for this for days, weeks. His eyes lift, holding me hostage with his gaze. I try to wipe my face of all emotion. It's been only a couple months since Mason was shot, and everything has fallen apart. For years, I've kept shit together, kept my act up, kept moving forward. Now my life is in shambles, what's left scattered at my feet.

"Tell me, Sam, do you know how many surrealists it takes to change a light bulb?"

I blink, connecting the dots. Ren is the one who's been hiring me all these years, sending a riddle just for me. I should have realized it years ago, but I never wanted to look too closely, afraid of what I would find.

"Interesting."

I try to look away but fail. "Yeah, you've said that before."

"You don't come across as ruthless."

"Looks can be deceiving. Shane thought I was a useless socialite until like a week ago, so . . ."

"Being the Wraith is a little more intense than playing at being an airhead, wouldn't you say?" he retorts, the corner of his mouth twitching.

And there it is. I'm finally able to break the connection, tipping my head back, thumping against the door. Denying it is pointless. I'm sure he confirmed with Helms. He was bound to find out if I stuck around long enough, but it's still jarring. At least he hasn't told the others yet. I'm sure I'd be dead if he had. I huff before deciding my next course of action.

"If you're thinking you can get rid of me quietly, I think you should know I'm much harder to kill than you'd think." My eyes drift down, trying to track if he's reaching for his gun.

Bewilderment fills his face instead. "What? Why would I kill you?"

His hands fall, which makes me flinch. He lifts them defensively, shock replacing the confusion. He reaches behind him, and I tense, ready to roll out of the way. I'm hoping the adrenaline will carry me if my stitches rip. Calmly, he pulls his gun out and sets it on the shelf before stepping away.

I narrow my eyes. "I'm not telling you anything about my assignments, so you're wasting your time."

"I didn't ask you about your assignments. I am curious why you think I'd want to kill you, though."

I cock my head. I don't have an answer. It's what Mason told me. I don't tout it around to random people, but he was adamant about not telling the Kings. Maybe it isn't Ren but Shane. At this point, I need to run. I still don't have anywhere to go, but once Ren tells Shane . . . I still need the info Ren has, though. My mind races, planning escape routes and backup plans. I can have him show me the videos, then make a run for it. I lament, leaving behind all the clothes stuffed away in Shane's room, but I'll survive; I always do.

"Why don't you show me the videos, Ren?"

"Oh, no. We're going to finish this first. We're not going to kill you." His intense eyes bore into mine.

"You're right, you're not. I'm sure you could try, but again, I'm not easy to kill."

"What the hell, Sam!" he yells, catching me off guard.

I jolt, though I try to hold it back. I've only heard him this heated from the other end of the phone. I drop my arms, trying to casually reach for the handle. At some point, I'll have to leave, but if he's not going to show me anything, it'll have to be now. I can't shoot him, can't kill him. I'd never be able to pull the trigger. That's the point I've come to with these men, even if they would put me in the ground, were the roles reversed.

"Sam, don't." His voice shakes. "Don't run. I don't know why you think we'd hurt you, but please, don't run."

He takes a step toward me, and I tense. His serious tone, coupled with the strain, is more than I've ever seen from him. His eyes plead with mine. My gut tightens, but I believe him. I'll wait and see what Shane and Alex's reactions are before I relax, but I nod to Ren. For some reason, through all this bullshit, I actually fucking trust him. I just hope doing so doesn't get me killed.

"So, the videos?" I ask, trying to steer us back on track. I don't know what to say after our conversation. I don't know how to reign in my chaotic thoughts. They're seesawing in my mind: trust—don't trust, up and down, back and forth. I'll probably fail at pushing them away, anyway.

He tips his chin to the door, still watching me. "Across the hall. Don't take off, Sam, please."

I step to the side, letting him lead the way. A keypad I hadn't noticed before is nestled next to the door, and we walk into the dark, making me tense again. Seconds later, soft lights flicker to life overhead.

I expect an office like Shane's but am dumbstruck when met with a wall covered in screens. A long desk runs underneath, and I follow it with my eyes, trying to map out the space. I spot the books—hundreds, neatly shelved along the opposite wall. The desk is bare. The walls are bare. The books are probably in alphabetical order. Like his room, the entire space is organized to within an inch of its life.

"Wow . . . this is quite the, uh, setup you've got here."

I scan the room again, trying to find another way out, but there's no way into the tunnels, no windows to sneak through, nothing other than the way we came.

"Sit down." He points to the only chair, and one of the screens flickers to life.

I opt to hover near my escape.

A few clicks later, a video pops up. People are streaming from a building, but I don't recognize it from the angle. Another person fills the screen, then after a bit, walks off screen. An inkling tickles my brain, trying to tell me something, but I can't put my finger on why it matters.

"Can you rewind it?" I ask, my curiosity reeling me in closer. "Who is that?"

"No idea. I was hoping you'd know."

"I don't think . . . there's something . . ." I narrow my eyes, trying to place why the figure feels familiar. "It's the way he walks, I think. There," I say, pointing, "but I can't figure it out."

After watching twice more, I give up, focusing on the other clues. The cars, the men, the drugs—those are undeniably drugs. Oracle. I need to go back to the Barrens, talk to the Byrns' local gangs. A few people who won't tell Victor I stopped by comes to mind. TJ would keep my whereabouts quiet. I should stop by his waystation again.

"This is the other one," Ren says, pulling up another video, "but I'm not sure you're going to want to watch it."

I scoff. "Show me."

"I'm serious, Sam, I can tell you . . ."

"Hit play, Ren. Now."

He shakes his head and presses the button, and I'm instantly thrown back to the night my brother was shot. It's strange watching it from a different perspective, knowing I was there. It's muted, but the clash in my memories from that night fills in the gaps. The light glinting off their guns, the way they pull the dead bodies away when they rush to the window.

"We don't know why they ran," he says, his eyes fixed on the scene.

"I do," I whisper, watching it all unfold again as it restarts. "They threw a smoke bomb in. They thought it would be enough to disorient everyone from returning fire, thinking we'd be afraid of hitting our own in the haze."

"Why did they run?"

"Because they didn't count on me."

"What do you mean?"

"I was on a beam, above the smoke. Those guys," I say, pointing to the ones falling on the screen, "are dead because of me."

I feel no remorse. They attacked us, unprovoked. Seeing it again fills me with rage. The need for revenge threatens to choke me. The Guild did this. They walked into my city, shot my brother, tried to kill Helms, and Colin . . . tried to kill me. Several times over, they've tried to kill me. When I glance at Ren, his eyebrows are low, contemplation on his face. My anger gutters when I remember Helms took care of the men running away on the screen.

His mouth turns down. "We need to talk about your extracurricular activities, Sam."

"No, we don't. You know my secret. I'd prefer you to keep it to yourself, but I have a feeling you won't. So, to make things even, how about you tell me a secret about you?" I swivel to face him, the video still looping over and over in the background, the screen lighting up the space.

"What makes you think I have a secret?" he quips, working to shut things down.

I stroll over to the bookshelf, pretending to peruse the titles, but my focus is on him.

"Guy like you—oh, you've absolutely got secrets. It doesn't need to be something as monumental as mine, just something you haven't told anyone else." I turn, ready to lean against the spines, but I flinch, finding him right in front of me, glaring.

Someone sneaking up on me is not normal. How they keep doing it is beyond me.

"Why would I tell you anything, hmm?" Ren snarls.

"Because I asked."

He narrows his eyes. "No."

"No? Seriously, I tell you I'm the Wraith, but my confession doesn't afford me anything?"

"You didn't tell me you're the Wraith. You confirmed my suspicions. I'm not going to hand you ammo to use against me later." He turns away.

Crossing my arms, I glare at him. "Fine. Don't tell me. See if I fucking care."

Slowly, he swings back, stepping fully into my space, not touching me but close enough that my pulse skips. The glint in his eye is almost menacing, and I suppress a shudder.

"Oh, I think you care very much. I don't think you've ever been told 'no,' so you throw a little temper tantrum, thinking you'll get your way." Ren's hand snakes up, wrapping around my throat. He isn't squeezing, but the look on his face tells me he will, if I give him a reason.

I swallow hard, his hand contracting with the movement. My voice will be anything but steady if I speak. Tingles shoot through my body.

The way he's looking at me, his face half shadowed, makes me clench my thighs together, and I pray he doesn't sense my reaction. I should be worried, scared, but I'm not. This man should intimidate me, put me on edge, especially since he knows things few other people do, but I can't seem to drum up anything but lust for him. He leans in, cedar filling my nose, making me lightheaded.

"Isn't that right, Pet?" he purrs in my ear.

I faintly shake my head, though I have the urge to agree. He growls softly, the sound reverberating through my body. I want to close the distance between us, regardless of his words. He tightens his grip, then abruptly releases me. By the time I've recovered, he's across the room. He's trying to appear unaffected, but he flexes his hand over and over, as if he still has me in his clutches. The ghost of his hand wrapped around my throat remains, imprinted on my neck. Subtly, I draw in a deep breath.

I still haven't moved when he acknowledges me again. He stares at the screens, mostly dark, but his voice is steady when he says, "We need to tell Shane and Alex who you are. They'll probably freak out at first, but we can definitely use you to take out the Guild."

My stomach rolls, then drops. Of course he's going to tell them, and he's only contemplating how he can use me. I doubt Shane will go along with Ren's plan, though. My eyes fall shut, trying to find my center again. This whole fucking day has been a rollercoaster, and it still isn't over. Ren's behavior is another thing to survive. I need to be worried about how the other two will react to Ren's revelation rather than how my body reacts to him. I need a fucking plan.

He's sitting at the computer when I finally open my eyes, working away as if I'm not in the room anymore. I slip out before I can make things worse than they already are. It hits me as I pull the door shut. This is where we've been heading all along, and I was too blinded by my emotions to see. It's time to stop letting my feelings override everything I've been taught. It's time to be the Wraith.

FORTY-ONE

SHANE

“**W**as that as weird as it felt?” I ask Alex after Ren and Sam leave—separately. I wasn't surprised by anything Ren had told us, which made my mind wander while he was talking. It only highlighted the strange behavior between them.

“You mean how Ren made sure to never look at Sam, even when she was talking? Or how Sam kept glancing at the door like she was going to bolt? Maybe it was the way, as soon as we were done, they both were ready to run for the door but then *both* sat down again, like they didn't want to leave together?” Alex raises his eyebrow, a sarcastic smile flirting around his mouth.

“She kept watching Ren, too. I think something happened between them. Any idea what?”

“Nope. Maybe they fucked? She's a little skittish with that shit,” Alex comments, pulling out his phone.

“They definitely haven't. Wait, what do you mean?” I ask, frowning. She wasn't skittish with me.

"Pretty sure Victor's bitchy statements got to her. She said she should feel weird about sleeping with both of us. Might be good if you told her, you don't give a shit."

"What the fuck did he say this time?"

"Called her a useless whore. Why do you think I beat his ass?" Alex shoots me a grin before refocusing on his phone.

I lean back in my chair, scrubbing my face. I wish we could force a regime change. Shit would be a lot easier if Colin was in charge.

"Think we could take Victor out? Install Colin in his place?"

Alex snorts but doesn't respond. Right. This isn't the time, but after we've dealt with the Guild, maybe we can set things in motion. At this point, I don't think Mason is ever going to come out of the coma. I can't deal with years of Victor leading the Byrns. Hell, I'd put Sam in charge before I put up with Victor's shit for the next five years until someone takes him out for being a douchebag.

"Want me to go to the Barrens tonight instead?" he offers, rising to his feet.

"No. I need you talking to the south side gangs. Take Ren with you. I'll go to the Barrens."

"You going to leave Sam here? Cause you know shit won't go down well if you try to leave her behind." He grins. "She can come with us."

"I'm taking Princess with me. She's got better connections down there anyway," I admit, closing my office door behind us.

"Holy hell, was that a compliment, boss? I feel so special!" Sam says.

I spin, finding her in the chair immediately by my office door.

Alex laughs. "You two have fun." He strolls away.

"What's the plan, boss?"

"Stop calling me that," I say, heading to my room.

"We going to the east side? The Barrens? A club?" She skips to my side, excitement rolling off her.

"Why are you so . . ."

"Amazing? Don't know. Just born this way." She laughs with a wink.

I decide to ignore it, ushering her inside my bedroom. Once there, though, she steps to the side, hovering by the door. I give her a look before going to the closet. Not like she's never been here before. She's spent enough nights with me. She should feel comfortable being in my room. Remembering Alex's comment as I open my safe, I'm beginning to understand what he meant by skittish.

"Come here, Princess," I call out. I wait, still rifling through my weapons. No answer.

"Sam!" I shout.

"What?" Spinning around, I find her directly behind me.

"What the fuck. Make a sound every once in a while."

She grins. She's starting to freak me out. This isn't a side of Sam I've seen before. I grab a gun and hand it back to her, along with an extra magazine.

"Expecting trouble?" she questions innocently, slipping the gun behind her.

"With you? Always," I reply, closing the safe and spinning the dial. "We're going to the Barrens."

"Got any cookies?"

"We're not bringing snacks," I growl, leading her out, which makes her laugh.

A knock on the door cuts her off, forcing me to glance back. Her face is blank, a mask. I pull it open to reveal Ren. He spots Sam behind me and lurches back, avoiding her eyes.

"We need to talk," he says, looking off down the hall. "Privately."

Sam's face shutters more as she pushes past us and heads for Alex's room. She doesn't knock, just waltzes right in. Seconds later, a shirtless Alex is pushed out, and the door is slammed shut, the lock echoing into the silence.

"What the fuck was that?" Alex asks in bewilderment, pulling the shirt in his hands over his head.

"What's going on, Ren?"

Ren turns, heading to Alex's office, closing us inside. The space is bare. When Ren took over his space, I thought Alex would need an office, but it ended up being a bust. He never comes in here.

Ren shakes out his hands, making me catch Alex's eye. Ren taught himself long ago to come across as an emotionless robot to most people, but he never could break the habit he's engaged in, cracking every knuckle, rolling his head back and forth. We wait, knowing he won't talk until he's worked everything out in his own head.

Finally, he stops and drops a bomb. "Sam is the Wraith."

Stunned silence follows his announcement. Alex's mouth drops open. My first thought is to deny it. When he said he knew the Wraith's identity, it crossed my mind, but there's no way the Byrns' princess is a lethal psychopath. She's too . . . emotional. I shake my head. When I spot Ren's face, I freeze. This isn't a theory he's come up with. He knows, which means . . .

"She told you?" I ask.

He nods before I've finished my question.

Alex's mouth turns down, muttering, "Well, that explains a lot."

"What am I supposed to do with this, Ren?"

I honestly can't figure out how I feel about it. I'm housing a goddamn assassin. I've fucked her. The questions run through my mind, demanding answers. First the Guild, now this.

"You needed to know. I think we can use her against the Guild."

"Are you fucking serious?!" Alex yells. "Use her? She's not a fucking weapon."

"Calm down, Alex," I scowl. "Why is she hiding in his room?"

"For some reason, she's under the belief we'll kill her." His voice comes out calmly, but he's still cracking his knuckles.

Alex storms toward the door, muttering, "Fuck this."

He's halfway across the hall before I register the implications of Ren's words. By the time I follow, Alex is pounding on his door, shouting for Sam to open up. My eyes find Ren, still standing in the doorway of the office. His eyes narrow and connect with mine. We're both thinking the same thing: Sam ran.

Of course she'd bolt. The smartest thing would be to get as far away as possible from us if she thinks we'll try to kill her for being the Wraith. And Ren knew. He orchestrated it perfectly. I rarely question my two best friends; I trust them with my life, but Ren set something into motion I don't know if we'll ever be able to stop. As capable as Sam is, she's only one person, and Ren has fed her straight to the wolves. If the Guild gets a hold of her . . .

"You fucked up," I seethe.

Ren nods while Alex continues to pounds on the door, pleading with Sam to let him in. I'm about to turn away to try to find her before she gets too far when a thump reverberates from the other side of the wood. We all freeze, waiting for any sign she's still here.

"What." Her muffled voice reverberates through the wood.

"Hey, Bug. Can you open the door?" Alex's head rests against the dark panes, trying to get closer to her any way he can.

"Why?"

"We want to talk," I tell her, praying my voice doesn't crack. I was pissed when she took off before. Now all I can think of is all the people who want her dead. In a couple days, she's become someone I need to keep alive, which makes the snort she lets out at my words all the more frustrating.

"Bug, please. Just open the door," Alex says.

Looking back, I find Ren gone. Their behavior earlier makes more sense now. I have no idea what he'd said to her before, but the fact he left us to deal with whatever he fucking did infuriates me. Then again, he convinced her to stay until he told us.

A squeal rings out from inside the room, and the lock clicks open. Alex rushes through the door, revealing Sam, who is wrapped up in Ren's arms. If it wasn't for the murderous rage on her face, they would look like they're in a loving embrace. She's struggling, but his hand is around her throat. She's not trying that hard to break free. No way she'd allow him to sneak up on her, catch her, keep her, if she were really the Wraith.

"Let her go, Ren," Alex growls.

Ren peers down at Sam, saying, "Oh, I think she likes this, don't you, Pet?"

Sam shudders, casting her eyes down. She tenses before twisting out of his hold, shoving him aside and retreating, a snarl escaping her throat. She produces a knife from god knows where and backs up to the wall. Alex, who was reaching for her, stops in his tracks.

"Sam, I don't know why the hell you think we'll hurt you, but that's not going to happen. If we wanted you dead, what's stopping me from putting a bullet in your brain?" I say, trying for logic.

"To do the dirty work of taking down the Guild," she sneers, swinging her head, trying to keep us all in sight.

Alex glares at Ren. "We don't want you to, Bug."

She rolls her eyes, fixing a stare on Ren, who has the good sense to grimace, ducking his head.

"I didn't mean it like that."

"Oh? Then what did you mean?"

Alex takes a step toward her, making her tense, but she keeps her weapon at her side.

It hits me: she doesn't want to hurt us.

The emotion in her eyes isn't the rage of someone who's cornered; it's sorrow. She stayed, not because of anything Ren said, but because she doesn't want him to be right.

"He's an idiot, Bug." Alex tries to mollify her.

She relaxes a bit, giving me hope she won't do something rash, like stab him.

Ren chimes in. "Clearly, you feel adrift, with your brother no longer leading. It's also quite obvious you don't feel as if you are seen as worthy, even though you are more than capable of taking care of things. You fail to see the freedom in being the Wraith. So, it stands to reason, giving you a purpose would allow you to feel as if you belong here."

Sam's mouth drops, then she snaps it shut, her eyes spitting fire again. Ren turns to me, confusion clouding his features.

"That is . . . it's not . . . I don't feel like . . . ugh!"

"You wanted a reason. I gave you the reason. I don't see how these two knowing affects anything. You've put two devils into hell, so I'm sure it won't matter," Ren says before walking out.

Sam bursts out laughing, clamping her hand over her mouth to stifle the sound, but it's too late. As he reaches the door, I catch the start of a grin teasing the edge of his mouth. The tension seeps from the room with her response.

"What the hell just happened?" Alex asks.

"I think Ren made a joke," I respond, my eyes fixed on Sam.

"I don't get it."

"Neither do I, but apparently, Sam does."

"Well, that was unexpected." She sighs out another chuckle. "We on the same page, then?"

"Uh . . ." Alex looks to me, panic lining his eyes.

"About not killing you?" I ask.

Sam tilts her head, a condescending smile on her lips. "Trying to kill me, but yes."

"Who else knows, Princess?"

I have my own suspicions. The only person who would have warned her away from us is laying in a hospital bed. Anyone else who knows she's the Wraith will determine who the hell I have to keep an eye on.

Sam rolls her eyes, saying, "Ryker Helms."

I wait, but she merely places the knife on Alex's dresser. My eyebrow twitches up, demanding more.

"I don't know what that look is for, that's it."

Alex questions, "Colin doesn't know?"

"Nope." She pops the *p*, avoiding us both as I scowl.

"How is that possible? Seems like it would be something to share with your brother's second."

"I'm not an idiot. The less who know, the easier for me, the safer for me. Helms and Ren figured things out. No idea how the president of the Reapers did, but he hasn't ratted me out so far, so I let it slide." She pulls out her phone, wrinkles her nose, and slips it back into her pocket.

"Why did Mason tell you we'd kill you?" I question.

"If I knew, I either would have ignored the rule, or I would have ignored you. Duh." She picks the knife up again and flips the blade around as if she can't sit still.

"Would you knock it off?" I gripe, scowling.

She smirks and sets it down.

"Bug, I don't get it. You had rules?" Alex's face is falling the more she reveals, and the fallout from this might break him. He cares for her, so her answers are hurting more than any revelations we find.

"When I was younger, they were . . . rigid. I understood, because things were so new after the shit with the coup. After I was . . ." she says before biting her lips, "trained, he was insistent I tell no one, but especially the Kings—you guys. He never told me why."

"Sam, we wouldn't hurt you, we'd never kill you. Would we, Shane?"

I know he wants me to reassure her, but guilt seeps through me. I've already hurt her. Not in the way Mason meant, but I did. I have to live with the regret, but I don't know how to repair the damage, so I shove them aside. My actions will have to speak for themselves.

"Of course not. We don't have time for this. Get changed, Princess. We're going recruiting," I state, striding from the room and getting halfway to my office before I find she hasn't followed me. Tipping my head up, I take a deep breath before spinning back the way I came.

Coming around the corner, Alex has her pinned against the wall, his head buried in her neck. They didn't even bother shutting the door, for fuck's sake. As he pushes a leg between hers, I find Sam's eyes on me, lust and fire and something else, a question.

I smirk, leaning against the door frame, waiting for their interlude to be done. She certainly doesn't seem skittish now, with Alex's hand cupping her tit, and his other sliding down, disappearing between their bodies, making her whimper.

I clear my throat so I don't get any harder than I already am. Alex barely pauses before glancing over his shoulder, a stupid fucking smile on his face. I tilt my head and gesture for him to hurry up. We're out of time, whether I wanted to let him finish or not.

"Wanna join? I'm sure we could make her come fast enough to still get shit done," he remarks, rubbing her through her leggings.

"We both know we wouldn't be going anywhere if we stripped her down and fucked her right now. Leave it for later." I watch as her eyes widen, her breaths coming faster as Alex continues his torture. "Let's go, Princess."

Alex groans, swooping down and kissing her hard before stepping away, adjusting himself as he passes me. Sam's blush splashes across her cheeks, but whether from embarrassment or because she's so worked up, I can't tell.

"Sorry," she mutters, not meeting my eyes.

"What the fuck are you apologizing for?"

Her head snaps up, glaring at me. "I'm not."

"Pretty sure you just did, Princess." I chuckle, turning to go. "Hurry up."

"You think because you know my secret you can order me around now?"

I spin back, finding her planted, hands on hips. My eyes travel down her body, and follow the renewed flush coming over her until it reaches her cheeks. Her nose flares, and I have to stop myself from grinning. She plays the part well, but her body always gives her away. I stalk toward her and wrap an arm around her waist, hauling her to my chest, our bodies fused together so close she has to tip her chin up to see my face.

"First of all, Princess, I didn't order you around. I told you what we were doing. If you have a problem with it, you should speak up. Second of all, if I did want to give you an order, I would, since you're in my house, but I wouldn't. Neither of those things have anything to do with the Wraith and everything to do with you being your own goddamn person. The only orders I want you to follow are the ones I give you when I'm fucking you. Now get your ass in my room and change, so we can get this shit over with. I want to hear that gasp you make when I'm deep inside you again."

FORTY-TWO

SAMANTHA

I keep sneaking glances at Shane. He catches me every time, but I can't stop. I keep expecting him to turn on me, take back his words, and betray me. It says more about me than him. I'm lost in my thoughts, focused on Alex as Shane drives through the streets. Alex was upset before he pushed me against the wall, his hands caressing my body. The betrayal of not sharing my secret with him was written all over his face. He wanted me to trust him, but how could I when Mason pounded the rules in my brain with a rubber mallet? They'd hurt me, use me, kill me. Pain radiates through me, wondering if I'll ever be able to ask Mason his reasons.

Shane's voice cuts through my musings. "Did Alex talk to you before he started ravishing you?"

It takes me a minute to accept he's read my mind before I answer, "Yes."

"Is he upset?" His face is turned away, so I can't read him. His voice is neutral, but it could be an act.

"Why does that matter?"

"I want him to be on point tonight. He's more likely to get himself shot if he's upset. I'm sure we all can agree we only want one gunshot victim in the house at a time."

"Oh. Yeah. Sure. He was, but he got over it," I say, wondering why my stomach is flipping at his explanation. Of course he's concerned with Alex's state of mind. It has nothing to do with me, but I try not to dwell on my feelings. Shane cares about Alex. It makes sense. No reason to be upset. I'm not exactly happy with them labeling me a victim though.

We pull up to the edge of the Barrens. He parks and turns to me. "Sam."

"Yeah?" I don't look at him, trying to be busy while digging around in the glove box.

"Look at me."

I glance up, his blue eyes pinning me in place. I still can't read him, which worries me more. I can react accordingly if he's pissed. I wonder if this is it. Is he going to kick my ass out? Leave me in the Barrens? Shoot me instead of deal with my being the Wraith?

"You gonna say something, or are we going to stare at each other all night," I rasp after a full minute of waiting for him to continue.

He sighs. "We're not enemies," he grinds out.

"Uh, yeah."

"We weren't enemies before, and now, we definitely aren't, but you keep treating us like we're going to turn on you the second we're presented with an opportunity. We're in this together for now. We all need to start acting like it."

I nod as my stomach drops, and tears prick my eyes. I glance away, fighting for control. He's right, we aren't enemies, but it doesn't make us friends, either. Shane says we're in this together *for now*, which tells me that, after the Guild is taken care of, we won't be. I didn't realize I wanted to stick around until the option is ripped away. We were thrown into this situation without warning. Working together, being together, is convenient. They don't have to like someone to fuck them. I should be grateful he's willing to help me now, but the pain inside overwhelms me.

I'm sucked too far in. I'm not getting out of this unscathed, and I have no idea how I'm going to handle the fallout. I thought I could push it off, push it down, deal with it later.

Alex and Ren pull up next to us, and Shane pops his door. He goes to Alex's window as I heave my own door open, hesitating. I don't want to hear what they're talking about, so I lean against my door, watching the dark river. A shadow falls over me, and I glance up, finding Ren leaning next to me.

"What's up?" I ask.

The last day, waiting for him to reveal his big news to the others, was like walking on eggshells. I kept expecting him to throw the news out, every time we were together. I'm still coiled tight from the whole ordeal. Then Ren accused me of being unmoored, and he was right. I am unmoored, but not because Mason isn't here.

It's them. They don't react how I expect them to. They don't say what I anticipate. Every time I talk to them, I become a little more isolated yet complete. The whole situation is confusing as hell.

Ren doesn't answer, just hands me some small plastic bags. At first, I think he's giving me pot but then I see they're full of brownies. My lips twitch, thinking back to our conversation.

"These pot brownies?"

He smiles. It's the most I've ever gotten out of him. I try not to stare, but it changes his entire face. Instead of the brooding, tatted man, his gray eyes dance with mirth, aimed directly at me. My heart jumps.

"I didn't have time for lemon squares. Hopefully this works." His smile fades, turning back to the river.

"Did you make these?"

He barks out a laugh, startling me. A half smile and a laugh? Not a snort or chuckle, an honest-to-god laugh. My mouth falls open and then I grin, too. I'm going to revel in this moment, remember it next time he's yelling or ignoring me.

"I'm not a baker, Sam. They were in the kitchen." He eyes the bag in my hands. "Come to think of it, they might have pot in them."

I laugh. "I'm sure that will go over well. Don't worry about it."

He pulls one more bag out and hands it over, not meeting my eyes.

"Is this trail mix?" I ask, confused. "Um, is this for me?"

"You didn't pack any snacks," he explains, ducking his head.

"Thanks," I whisper, taking a deep breath. The rollercoaster of today is taking its toll on my emotions. Was it really only yesterday we went to save Alex from the Depot? It feels like it's been a lifetime.

"Good thing you didn't run, huh?" he whispers back before walking back to his car.

I watch him slide in, say something to Alex, and they all laugh. They make me want to belong, but I'm still an outsider, staring in at them. I doubt I'll ever be let in.

It isn't jealousy coursing through me this time; it's heartache. That deep, bone-chilling realization I will never have what they have. A connection so clearly defined they know they have each other's backs. Mason has too many other obligations. He can't give me what I need. I've already realized Colin isn't a substitute.

Loneliness seeps into me as I, at last, acknowledge I want to be loved. So deeply and unconditionally I never have to question their loyalty. I can trust them with everything I am and everything I'm not, and they'll still accept me. Someone who wants me. Not because I'm the Wraith, not because I'm Mason's sister, not because of my last name, but because I'm me.

My whole life, I've been running from the truth. Ren is right, the attempt on Mason's life undid me, shoving me into a world I no longer understand. I don't feel worthy or useful, not in the way these men are to each other.

Shane was right, too: I might be the Wraith, others might fear my arrival, but no one knows I'm her.

As Sam, I'm forgettable, replaceable. He apologized later, but the truth in is words were why they affected me so acutely; why I cared about what he said when other's opinions didn't matter. I want his approval, but I'll never get it. I don't know which I should believe anyway—the Shane before or the current one.

They want a warm body, a short-term alliance, and I need to brace myself for when everything inevitably ends. I won't survive if I let myself be lured in by them, fall in love with them, and they walk away when it all comes crashing down around me. The essence of myself will float away.

I'm deep in my thoughts, but I register Ren driving off, taking Alex with him. Shane rustles around in the car, and I drag myself to the present, deciding to protect my heart at all costs, but I'm afraid it might be too late.

"You ready?" Shane calls.

"Yeah." I mentally shake myself. "Yeah. You got a plan?"

"Think you can get us into the Egg?" he asks, a smirk playing on his lips.

"We'll see. They don't care who you are. They might make you stay outside, though, so don't get cocky about shit. I know that's hard for you."

We start to walk, the lights winking out as we travel deeper into the Barrens. Shane keeps sweeping back and forth, trying to make sure we aren't being followed. After several blocks, I can't take it anymore.

"Will you knock it off? You're annoying the hell out of me," I grumble.

"Sorry I wanted to keep us from being ambushed, Princess." His reply drips with sarcasm.

"You look like you've never stepped foot in the Barrens. It's distracting, not to mention fucking stupid. No one is going to sneak up on us."

"Oh, you have a crystal ball I don't know about? Did you consult a psychic who told you tonight would go swimmingly?"

"Oh, fuck off." I wave my hand at him. "I know because no one *can* sneak up on me. Not here, anyway. The people who live here wouldn't try, and the Guild wouldn't sneak. They'd try to shoot us outright, but I'm sure the residents blocked most of the way by now."

"Why would they do that?"

"Just because they're poor doesn't mean they're stupid. I doubt we'll be able to tell them anything new. They'll be able to tell us what's going on, if anything. You think you're going to recruit them? For what? They won't join you or your war. They'll do what's best for them."

"My war?" he questions, looking behind us once again.

I don't bother to answer—I don't know how.

The Egg comes into view, more subdued than the last time. A handful of groups mill about. I remember it's a Monday, which explains the lower numbers. I spot Nicki, but she's not working, thank god. I side-eye Shane, knowing being off the clock won't stop her from trying to make a dime off him.

"Maybe you should stay here. Let me go figure shit out," I say, trying to convince myself it's because I don't know if they'll let him in, but it's because of her.

All the years she's spent in the Barrens haven't diminished her beauty, which is how she keeps making money. She'll try to pick up Shane . . . I wrap another wall around my heart, reminding myself he isn't mine. I have no right to be upset if he wants to go off with her. It doesn't help.

"Stop stalling, Princess." He gestures me ahead.

"Fine," I snap. "But let me do the talking. You'll get yourself stabbed if you open your mouth."

Approaching the gate, I recognize the guys on duty and explain Shane's presence. They scan him up and down, judging him, and I suppress a giggle. Shane's stony expression is more than worth trying to get him in. To my surprise, though, they wave us through. One of the regulars stops Shane and gives him the rules, and that he will never be let in without me. I stick my tongue out, crinkling my nose to rub it in. He rolls his eyes, but a smile forms again, right at the edge of breaking out.

I hand off one of Ren's bags, the others crowding around and divvying up the brownies. Ren probably gave me the treats for Shane to hand out, not me. I push the thought away as my fingers brush the bag of trail mix in my pocket.

"Girl, it's been a minute since I seen you. How you been, sweetie?" Nicki calls out as we roam closer. I can tell when she spots Shane, going from relaxed to seductive in three seconds flat. She drops the dopey smile she's plastered on for me and is licking her lips. I fight the urge to glance at Shane and see if he's buying what she's so obviously selling.

I'm about to answer her, when she says, "And who is this fine specimen?"

"This is Bob. He doesn't speak." I hear Shane snort behind me but keep my eyes on Nicki.

"Well, hello there, Bob. I bet you have other ways of showing what you want, don't you?"

I sigh, stepping to the side, looking over to the group at the next stall, I see them whispering together, glancing at Shane now and then. Their big business is weed, but they've been known to dabble in harder stuff. I'm about to go over when Shane wraps his arm around my waist, pulling my back against his chest.

"Sorry, Nicki. I got my hands full already." His hand slides down, squeezing my hip enough to show me how pissed he is.

"Uh, I need to know how business has been."

Shane tries to hide his shock at my question but fails. No wonder he thought I was an airhead. He puts people in neat little boxes and can't accept they're more than he sees. Nicki melts back into her normal self now that a customer isn't on the line.

"Pretty much moved along. There was a little scuffle at the docks, but things got cleaned up quick. We need to make the call, you think?" Her eyes dart to the men next to us. They're quiet and trying very hard to not look interested in us anymore. I slip out of Shane's hold, stepping closer to the woman.

"Might want to see what you got. Lots of other places to find it, though . . ." I shoot Shane a smile over my shoulder. Confusion swirls in his eyes, but he's schooled his face at least.

"Oh, sweetie. You can look, but you know how those others are. Always promising things they can't deliver on. You came to the right place—the Egg is beyond compare, don't you think?" she says with a wink.

"I would have to agree. This might seem like a silly question, but do you have protection? I'm not wanting to catch anything."

"I got you covered. If you're into kinky shit, though, you'll have to search in the east side. They get some crazy fuckboys over there."

"All right, thanks, Nicki. I think we might discover what they have to offer." I toss her a bag and walk away, beckoning to Shane.

I meander away from the men when one of them breaks away. He's trying to be casual, but his body language is off. I stop by another stall, chit-chatting with the two brothers there. They stock the warm stuff people in the Barrens need: everything from coats to small gas-powered heaters. I try to signal to Shane to keep an eye out, but he turns away, and I have no idea if he caught it. We're going to have to talk about hand signals or something, especially if I have to save his ass.

"You guys stay out of the river," I tell them, ready to move on, but one stops me.

"Run the gamut, girly."

I nod, tugging on Shane's sleeve to get him going. We're in deeper shit than I thought.

FORTY-THREE

ALEX

We pull up to the compound, bullet holes pepper the front of the building, plywood covering two windows. Ren's eyes meet mine, both of us wondering what the hell went down here. I tilt my phone to him, showing him Shane's most recent text.

HA: running the gamut.

"What the fuck does that mean?" Ren spits out, pulling out his own phone.

"Obviously, 'high alert' but running the gamut? No idea. Let's get this over with," I reply, shoving open my door, Ren following suit.

We make our way to the side door and walk in after we've put in the code. Most of the buildings in the south side don't have such sophisticated technology, but since this is more of a central hub, Ren had it installed.

Inside, it's quiet, the usual music and conversation that fills the place noticeably absent. I palm my gun and nod to Ren. Making our way down the hall, the murmur of voices filters from the back. I peek around the corner, seeing our guys sitting around a table, playing cards.

I jerk my head at Ren, who slips around me, waltzing into the room without a care as he tucks his gun away. I stay back to make sure we're not about to be ambushed. We trust these guys to run guns for us, but I'm not about to risk my life for them.

Ren grills them on how business is, talking to the leader, Big John, as if this is a normal check-in. He's thick and burly but also the smartest out of this bunch, which is why he's leading. Plus, he's loyal, and that's not always the easiest to find, especially these days.

Quake is living up to his name, practically shaking out of his boots while he keeps a lookout from the window. One of them drops a bag, and half of them jump, scanning the small area as he mutters out an apology. I have no fucking clue what happened, but I'm itching for Ren to get to the goddamn point. He's still talking about the latest shipment and where it should go. Shane wants most of it dispersed to the various compounds until we can finalize the plan to hit the Guild, but Big John wants to keep it here, as if he has any say in the matter.

"That's not going to work. We're not prioritizing one station over another because you're paranoid. What the fuck happened here?" Ren's voice rings with annoyance.

"Those assholes tried to take us out!" Quake bursts out, and Big John glares at him.

Ren pins John with narrowed eyes. "Start talking. Now."

"Couple weeks ago, 'nother group came sniffing around, trying to recruit us. We thought it was Byrns' guys. We declined. They didn't like that and tried to shoot the place up," Big John says nonchalantly, like this isn't something he should have run up the chain. Dumbass.

"Quake," Ren's says, voice cut off whatever bullshit the leader is about to keep shoveling, "the whole story."

"A couple guys went with them. I wanted to take the fuckers out, but Big John said no."

My mouth drops, forcing myself to stay where I am. Ren, to his credit, barely registers the revelation, blankly watching the leader.

"And then?"

"Then those fuckers tried to take our families! Our girls, kids, parents, whoever they could get their greedy fucking hands on. What the hell is going on! I got my girl in a safehouse with her cousin and three other families. We're running out of space, and I don't know how safe it even is. Why the hell aren't you guys doing anything?" Quake is quivering with anger, but a sheen of wetness wells in his eyes.

Ren doesn't answer, merely leveling a look at Big John, who stupidly shrugs his shoulders, as if this isn't a big fucking deal. One of Ren's eyebrows twitches up as he waits. He's always better at delaying the inevitable until he gets the whole story. My fists would be flying by now. My phone vibrates in my pocket, but I leave it, not wanting the distraction.

"I suggest you explain yourself, Big John."

"Don't know what to tell you, boss. Shit happens." He shrugs again as they glare, murderous intent in their eyes.

"You're right. Shit does happen," Ren quips, sidestepping as I slide around the corner and put a bullet in his head.

The rest scatter as the report of the gun echoes through the room, Quake yells and trips over his feet, landing on his ass while fumbling with his gun.

"Hello, boys. Sorry for the delay. Who's going to take out the trash?" I ask, casting a psychotic grin around the room.

"What the fuck, Alex?!" one of them yells.

Big John's body slumps and slides out of the chair, blood leaking from the hole in his forehead. I swing around, eyeing each of them. They should be used to this, but apparently, seeing one of their own being taken out is a bit too much.

"Shit happens" is all Ren says before he fixes Hermit, Big John's second, with a stare.

"Wanna play a game, Hermit?" I ask slyly, as he swallows hard and shakes his head.

"You're in charge," Ren tells him. "See this gets cleaned up. None of this would have happened if someone would have opened their fucking mouths, so let's learn from this, hmm?"

A chorus of "yes sirs" rumble, and several of them move to deal with the body languishing in front of us. Ren moves to Quake in the corner to talk him off the ledge. Hermit has two newbies dragging Big John's body away to dump in the river, but he's skirting around me.

"Hermit."

He freezes, turning slowly to face me. "Yes, sir?"

"You got something to say?"

"No, sir."

"You should. Seems a lot of you aren't exactly happy with how we've been running things?" The last thing we need is for them to go rogue. We keep information in the lower gangs to a minimum so that, if one of them goes down, we don't go with them. But there's still shit out there, shit they can sell or can get beaten out of them.

"I'm not a snitch." He glares.

"Wouldn't be leading if you were. But you'd better start talking before Ren gets back. He's not as good a listener as I am," I say, crossing my arms.

"Uhh, well, it's just . . . what the fuck is going on?!" he bursts out.

"Ah, Hermit, if only I could tell you. We got some fuckers we're dealing with. You'll know when we need you, but I need you to hold these guys down until, then. Keep things moving, and we'll deal with the big shit."

"Not an answer, King. We're the ones getting hit out here. There's been raids and kidnappings and drugs going missing. I think we deserve to know what we're up against."

I eye him, debating how to handle this. Killing Big John had to happen. No question his loyalty was compromised. But these other guys? They're trying to keep their families safe the only way they know how. But I can't have Hermit disrespecting us, either. Decisions, decisions.

"Listen up, Hermit. I don't owe you a goddamn thing. If I tell you we got shit under control, it's your job to trust that. You do your job and we'll do ours and everything will work out. Stay the course and everything will be fine."

"I hope you're right, 'cause shit is poppin' off down here."

I clap him on the shoulder, hoping I'm right too, and we can move these fuckers along without losing too many people. He nods before going over to Ren and Quake. My phone goes off again, and I lean against the wall to pull it out. Reading through the messages, I swear under my breath and catch Ren's eyes, motioning we have to go. *Now.* I bolt out the door.

I stumble into the car, my leg jiggling while I wait for Ren to hurry his ass up. My foot hits the gas as soon as his door clicks shut, and we're speeding away from the compound. Ren's focused on his phone but shakes his head.

"What's going on? They tell you anything?" Ren demands, scrolling through his messages.

"Shane and Sam are in trouble. Some guys made them at the Egg. Not sure who the men are, but my money is on the Guild. Shane called for an out," I explain as quickly as I can, concentrating on dodging the few cars around us. We leave at least one accident and a fuck ton of angry people in our wake, but they're the least of my worries.

"Where are they?"

"Not sure, but they're north of the Egg, deep in the Barrens. Sam won't tell him where she's leading him, though."

I glance at Ren, trying to gauge where his head is, but he's buried in his phone, fingers flying across the screen. He curses and pulls his tablet from the glove box, most likely to check the cameras. I'm not about to try to figure that shit out. Shane wasn't exactly happy she was leading, but I trust her even if the other two aren't sold yet. She won't turn on us.

"You're not going to be able to track them on cameras. There aren't any down there," I remind him.

"I know that dickhead. I'm tracking Shane's phone, but it's not pulling up. Hold on." He's pounding on the screen before he rattles off a street name.

"That where they are?"

"Yeah, but they're moving. I got Sam, so hopefully they're still together."

"You put a fucking tracker on her phone? Why the hell would you do that?"

"Clearly, for this exact reason. Do you really want to be in the position we were in before? When she was fucking dying, and we couldn't find her? Because I'd rather skip another adventure like that, wouldn't you?" Ren snorts.

"Of course, but you can be damn sure, if I did, I'd tell her. Bet you didn't, though, did you? I bet you grabbed her phone when she was sleeping, and she's got no clue you're tracking where she is. That's fucked up, man."

"I did it right in front of her, actually. As soon as I'm confident she won't run, I'll tell her. Until then, you're going to keep your mouth shut."

It's pointless to argue with him. This is Ren's version of keeping her safe. I can't argue with his logic. I feel better knowing we can always find her, but I won't admit it to Ren. He's already got a fucked-up view of what we should do with Sam.

"Fuck!" I yell out.

Ren's head snaps up. We're completely boxed in. I have no idea where the hell all these people came from, but more cars pull up behind me. There's nowhere to go, traffic is gridlocked all around us.

"Alex, get us out of here."

"And how the hell would you like me to do that? Maybe I could see if your car floats in the goddamn river." I lay on the horn, knowing it won't do any good, "What the hell is going on? Where did they come from?"

Ren swings the tablet to me, showing me a flyer for a club event, and it let out ten minutes ago. I grab my phone, shooting a text to both Shane and Sam. I'm debating abandoning the car and going on foot. I grab the handle when Ren's hand shoots out, stopping me.

"Don't. We need to stay together. Shane and Sam are going to need to deal with shit on their own until we can get there. I told him to try to head south and haven't heard back," Ren states evenly, concern stirring his eyes.

"If we're too late . . ." I sigh.

"We won't be. They can handle it."

I don't know if he's trying to convince himself or me.

FORTY-FOUR

SHANE

I trail Sam into the shadows surrounding the rundown building, glancing back to see if the men are still tailing us. When I turn back, though, Sam is gone. I hurry my pace, trying to navigate in the dark. I have no idea where the hell we are. We've been running, slipping in and out of shadows, for the past thirty minutes. We can't shake the men who followed us from the Egg, and now I've lost the one person who might be able to lead me out of this fucking maze. I curse under my breath, not wanting to call out, fearing they're close enough to track us.

I peek around the next corner, and the hairs on my neck stand up. I swing around, lifting my gun wrapped in my fist instinctively, but it's knocked away, and I'm met with Sam's glare. She mouths "what the hell" before pushing past to take the lead again. I glance back, trying to figure out where she was hiding but hustle after, not wanting to lose her again.

My phone vibrates in my pocket, but I leave it. The last thing we need is a beacon announcing our location. I'm sure it's Ren, but I trust he'll be able to track us. It's not like I can tell him where we are. I can't make heads or tails out of this place, especially with all the street signs missing.

I snag the back of Sam's hoodie, yanking her back into my chest, and put my lips to her ear. She shivers when I whisper, "Where are we going?"

She shoots a look at me and tugs out of my grasp, heading into another tight space between two ramshackle huts. I don't know if anyone is in them, but if they are, they stay inside. I wonder how often this happens, that they are used to people sneaking around outside their doors.

Sam pauses at the opening, checking left and right, then dashes across the short opening to the next street. This time, she waits, eyes fixed on me while I copy her. I try to keep my steps light, silent, like her, but she has some freaky magical ability I don't possess. I'm not loud—we were taught how to move silently from space to space, but Sam melts into some ethereal figure and blends in with the night.

The farther we travel from the Egg, the more she slips into the Wraith. Knowing who she is and seeing it are two very different things. I thought the Wraith was a psychotic phantom, not quite human, a sociopath at best. I haven't wrapped my head around the fact Sam and the Wraith are one and the same.

The Sam I know is emotional and doubts herself, as much as she tries to hide it. She's passionate and persistent. I almost convince myself Ren is wrong. Sam lied because what I know of the Wraith doesn't align with the woman who had spent last night in my bed. Seeing her slough off everything she is, leaving the Wraith in its place, hits me how it's possible. I believe it now. Her ability to go from socialite to phantom is insane.

The buildings grow taller the farther we cross the Barrens. I keep looking behind, expecting to spot the men. They've disappeared. I breathe a little easier every time, relaxing bit by bit. If we can hold out until the guys can pick us up, we won't have to deal with them, at least not yet. As much as I trust Sam and her abilities, we can't take them all on. Six trailed us, with however many more hidden.

"Shane, pay a-fucking-tention."

I jerk forward, and Sam is glaring at me again. She's told me at least a dozen times—in words and with the nasty faces—to keep moving, but I'm not about to be ambushed. The last thing I want is to be shot in the back. I don't say anything, though. The last time I did, she snorted and rolled her eyes, as if it isn't a valid concern.

"Where the fuck are we going, Sam? I feel like we've been walking in goddamn circles." I don't tell her I have no clue where we are or how I don't know how to get out of this labyrinth. I know the rough way to the river, and that we're heading north, but that's about it.

"We're not—well, sort of not."

She dismisses me, pulling herself on to a dumpster and using the height to scan the next alley.

"That's not a fucking answer!"

"Can you climb?" Sam glances back, scanning me up and down. "Never mind."

"Why would I need to climb?"

"Stop talking." She hisses under her breath—something about hand signals but then she's off again, launching off the dumpster and landing without a sound halfway across the space, then sprinting the rest of the way. I skip the dumpster, checking the corner, but stop when a purring engine echoes through the quiet.

My eyes shoot to Sam, but she's gone. I don't know if she melted into the shadows or kept going, but either way, she's vanished into thin air. I hold my breath, closing my eyes to concentrate on where the car is. I shake out my hand gripping my gun and palm it again. With the complete silence in this part of the city, I thought it would be easy, but the sound reverberates off the tin-roofed hovels and the concrete remnants of businesses long since gone, making it impossible to decipher anything other than they're out there, searching.

I debate the three options: sprint after Sam, go back the way we came, or stay put. I peek around the corner, but another pile of trash blocks my sight. I curse softly, trying to pierce the darkness where Sam disappeared. I don't want to lead them toward her if they've spotted me.

I shuffle back a step, deciding to go down a block and loop around to her, when a pop rings out ahead of me. I haven't even fully comprehended what I heard when my feet are moving toward Sam. I don't think, only react, intent on reaching her.

If they've shot her . . . I stop those thoughts as I launch into the dark opening, knowing I'm making too much noise, but not caring. All that matters is finding Sam, ensuring she's okay.

The moon gives off enough light to spot the end of the alley, which opens to another street. The next building is farther away this time. I slow, but I don't stop—I can't. As soon as my feet touch the sidewalk, I'm shoved to the side, going down hard. I keep hold of my gun, rolling to my knees, and swing it up. The weapon is knocked from my hands as I'm kicked in the back, narrowly missing face-planting onto the concrete. I try to roll again, away from my attackers, but several hands grab me, wrenching my arms behind, hauling me to my knees in the process.

"Well, boys. Look what we've caught," a nasally voice sneers out. "Shane King, fancy seeing you here. Not exactly your neck of the woods now, is it?"

He's hidden in the gloom, the single streetlight buzzing across the alley, but I recognize his voice regardless. He was with the Byrns at one point, but they banished him. For what, I don't remember. There aren't many ways to make us banish someone without killing them. The only reason I remember this guy is because he tried to defect to the Kings. I told him we don't take rejects. I resign myself to hearing him tout for the next however long before I can get away. I remember he's a talker. I fucking hate people who talk to fill the silence, but in this case, it'll give me enough time to plan.

"Aw, come on King, don't be like that," he says, stepping out of the shadows. His face matches his voice, almost rat-like. I stay quiet, canting my eyes around to gauge how many guys are with him. I count eight, and I hope to god there aren't more tracking Sam.

"Nothing to say? You thought the Kings were too good for me, but don't worry. I found something better, didn't I, boys?" The rest of the men chuckle as his lips curl into a sneer.

"What we going to do with him, Bull?" a guy to my right asks.

Bull, what a shitty name for this piece of shit. I peer at the guy who asked out of the corner of my eye when I catch a shadow a little darker than the rest tucked away in the opposite alley.

Sam.

I roll my eyes to the side, trying not to give away her position. I have to force her to run. There's no way she can take on all these guys, especially if I'm not capable of helping. Bull is talking, but I'm not paying attention. Instead, I focus on my plan. At least Sam will be free, I hope.

"Why don't you guys fuck right off. How about that?" I cut him off, my lip curling.

"You think you're some tough motherfucker? The big Shane King. I should shoot you now. Take your little gang from you." His face turns blotchy.

I burst out a laugh, knowing it'll piss him off. He's delusional if he thinks he could take over the Kings. It might be the craziest thing about tonight.

"You? A little rat like you thinks he could run *my* empire? That's funny. I mean, I knew you were a little pissant when you came begging me for a job, but this tips it over the edge. I can't wait to tell the guys about this." I chuckle again, eyeing the shadows.

I breathe a sigh of relief when I don't find her. My chest aches, though, knowing I'll probably never see her again, unless these guys intend on giving me over to whoever they're working for, in which case, I might be able to escape, but the odds aren't looking good.

Bull is trying to pull himself together, when one of his men, a tall, beefy man bends down to whisper in his ear. Bull's beady eyes fix on me, and I yank on the hands holding me, but there's no give at all. My arms are aching from their restraint.

"Where's the girl?" Bull demands, waving away the enforcer.

"What girl?"

"Don't bullshit me. Samantha Byrns. I was surprised to see you guys running together, but a slut like her gets around to all sorts of places," he guffaws loudly, the others joining in while I grind my teeth. I set my face poker face, though.

"Don't know. She's got a habit of disappearing, though, so not surprised she left me here."

"Trouble in paradise?" He cocks an eyebrow at me.

"She's more trouble than she's worth." The words turn to ash in my mouth.

If Sam's still out there, listening, hopefully my words will make her run. I'd rather her hate me and live.

"Most women are," he spits, swiping his hand across his mouth. "How about you give me your contact for Oracle?"

I struggle to keep the confusion from my face. I assumed they were from the Guild, but why would they need to ask me about a drug they're supplying? No way Bull has pulled his own crew together. He's too stupid to pull something like that off.

"Who are you running with these days, Bull?"

"Wouldn't you like to know."

"Precisely why I asked, dumbass." I roll my eyes.

"Fuck you. I ain't tellin' you shit," he spits out, stepping closer to me.

"Why would I give up my contacts if I don't know who I'm giving them up to? That's bad business, Bull."

The cold is seeping into my knees, and if I don't move soon, my muscles will cramp.

"Because if you don't, I'll put a bullet in your brain, King."

Bull steps up, blocking my view of the other men, pressing the barrel to my forehead. I stare into his crazed eyes, hoping he shoots me and praying he doesn't. Pulling the trigger will give Sam time to slip further from their grasp, but he's going to look in my eyes as he does it.

He pulls back the hammer, and I tense, waiting for the explosion, when one of the men holding me shouts, and his hands go slack. I yank my arm forward, causing the other man to stumble and free my hands. I use the momentum to push Bull back. His arms flail, trying to catch his downward path. A shot rings out from his gun, echoing in the chaos of the others yelling. I scramble to grab it, wrestling the weapon from his grasp, then pistol-whip him directly in the face, causing his nose to break, blood spraying and splattering on me. I'm about to shoot him when he starts sobbing. Huge fearful hiccups are bellowing from him, and a look of disgust crosses my face before I hit him again, and he falls silent.

I scan the area, finding Sam covered in blood and surrounded by bodies. The two men who were holding me turned tail and ran for their lives, but Sam pulls a knife from god knows where and hurls the blade toward the farther one. He goes down, the knife sticking out the back of his neck. If he's not dead, he will be soon. I aim at the other, who stumbles when his friend goes down. Before I can pull the trigger, another knife flies through the air, inches from my ear, and he falls two feet from the other body.

I whip my head back to Sam, mouth agape. I have no idea how she took out eight guys by herself with only a couple knives. She's staring at me, a wariness in her eyes that wasn't there before. I rise, kneeing Bull in the balls before I go. His body flinches, but he doesn't wake.

She tenses when I stalk over to her, as if she wants to run, but is forcing her body to stay and wait for my verdict. I run my eyes over her body, trying to decipher if any of the blood is hers. She looks unharmed, but until I see with my own eyes, I won't be satisfied.

"Did they hurt you?" I murmur.

She lets out a huff, turning her head away. Slowly, I tuck my fingers under her chin, guiding her eyes back to mine. She shakes her head, trying to duck her head, but I keep a firm grip, enough to keep her looking at me. A groan interrupts us, making her jolt.

"Sam . . ."

"What?" she whispers.

"Thanks."

Her eyes widen before she nods, a small smile playing on her lips. I swoop down, claiming her mouth to remind her that I'm here, and I'm sure as fuck not going anywhere.

FORTY-FIVE

REN

Alex whips the car around the last corner and screeches to a halt before launching out and rushing to Sam's side. I stay put, trying to settle my racing heart. The last hour was a living nightmare, reminding me of our mad dash across the city to a burning house. Staring down at the device in my hands, I notice it's shaking—my hands are trembling. I throw my head back, slamming my eyes closed. It's hard enough to worry about my brothers. Our work isn't what one would call safe. To add Sam to the list of people I actually care who lives or dies . . . I don't know how to deal with the rolling emotions inside me.

I tried to ignore it. I solved the mystery of her. I thought once I put together the puzzle of Samantha Byrns, I could go back to not caring, barely registering her presence, like most people in this world. Somehow, she's become essential, something more, and it's freaking me the fuck out. It isn't her relationship with my brothers anymore. It's my own feelings for her. Even if I have to keep hiding it from her, I can't keep lying to myself.

I squint out the window and catch her throwing her head back, laughing at something Alex says while Shane is on the phone, calling in the cleanup. She's covered in blood, surrounded by bodies. I'm sure she's taken care of herself. The pure joy radiating from her is enchanting. Alex loops an arm around her waist, tugging her close, regardless of the mess. She attempts to push away but is still laughing. Shane hangs up and kisses her head as he passes, making his way to me. In the last several hours, it seems their insecurities have dropped away, leaving just the three of them content. I look away, my stomach turning with jealousy. A knock brings me back, and I push open the door to step out. Shane turns back to watch the other two, concern lining his face.

"You think more are out there?" he asks, scanning the area.

"Probably, but I doubt they'll try anything with us all here," I reply, forcing my eyes from Sam.

"I got Graves coming to deal with this. He'll haul Bull back to the compound, too, see if we can coerce anything from him. I want to move before anyone else shows up," he says, his eyes fixed on Sam.

"They won't know it was her," I murmur.

His eyes meet mine. "Not willing to take that chance."

"So, you're good, then? Not worried she'll smother you in your sleep?"

"I can think of worse ways to go," Shane chuckles, his eyes lighting up and back on Sam.

I shake my head, knowing he's not imagining a pillow suffocating him.

"She'd try to hover anyway," I quip before making my way to the driver's seat. Alex tries to slip in the back next to Sam. Shane snags his neck and pushes him to the front, while they both laugh. I flick my eyes to the rearview mirror and catch Sam staring back, no longer laughing.

I pull my eyes away, turning the key, vowing I won't look again. A *pop, pop, pop* erupts from behind us, and I slam the car in gear. It doesn't sound close, but with the mess we're leaving behind, I'm not willing to risk the gunfire is normal Barren activity. Shane yells at Alex to put his seatbelt on as I take a curve, heading toward the river. Sam leans forward, but Shane slams her back, snarling before he shoves her head down.

"What the hell, Shane! They're not even shooting at us! Let me up!" she shrieks.

I can hear her struggling against him while Alex's laughter peals out around us. Stupid fucker always loves the rush of a fight.

"Stay the fuck down, Princess. Last thing I need is you getting a bullet to the head because you didn't want to duck when someone is shooting."

"You are such an asshole. We're not in the middle of a shootout. You're so fucking paranoid!"

After several more turns, we hit the bridge, and I slow. This is one of the lesser-used ones, so I don't have to worry about traffic, but I'm not about to call more attention to ourselves than necessary. Alex is still grinning, craning his neck to watch Sam struggle out of Shane's hold. I meet her eyes again, filled with ire, but there's a hint of a smile on her lips.

"Fuck this," Shane grinds out, and he's hauling her up onto his lap, slamming his mouth on hers. Her groan fills the car, mixing with Shane's.

"What the fuck, Shane! No fair!" Alex whines, but he's met with Shane's middle finger. I fix my eyes back to the road, trying to ignore the desperate sounds coming from Sam. Alex is ready to crawl in the back and join. I swear I'll pull the fuck over and shove his ass out if he does.

There's a click, and Shane slides over, setting Sam on his seat as he repositions himself behind me. I can't tell what he's doing, but the sound Alex makes in his throat tells me all I need to know. I slow at a stoplight, and another car pulls up beside us just as a flash of Sam's hair comes into view. Her flushed face fills the mirror. Shane has her back on his lap facing forward this time, in a perfect position for Alex to watch while Shane fucks her.

I almost miss the light turning green I'm so mesmerized by the pleasure flooding Sam's face while Shane fills her over and over. Her eyes never leave mine, even as she tips her head back. At this point, I'm thankful it's so late so I can watch her instead of worrying about rear-ending someone. Alex is whispering to her, most likely dirty things he would do if he were back there, but I can't make out the words over the roaring in my ears.

I see the exact moment before she explodes, the tension, the shuddering, eyes finally falling closed with a gasp as Shane's grunts fill the small space. Her body goes limp, draping over Shane as he presses his lips to her neck, both catching their breath.

"Well, that was hot as fuck." Alex grins at me.

I'm too busy trying to keep my shit together to respond. I hear more, then I see Shane settle Sam behind me, clicking her belt on again while he slides behind Alex. I'm struggling not to speed home, whether to run away or something else—I don't know. I could scarcely keep a hold of my emotions before, but after watching her lose herself, they're out of control. I'm practically vibrating in the seat, straining to keep my face neutral.

I'm determined to walk away as I fly into the driveway. I will bolt from the car and not look back. The push and pull of this woman is too much for me, and if I give in now, I'll never come back from it.

I slam the car in park and reach for the handle, glancing in the mirror one last time as Sam's eyes burn into mine. Desire pours out of her, begging me for something I'm not sure I want to deny her.

All my plans of staying away rush out of me, and I pull her door open and yank her out. I throw her over my shoulder and charge up the stairs, leaving hollering and chuckles behind. Sam doesn't say a word as I bound up the stairs, but her arms wrap around my waist, pressing her face into my lower back.

I kick the door shut when we reach my room and toss her on the bed. She plants herself up on her elbows while I stare at her, breathing hard. Her cheeks are still flushed, eyes still burning. I want to ask if she's sure, but I'm fearful of the answer, so I spin and stalk into my closet.

I try to calm my racing heart, bracing myself on the shelf, to regain my composure I usually keep so close. Around this woman, I can't trust myself. Sam sends me to the edge of the unknown. I'm still not sure I want to try. It's a mysterious darkness, placing my trust in her. A trust I've never handed over before; she will strip me bare and gain a power of me I've never given to another person. She won't settle for a mindless romp, a fling, like every woman I've had before. She's already burrowed deep, and taking this last step—there'll be no turning back for me.

A soft knock makes me tense, but I stay where I am, head hanging, heart still racing. I feel her as soon as she enters. I always know exactly where she is. More proof of how much she's infiltrated my senses.

"Ren?" she calls softly. "It's okay. I can go if you want me to."

I shake my reeling head, not wanting her to go, but how can I let her stay?

"Is it because of . . ."

I know what she's getting at.

"No."

"Do you want me to leave?"

"I don't know," I whisper back. It's the most honest statement I've ever said to her. Not knowing my own mind is the worst possible position I can be in. I thrive on being in control of my thoughts. The chaotic world we live in forces me to crave it. Sam is just another thing I can't predict, can't control.

"I can leave. You don't have to see me again. It's okay," she chokes out, and it clicks.

She isn't telling me she'll walk out of my room. She's willing to leave us, to make me more comfortable. That realization has me reaching for her, pulling her into my arms and holding her against me.

"No," I hum, burying my face in her hair. "Don't disappear on us again. I can't handle that. I need . . ."

I don't know how to finish, so I hold her instead. She wraps her arms around my waist, and I press her head to my chest, breathing her in.

She drops her hands, her muffled voice sighing, "I should shower at least."

I gather her up and walk her to the bathroom, setting her on the counter before turning to the shower. I keep my mind on the task at hand, instead of Sam watching me. I turn when I have everything, finding her right where I left her.

I gesture to the running water, choking out, "I'll be here when you're done."

I flee the room and shut the door behind me with a soft click. I wait for the lock, but it never comes. Instead, the shower door closes. I slam my eyes shut, hand still on the knob, I imagine what she's doing: stripping down, stepping under the spray, sighing at the hot water, suds flowing down her . . . I halt my line of thinking and drop my hand before I march back in there and take her against the wall. I pour myself a drink and wait.

I don't turn away from the window when she emerges fifteen minutes later. It's late, the world outside sleeping in this part of the city. I should send her to bed, even if it isn't in mine. She must be exhausted after everything tonight. Hell, she's only had a few days to recover from getting shot. My thought jolts me into action, spinning around to check her stitches after her fight. I stop when I see she's only in a towel, hair still wet. Her bare feet affect me the most. Knowing she's standing here barefoot makes her seem at home, comfortable.

"I don't have any clothes in here."

I motion her back to my closet, trailing behind, curling my hand into a fist if only to stop myself from ripping the fabric from her body. I pull open a drawer, and she squeaks, looking from me to the drawer.

"Ren . . . are these . . . you know what, I don't want to know." Her nose crinkles as she reaches for a shirt on top.

"They're yours."

"And who's were they before? Wait, don't answer that."

"They've always been yours," I murmur.

"Wait, this *is* mine!" she says, examining the shirt.

"That's what I said."

"Where did you get this? I left it . . ." Her astonished eyes meet mine.

"I went to get some of your things when you were at the safehouse. I didn't think you'd want Victor burning them. I knew you'd need clothes at some point, and it's always better to have your own things," I explain, looking away, rubbing the back of my neck.

"You always knew I'd end up here, didn't you?"

"It seemed inevitable by then."

"But you knew before."

I stare at her, not willing to answer. It isn't that I knew, even back then, but I think I hoped she would end up with us.

"You have pretty eyes," she murmurs, sending a shiver down my spine.

She shakes her head, turning away to grab more things from the drawer while I go to leave.

I reach the door, and her towel flies past me, landing on the floor by my feet. My cock hardens as I blink at the fabric, imagining her naked behind me, knowing she's giving me the option to turn around. I won't get this opportunity again if I walk away now.

Five seconds is all I need to decide. With as much as I've tried to talk myself out of it, I knew all along we were hurtling toward this. I spin and march back to her. With a cursory glance at her flushed skin, still pink from the shower, I snatch her up and pin her to the wall as my mouth descends on hers. She wraps her hands around the back of my neck, holding on while I devour her. My tongue prods her lips, and she opens. My hand slides up her soft skin, tangling with her hair and tilting her head to the side, all while kissing her deeper. I can't get enough of this, of her. The desperate whimpers escaping her are driving me insane.

I haul her up, snaking an arm between her legs, and carry her, mouths still fused together. Out of the closet, I sit on the edge of the bed, settling her to straddle me. She tugs at the hem of my shirt, and I yank it up, my mouth molding to hers again, then traveling down her neck. I wrap my hand around her throat when I reach her nipple, holding her waist and forcing her to arch her back, darting my tongue out to encircle the hard nub. I latch on, swirling and biting, and she cries out, her hand flying to my wrist, still holding her in place. I slow, sure she's about to pull my hand away, but she holds on, arching her back again, begging for more. I happily oblige, moving to the other nipple before righting her again, staring into her eyes brimming with desire.

A tremor runs through her as her fingers trace my chest, down my stomach, and up again. Her hips are moving, greedy for the friction. I fall back, pulling her with me and setting her on my stomach while I wrestle my pants off. I can feel her warm arousal on my abs, while I fight to remove my socks. Sam huffs, leaning over me, burying her face in my neck, hair tickling my face, then she shakes. I freeze, one sock on, pants around my ankles, trying to figure out what's happening when she giggles, sucking it in before it fully escapes.

"Something funny, Pet?" I grumble.

"Do you . . ." She giggles again. "Do you need some help there?"

I roll us over, pinning her beneath me as a growl escapes my lips, while I kick my pants the rest of the way down, along with the remaining sock. Her eyes fill with glee as she grips my biceps, nails digging in as she swallows another laugh. Settling my body over her forces a gasp from her lips, all traces of mirth gone when I glide my cock along her slick pussy.

"Do I look like I need help?" I ask, latching on to her nipple again. Any answer she would have given is lost among her whimpers, and she lifts her hips up, seeking more. I rise to my knees, grabbing her hips in a bruising grip to still her. I expect her to complain, but she runs her hands up my arms and scrapes her nails down my chest.

"Now, now," I say, encircling her wrists and trapping them above her head. "I am going to need you to follow directions. You think you can?"

Her wide eyes meet mine as her head bobs up and down.

"Good girl." I swoop down, capturing her mouth again, resisting the urge to plunge into her.

"Ren." She breathes as I suck on her neck. Biting the soft juncture, I leave it red and swollen. Leaving my mark on her, branding her as mine.

"Hmm?"

Her wrists are twisting in my grip, body begging me for release, but I'm not going to rush this. I want her begging before I give us both what we crave.

"I need . . . I can't . . ." Her hips press up.

"I know what you need. I'll give you exactly what you want and more. This will be a sweet, slow torture, my pet. The other two might allow you to make demands, but tonight, you're with me. And you'll do as I say."

"If I don't?"

"Then, I'll leave you aching and empty, begging me to make you come. I'll bring you right to the edge, over and over, until you've learned your lesson. Pick which way you want this to go now," I purr, a shudder running through her body.

"Slow torture, please," she gasps out as I pinch her nipple, hard.

"Good choice. Now, don't move."

I release her hands, skimming my hand down her pliant body. Her soft skin, flushed from either the shower or her arousal, maybe both, is intoxicating. Her heavy pants push her tits up, begging me for more. Sitting back, I contemplate what to do with her now that I have her here, in my bed. There's been so many fantasies, it's hard to choose which one to fulfill. My eyes meet hers, and I jolt at the uncertainty filling them.

"What's wrong?"

"Can I put my arms down?" She bites her lip, her gaze casting away from me.

"Why?"

"No reason."

"Bullshit. What's wrong, Sam," I demand.

"I'm just a little . . . exposed." Her cheeks redden more with her admission.

Understanding flows through me. As open as Sam is, she still doesn't see what we see when we look at her. That one statement tells me more about her than anything else has.

"Do you feel like this with Alex and Shane?"

"No, but they don't sit there and stare at me."

I settle my cock between her legs, bracing myself above her and cupping her face, forcing her to meet my eyes. As confident as Sam is, vulnerability swims in her eyes. I kiss her lightly, once, twice, before pulling back.

"I'm not going to mindlessly fuck you, Sam."

"Why not?!" she squawks.

"Because that's not what you need, and I told you I was going to give you what you need."

I grab her knee, pushing it to her chest to spread her wider for me as my cock throbs, feeling her heat against me. I capture her nipple again while I run my hand down, cupping her pussy. She's pulsating and twitching against me, when I slick a finger through her folds, pinching her clit. She jolts before snapping back toward my fingers while she whispers my name. That feeling comes back——the one I always have when she says my name, the one I can't quite name but makes me tremble.

Her hands fasten on the headboard, knuckles turning white as I gradually build her body back into the frenzy I had her in before. She grunts when I pull my fingers away from her center, complaints dancing on the edge of her lips, before she presses them into a thin line. I smirk as I slide down, nipping here and there as I go.

"Begging is encouraged, Pet."

Her eyes narrow, mouth set, keeping her pleas to herself. I'm not worried. She'll be begging by the end. I throw my arm over her hips moments before I pinch her clit, making her lower half thrash up, but I hold her still. I suck it into my mouth, swirling before I nip down. Just enough for her to know who's going to be responsible for all her orgasms tonight.

I hum against her while she bucks. "You sure you don't want to beg?"

Sam whips her head back and forth as she writhes under me while I keep up my assault on her pussy. I close my eyes, burrowing into her pliant flesh, wondering if I will ever be sick of having my face buried between her thighs. I slip a finger in, then two, and she clenches down, her legs shaking. She cries out in frustration when I stop, pulling my face back and stilling my fingers. Sam slams her palms on the bed, glaring at me.

"What the hell, Ren?"

"I told you what the punishment would be—can't say I didn't warn you."

I crook my fingers deep inside her, rubbing them along her inner walls. Her hands fly back to the headboard, holding on as if her life depends on it. If not her life, definitely her climax.

"Ren . . ." she whimpers.

"Yes?" I press a thumb on her clit, still stroking inside her steadily.

"I . . ."

I wait, keeping my strokes slow and deliberate, waiting for her to break down those walls to no longer be ashamed.

When she doesn't finish, I lower my head, nipping her thigh, saying against her flesh, "If you want something Sam, ask for it. I'll give you anything—everything." I kiss my way back down, giving her plenty of time to respond.

"I want . . . I want to come. I want you to make me come. Now."

It's a whispered confession, but it's enough. I swoop down, tongue delving into her heat, and thrust my fingers deeper, faster, her breath matching my pace. Her pussy tightens, and I suck hard on her clit, locking my arm on her hips as she cascades over the edge, crying out her release.

Before she has a chance to recover, I'm on my knees, pulling my fingers out and burying my cock inside her. She gasps, and my eyes roll back as I let out a sigh of satisfaction at finally filling her. I roll my hips lazily as she pulsates around my cock. Intoxicated, I pull out inch by inch and slam back in, relishing in the feel of her. Sam chants my name, begging me to go faster, harder, deeper. I hold back, wanting to erupt, basking in her body instead.

I pull her up, fusing her body to mine, and thrust my tongue into her mouth, matching the rhythm of my length embedding into her, sparking an inferno in both of us. Grunting, I bury my face into her neck, biting hard enough to leave another mark. I want the other two to know who's been in her last, who's name she screamed, who's responsible for her orgasms tonight.

I stop as she's on the edge again, and she starts cursing me, trying to gain the leverage to keep the friction going, but I slip out quickly. Sam moans out in protest as I spin us around, her back to my chest, positioning her in front of the mirror atop my dresser. Our eyes meet in the reflection as I fill her again. Her mouth falls open, and her head tips back against my shoulder as I encircle her waist to keep her steady.

I wrap my other hand around her throat, forcing her to watch as I bury my cock into her over and over, harder each time. She digs her nails into my arm at her waist, forcing me to focus on the bite of pain instead of shattering inside her. I need this to last as long as possible for us both. We will never get this first again, and I want it engraved in our memories forever.

"Look at you, completely at my mercy. Your pleasure, mine to give. Watch yourself." My hand contracts at her throat, forcing her eyes back when she tries to glance away. "Keep watching. Until you see what I see. Until you feel what I feel when I see you like this. Beautiful in your submission."

Her eyes glaze over as she comes at my words, sparking my own release. My teeth sink into her skin as I groan. A weightlessness settles over me, my breath coming out in harsh gasps while I hold her limp body to mine. I lower her to her stomach, stroking her flushed skin as she quivers, my cock still deep inside her. I kiss her back over and over, shallowly driving into her still, pulling out her climax as long as possible.

I ease out and lie next to her, nuzzling her neck, and she turns her face to me, so I kiss her delicately. Her eyes are slits but intently focused on me. I glide my fingers up and down her flesh, kissing her again and again. In this moment, I know this is it. She's it. I was prepared to do whatever it took to keep her with us before, but now—now, I will burn the world down just to keep her.

FORTY-SIX

SAMANTHA

My buzzing phone pulls me from sleep, and for a moment, I don't know where I am. The disorientation persists until I spot Shane's sleeping form tucked under the comforter next to me. He's been different since our trip to the Egg. The last week has been a whirlwind of meetings and phone calls, gathering information from the streets and other major players, and he's included me in every single thing. He listens when I speak, even asking for my opinion. I don't know what's changed, but I can almost taste it in the air. I've never had this level of involvement before. Mason tolerated when I spoke up, but he never encouraged it. These men crave my thoughts, my attention, my body.

I never know when I'll be pulled into a random room, mouth on my skin before I can even register what is happening. Alex's hands roving over my body, working me into a frenzy before walking away without release, cocky smirk plastered on his face. Shane pushing me against the wall, thrusting in from behind, whispering all the things he loves doing to my body. Ren, though, drops to his knees, devouring me inch by inch, until I'm screaming his name. Sometimes, he'll happen upon me with one of the others, and he watches as I unravel under their hands and teeth and cocks. Those nights, he throws me over his shoulder, demanding everything from me, while he worships my body.

I still don't know where this whole dynamic will go when we've finally dealt with the Guild. I'm trying to protect my heart, while enjoying the completeness enveloping me. It's hard to separate the two. I feel myself slipping, my walls cracking with every smile, every whispered word, every passing day. I'll be lost forever if I don't gain some distance soon.

My phone buzzes again but goes black before I notice who the text is from. I slip from the bed, tiptoeing to the bathroom. Ten texts from Colin. He's been silent since Ren, and I sprung Alex from the Depot. Three apologies, four pleas, two guilt trips, and one request: a meeting. The two of us, no one else. There's no way I'll be able to convince any of the guys I should meet him alone.

Regardless of my trust in Colin, Ren, especially, is leery of anyone outside of their circle. Sometimes, I'm included in their group, but I realize that's only for now. I could be dressed and gone before anyone knows, but the fallout isn't worth it. I would be on the outside of the circle for sure if I went gallivanting off at dawn to meet with my brother's second. I hear the door, but don't turn when Shane comes in.

"What's up, Princess?" he asks, hovering by the threshold.

"Message from Colin," I reply, facing him.

"Were you going to tell me?" I study his face, trying to decipher the emotions there, but he glances away.

"I just did. Why wouldn't I tell you?"

Shane glances up, eyes hard. "Because you didn't tell me about texting with Emma. Seems like something I should have been informed of, don't you think?"

Shit. I knew it was a risk, but I was afraid if I ignored Emma's attempts to talk, she'd take matters in her own hands and try to sneak back to the city. Shane may think sending her two hours away is good enough, but Emma won't let the distance deter her.

"What did you expect, Shane? You could shove her off on some batty old lady, and she'd be cool? She was threatening to hitchhike back. I figured the safest option was to talk to her, keep her there. She asked me not to tell you. There wasn't anything you needed to know, so I respected what she wanted. If something came up you should know, I would have told you."

"Who she talks to *is* something I need to know. Every fucking time, Sam."

"It was just me. It's not like I passed out her number at the club, for fuck's sake." I throw my hands up.

"You think you texting her is any better?"

I flinch back, immediately gutted. My mouth drops, but I snap it shut.

"Fine," I grind out.

"Fine? What the fuck does that mean?" The angrier he gets, the more detached my body becomes.

"If that's how you feel, I won't talk to her. Now, if you'll excuse me, I need to get dressed," I huff, fixing my gaze behind him, praying he'll move so I can escape.

"And I'm supposed to trust you? You knew I wouldn't like it, and you did it anyway, but now I'm supposed to believe you?" he scoffs, folding his arms.

"Believe whatever you want. Now move," I hiss, mask falling into place.

"Where are you going?"

My heart cracks at the suspicion in his voice. I thought we'd overcome this, moving past the mistrust and accusations. There's always something else with him. I should have anticipated this outcome. I thought I'd protected myself enough to not be hurt this time, but I imagined the consequences coming during the after. After the Guild, after Mason woke up . . . just after. I didn't think it'd be something as stupid as texting his sister.

"I'm going to find Alex," I say, pushing past him when he still doesn't move. I throw on whatever I can find scattered on the furniture and flee out the door. I'm about to knock on Alex's door when Ren's opens down the hall, and I change directions.

"Hey," I say, falling in line with him. Ren stops, looking me up and down before he grabs my elbow and leads me back to his bedroom. I shiver, funneling the adrenaline from my fight with Shane into the anticipation flushing my body. Ren's need for control in the bedroom is precisely what I need after Shane's accusations.

Ren steers me to the closet, grabbing me new clothes. He hands them to me and leans back, waiting for me to change. I hesitate for a second before I comply. It's getting easier to be completely bare for him. He watches enough I don't blush anymore when I'm naked in front of him at least. And he watches a lot: dressing, showering, fucking.

"You going to tell me why you're wearing the same clothes from last night, even though you have some in Shane's room?" he probes, crossing his arms.

"I just grabbed what I saw," I reply, pulling the shirt over my head.

"Which means you were leaving in a hurry. So, again, why?"

"Shane got pissy. I left."

"Sam, you can't just leave every time someone says something you don't like."

"You don't even know what the hell happened, so don't come in here, lecturing me like an errant child."

I yank on my pants, waiting for him to continue, but he tips his head back. I thought, out of anyone, Ren would at least gather all the facts before passing judgment. I throw the clothes into the hamper and stomp off to find Alex.

"Sam, wait," he hollers, but I don't stop. This whole day is going to shit, and I haven't even eaten breakfast yet. Ren catches me as I reach his door, crowding me between his body and the wood.

"Ren . . ." I warn, face pressed against the cool wood.

I don't know what I want him to do. Apologize? Defend himself? Make me forget?

He buries his face in my neck, breathing deeply before mumbling, "I shouldn't assume. I don't like it when you walk away."

"Then, you should ask me shit before you assume I'm at fault."

Ren spins me, pressing his body back into mine, tightly gripping my hips. His forehead rests against mine before kissing me lightly.

"Tell me what happened."

"Colin texted me," I say.

Ren's lip curls.

"Which I told him about, which led to him finding out I've been talking to Emma. He wasn't happy about it."

"That's not all, is it?" I roll my eyes. Of course Ren picked up on the fact I'm not angry, I'm hurt.

"He may have insinuated I wasn't good enough to talk to his sister. I thought . . . well it doesn't matter. He made his point, and I remember my place now. So, would you like to go with me when I meet Colin? He wants me to come alone, but I figure it wouldn't be in good form." I hold my breath, hoping he drops the subject.

"Your place?" His voice is eerily calm, forcing goosebumps to erupt along my arms.

"Temporary. I get it. I just forgot for a minute. Did you want to go, or should I ask Alex?"

"Interesting."

I turn my head away, if only to escape his gaze. Heat flashes through my body, no longer in anticipation but in . . . something else. Shame or embarrassment or rejection, maybe all three. There's been no indication this situation is anything more than a fleeting moment. I knew, going in, no matter how many things change along the way, the chances of this being permanent is slim at best. Doesn't mean I wanted to admit those facts out loud, especially to one of them.

"Can we drop it? Don't worry about it." I squirm, trying to put space between us.

"Oh, we'll be revisiting this, but for now, let's go see what Colin wants," he says, stepping away.

Twenty minutes later, we park outside a house that's seen better days. It's probably another safehouse. We have so many I can't keep track of them all. Why Colin picked this place instead of a public space makes me nervous. I don't want us walking into an ambush.

"Do you think he set us up?" Ren inquires, breaking the silence.

"No, but I'm worried this is a ploy from Victor. Colin might not be in there."

Ren nods, going back to his phone.

I pull out my own, seeing several more texts from Emma. I leave them unread, though. I don't want to block her, but I'm trying to respect Shane's decision. I don't want to be yelled at again. He doesn't trust me, fine. I thought we worked all our shit out, but it doesn't matter either way. The end result is the same. I pray she doesn't do something rash, though. The last time she ran headlong into a situation, she almost got kidnapped. If I'm not there the next time . . . I shudder, trying to force the flashes of what the Guild would do to her from my mind.

"Ready?" I ask as Colin's text comes through with the door code.

"Let's get this over with."

Ren's slips his hand into his jacket, palming his gun as he punches the buttons. I want to tell him he won't need it, but I remember Colin pressing his own weapon against Alex's head and hold my tongue. Colin is in the kitchen, eating a breakfast sandwich. He doesn't look up when we come in, and I plop down across from him.

"Thought I told you to come alone?" Colin says around a full mouth.

"We both know that wasn't going to fly, Colin."

"They your keepers now? That how it works over in King territory?"

"No, but I'm not stupid enough to go off on my own with people actively trying to kill me."

Colin's head whips up at my statement. Apparently, he wasn't informed. I won't fill him in. It hits me then—I'm pissed. He had so many choices, chances to help me, to protect me, and he left me. He left me alone to deal with everything. He's supposed to be my family, but he's done a piss-poor job.

"I wasn't aware."

"I'm sure there's a lot you're not aware of, but that's the nature of things, isn't it?" I glance at Ren leaning against the counter. Bringing him was the perfect choice. He'll let me do the talking without trying to take over, whether in a dick-measuring contest or to protect me.

"What the hell is that supposed to mean, Sam?"

I swing my head back and narrow my eyes. "You fucked off. You handed the Byrns' empire over to that greasy, misogynistic bastard without a backward glance. Oh, sure, you said it was to keep the peace, but we both know that's shit. If you stepped up, like you were supposed to, the lower gangs would be in order, things would be running smoothly, I wouldn't have been fucking shot. The Guild would be taken care of, Oracle wouldn't be flooding the streets, and things would be fine."

And you would have never crossed paths with the Kings, a voice in my head whispers, but I banish it before it can take root.

"It's not that simple. I don't expect you to understand."

"Don't talk down to me like I'm some naïve, little girl, Colin. Own your shit. Regardless whether you took over or not, you should have fought more. Instead, you went along with whatever Victor wanted and left me to figure shit out on my own. You don't get to piss all over my choices. And for your information . . ." I pause. "Never mind. Tell me why the hell we're here, so I can go."

"Back to them?" he asks, but the fight is draining from him.

"Yes, for now." I say, glancing at Ren.

Ren tenses.

Colin hesitates, looking between Ren and me, before saying, "Things are bad, Sammy. I don't know what you've found out, but it's worse than whatever you've discovered. Nothing is going to plan, and I don't want you stuck in the middle of it. I'm sure your *friend* will disagree, but I think it's time for you to think about getting out of Synd."

I sit back, stunned. Out of all the possible reasons I thought he reached out, him asking me to run wasn't on my radar. I try to collect my chaotic thoughts as Ren pulls out his phone. He always thought I was going to take off, and Colin's suggestion is sure to trigger a chain reaction.

"That's not going to happen. I appreciate your concern for me, but," I say before clearing my throat, "you should know me better, Colin."

He nods, as if he expected my answer. The thought of leaving, when my family, my friends, my city is in danger, is ludicrous. Leaving my brother, who's still laying in the hospital? I'd never do that. Leaving Shane and Alex and Ren? I'm not ready to make that decision, might never be.

"Just think about it. I grabbed one of your bags from under your bed. Thought you'd like to have something of your own. I think someone went through your room, though, some of your things were missing," he says, setting a bag on the table.

"Thank you."

I grab the bag, standing, ready to be done with this whole interaction. As I pass Ren, he snatches it from my grasp and hauls it on his shoulder, gesturing for me to pass. I stop when we reach the threshold, casting my gaze back.

"Colin, try to talk some sense into Victor. I don't know where he stands, but we're going to need all the help we can get. This isn't something the Byrns can take on by themselves."

"Victor and I haven't exactly been on the same page the last few weeks," he says.

"Maybe it's time to step up, then, force the conversation. They won't distinguish between east and west when it comes down to it."

I walk out before he can respond. Ren places the bag on my lap when he slips in the car. I thought he'd go straight to the Kings' estate, but instead, he parks next to the pond we had our first conversation at. We sit in silence, staring at the half-frozen water, both lost in our thoughts.

"What's in the bag, Sam?"

"If he didn't go through it—some clothes, cash, first aid kit, a gun, and some knives. Couple other random things." I wait a beat. "And a phone."

"Open it. We need to make sure nothing extra was added."

Pawing through the pack, I see everything is the same as when I'd originally packed it. I pull out the gun and knives before zipping it back up. I pull out the phone out of the side pocket and drop everything on the floor. I fling open the car and throw the bag in the pond before I can think twice about what I'm doing.

When I get back in, Ren nods to the pile at my feet. "You should get rid of the phone, too."

"No need. It's heavily encrypted. Your mysterious hacker wouldn't even be able to get into this thing."

"Impossible."

"Improbable, not impossible. Go ahead." I smirk, tossing the phone to him.

Ten minutes later, he gives up, handing it back to me with a scowl. I unlock the screen, grinning, and see dozens of messages unopened, all addressed to the Wraith. I scroll through them. They start off as normal requests for a hit on various people, then move to pleas for help. Every one of them, toward the end, are requests to find someone. No one is asking me to take someone out but to return a loved one. The Guild's reach slithered out of the Barrens, infiltrating the suburbs, entangled itself within the rich and powerful of the city. While we gathered our information, they were expanding without us realizing. My other phone vibrates, showing a text from the last person I ever expected to reach out.

Ren, we need to call a meeting. Now.

FORTY-SEVEN

SHANE

"Helms, we need to get this meeting sorted. Now. I'm done fucking around with Victor and his asinine requests. The meeting is in three days here, and we're doing it with or without him. You got a problem with any of that?" I bark into the phone.

"Fine by me. My people are coming in tomorrow, so we'll be ready. If anything, we can loop Colin in. He might have to substitute for Victor if the asshole can't get his shit together," Helms replies.

"We'd rather not. His position is unstable at the moment."

It's the most diplomatic way I can say Ren thinks Colin's a shit person who shouldn't know anything. I don't agree, but I trust Ren. If he says we keep Colin out, then he's out. I assume Ren went with Sam to whatever meeting Colin wanted to have, but he hasn't mentioned anything, and I'm not bringing it up. The last thing I need to do is discuss the shit happening between Sam and I with him.

"What's Sam think about him?"

I pause, trying to figure out how to word my response. I haven't kept her from the meetings, but I haven't been seeking her out, either. She trusts Colin, regardless of how Ren feels, but she respects him enough to not tell Colin anything. I wish she respected me enough when it comes to talking to my sister.

"She's good with the plan."

"You might want to work on your delivery, King. Sounded a bit hollow. Trouble in paradise?" Helms laughs.

"Fuck off. Everything is fine. I'll see you at the meeting."

I hang up before he can bust my balls anymore. His comments during the entire conversation kept bringing Sam to the forefront of my mind, no matter how much I tried to push her away. We haven't talked in days unless it's about the Guild or the upcoming meeting. We haven't fucked in almost a week. I caught her slipping into the others' rooms or them pulling her from the hallway. Jealousy burns in my gut knowing I can't keep going like this. It's more than getting laid; it's the distance. I want to blame her for it, but we're both at fault, not that I'll admit anything.

I sigh, scrubbing my hands down my face, when there's a knock at my door. I contemplate ignoring him, but Ren knows I'm in here. He's been dogging me, but I keep putting him off.

"Yeah?" I call out, fixing my gaze on my laptop, trying to look busy.

"What'd Helms say?" Ren asks, dropping into a chair.

"He's a go. He'll relay the info to Victor. I don't think I can handle another go-around with the fucker."

Ren nods, peering around my office. A memory hits me out of nowhere: Ren sitting in the same chair but smaller, wide gray eyes staring at my father, who once occupied the seat I'm in. I shake the memory away.

He breaks the silence. "You still going to be an asshole about this?"

"No idea what you're talking about," I hedge, training my eyes on the screen.

"Sure you don't. You realize you hurt her feelings, right?"

My chest twinges, but I ignore it. "She's a big girl. She'll get over it."

"I don't think she will, Shane. After everything you've said to her . . . she thinks she's temporary," Ren confesses.

"I know." I didn't know, but I can't admit that to him.

"No, you didn't, but whatever. You need to figure out what's more important to you, being right or being happy," he sighs, pushing himself up.

"I have to protect our family, Ren," I say when he reaches the door, making him turn back.

"When are you going to see it, Shane?"

"See what?"

He shakes his head. "Figure it out."

I curse as he closes the door. Of course, he'd leave me with a riddle instead of answers. None of them understand the pressure I'm under. Protecting Emma is at the forefront of my mind. I don't want this life for my little sister. As much as Sam fits into our world, I don't want Emma to fit. It's dangerous and hard. I've seen what it's done to Sam, and I can't put my sister through that willingly, regardless of what she thinks she wants.

Alex doesn't bother with knocking, collapsing with a groan in the seat Ren left vacant. His usual grin is nowhere to be found. He levels me with a look before dropping his phone on my desk and pushing it toward me.

"I don't have time for this, Alex, tell me what you want."

"Oh, you don't want to see what Emma's been texting me? How she's begging me to talk some sense into you? Pretty sure she implied bodily harm to various parts of your anatomy, but I can't figure out half the shit she's saying. Kids these days don't know how to fucking talk."

"She's been texting you?" I glare, an ache burning in my lungs.

She refuses to respond to my messages or take my calls. I assume Sam told her I'm the reason she won't be talking to her anymore. Or maybe Sam is still texting her, and Emma is covering for her. I don't know.

"Yup, like seventeen thousand times a day. It's annoying as fuck, but since you cut off her only source of communication, she's turned to me. So, are you going to pull your head out of your ass and let Sam take over again? 'Cause I'm losing my mind here," he complains, tipping his head back.

"Oh, I doubt Sam listened to me. She's probably texting Emma as we speak, giving her pointers on where to stab a man to make it hurt the most." I roll my eyes, focusing on the screen.

"Are you for fucking real? I swear, I knew you were dumb, but this is insane, even for you. What the fuck happened to make you suddenly not trust her?"

"Fuck you. I'm not going to discuss this. You can handle your relationship with her any way you'd like, but don't come in here talking shit to me. You didn't want to be a matchmaker before, so don't start now."

"Well, your shit is getting in the way of my shit, so . . ."

I lean back, rubbing my temples. I can't handle all this at once. Between the Guild, coordinating all the various factions, and this thing with Sam, my head throbs a little more every day. Add in keeping my sister safe—it's too much. I can't deal with the bullshit between Sam and I. I don't know if I want to. My family has to come first.

"I don't have time for this. Dealing with the Guild is first priority, not some woman whose feelings got hurt." The words burn coming out, but I won't take them back.

"Some woman? Is that really how you see her? Just some woman? Wow. Just . . . wow. I'm not giving her up because you're a fucking bastard. So, figure it out. I get it, pushing the Guild out of our city needs to be number one, but if you fuck this up with Sam in the process, you'll only have yourself to blame in the end," he says, shaking his head and getting to his feet.

"Meeting is in three days," I respond.

The click of the door is his only acknowledgment.

Ten minutes later, I'm still staring at my computer, not doing any work. Ren and Alex's words keep spinning through my mind, making me question whether I'm right here. I can't see another way to keep Emma safe, though. Sam may be exactly what they need, but I don't. She'll only pull Emma further into our world, and I can't have that, no matter how much I wish things were different.

Another knock rattles my door, but this one is tentative. Sam used to waltz right in like she owned the place, but ever since our fight, she's backed off, leaving the room when I enter, barely speaking when we do end up together. I hate the distance, but I don't know how to get her to see things from my point of view.

"Come in," I call out.

Sam glides in, avoiding eye contact, holding a folder. She drops it on my desk and folds her arms, waiting.

"What's this?" I ask when the silence becomes too much.

"Don't know. Some guy at the gate dropped it off," she replies, peering out the window.

"Why were you at the gate?" Suspicion riddles my voice, and she flinches.

"I wasn't at the gate. I was downstairs. I'm the first person they found to pass it off to," she explains, exasperation bleeding into her voice.

"Did you open it?"

I can't stop asking the questions I know are going to piss her off, push all her buttons until she finally breaks. My chest burns, and my spine straightens as shame flows over me. I don't want to break her, but I keep lashing out, knowing I'm causing her more pain.

"No, King. I didn't. I don't fucking care what's inside. Anything else?" It's my turn to flinch at her flippant use of my last name as she spins, not waiting for my response.

"Actually, yes, there is. The meeting is in three days. I expect you to be there," I command, pulling the folder toward me.

She whirls around, fire in her eyes. "You don't get to expect anything out of me. I'll be there because it's in my best interest but don't think I'm doing it for you."

"Oh, I hardly think there's anything you'll do for me, Byrns, regardless whether I ask or not."

"That wasn't you asking. That was you commanding. I'm a grown-ass woman. It'd do well for you to remember that when you're spouting off demands."

"I'm well aware of what you are. You're living in my house, in my territory. You'd do well to remember *that,* Samantha."

We're on our feet now, glaring at each other and waiting for the other to break. I wish I could rewind the days, go back to when she was stealing snacks into my bed, laughing at some joke Ren told no one else got, and putting Alex in his place when he got out of line. I wish I could stuff all the words I've spewed back in my mouth, but they're out there, waiting to explode like unattended bombs.

"It's a good thing I won't be here much longer, then, isn't it?"

"What's that supposed to mean?"

"You're a big boy. You can figure it out."

"Oh, I most certainly can. Like you said, you're a grown-ass woman. You can make your own decisions."

"Not going to try to command me?" she snarks, eyes glittering with malice but lined with pain.

"I don't care what you do, Byrns," I sneer. "The fact you think your presence here has any effect on me is laughable. I couldn't care less if you leave. We'll be just fine when you take your ass back to your side of the river. In fact, I can't wait until you do." I heave out the words, and watch as her face shutters, all emotion draining from her, before she calmly turns and walks out the door.

Remorse chases the bitterness, and I sag in my chair, my hand covering my mouth. I want to run after her, beg forgiveness, let her rage against me, give her anything she wants if she'll let me take back my words. Instead, I'm frozen, staring at nothing and reliving the break I saw in her eyes before she shut herself off. Even if I went after her, I doubt there's anything I could say she would believe. The things I've said to her before were harsh—cutting, but we didn't know each other yet. We were merely two people, living in the same world.

This is different. We're different.

I don't know if we'll ever get back to how we were just days ago, even if she wanted to.

It's better this way.

The longer I sit here, the less I believe those words.

FORTY-EIGHT

ALEX

"Bug," I grumble, tugging Sam's body back under the covers. I nuzzle her neck as she shivers and throws my leg over hers to keep her from escaping.

"Alex, I have to get up."

"Why," I whine, locking my arms around her.

"The meeting is today. We can't all stay in bed until ten minutes before it starts."

The door swings open, and Ren stalks in. I mutter a "morning," then turn my attention back to Sam's warm body. Ren usually knocks, but since Sam has been occupying our beds, he's taken to barging in whenever he pleases.

"You coming, Sam?" he asks, stopping in front of us

"Not yet, but she will be soon," I reply, grinning.

"Alex!" she squeals, trying to pull away.

"Want to join?" I entice him, ignoring her indignation.

"Only if I can be in control," he replies as he closes the door. The lock clicks, sending another shiver through her body. The quickness of his reply makes me think he planned this all along.

"Wanna play, Bug? I mean, if you insist on getting up instead, we could always finish this later."

I untangle my limbs and lay back, tucking my hands behind my head. Ren pauses, halfway through taking off his shirt and waits for her answer. She's deliciously rumpled, dark hair a riot on the pillow, and she bites her lip, brown eyes widening when she sees what Ren is in the middle of. He gradually pulls it the rest of the way off and reaches for his pants.

"I'm sure whatever I was going to do can wait."

"Good answer, Pet," he quips as his pants join the pile on the floor, "But you're wearing way too many clothes. Alex?"

I move before he finishes speaking, straddling Sam and peeling off her tank top, leaving her only in a little thong. I'm already hard, my imagination running overtime, but seeing her splayed out underneath me, and I'm practically salivating. Sam reaches up to touch me, but Ren's hand is there, wrapping around her wrists and forcing them above her head.

"Ah, ah, little pet. No touching."

"What? Cruel," I protest.

"Get up, Alex, you'll thank me later."

As I stand next to him, we shuck off our boxers, Sam's eyes fixed on us. Her tongue darts out, licking her lips when I spring free. My cock reacts, and we haven't even done anything yet. Ren pulls off her panties, leaving her bare for us.

"On the floor, Pet—knees," he demands, kneeling behind her when she complies, then holds her arms back. Her eyes dance between my face and my erection, and I almost miss Ren telling her to open up while his hand travels down her body, pinching her nipple before going lower.

Her mouth on my cock has me groaning and tipping my head back as she swirls and licks the tip. She's watching me, Ren's hand tight on her hair, guiding her movements.

"Such a good girl," he croons. "You like his cock in your mouth?"

She hums in response, making me grunt at the vibrations. I'm struggling to keep myself still, letting Ren set the pace. She's clasped her hands behind her back, letting him take over her body. He dips a finger between her legs and pulls it out, glistening with her arousal, then pops it in his mouth, humming his satisfaction.

I pull out, not able to take much more without coming down her throat, and a cry of protest falls from her lips. I drop to my knees and pull her face to mine, thrusting my tongue in, like I want to do with my cock. Ren's hand drops back to her pussy, and he rubs along her slit, while she chases his fingers. Cupping her tits, I switch to her nipple, as she tips her head back. Hearing her cries of pleasure has me twitching, and I reach down, squeezing my cock to relieve the pressure. Sam's body quivers, and her fingers are suddenly digging into my hair, holding on as her orgasm overtakes her.

"Where is it, Alex?"

"Where's what?" I ask, mouth still attached to the hard nub.

"Lube."

I jerk my head up, looking from one to the other. I've fucked Sam in multiple positions now, but I stay away from her ass. I don't want to scare her, and it isn't something one just brings up casually.

"Sam?" I ask, meeting her glazed eyes.

"Bedside drawer," she gasps before pulling my mouth back to hers.

He clambers up, so I pull Sam with me on to the bed, putting her on her knees in front of me, then cup her face, silently asking her if she's okay with all this. Her eyes flash with lust, and I swoop down to capture her nipple between my teeth, nipping until it's hard.

She leans in, jolting as Ren whispers in her ear from behind, getting her ready. I can't hear what he's saying over the roar in my ears, but her body tenses, then melts. Grabbing her hips, I catch Ren's eyes over her shoulder, a wicked grin on his face, and he nods.

I grasp her hips hard, embedding myself in her soaking pussy, and she clings to me. I wait, reeling in the feel of her wrapped around me, leaning back to give Ren access to her. Her pussy tightens and spasms as he eases into her, needy notes falling out of her mouth the more he inches in.

"You good, Pet?" he gasps, voice strained.

She nods, hips jerking, desperate for more. I'm trying to be gentle as I delve inside her.

"Alex, faster . . . harder . . ."

I give her exactly what she's begging for, plunging into her, deepening my thrusts more each time. Sam tenses, craving more. Then Ren starts to move, pushing in and out shallowly, grunting with each movement. I smooth the hair sticking on her damp forehead and snake my hand behind her neck, tipping her head back.

"Is this what you wanted, Bug? Both of us fucking you?" I say, playing with her nipple as she tips ever closer to the edge. Her pussy pulses around me, and Ren wraps an arm around her waist, keeping her still as we possess every inch of her.

His hand finds her clit, rolling it between his fingers. "Come for us, Sam. Show us how much you love us inside of you."

She erupts at his words, sparking my own orgasm, and I let out a guttural moan, her pussy seizing around my cock. I'm drained, but somehow, I maneuver my legs out, still fully sheathed inside her, while she goes limp. I lay back, taking her with me, and Ren follows, grabbing her hips and thrusting harder. Her pussy twitches with each surge.

"Such a good pet, aren't you?" he huffs.

Sam whimpers, and her eyes fly open, locking on mine. Entranced, I hold her tight, watching her face as she hurtles closer and closer toward another climax.

"Oh god," she moans, spasming and clenching around my cock. Ren pulls out and pumps his fist over his cock, spreading his cum on her back, a possessive look overtaking his face as he leans back, admiring his work on her skin. Sam is purring, lax and exhausted, pussy still clinging to my cock.

"Goddammit, Ren, now I have to change my sheets!" I grumble when I see the mess he's made.

He barks out a laugh, grabbing the corner of my comforter to clean Sam up. I lift her off me gently, tucking her close to my side, and she burrows in, throwing a leg over mine. Ren collapses next to her, petting her skin. We lay, basking in bliss. Minutes pass, and I'm sure she's fallen asleep again, body sated.

"Well, that was unexpected," she murmurs.

"Not really," Ren jokes.

Her head sweeps around, pinning him with a glare. "Are you telling me you came in here just to tag team me?"

He grins, kissing her swiftly before vaulting off the bed for his clothes. The more time he spends with Sam, the more he falls into how he is with Shane and me. Other people see the mask—cold, controlled, emotionless, but we see the real him beneath. Sam brings out a side of him I haven't seen in years, though. I don't know how she did it, but she fills something in each of us. I can't lose that. None of us would survive.

"Up you get, Bug. We have a meeting today, you know," I tease, pinching her side. She squeals, leaping off the bed and into Ren's arms. He laughs again, kissing her soundly before passing her back to me and strolling out, a smile playing on his lips.

"Put me down, Alex."

"Nope. You're all icky, but I'll fix you right up," I say, carrying her into the bathroom and straight into the shower. She shrieks when I turn on the water, the crisp spray soothing my overheated skin.

"Alex, please!"

"Begging for it again, Bug? Did we not make you come enough? Greedy girl."

I crowd her against the cold tiles while she yelps, trying to jerk away from the chill, but I push in closer, warming her body with mine as the water heats up. I stroke her side, swooping down to nibble on her ear. She shudders, running her hands over my shoulders, tipping her head to give me more access to her delicious skin.

I can't get enough of this woman: her body, her essence, everything she is. Sam wraps her hand around my cock, squeezing hard before working her hand up and down my length. It doesn't take long before I'm hard for her again.

"Tell me, Sam, have you fantasized about us both taking you? Filling you up? Making your body sing for us?"

I don't expect an answer, Sam's not very vocal in bed, content with me telling her all the dirty things I want to do to her, but her hand pauses, and she looks in my eyes.

"You have no idea. Every time I see you together, I wonder, but I didn't want to ask," she replies, the words falling out of her before she tucks her face in my chest.

"Oh, Bug, don't do that. Don't hide from me. I want to hear all your dirty fantasies. If I can bring them to life, I will."

I tip her chin up and kiss her softly, and she melts a little more into me. No matter what's happening around us, I want to live here, knowing she trusts me to take care of her: her needs, her wants, her desires.

"Alex," she murmurs against my lips.

"Yeah?"

"I want . . ." She stops, tucking her head again.

"Tell me."

"Bench." Her answer makes me grin. I have never been happier for the large ass shower I have, complete with a bench to perch her ass on. I spin us around, crowding her back until her legs hit the wood of the seat. She huffs out a laugh when I guide her down, but she stops when I drop to my knees in front of her, spreading her legs wide for me to see her pretty pussy.

"This what you want, Bug?" I ask, before grabbing her legs and throwing them over my shoulders, sliding her until her ass is right on the edge and bury my face in her folds, sucking and licking as her thighs squeeze my head. I could die happily with my face buried between her legs. She chants my name, latching on to my hair, and her hips move up and down, using me to get herself off. It's intoxicating knowing I can make her come over and over again.

Her voice echoes, bouncing around the small space. "Alex, wait."

Immediately, I stop, jerking back and releasing my hold on her. She's never told me to stop before. Alarm floods me, and I gaze up at her, waiting, but she just bites her lip, concern filling her face.

"Are you okay? What is it?"

"I . . . this is amazing, but . . ."

"But?"

She's killing me here.

"But I wanted to fuck you while you're sitting," she admits in a rush, covering her face with her hands. I stand, grinning, and tug her up to trade places. The steam is thickening, coating the glass and transforming the shower into our own personal bubble.

"Your wish is my command."

She smiles, pressing me down and climbing on top of me. Her tits end up right in my face, and I have to agree this is way better. I suck in a breath when she grabs my cock, lining me up to her center. I expect her to sink down slowly, but instead, she surges down, my cock impaling her in one stroke. I grab her waist, forcing her to stay still while my breath stutters out of my lungs.

"Did you like watching me fall apart while you and Ren fucked me?" she whispers in my ear, making me jerk. I don't know where this side of her is coming from, but fuck me if I'm going to stop it.

"Bug, you have no idea how incredibly hot that was. I can't wait to do it again." I skim my hands up, trying to pull her closer. She resists, planting her hands on my shoulders and shuddering as she heaves up, lingering before sinking down again, forcing a hiss out of me.

"You're going to sit back and take it, Alex, whatever I want to do to you."

"Yes, ma'am," I drawl out, leaning back but keeping my hands around her waist. The last thing I need is her slipping off.

Sam moves faster, pants falling from her lips, and I can't help but move my hips, burrowing deeper into her with every thrust. She throws her head back, bracing her hands on my knees, and moves. I've never seen her sexier than right now, throwing all her inhibitions away and riding me, bringing herself closer and closer to climax.

"Fuck, I love feeling your pussy squeeze my cock." My words make her clench around me, but she doesn't stop. "I love watching you ride me." I dip my head, scraping my teeth along her nipple.

"Alex," she stutters out, her movements faltering, "fuck me."

Her words undo me, and I tighten my grip, holding her still while I ravage her. She moans, fingernails digging into my legs, and I plunge into her harder, possessing every inch of her. The tingling starts in my base. I'm close to exploding, and she'll erupt with me based on the needy sounds falling from her lips.

"You going to come for me, Sam? You going to show me how much you love my cock filling you up?"

She shudders, gasping, and she snaps, soaring over the edge while squeezing me so tight I come with her, grunting and jerking before she collapses on top of me, utterly spent. I don't know how long we sit, wrapped in each other, but I don't move, craving the feel of her in my arms a little bit longer.

FORTY-NINE

SAMANTHA

I imagined this meeting going to hell in a handbasket, but not quite like this. When Victor texted me, politely asking for the contact protocol with the Kings, I figured he would be his smarmy self, full of air and bravado. Instead, he was civil, following every rule I gave him, going so far as to thank me when we were done. Why he decided to text me instead of asking Colin is beyond me.

Shane has been less polite, which isn't surprising, seeing as how he isn't getting laid at the moment. Neither of us have tried that hard to deal with the elephant in the room, and after his little temper tantrum the other day, I have a feeling we never will. He made himself pretty clear on where we stand, so there's not much more to discuss.

I'm not going to apologize for talking to his sister. He isn't going to back down that he's right. Typical Shane: always needing to be right, even when he's wrong. It's better this way. He'll have an excuse to point to when this whole mess is settled, and we can go our separate ways. Just a few more days, and I'll be gone.

A sharp pang shoots through me at leaving them. I have no idea where I'll even go. I could go back to the estate, since Victor seems to have calmed his shit down.

Letting go is easier said than done, especially when I'm constantly running into Shane in meetings, in the hall, in the kitchen, in the other guys' rooms.

Heat rushes to my cheeks, remembering Alex and Ren and what we did earlier. As much as I enjoyed it, when Alex left me to finish my shower in peace, the tears came. With every passing day, I'm one step closer to leaving. One step closer to disappearing from their lives. My emotions are jumbling more with every encounter. Ren and Alex fucking me together was a fantasy I'd dreamed of, but it was missing one thing. Shane not being there sent me into a spiral with how we left things for almost a week, knowing we won't get back to where we were. Thankfully, the redness around my eyes faded by the time I left the bathroom, but Ren's eyes have been tracking me from the minute I stepped in the room. He knows something is wrong. I hope he doesn't think I'm regretting them.

"Victor, you said you had actual information for us. If you can't contribute to this fucking meeting, why the hell did you call for it?" Shane demands, leaning across the table from my uncle.

All the major players are sat at the conference table, but Shane is the only one who's flanked with others, Ren and Alex. Everyone else is scattered along the wall, trying to pretend they aren't eyeing each other. The tension is probably the same as it was last time they had met up. I post myself next to the door, praying I can make a quick getaway when this shit show is finally over.

"I think what King is trying to ask is what prompted you to ask us to meet, Victor?" Helms placates, the reluctant peacemaker. He has rolled his eyes fourteen times in seventeen minutes . . . not that I'm counting.

"Well, this whole situation is obviously more than we are able to handle . . ."

I can't see Victor's face, but his neck is bunching. He's hiding something, but I keep my mouth shut. Shane warned me to listen instead of speaking. I can't figure out if he's trying to protect me or himself. Maybe he doesn't want people to know how deeply we're connected . . . were connected. He must be regretting his demand I be here altogether.

"Clearly. We all warned you. What changed?" Alex speaks up, raising an eyebrow at the older man.

"I thought the Byrns' crew would be able to handle things on the east side, without interference from the west. That's how we've always done things. With the Guild coming in, though . . ."

Victor pulls at his tie. I bite my tongue.

"It wasn't always this way," Helms admits.

"What do you mean?" Ren asks, his eyes finally leaving me to focus on Helms.

"When the Kings and the Byrns came to town, they worked together. It wasn't east and west. It was just Synd"—he shrugs—"things changed, but no one remembers why."

Shane waves away Helms's history lesson. "Regardless, we need to know what's brought you here, Victor."

"I told you," he sputters, his neck flushing as he smacks the table. "I want to know what's going on."

"Spit it out, Victor," I chime in.

His body tenses more. "I don't know what you're talking about, Samantha."

"We've all been waiting to hear what the hell happened to make you request a meeting; to reach out to *me* of all people, so spit. It. Out."

He stays silent, and all eyes are on me. I wait, knowing he'll break before I do. I cross my arms, leaning against the wall. A full minute passes before he mutters something and shakes his head.

I sigh. "How about I guess, and you can tell us if I'm right. The Guild started hitting you hard, talking to the lower gangs and luring them to their side. Then, they hit a couple safehouses, brought in more Oracle, maybe floated some of the gunrunning. But those things didn't sway you enough to seek out the Kings. No, that wouldn't be enough. It wasn't until they went balls to the wall that you got spooked."

"I don't know what you're referring to."

"They took it, didn't they?"

"Took what?" Alex frowns.

"The Depot," I answer, focused on the back of Victor's head, which slumps at my words.

"For fuck's sake," Shane says, throwing his hands in the air.

Everyone starts talking at once until Helms slams his hand down. "Shut the fuck up and let's come up with a game plan."

Another hour in, and I'm bored to tears. If I can slip out, make myself something to eat, I'm sure I can make it back before I miss anything important. They've been going in circles, arguing about what to do, who is going to do what, and why shit won't work. With Victor here, it's more chaotic than our previous meetings. He has a problem with saying stupid shit, then getting defensive when someone tells him it's stupid. The only thing they've agreed on is the last-ditch effort, which is just to blow shit up. They didn't even have to come up with the plan, since it's a holdover from the attempted coup ten years ago. I'm about to slip out the door in search of a snack when Alex loses his mind, so I settle back, content to watch him go ape shit. It's rare, but a thrill rolls through me, and I hide my smirk behind my fist.

"What the fuck are we doing here? We've been talking for fucking weeks now. Can't we just get this shit going and burn the fuckers to the ground? This is fucking ridiculous!" he yells, chucking his water bottle against the wall, narrowly missing some woman Helms brought. She yelps, and Helms jumps up, glowering at Shane's second.

"Watch yourself, King," he snarls.

"Sorry," Alex says to the woman before retreating to his seat, cheeks flushed.

"Let's go over it again, figure out where we can agree." Shane rubs his hands over his face and looks to Ren.

My phone buzzes, and I pull it out, seeing a series of texts from Emma. I've been ignoring her, but I keep reading the previews. I'm trying to skirt the line Shane drew in the sand, but it's been hard. I know what it's like to be on the outside looking in. The messages before were borderline whining. The ones I'm getting now, though . . .

Im sry. Pls answer

What did I do wrong?

I pull them up, swiping through, praying she's not saying what I think she is.

U arent answering. I cant stay here

Im coming home

Think Im being followed

What do I do?

I push off the wall, about to show Shane, when the latest one pops up.

Help

I glance up, the meeting still in full force around me. While I'm falling into panic, they're still embroiled in their schemes. I try to will Shane's eyes to me, but he's intently listening to something Helms is saying. Glancing down again, the last message is longer, and not in Emma's shorthand ways.

Hello Ms. Byrns. You're a hard woman to find. Fortunately we've found someone else. Please come and retrieve her, and we can have a little chat.

They've sent an address, which is unnecessary, since I practically grew up there. My blood runs cold as I look up at Shane. He's still in deep conversation with the others. No one is paying me any attention since I've extracted the information they needed from Victor.

I'm about to say something, go to him, anything to get his attention, when my mouth snaps shut. They're all talking about infiltrating the Depot, hitting them with an attack, much like the hit on my brother months ago. Emma could get hurt if they do. The guys . . . they could die. It's foolish to think, in an attack of this magnitude, they'll all walk out without a scratch. Even if they do, if something happens to Emma . . . Shane was right. I should have left well enough alone. Regret slams into me, seizing my lungs and freezing me in place.

I give myself thirty seconds, my eyes bouncing between the three men who have changed my life. Even if I don't want to admit it, they've swooped in and made me come alive like nothing else in my existence. Those thirty seconds is all I allow before I snap out of it and slip out the door.

I rush down the empty hall, charging into Ren's closet to change and raid his supplies. I push the thoughts of the men down the hall aside, focusing on a plan. The Guild thinks I'm some mafia princess, like Shane. What they'll encounter is the Wraith. I'm not going to cower or turn myself in. I'll be a shadow, seeping through the cracks, snatching their prey away in the dead of night.

I take the tunnels, using my phone to light the way to the garage. I hesitate for a second before placing my phone on the bench. Seeing Ren's setup, I know he can track me, but I need to do this alone. I snatch one of the key rings and hit the button, cursing my luck when Ren's Maserati lights up. I debate whether to try to find another less noticeable vehicle, but I slide in the driver's seat. As obnoxious as it is, at least it's comfortable. The sensor for the garage pings. I race through the suburbs and into the lengthening shadows of the fading light.

The Depot was built years ago, enhanced along the way, but it holds the same secrets the estate houses do. Hidden entrances and escape routes are tucked everywhere. Mason added more after our father died.

As I approach one, folded into the shadows of an alley, I pray they haven't uncovered those secrets. The keypad stays dark even as I press the buttons, a dark blue pulse the only indication I'm in. Darkness envelops me as the door whooshes closed, but I know where I am. I bound up the three flights and come out by my old room. I contemplate going in to retrieve my knives but think better of it. If it were me, I would have put an alarm in there, hoping my prey would come back at some point.

Following the U-shape of the building, I get closer to the main room, knowing I'll have to backtrack and cover all the levels on this side before I attempt crossing the open mezzanine to reach the other rooms. The farther I travel, the more aware the oppressive silence presses down on me. I assume they've moved their men here, but everything is silent. Finding Emma in this compound, stifling every potential noise along the way, is going to test everything I've ever learned. I creep down after checking the stairwell, palming a knife as I go.

I clear two floors before I encounter anyone. Either these fools don't have enough men to cover the roof, or they never thought someone would scale the side of the building. A stout man leans against the wall facing away from me, fiddling with something in his hands. He doesn't hear me, and the only sound he makes is a gurgling as my knife slides across his throat. I try to ease him down, but he's huge compared to me. I end up fumbling with his limbs, and he plops on his ass, still leaning sideways against the wall. I leave him, unwilling to heft him into a room.

The first floor is as quiet as the others, but more men mill about. They seem strangely at ease, as if this is any another night. Their silence is creeping me out, only nodding when they pass one another. I leave them, easing back around the corner and up the stairs.

Coming up to the fourth floor again, I sneak around the corner, eyeing the open space. These hallways overlook the warehouse floor. The doors lining the other side are closed, with no one in sight. Halfway across, a strangled sob reaches me, not from the rooms, but from the open area four floors below. My head whips around, peering between the rails.

Horror flows over me at the sight. Dozens of people, men and women, shackled together, their wrists bound, lined up in neat rows. Some are slumped over, others' shoulders are bowed. A girl, no older than ten, is crying, lips pressed together to keep in her sobs. Two dozen men line the walls, guns hanging from their fists as they watch over their prisoners. The numbness seeping into me flees, replaced with rage. It's one thing to know the Guild is snatching people off the streets and out of their homes, but it's a whole other nightmare seeing it played out in front of me.

I reach for my phone to text Shane but then remember I've left it behind. I never thought the Guild would have all these people here yet. Of course they would gather them in one place, move them out for the Trade in other cities they hold in their wicked grip. The Auction will be held in Synd, VIPs traveling from all over the country to purchase those they want to control, break, bleed. Their efficiency in moving them in speaks to how many times they've done this before.

I wheel in the chaotic thoughts, trying to focus on why I'm here: Emma. The sooner I get her away, the quicker we can come back to save these people before they're shipped out to whatever new hell the Guild is sending them to.

With a renewed sense of urgency pushing me, I trust my gut Emma is in one of the first-floor interrogation rooms, like Alex was. I take the stairs two at a time, easing around each corner and bounding down again when the way is clear. I ease the door open a crack, seeing empty space, but the lights are on, at least. It's a blessing and a curse. I can search two rooms before I'll be exposed to the warehouse floor.

As I approach the first door, a soft cry echoes from behind the wood, making me freeze. Shaking out my arms and grabbing one of Ren's pistols, I glance back and forth, making sure no one is coming before inching the handle down and opening it enough to see inside. It appears empty, but I can't see the whole area.

I brace myself and barrel through, swinging the gun up and scanning the space. A squeak of fright rings from the corner where a small figure is crouching. Emma is up, throwing herself at me. I wrap my arms around her, trying to keep the barrel away from her.

"Shh, it's okay," I whisper.

"I'm sorry, I'm sorry . . ." she cries over and over, body trembling against mine.

"Emma, take a deep breath. We still have to get out of here."

I give her another ten seconds before pushing her away, still gripping her arm. She doesn't look hurt, but we don't have time for an assessment or a heartfelt reunion.

"How'd you get in here? They've got cameras and men everywhere." Her voice is steadier now, but she's still shaking.

"Doesn't matter. They got the cameras working?" Protocol is for Victor to shut the system down, but the doors are working, so there's a good chance the Guild accessed the cameras by now, too. Which means they could already know I'm here. Shit.

"I don't know. They said they'd be watching, though. Sam, I want to go home," she says, tears streaming down her face.

I pull her in for another hug, knowing we're wasting precious time, but she'll slow us down if she's breaking down in an open area. I tug her behind me, putting a finger to my lips. Peering out the doorway, I scan the hallway. I edge around, Emma close behind. I contemplate giving her one of the many guns on me, but the last thing I need is to be shot again. I curse Shane for not training her properly as we make it to the stairs, and I lead us up, all the way to the fourth floor.

"Where are we going?" she mumbles when I hesitate at the top.

"There's a back way out, but it'll take us across the mezzanine. I don't want to risk it, but the rest of the ways out of here are behind those doors," I explain, gesturing toward the hall lined with bedrooms.

"You don't want to risk anyone being in there?"

"Nope, but we might have to. I don't know if they've blocked those exits, either."

I stare at her, deciding the risk of being spotted from below is less than waking a sleeping giant in the rooms and steer my way toward the open hall, hoping Emma keeps her eyes on me. Her gasp when we clear the wall tells me she didn't, but she keeps moving. I take every few seconds to spy on the people, trying to find out how soon they'll be moving their victims, but it's hard to tell. I can't even guess how long they've been there, tied together like cattle. When was the last time they were fed? Bathed? When were they taken? Disgust crowds in my throat, making it hard to breathe.

We're almost to my room when a commotion behind has me whipping around. I shove Emma behind me and raise my gun. Footsteps pound up the stairs, and I herd Emma toward the stairwell.

"Emma, when you see them, run. Don't wait for me, just run. There's a door at the bottom, tucked under the stairs. It's like the ones at the house—push, and you're out. Run to the club two blocks down, hail a cab, and get home," I hiss.

"What about you?"

"I'll be fine. Tell your brother . . ." I swallow. "Tell him about the people. They need to move now."

I push her through the door, hoping no one is waiting at the bottom. I prop it open an inch, enough to be able to tell her when to go.

Guilt slams into me, knowing I wasted so much time bickering about stupid shit with Shane, but I can't unload my regrets onto Emma. It wouldn't be fair to her or him to hear my words from his sister. The possibility of getting both of us out is slim, but at least I'll take some of them with me. Emma will carry the Guild's plans back, and my guys will be able to strike at the them. I'll leave them in the best possible position I can. Somehow, I don't think this is how Ren wanted to use the Wraith.

The security door slams open across the way, and my eyes meet hers. I nod before I pull the door shut, willing her to listen as I punch my fingers on the pad next to my room. I swing my gun up and pull the trigger. A strangled cry tells me I hit at least one. It beeps, and I'm in, slamming the door as their shouts break through the silence. Bullets ping off the metal, and I push the bed aside to squeeze into the tiny space, flipping the latch hiding the crawl space. It doesn't go far, but it's all I have at this point. They're still trying to force their way in the room, shooting and kicking at the steel, but they'll never break through. Then again, I didn't think anyone could get in here before either. The only option is to override the system, and I'm hoping they haven't figured out how to do that yet. It would explain why they weren't able to lock the room Emma was in. I pray they focus on me instead of going after her.

I shimmy in, wiggling my body into the dark space, using the studs to pull myself along. It feels like forever passes before I'm reaching the emptiness of a sudden hole, but I breathe a sigh of relief. Carefully, I hang over the void until I can work my way feetfirst and brace myself, sliding down the long drop. There's more space on this level but not much. I kick once, twice, and the latch pops off the other side of the small door, making more racket than I want. I duck down, expecting a bedroom below mine, but there's no bed. I see a desk, two chairs . . . someone made this room into an office, and right next to a stack of papers sits a steaming cup of coffee. I jerk back as the smell burns in the back of my throat.

There are no secret tunnels here. No escape hatches. The crawl space I came from one goes only one way. The only option I have is the door. I rush forward, trying to control my breathing. I can't panic, but I'm as close as I've ever been to having some sort of mental breakdown on a mission. The anxiety coursing through me throws me back to my job to take out the commissioner, and I'm not ready to relive the feelings.

As I turn the knob, it's ripped from my hand, and I stumble back, bringing my gun up. I'll take as many of these fuckers as I can in the process. I'm about to pull the trigger when I swing the gun to the side, Colin framing the doorway, a manic look on his face.

"What the fuck, Colin! I almost shot you!" I hiss, voice laced with panic.

"Goddammit, Sam, you couldn't leave well enough alone, could you?"

Questions crowd my mind, screaming for answers. I don't have time to question why he's here, how he got in, what the hell he's been doing lately. I need to get us out. I march up to him and then peek out to see we're alone.

"Let's just get the hell out of here. Now," I say, turning to face him.

He grabs my shoulders in a bruising grip and shakes me, mania shining from his dark eyes. "Why are you here, Sam?"

I snap my arms up, breaking his hold on me. "Colin, snap out of it. We don't have time for lectures. We need to get out. This place is crawling with the Guild's men."

He sighs, glancing over his shoulder at more footsteps echoing around us. "Let's get you out of here."

I eye him, wondering how he found me, but I want to find Emma if I can. Hopefully, she's far away by this point. I swing around, pausing to listen. The stairs are quiet, thank fuck. Another handle, another surprise. Before I can respond, fight—yell, a burst of pain radiates from the crown of my head, and my world goes dark.

FIFTY

SHANE

I swear, if Victor doesnt shut the fuck up soon, I'm going to shoot him.

Alex's phone vibrates next to me, and he reads my text, trying to hide his grin behind a hand. I glance at him out of the corner of my eye before turning my attention back to Victor, who is still droning on about resources and how he can't deplete his own. Helms is scrubbing his hands over his face, clearly as close to losing it on the older man as I am.

"Victor, we're not fucking stupid. Stop treating us like we don't know how to handle our shit," Helms says, looking back at the allies he's brought with him. I don't know them, but the leader of the Reapers said they're trustworthy, and he hasn't given me any reason to doubt him thus far.

My phone buzzes, and I pull it out, ignoring their bickering. Confusion fills me as I read it once, then twice, until it clicks. I pass the phone to Ren, who reads it, then show it to Alex before he's typing out a response.

"Something you'd like to share, Shane?" Victor's nasally voice interrupts the plans whirling in my mind.

"If I wanted to, I would. I'm not exactly in a sharing mood these days," I say, fixing him with a bored look.

"Certainly not what I've heard . . ." he murmurs, making my eyes narrow. The longer this meeting goes on, the bolder he becomes with his snide comments. I've let it slide up to this point, if only to keep the peace, but I'm fucking done.

"I'm going to tell you this once, and only once, Victor. Keep your bullshit comments to yourself. What I, or my brothers do in our personal lives is none of your concern. If you continue spewing your vile filth in my house, I'll . . ."

"You'll what?" he laughs. "Kill me? I doubt it."

I open my mouth to respond when Ren's voice turns deadly. "We'll eviscerate you. We won't need to kill you; you'll do the job for us. There are much worse things than death, which I'm sure you remember, Victor."

Victor blanches, the ghost of his encounter with Devil's Breath dancing in his eyes. My wicked smile makes him flinch. He looks to Helms, who smirks, refusing to come to the older man's aid.

"Now, let's get back to business, shall we?" I say, gesturing for him to continue. He stutters but picks up where he left off.

Ten minutes later, he's still droning on about how he can't imagine it will be hard to take back the Depot when Helms cuts him off, asking about manpower and where Victor intends to put his men. We're trying to make a plan, but with so many factions here and Victor not wanting to give any hard numbers, we can't get anywhere. I'm about to tell Victor to fuck off, and Helms and I will do it alone, which leaves the people in their territory vulnerable, and I'd rather not have them helpless. Plus, he technically holds the Depot, so I probably shouldn't step on his toes, but I'm close.

"Can you at least put some fucking men in place to block off the bridges?" Helms demands, frustration leaking out.

"That's taken care of. We don't need to worry about the bridges or the Barrens," I say.

"We need all the manpower to hit the Depot, King."

"I know. We've got it covered. We'll have enough men to do both." I give him a look, and he drops it.

"Victor?"

Victor ignores him, directing his questions to me, like I give a shit what he has to say. Leaning forward, I wave him off when the door slams open. Guns appear in everyone's hand before I register Emma standing in the doorway, followed closely by Titus, who is looking guiltier by the second.

I rush around the table, and she crumples in my arms. She doesn't look injured, but she's shaking and crying, gasping for breath. She coughs, and Ren shoves a bottle of water in her hands. She snatches at it and drains half the bottle before turning her eyes to me, tears falling down her face.

"I'm sorry. She told me to run. I'm sorry," she chokes out before breaking down again.

"What? Emma. Tell me what happened. Who told you to run? How did you get here?" We have an audience, but at this point, I couldn't care less.

"Sam," she admits, voice quivering.

My vision goes black, chest seizing.

Alex grips my shoulder, pulling me back to the present. My head swivels around, looking for her among the others, but she's not here. She's slipped out; I don't know how long ago. I thought she was going to the kitchen, but with all the bickering, I failed to see her return.

"Emma, you need to tell us what happened. From the beginning," Alex tells her. Ren's fingers already flying over the screen of his tablet. Searching for Sam, no doubt.

"She wasn't answering me. I thought . . . I'm sorry, Shane. I got on a train and came back but then I thought I was being followed, so I texted Sam. They took me to this big building and stuffed me in a room. I didn't know what was happening. They laughed, saying they use me to lure her out and how they can take the city. I'm sorry, Shane," Emma says.

"The Depot? In Byrns' territory? Was that where you were?" Helms asks, looking at Emma. His voice is softer than I've ever heard it, and I'm grateful. If someone starts barking at her, she's likely to dissolve into a puddle.

"I think so. She told me to tell you that's where they've got the people. They're all tied up together in the big area. She said you have to move now."

Her blue eyes glitter with guilt, tearing at my heart. All I ever wanted was to protect her, but I couldn't even do that.

"It's okay, Emmie," I say, hugging her.

"Where's Sam?" Alex's voice is gruff.

"I don't know. She told me to run, so I did. They were coming, but maybe she got away?"

"Shane," Ren murmurs, tilting the tablet toward Alex and me. The blue dot centered on the map is directly over our house. I curse, knowing she left her phone behind for this exact reason; she knew we would track her.

"Why did she go alone? Why not tell us?" Alex demands.

I don't answer, gathering Emma up and depositing her into Titus's arms, telling him to take care of her. Rage courses through me, directed at Sam, myself, Ren, and Alex. All the plans we've come up with over the last four hours are dead. All I care about now is getting her back, and no one will stop me.

"Get your people ready. Now. We're going to the Depot. We'll meet you there." I nod to Helms, hoping he can get everyone else in line.

Victor sputters, "This is ridiculous! We can't just go running in there without a plan."

"What the hell do you think we've been doing here all damn day?" Helms's lip curls, derision dripping from his voice.

"We know where they are, most of them at least. We should enact the protocol and blow it up."

Alex slams Victor against the wall before he's finished speaking, his forearm pressing into the older man's neck while Victor's toes scrape the ground, trying to find purchase with his cheap loafers. His face is turning red as his throat constricts. Alex eases off slightly, enough for him to not die—at least not quickly.

"Your niece is in there, Victor, along with dozens of innocent people," Ren informs him.

"An unfortunate sacrifice," he chokes out.

Alex snarls, baring his teeth, "Say that again, and I'll rip your tongue from your fucking mouth."

"You have two options, Victor," I state calmly. "You can start acting like the head of the Byrns' family and offer up your men and resources, or we will take control of the east side of the river. This city has been divided long enough, don't you think?"

His eyes grow wide at my words, and he struggles for another minute before the fight leaves him. He slumps in Alex's grip and nods, no longer willing to make eye contact.

"Well, this is a lot more fun than I thought it would be," the woman with Helms mutters.

"Shut up, Kenzie. Shane, one of you needs to stay, lead your men." He leans in, speaking softly, but his eyes burn into me.

I should. I can't go tearing after her, leaving the King men to figure shit out for themselves, but . . . "I can't."

Ryker nods, looking at the girl behind him, and spins back when she catches him. I don't know what the hell is going on there, but it's the least of my problems.

"Go. I'll figure shit out here. Make sure Ren does what he needs to get them there."

"Helms, the Barrens is covered. They'll take care of shit. Guild won't be able to go through there," Alex mutters.

He nods again. "Go. Get your girl back. And don't get fucking killed. I don't want to have to deal with dickhead on my own." He walks away before I can thank him.

I stride from the room, and I hear the others leaving, heading out to hopefully pull their people together and hit the Guild. Alex and Ren follow me to my office, through the bookshelf and into another room, lined with weapons. Methodically, we grab what we need, not willing to voice any of our fears out loud. When we enter the garage, Ren's cursing rings out.

"She took my fucking car," he shouts, snatching Sam's phone from the bench along the wall.

"Don't you have a tracker on your car?" Alex grins, but it falls flat, dropping from his face.

"Yes, yes I do."

Alex is demanding Ren to find her as I pull out the driveway, heading toward the Depot. His emotions are always close to the surface, but Sam coming into our world has them boiling over. I want to tell him to shut the fuck up, but he's matching my inner turmoil, saying the things I can't put into words. He'd probably explode if he doesn't let them out.

"Shut up, Alex!" Ren snaps. "I can't find her any faster with you yelling."

"This can't be happening again," Alex mutters, leg bouncing.

Ren drops a bomb on us. "She's not at the Depot."

"What do you mean she's not at the Depot?"

"Unless someone stole the car, she's not at the Depot."

"Then where the hell is she?" I'm ready to snatch the tablet from him at this point, regardless of whether I'm driving like a lunatic through the dark streets.

"She's at the Byrns' estate. Shane, this could be a trap."

My mind races, trying to put myself in her shoes. Why would she go to the house when she could have come home? Was she being followed? Was it faster to go there than to us? I refuse to believe she ran, not after all we've been through together. I trust her, even if I've fucked things up. Regret slams into me, thinking of our fight. Our stupid, ridiculous fight, which doesn't mean shit now. I whip the car around a corner, making for the nearest bridge to take us to the east side.

"Shane, what about the Depot?" Ren questions, breaking through my chaotic thoughts.

"Who cares about the fucking Depot? We need to find Sam," Alex bellows.

"I understand, but the Guild is going to sell the people there. The others are going to be waiting for us. We told them that's where we were going."

"Fuck them. And fuck you, too, Ren. They can take care of shit. We're not leaving Sam to deal with whatever is going on at the estate."

"Sam is quite capable of taking care of herself, Alex. She didn't acquire the reputation she did without being able to deal with shit on her own."

Alex scoffs, shaking his head and looking to me. I'll be the one to make the decision. Glancing in the rearview mirror, I meet Ren's eyes and see something I've never seen before: desperation. He might be countering Alex's arguments, playing devil's advocate, but he wants us at the estate. He won't admit it, but he needs Sam just like we do. We can't live without her now.

"Shane?" Ren prompts, while Alex holds his breath.

"Ren, text Helms and tell him we'll be a little late, and keep an eye on your car. I'm not going on a wild goose chase trying to find our girl."

Alex deflates, shaking out his hands and leaning forward. With the decision made, he might jump out and run the rest of the way. Ren's head is buried back in his electronics, furiously contacting the others.

"Do we call Colin? He might be at the estate, right?" Alex directs his words back to Ren.

"Victor said he's at the hospital, keeping an eye on Mason. I'm sure Victor will talk to him. He'll be needed at the Depot anyway," Ren answers.

"How did Nicki get my number?" I ask, using any excuse to keep my mind off worrying about Sam.

"Sam. She passed it along." He meets my eyes in the mirror. "She told her yesterday, Shane."

"You think she planned this? Go to the Depot while we were at the meeting?" Alex is practically vibrating in his seat.

"No, I don't. I think the opportunity came, and she seized it, for whatever reason," Ren answers.

"Emma. She did it for Emma," I choke out. She didn't tell us because of me. If I had done things differently, they wouldn't have taken Emma; Sam would have come to me. We could have dealt with everything together. I have to find her, tell her I want Emma to be like her, tell her I trust her, tell her I shouldn't have pushed her away. I'll say anything, do anything. Racing through the streets, I wonder if I've fucked up my last chance.

FIFTY-ONE

SAMANTHA

My ears ring and my throat burns when I come to. The grinding in my neck when I lift my head is worrisome, but I can't remember why. The darkness doesn't change as I look around. I ache in places I don't remember having, but the lack of any light is more distressing than anything. I try to pull my body back under control, taking deep breaths. My eyes itch, but when I try to shake out my arms, I find them tied to a pipe, cold beneath my touch, zip ties digging into my wrists.

Whoever took me didn't know who they are dealing with, since they haven't secured my feet, and my hands are trapped in front of me. Rolling my neck, I close my eyes, concentrating on any sounds as the whistling in my ears subsides. Other than the dripping water on my left, the space is silent.

I cough, mustiness overwhelming my senses, but underneath is a layer of chemicals and something tangy . . . blood. My eyes shoot open, frantically trying to pick out something—anything in the emptiness, but it's black, not a glimmer of light seeping in. The Depot has a concrete room like this, for more intense interrogations. I can't remember if there's a way out, though. My mind is too jumbled.

A thought skitters across my mind, and my breath hitches. *Where is Colin? Did they grab him, too?* My heart pounds, imagining what they could be doing to him. He's high up in the Byrns' organization, so they'll keep him alive and force info from him—maybe ransom him off. I'm pretty sure they'll send me to the Auction, if only to watch someone break me. The Guild is known for taking those who resist and put them on display. The fact they knocked me out instead of killing me outright tells me I'm headed to the auction block. At least it gives me time to escape.

I can only hope the guys don't try to do anything heroic. I let out a snort when the thought crosses my mind. Those three are anything but heroic. As intertwined as we are, they know the risks in coming after me. They won't gamble their hold on the city to save me. I would save them if the roles were reversed, but I'm not the head of a family. I'm not the leader of a mafia. I'm just me. My skills give me the power to do whatever I want. It isn't something I thought of before—the independence. I was so focused on living in the shadows that I've forgotten the shadows let me live without shackles.

Ren's voice echoes in my head, and I wish I could tell him I understand now—the freedom of being the Wraith.

A choked sob works its way up my throat, and I wonder if I'll live long enough to tell him—tell *them*, how they changed me. Or maybe they merely helped me see who I am, not a Byrns or a mafia princess or the Wraith. Just Sam. They shifted something inside me, allowing me to look at myself clearly, without the lens of the titles I hide behind. I'd like to believe my revelation would mean something to them, but maybe I really am nothing more than a distraction for them, and they'll be glad they don't have to deal with the aftermath of letting me go. Either way, I need to find a way out and save Colin from whatever fate the Guild has in store for him. I won't lose someone else to them.

With a new resolve, I work on getting my hands free. Whoever tightened them did a good job, but I've been in worse situations. After several minutes and more than one muttered curse, one hand slips free. Before I can start on the other, a muted scuffle from beyond the room breaks the silence. I renew my efforts while trying to listen. My left hand pulls free, the zip tie taking skin with it, leaving a burning sensation in its wake, when a single overhead bulb flickers on. I slam my eyes shut, the light sending bursts of colors behind my lids. I blink, looking away and trying to regain my sight.

"Why is it every time I think I have you figured out, you go and surprise me again, Sammy?"

His voice rings out, disappearing into the concrete walls, but I know who it is. I grew up listening to him, training with him, growing with him. My heart shatters, wishing there was another explanation to who is in front of me, who hurt me and took me, shackled me to a pipe, and left me in the inky blackness. I want to cry out for the dark, where I was ignorant to where I am and who betrayed me. I want the Guild to be the only villain in my world that matters.

I steel myself to face the truth and open my eyes. I take in the sandy mussed hair and deep brown eyes that once held so many emotions but are empty now—soulless. He's not how I remember him, how he was the last time I saw him. He seemed beat down then, but the madness was missing. The frenzy is radiating from him now, showing through the mania in his eyes, the twitching of his limbs, the jerkiness of his stride. He stops, gazing down, a crazed smile playing on his lips.

"Colin . . ." I breathe out, the rest of my intended words crowding in my mouth, refusing to spill out.

"Am I going to have to tie you up again? Or can you behave?" he asks, cocking his head, and I shake mine.

He holds out a hand, and after a second's hesitation, I place mine in his. He tuts over the blood seeping out of the wounds on my wrist but releases my hand and turns away, settling himself in one of the two chairs in the room. He gestures for me to take the other, facing him. I glance around, taking my time. We're not at the Depot. This room is deep in the bowels of my family's estate, below the tunnels, buried under layers of dirt and foundation. The perfect room if someone is worried about the neighbors complaining about the screaming. Only a bench and chair occupies the space, along with the stains flowing into a drain built in the floor.

"Why am I here, Colin?" I ask, perching on the chair bolted to the floor.

Of course he's blocking the door, but now, the shock of finding him here is wearing off. I'm calculating the chances of reaching it before him. My eyes dart over his shoulder, and he moves, pulling a pistol from behind his back. Inwardly, I curse for not seeing it earlier when his back was to me.

"It wasn't supposed to go like this. It got off badly from the beginning, really. Mason wasn't supposed to be shot, just spooked. I hope you know that." He looks at me from under his lashes, then focuses back on the gun laying on his lap. He doesn't point the weapon at me, but I won't be able to rush past him before he shoots me. Besides, I want to know how the hell we got to this point.

"You ordered the hit against my brother."

"No, but I had a small hand in it. He wasn't supposed to be hurt. I thought he would listen to me when I told him to hide, but he had to try to go and save you. Too worried about his little sister to keep himself safe. The hit was only to force him to see," he spits out, turning hard eyes to me.

"See what?"

"We aren't meant to share!" Colin bursts out, exploding from his chair and gesturing wildly. Instinctively, I duck, waiting for the burn of a bullet, but he shoves me farther on to the chair. My head careens back from the force, slamming against the edge of the metal. My head spins, vision blurring, and I hold back the groan threatening to leave me. My muscles tense, anticipating the next blow, but only his harsh breathing fills the space. He steps away, closing his eyes, sucking in a gasp of air before settling back into his seat, calm once more.

I wait until my head stops swimming before I gasp out, "I'm sorry Colin, I don't know what you're talking about."

"Of course you don't. You aren't privy to these sorts of things, are you, Sammy? I wonder if I should have informed you, if you would have still made such a mess of things. I did warn you, though. I told you to leave things alone, but like the stubborn bitch you are, you couldn't. I'm not surprised. Mason let you get away with far too much. I told him to put a tighter leash on you, but again, he just wouldn't listen. We could have had it all. We could have ruled all of Synd, but he wouldn't break protocol."

"You mean he wouldn't kill the Kings."

"Ah, the Kings. I wondered when we'd come to them." Colin's eyes glitter, piercing me with malice.

"What about them?" A protectiveness rises in me, filling me, threatening to flood the room.

"I told you to stay away. They weren't for you. I shouldn't have been so blindsided when you didn't listen. I thought you were smarter than that, but maybe Victor has a point. All it took was one look from those three, and you were spreading your legs for them, weren't you? I can't blame you, but honestly, Sammy, how cliché. You can't seriously believe they would have kept you. Girls like you are always replaceable to men like them."

Colin's words pierce my heart, but I steel myself against the vitriol he's spewing. While Colin smirks, trying to tear me down, the only thing I feel is a sharp bitterness by not telling them that, if I had the choice, I'd stay. If it was an option, I'd be with them for as long as they'd let me. My heart aches for the boy I grew up with, too, wondering where the hell we went wrong. When did he go from the boy who protected me to this crazed man before me?

"Why the Guild, Colin? Mason didn't listen to you, so what? Are you really that greedy you had to try to take the whole city, and when you couldn't, you brought them in? To what end? To bring us all down with you?"

"We could have taken them out! They weren't supposed to make it this far. It isn't my fault. I only did it to force Mason to do something—anything. And instead of talking to *me*, he went to that bastard, Helms; kept talking about going to the Kings," Colin hisses, pacing back and forth in front of me. "I could have taken care of the Guild. *We* could have taken care of them, but he . . . he . . . and then you . . . you went running to them, too, but I can fix this. I can handle the Guild and them and you. I can deal with it all. When Mason wakes, he'll see what I did for the family, for him, and he'll finally see what he didn't before."

"What's that?" I whisper, morbid curiosity pushing the words from my lips.

"Me. He'll see me. You don't get it, Sammy. I was fine living in his shadow. I'm content to be his second, to never lead. But he doesn't get it, he needs me. No one else can do what I do for him . . ." He shakes his head. I'm not sure he remembers I'm here anymore. He's still pacing, muttering to himself.

"How are you going to handle all of it alone, though? I think you need help, Colin. All you have to do is ask. The Guild is too big to take on all by yourself. Let me help you," I say, hoping to convince him to let me go. His laughter rings out instead, filling the room with the demented sound.

"You? How could you help? You're nothing but a few years of training and an empty head. I kept telling Mason to find a better place for you, but of course, he wouldn't listen. You've played the part of socialite for so long I don't know if you remember who you actually are. Then again, maybe that's all you are, and everything else is merely an act. What is it King calls you? Princess? Fitting," he scoffs.

My skin tightens as my muscles bunch. Colin thinks he's hurting me with these poisoned darts he's throwing out, but the only thing they accomplish is to piss me off. I'll mourn the boy who was like another brother after I've killed the psycho who stands before me.

"Fuck you," I hiss.

"Never in a million years, Sammy."

"Don't call me that."

"What should I call you, then, Sammy?"

I take full advantage of his sudden stillness, erupting from my seat and slamming my hand into his chest. His breath burst from him, and he doubles over. I bring my knee up, and his nose crunches on my bones. The rush of hot blood flooding from him splatters over my leg to my feet. I shove him aside before he can grab me, reaching for his chair. Mine is bolted to the floor, but his isn't. I whip it around, crashing it into his side, making his body list. For growing up in the mafia, he's been particularly stupid, underestimating me every step of the way.

I pause, the severity of the situation catching up to me. I wait, watching him regain his senses. His gun clatters across the floor in our scuffle, and he casts his eyes around, trying to find it. It's in the corner behind him, though. There's little chance he'll find it, not without me getting to him first. I could run. I could dash out the door, but where would that leave me? Victor won't take my word over Colin's. The guys can't do anything about him. I'll just be placing another burden at their feet. Mason is still laid up in the hospital. At this point, I don't know who he'd believe anyway.

I sway, my head pounding now. I've stopped moving, and Colin launches to his feet in a burst of speed. He tackles me, and I barely stop myself from banging my head on the concrete. One more blow, and I'll be down. Colin straddles me, wrapping his hands around my throat, cutting off my breath. I struggle, hysteria momentarily overtaking me. I can't remember how to fight my way out of this. All those hours of training gone in the face of my panic. Fear crashes through my body, blinding me.

Instinct takes over. I punch up between his arms, and I snap the heel of my hand straight into his already broken nose. Colin's head snaps back from the force of my blow, and his strangled cry rings through the space. I lash out again, but he blocks my attack. I turn just in time for his fist to connect with my cheekbone instead of my nose. Pain explodes through my face. He didn't hold back, which tells me that, if I don't do something, he'll kill me. I stab my fingers into his jugular, and a gagging noise escapes him. He falls forward, and my knee connects with his dick as I buck, and he falls to the side, coughing.

I roll, ignoring the pain radiating through my head. I spy the shard of glass under the bench, and I snatch at it, the edges biting into my palm. I push up and spin toward him. Colin is bracing himself, trying to push to his feet. My head pulses, but I channel the adrenaline coursing through me and scramble behind him. His hand lashes out, and there's a burning sensation in my thigh, a knife handle sticking out of my flesh. I leave it, and smash my fist into his ear, which disorients him long enough for me to grab his hair, pulling him back to my chest. I bring the shard of glass to his throat, and everything freezes.

I don't know if I can kill him. Flashes of memories flit through my mind, reminding me of the life we've lived together: my brother, Colin, and I.

We were inseparable when we were young, forging through tragedy and pain together. How will I look my brother in the eye and tell him I've killed his best friend? His second? How can I explain the impossible situation to him? Blood trickles from my lip and down my chin, and my chest heaves. My eye swells, and my cheek pulses with every heartbeat. Only a few seconds have passed while I've contemplated ending things or searching for another way.

The door flies open, metal crashing against the wall in a dull thud. The fight seeps out of me, but I don't loosen my grip. Tears fill my eyes, and I grip the glass tighter as I take in my brother, awake and whole, gun lifted toward us. Colin sucks in air, throat scraping against the edge and then he's babbling.

"Thank fuck you're here. Mason, I tried to help her. She wouldn't listen. She's gone off the deep end. I was trying to protect her."

Mason's eyes track him, staring impassively as Colin spins his story of lies and deceit. He peddles falsehoods of how I couldn't handle my brother getting shot, and I ran to the Kings instead of him. How we aided the Guild to exact revenge on the Byrns. His eyes finally meet mine, and I stare back, waiting for him to say something. His gun hangs limp at his side now. Relief and all the pent-up grief I've been holding back all these months crash over me. Tears fall, unheeded, down my face, mingling with the blood. I'm trembling with the strain of keeping my shit together until Mason makes his call. Subtly, he shakes his head, and my heart splits in two. I don't know how he can believe Colin's empty words.

I suck in a deep breath, hand trembling, and lean down to Colin's ear. "You can call me the Wraith."

He chokes, but I step back, leaving a thin, bloody line on Colin's neck as I do. As much as I want to stab the fucker for all he's done, for all he's put us all through, I have to obey. Mason is the head of the family, whether he's been out of commission for months. Out of everything I've been taught, the most important is to always follow his lead. If I don't, no one will. It's ingrained so deeply in me there isn't a sliver of me willing to disobey, no matter how wrong he is. The utter ridiculousness of my thought process isn't lost on me, but I still follow his silent commands.

My emotions spiral out of control, and I gasp for air. The tears I've been holding back spill out, mixing with my blood more. I've stopped moving, and exhaustion threatens to pull me under, back into the dark. I sway to the side, struggling to keep my brother in focus. Concern flickers in his eyes before he turns his attention back to Colin, who is still on his knees, pleading with Mason to get me help, as if fucking the Kings is an addiction.

Black spots swim in my vision. I'm going to pass out if I don't get my shit together. Rationally, I know what to do, but when faced with the reality of not being able to breathe, I panic. Shane's face floats out of the darkness when I close my eyes, just the way he looked before he kissed me after the meeting with Helms, before there was anything between us, except animosity and attraction. A calmness sweeps over me, and I lift my lids in time to see Mason raise his gun methodically, gaze fixed on my face. I want to close them again, shut off the sight in front of me, and pretend this isn't happening. I could fight, but what's the point? Maybe it's better this way—an ending tied up in a bow with no heartache or regret. I can't imagine what mental state my brother is in right now. I won't blame him.

The room dims, and my head is floating away, no longer attached to my body. Everything goes black. I can feel my body falling. Distantly, the sound of a single gunshot bounces in my ears, filling my body, and I sink back in the shadows of my mind.

FIFTY-TWO

ALEX

I push open the hidden door to the Byrns' estate. The hallway beyond is empty, house silent. I forge ahead of the others, shoving my way into her room, but it's empty, her things strewn about like someone's ransacked the place. My heart stutters, wondering if she ran away from us. The last thing I need is to doubt her. Victor is obviously to blame for this mess, trying to ferret out Sam's secrets.

We sweep the rest of the floor and move down to the next, then the next. No one is here, and I'm starting to question whether she was ever here in the first place. It seemed the most likely conclusion at the time, but finding the house empty is making me rethink everything. The first floor is just as vacant as the rest, our soft footsteps echoing on the wood floors. The longer we search, the more frantic we get. Shane stalks from room to room, the scowl on his face deepening with every empty space. Ren's hand twitches, and I'm afraid he might shoot one of us if we get in his way.

"Do we check the basement area?" Shane's voice is jarring after so much silence. He doesn't wait for a reply, stalking toward the kitchen.

I stalk to the back corner of the room, heading for the door to the lower tunnels hidden in the wainscoting. With a click we're in, descending into the shadows of the belly of the mansion. It's musty and disused, which makes me more nervous than when we found the house devoid of people. We'll find an extra room tucked away if the houses truly are the same, made of concrete and steel, with a drain in the floor. I can't remember the last time we used ours, but our dads frequented it a lot when we were growing up. Those aren't memories I like to revisit.

I roll my shoulders, trying to ease the tightness in them, but I'm too anxious. We're almost to the bottom when I freeze at the sharp report of a gun, a thud, then a silence so deafening I fear my hearing has fled. Ren lets out a string of curses, and I'm flying down the stairs, not caring if I'm running into an ambush or not.

Not again. Please, not again.

Busting into a burning building to save her was too much; seeing her laying there, motionless, nearly ripped my heart from my chest. A world without Sam would be devastating. I've realized how integral to my life, to our lives, she is. I won't survive if she's gone. She means too much to me, to us.

The door ahead is ajar, with a body lying on the floor. It's not Sam, so I leap over it and come to a halt inside. Colin's body, blood leaking from the wound in his forehead, is crumpled on the floor. I start to shake, seeing Sam, my Bug, just beyond him. Shane lets out an anguished cry behind me, and his knees thud when he drops. Skirting the body, I kneel, reaching out to brush her hair back, and I suck in a breath. Her face is a myriad of bruises, blood trickling from the corner of her mouth, a cut gracing her cheekbone.

"Is she . . ." Ren's harsh whisper bounces off the walls. Glancing back, he checks Mason, who is laying in the doorway. I can't imagine what events lead up to them all being in this room together. The last I knew,

Mason was still in the hospital, deep in a coma. I turn back, gingerly picking up her wrist. Scratches and bruises encircle them, but I check her pulse and almost collapse when I find the strong beat of her heart.

"She's alive," I croak out, reaching to check for more injuries, but Shane is there, trying to pick her up.

I push him away, baring my teeth at him. He backs up, shock and agony etched on his face. I need to feel her in my arms, to assure myself she's going to be okay. Her black pants are wet, and my fingers come away with blood.

"Ren, call the doctor. Have him come here," Shane barks out, eyes trained on my hand stained red.

"We need to move them upstairs. Leave that one," Ren says, gesturing with a curled lip at Colin's body between us.

I gather Sam up, pulling her close to my chest. A choked sob leaves me when she lets out a sigh. The walk back to the main floor feels twice as long as the descent. I settle Sam on a couch in the library, keeping tight hold of her hand, eyes fixed on her chest rising and falling gently. I'm afraid if I look away, she'll stop breathing.

"What's wrong with him?" Shane questions Ren as he places Mason on the opposite couch.

"Well, my guess is he woke up, checked himself out of the hospital, and came straight here. Not a great medical plan for someone who just came out of a coma," Ren says ruefully.

"Have we heard anything about the Depot?"

Ren's phone is in his hand before Shane finishes asking, stepping to the window to have a hurried conversation with whoever he's called. I don't care what happened at the Depot. I peer at Shane to tell him I'm not leaving her, but his gaze is locked on her prone body, guilt and agony written all over his face. I sigh, knowing we're not going anywhere.

"Victor cursing us out for not being there, Helms coordinating everything. Looks like they got the people out. Most of the men from the Guild are dead. We'll have to wait to see if they pull out of Synd or if we have to hit them again," Ren tells us, coming around the couch and collapsing in a chair, head buried in his phone. I want to rage at him for not asking about Sam, but this is his way of dealing. I can't fault him for trying to protect himself, to keep his emotions from spilling over. One of us has to be sane enough to deal with plans.

"Do we have to worry about Victor coming home?" I ask, brushing a finger along her jaw.

"No, he got shot. Nothing serious, unfortunately. He's at the hospital, apparently. Helms said it was superficial, but he insisted on going," he scoffs, shaking his head.

My phone vibrates, and I pull it out, scowling down when the commissioner's name pops up. I shut my phone off instead of answering. I'm not about to deal with his bullshit blustering about us dealing with the Guild. We've kept them out of the loop thus far, and I'm not about to bring him in now.

A chime jolts me, and Shane stalks from the room to let the doctor in. Ren moves to the couch, resting a hand on Sam's ankle, but his eyes are fixed on the door, gun in his other hand. I should pull my own weapon, but I can't tear my eyes away from Sam's swollen face, the bruises deepening the more time passes. I trust Ren to protect us.

"Alex," he murmurs.

"What?"

"She's going to be okay."

I don't know if he's trying to convince himself or me, but I nod all the same. We sit, waiting for a new day to dawn. Praying for the girl between us will be okay.

An hour later, Shane escorts the doctor out, and I'm alone again. Mason woke minutes ago, disoriented and slurring his words, but our doctor told us it was normal and rest would help. Ren left, helping him to his room while Mason muttered about betrayal. He left me alone with Sam, a bright, white bandage covering the stitches closing the wound in her leg. I gather her up once more, making the trek to her room. When I step inside, I'm reminded it's trashed—clothing, books, and random bits scattered across the space. I spin around and find a guest room before tucking her into the bed. I pull up a chair over to keep vigil.

"It's going to be okay, Sam. We'll be here when you wake up," I murmur, gathering her hand in mine before kissing her head. I don't know if she can hear me, but I need to say the words crowding in my mind.

"I know you're hurting, but I'm not going anywhere. Just rest, Bug."

I want to tell her so many things. I don't want to say them while she's like this, oblivious to what I'm telling her. Promises stack up, one on top of another in my mind, threatening to spill from my lips, but I hold them in.

"Alex, why don't you get some rest?" Shane calls from the doorway.

He sighs, saying something to Ren, and footsteps retreat down the hall. I don't care. I can't leave her.

"I'll stay with her. Just take the other side of the bed, Alex," Ren says, resting a hand on my shoulder. I shrug him off but get up, trying not to jostle her as I climb in.

"You'll wake me if something happens?" Vulnerability burrows itself into my voice, but I can't bring myself to worry about what he'll think.

"Yes. I won't leave her," he says.

I heave out a breath, the tension of the night finally leaving me, and I relax, the sound of Sam's breathing lulling me to sleep.

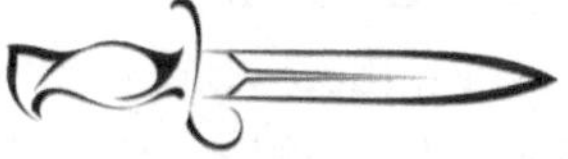

I'm disoriented when I wake. My brain skips as I try to process where I am, what time it is, why I'm so stiff, when the events of the night come rushing back. I whip my head to the side, seeing a still-sleeping Sam next to me. She's pale beneath the bruises, and I roll toward her, gingerly laying an arm over her waist. I close my eyes again, burying my face in her hair. Faintly, I pick up the smell of her shampoo under layers of blood and mildew.

"Do we know what happened?" Ren asks, his voice filtering in from the cracked door. I didn't even notice he wasn't in the room anymore.

"Mason said he's not sure. He remembers Sam holding a piece of glass to Colin's neck and Colin spewing some bullshit about Sam going insane. He's the one who shot Colin, though. He wasn't very coherent," Shane answers.

"Did he say why he shot him?"

"Something about Sam's eyes. He saw the bruises and blood and made a decision. He could see Sam starting to pass out, knew he wouldn't be far behind and wasn't going to risk Sam's life. I don't know, though. Do we really think Colin orchestrated this whole thing?"

"It's plausible. He's high enough up to be able to bring in the Guild. I don't think we'll know for sure until Sam wakes up. Hopefully, she'll know more about what happened. I never did trust him, though."

"I know you didn't. For once, I'm grateful for your paranoia," Shane chuckles, but he sucks it in quickly.

"She'll be okay."

"I know . . . she has to . . ." Shane pauses. "I have to tell her."

"Tell her what?"

"That I lied."

"Shane . . ." Ren warns.

"I told her we would be fine without her. If she left, we'd be fine. But I lied. I can't . . . I can't live without her. *We* can't live without her."

"No, we can't," Ren agrees, their voices falling silent.

I whisper into Sam's hair. "Hear that, Bug? We can't live without you. You need to wake up so we can tell you. We need you to be okay."

I pull back, but she's still and silent. I watch her as the light cascading through the curtains slowly fades, casting shadows around the room. I watch her as Ren and Shane filter in and out, exhaling words and promises and pleas.

I watch, waiting for the moment she opens her eyes.

FIFTY-THREE

REN

"With all due respect, Mason, you have no idea what's been going on." Shane's voice floats through the door. I'm posted in the chair, counting Sam's breaths.

"Obviously, I had no control over that, but I'm here now," Mason responds, his voice gravelly from disuse.

"Oh, joy," Alex quips, sarcasm dripping from his tone.

"Watch it," Mason growls out. "Sam is my sister. She's a part of the Byrns' family. She'll be staying here while she recovers."

Shane barks out a laugh, while Alex grumbles. They've been having this discussion for the last thirty minutes, going in circles the entire time. We want her home, with us, where she belongs. Mason wants her here. For some reason, though, her brother thinks she'll be choosing to stay here. I haven't argued with my brothers, but I can't convince myself she'll decide to come with us. The connections we made with Sam happened during such a tumultuous time that, when faced with the idea of making us permanent, I can't coax my mind into believing it. That coupled with her thinking her place with us is temporary stays my tongue. So, I leave the arguing to Shane and Alex. I wish I would have forced the conversation when she told me how she felt. I could have avoided these feelings, secure in the knowledge she'd choose us. Then again, maybe I read her wrong. Maybe she wouldn't have chosen to stay at all, and I only convinced myself it's what she wanted.

"You can't think she'll want to stay here. Her life was in danger here. *Your* second kidnapped her and almost killed her!" Alex scoffs.

Shane cuts off whatever Mason is trying to say. "And if she does decide to recover here, it will be because *she* made the decision, not because you say so. I won't overstep my position here, Byrns, but let me be perfectly clear: whatever Sam decides is what we'll be following, with no influence from you."

His footsteps fade away, and a dull thud of a fist hits the wall. It's clear Mason loves his sister, but I wonder how he'll feel when he figures out the truth about what's happened between us and her. Maybe he'll never know. She may never tell him if she stays here and cuts us off.

The dull ache in my chest spasms at the thought. Not having Sam in my life, living day to day without her, knowing she's on the other side of the river . . . I don't know if I could handle that. I've fought my feelings for so long, and when I finally crossed the final hurdle, I knew I was all in. To have her choose to leave . . . I don't know how to control the emotions welling inside me. I envy the convictions I had before. I didn't want her to get too close for this exact reason. I knew if I let her in, and she left, it would leave me bereft. If she was taken, I could use it to fuel the hate, the rage, the revenge. But if she takes herself away, there's no one to rage against, no one to hate, no way to seek revenge. I can't blame her if she decides we're not what she wants.

"Ah, Pet, what are we going to do? You've stirred the pot again."

I wait, but she stays frozen, not even a twitch.

"What are you going to do, Sam? Seems like we've been here before—you, sewn up with stitches and no pants, me begging you to stay without actually saying the words."

I lean in close, whispering in her ear, "I'll tell you all my secrets now. I made those brownies I gave you for the Egg. From scratch. I can make you all the lemon squares you want. I'll make you all the snacks you want. Just come back to me. Please."

I squeeze my eyes shut, the pulsing anguish wrapping around my heart. It's so small, the secret I've given her, but I've spoken the truth. I'll tell her everything. Every dirty little secret I keep locked tight in me. I'll spill my entire soul to her, my ugly, fucked-up childhood, the memories of her, the mistakes I've made. All of it. If she'll only wake up. Come home.

"Ren," Alex calls behind me.

I clear my throat before lifting my head. "Yeah?"

"Shane wants to talk to you. I'll sit with her. Keep your phone with you, though," he says, eyes fixed on Sam.

I wave the phone in my hand before leaving. I stutter at the door, glancing back. Alex is already settled in the chair I vacated, holding her hand and stroking her hair. At first, I don't know why I've stopped, but my feet won't move. It hits me: I didn't tell her I was leaving. It shouldn't be a big deal, but for some reason, I'm having a visceral reaction to not telling her I'll be back. She won't know either way if I'm walking out of the room, but the feeling remains. I think about going back but shake myself, forcing my feet to move away from her.

I shuffle down the stairs, then swing around the bottom and stop short. The false panel tucked away under the stairs is still there, all these years later. I can't remember being small enough to fit through the tiny hatch but memories of a small hand in mine, whispers of secret friends, and a promise to save me, echo through my mind. I shake my head, pulling myself back to the present. I spin away, not willing to relive more heartache.

"Shane, we need to do something about Victor," I remark when I find him tucked away in the library. I avoid looking at the bloodstained couch Sam was on hours before, keeping my eyes fixed on my tablet.

"I tried to talk to Mason about it, but the doc came back and interrupted us."

"I don't know how much longer I can keep him away. Mason needs to . . ."

"I need to what, Ren?" Mason calls out from the other entrance of the room.

I spin, looking him up and down. He glares at me, leaning on a cane. He thinks I'm being condescending, but I'm actually scanning for any signs of injury. The man was in a coma for months; to think he'll be able to bounce back without repercussions is laughable. His color has returned, but he's still listing. The fact he's walking at all is a miracle. I wonder what they did in the hospital to keep his muscles from losing the ability.

"Either cut him loose or deal with him. Letting him continue how he has been would be unwise," I state, clutching my emotions tight, locking them away. With Sam still unconscious, injured, I haven't felt centered since we arrived. At least dealing with Mason will help me get a grip on my emotions.

"Fortunately, for you two, that's my issue to deal with," he answers.

"Don't be an asshole, Mason. You and I both know it's sound advice. Plus, you need us," Shane spits out.

"I think what Shane means is there are a series of events we should inform you of before you make any rash decisions," I interject, shooting a look at Shane. "The last several months have been volatile, to say the least. Victor's involvement caused . . . unneeded grief for us but for your family as well—namely, to Sam."

Mason collapses in the other chair, raking his hands over his face. He's hiding the grief of shooting his second well. Tightness pulls his eyes, the twitch of his lip, the slight shake of his hands. Most would think those are from the aftereffects of the coma and getting shot, but he's soundlessly screaming his pain through his movements. Not to mention having to deal with his sister's injuries as well.

"This whole thing is shit. Fine, tell me what happened."

Shane sits back and starts telling him everything, while I chime in every once in a while. Every time he stutters over his words, I speak up, continuing the story before Shane can trip up and tell Mason we've been sleeping with his sister. Even if Mason would be fine with her being with us, the last thing he's going to want to think about is us being with her. He's also skirting around the fact we know Sam is the Wraith, which isn't hard, but picking and choosing what to tell him isn't easy.

"So, you're telling me Sam left the meeting, and you didn't notice?" Fire burns in Mason's eyes.

"I noticed . . ."

I break in. "She's a grown woman, Byrns. I understand she's your sister, but she can make her own decisions. She chose to go to the Depot alone. Nothing we would have said would stop her."

He sighs, nodding. "I know. It's the same thing I told Victor before I was shot. Hard, though, being her brother and protective and knowing she's the Wraith and capable at the same time."

I freeze, wondering if it was a slip of the tongue, him divulging Sam's secrets. He's the one who told her we'd kill her in the first place but then he flippantly lets out her identity? It doesn't make sense.

"Well, at some point you have to let go and let her make the choices for her own life," I hedge, pinning Shane with a stare. He shakes his head.

Mason eyes us before saying, "You're thinking I'm stupid for telling you she's the Wraith, right?"

"It is a little jarring, yes," I reply carefully.

"Well, Shane's not very good at lying or telling half-truths. I could tell you knew. I suspect it's fine to talk about if she didn't kill you."

"I'm curious—why did you tell her we'd kill her? You couldn't have thought we'd do it if we had known."

Mason's face fills with guilt before glancing away. I glance at Shane again, who is as confused as I am. It makes no sense. We're not enemies. We're not rivals. Perhaps he understands why our families parted ways all those years ago. Maybe his decisions stem from our fathers' actions.

"I needed her to be safe," he murmurs. "I knew I couldn't protect her, not the way I should. I had too much going on. So, I sent her to others. I had them train her so she'd never have to rely on me, on anyone, to be able to protect herself. It was a good plan. Sam is smart, a chameleon, adapting to any situation. She was always like that, even when we were young. She learned early masking your feelings kept her alive, and it morphed into something more, but knowing she'd be able to take care of herself and having her come back a different person . . . it was jarring. I didn't know her anymore, not really. As capable as she was, it still scared the shit out of me when she would slip into the shadows. So, I tried to protect her the only way I knew how, by drilling into her no one could ever know."

"But why us specifically?" Shane leans his elbows on to his knees, eyes intense.

Mason chuckles. "Oh, that was just . . . sorry. She was a little obsessed with you guys when we were younger, or I guess obsessed with everything over on the west side. She always wanted to know what was going on, who ran it, why we didn't go over there but then our fathers died, and we had the meeting. She saw you, you know. From her window when you came. I thought she'd start asking questions again, so I gave her a bunch of rules. When she came back from training, she asked about going over there again, and I freaked out. I didn't want Sammy doing jobs on the west side at all, but I knew I couldn't stop her, so I told her if you guys knew, you'd kill her. She believed me and always had a healthy respect for crossing the bridge. Seems stupid now."

"Yeah, thanks for that. I thought she was going to shoot me the first time I found her in my office," Shane quips, chuckling as Mason grins, but it slowly fades.

"What are you keeping from me?" he asks.

"Why would you think we're keeping anything from you?" Shane leans back and crosses his arms.

Mason raises an eyebrow before turning to me. "Tell me."

He knows the answer, but he needs us to confirm his suspicions, just like I did when I confronted Sam about her secret identity.

"Sam is . . . special to us," I hedge.

Shane groans, covering his face.

"Special, huh?"

I nod, not willing to give him more. He can make what he will of my statement. I'm not telling him anything else. Especially with Sam and Alex not here. If Sam wants to tell him more, so be it. I won't stand in her way if she wants to tell him everything.

"What if she doesn't want to be . . . special to you, now that I'm back?"

"We'll respect her wishes," Shane answers before I can form the words.

I want to rage against him, demanding he say we'll fight for her, but I can't. Not in front of Mason. That conversation is best left for another time. Regardless, I would find her, watch her, beg her to reconsider if I had to. That's not what Mason or Shane wants to hear.

Mason nods again and heaves himself out of his chair. He turns at the door. "Thank you."

"For what?" Shane asks.

"For taking care of her when I couldn't."

Silence falls as the door clicks shut behind him, both of us lost in our thoughts. I can't live in my head for long; I'll go insane. I'm about to go back to Sam when Shane clears his throat.

"What is it, Shane?"

"You had to go and tell him, didn't you?"

"He already knew. There's no other reason we would be fighting so hard to bring her home."

"Home," he echoes.

"Yes, home. The place where we live, where we built a foundation for our family."

"Which family?"

"What do you mean, which family? Our family." I glare.

"You mean the family with Sam? Or the King family? The King business?"

I pause. Admitting my intentions out loud solidifies them. I'll have to live with the words being out there if Sam doesn't choose us—choose me. I can't deny them, regardless of how much the potential hurt scares me.

"With Sam."

"Down the rabbit hole we go, huh?" he chuckles.

"I'm more than willing to live there as long as she's there with us."

"Fuck the ducks," he mutters, making me grin.

The door opens, admitting Alex, whose usual swagger is buried deep under layers of anxiety and exhaustion. He drops in Mason's empty chair, tipping his head back and closing his eyes.

"Anything?" Shane tenses.

"No. Mason is with her. I'm worried. Maybe we should take her to the hospital."

"The doc said it's normal. We don't have a reason to be worried yet."

He snorts. "As if we haven't all been fucked out of our minds since yesterday when Emma showed up."

"She'll wake up and be fine," Shane answers, but the more he says it, the less confident he sounds each time. So, we sit, waiting for Sam to open her eyes and tell us to take her home.

FIFTY-FOUR

SAMANTHA

The darkness is lifting, little by little; it's different from the last time. A jumble of memories or dreams, I'm not sure which, float by: Alex's whispered words, Ren's secrets, Shane's confessions. I don't know what's real versus what my mind's fed me to keep me sane while I swim through the shadows in my head, but I cling to them, those promises and admissions, a lifeline under the shadows.

When I open my eyes, blinking away the fuzziness around the edges, I'm met with my own eyes staring back from my brother's face. The memory of those eyes, filling with guilt before he lifted his gun, seizes me, but I'm unable to move my heavy limbs. He didn't shoot me, I'm pretty sure, but the terror of the moment takes hold.

Mason leans over, shushing me, as strangled sobs leave my lips, tears spilling down my cheeks. His reassurances come out in a hushed tone, and they settle in my brain, seeping into my bones. He's whispering "I'm sorry" over and over, like if he repeats it enough, I'll believe him.

"Mason," I croak, my dry throat strangling the words.

He grabs a glass of water, then helps me up. I try to drink the whole glass, but he stops me, taking it away before I'm fully sated.

"You have to go easy, Sammy."

My eyes fill with tears again, hearing my name on his lips. I tried to hold on to the hope he would get better and wake up. I imagined things would go back to normal, but as each day passed, my hope diminished bit by bit until it was a sliver in my heart. Now that he's here, it hits me. I don't want to go back to normal. Guilt crashes into me, making me dissolve again. I want to explain or at least ease the concern on his face, but I'm hanging on by a thread.

When I've caught my breath, calming myself enough to think coherently, I glance around, seeing the familiar space through new eyes. I'm in my room, but a lot is missing. Pictures and paintings are gone from the walls. My closet, sitting open across from me, is woefully empty.

"Why am I here?" I ask, confused.

"What do you mean?"

"I should be . . . I . . ." I meet Mason's eyes, and it hits me. I almost said I should be home, but this is my home. Not the Kings' estate. Not with Shane and Alex and Ren. I glance around again, half expecting them to be camped out, but of course, I find it empty.

"Sammy . . ." He hesitates. "Are you okay?" He sighs, as if that isn't the question he wanted to ask.

"Sore. But I'm okay. Sorry, it's been one helluva day." I try to bluff my way out of this feeling of emptiness, but Mason's look tells me I'm not convincing him with my fake smile. It feels forced, even to me.

"You wanna tell me what happened?"

I struggle to sit, and he rushes to help me. Settling back against the headboard. I don't know where to start, much less what he's already been told.

"Have you talked to anyone?"

Have you talked to Shane?

"A little, but I trust you, so I'd rather you tell me."

I sigh, leaning back and closing my eyes before I tell him everything from the moment he got shot. Several times, I have to stop, but he waits, never commenting. I keep my emotions at bay, and I think of how proud Ren would be I'm able to lock them down. I leave large chucks of time out of my story, trying to keep in what happened between the Kings and I.

When I get to telling him about the Depot, it hits me. I have no idea if anyone was hurt, if Emma got away, if Colin is still alive. My head throbs, reminding me of getting pistol-whipped after being stabbed. I turn my frantic eyes to Mason, practically climbing out of bed to find my clothes, but his hands press me back, keeping me in bed.

"No! Mason, the Depot. They're at the Depot. And Emma . . . and . . . and . . . I have to tell them!"

Panic fills me at the thought of my guys being there getting hurt, and I'm not there to help them.

"Sam! Calm down. No one is at the Depot. It's been almost a whole day since you got Emma out. She's fine. Everyone is fine. The Guild's is on the run—for now, at least. Everyone is okay, except . . . Colin." His voice catches on Colin's name.

His words should soothe me, but my hysteria wells up, threatening to pull me under. Mason is telling me everyone is okay, but what does that mean? Alive? And who is everyone? He doesn't understand. He can't.

"You don't get it!" I yell. He rears back. "I can't . . . I have to . . ." I can't force the words out. For some reason, they still feel like a betrayal. He tried to keep me from them for so long without a reason. I never questioned it, but now, I wonder why. How could he keep me from them? How could he ask me to not be with them? My mind is a jumble, the past and present mixing together, and my vision blurs. I suck in deep, gasping breaths, trying to get my shit under control.

"Sammy?" he asks helplessly, holding his hands out.

I take a deep breath, holding it, then slowly exhaling. "I'm sorry. I need to know if anyone is hurt. Or . . . or dead. I need to . . . Please, just . . . tell me."

"Victor got shot, nothing serious. We all lost some guys, but that's the worst of it, really. There's a few more bodies in the river this morning, but nothing we can't handle. Apparently, they were going to blow the Depot up as a last resort, but they didn't have to. The people in the Barrens blocked the bridges, forcing the Guild back toward our side. Helms and his men are fine. The Kings are fine. Actually, the Kings weren't even there."

My head whips around, glaring at him. "What do you mean, they weren't there? Where the hell were they?"

"Oh, Sam," he sighs, pity in his eyes. I close my eyes, shutting myself off from him. I can't handle more news when I'm still trying to keep things from him. It's pointless pulling information from Mason, not when I can't tell him why I care so much. I don't understand so many things, my mind feels like mush. I don't understand how I made it to my bed. I don't understand how Mason got out of the hospital. I don't understand where my guys . . . no. They're not here, so are they even mine? Do I have the right to demand where they are or if they're okay?

"I'm tired," I whisper.

I clamp my mouth shut, but my emotions dip again. Despair overtakes me. I try to reassure myself they're alive, and I got Emma home safe. I can't imagine why they weren't at the Depot, unless Victor derailed the whole meeting. I wouldn't put it past my uncle to sabotage everything, so he comes out on top. He must have pissed them off for them not to come, or maybe it was me.

Did Shane blame me for Emma getting kidnapped? He should. I do. Maybe they needed to stay with Emma, keep her safe, something Shane would do. He's been set on keeping her safe from the beginning, since before all the shit went down. Why they're not here now has nothing to do with Emma and everything to do with me.

Did they decide my disappearing was the perfect opportunity to end what was between us? Pain bursts through me, taking my breath away. Whatever they were doing, it wasn't for me. I tried to shield my heart from them, but they snuck in, wrapping themselves around me, refusing to let me go. I never stood a chance against them. My useless heart shatters, filling my body with shards of misery.

They didn't come for me.

The door clicks, but I keep my eyes shut tight. I don't want an audience as I fall apart, but I also don't want to be alone. I wish I would have run when Colin told me to. It would have been better to have never crossed paths with the Kings; I wouldn't have to feel this pain, knowing I'm never going to be good enough for them to keep. Shane told me, but I pushed it away and ignored his promises. I should have. He proved over and over he'd choose the Kings over all else, including me. I can't even be angry about it, since he told me every step of the way. I can't blame them for making the choices they did. No one made me any promises. Ren fought so long against the pull between us, I doubt it was a hard decision for him to make. I have to admit to myself Alex might have told me the things I wanted to hear instead of what was real. I slide down, burrowing into sheets that smell like another time, and let the darkness drown me, whisking me away from the heartache I can't outrun.

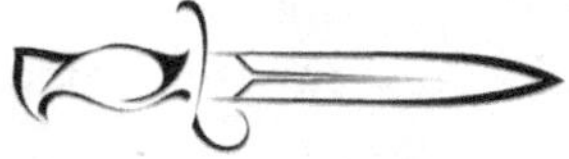

Hours or days later—I can't tell—I open my eyes again. At least I don't feel so bereft, so emotional. My room is brighter, the sunlight casting soft beams over the space, which at one point, felt like home. Now it feels like a prison. I no longer understand my place in this world, in the Byrns' family or the business. I've felt so off balance since Mason was shot, and I don't know how to realign myself. I'll need to find a way to navigate this new world. The world without Colin, without Shane, Alex, and Ren. One where I'm alone again.

Adrift, Ren's voice sounds in my head.

He was right. He saw it, and I thought I had come to grips with it, but being back here, knowing my brother is alive and well, I thought everything would feel normal. I thought I would be normal. Now all I see is how lonely I was, how starved I was for a direction, for a life of my own not under the heading of being a Byrns. I can't play the part of a socialite anymore, with no worries other than the next party. I don't know how to act like everything is okay when it feels like my entire world is imploding.

It's more than the guys not being here, not choosing me—it's my entire existence in this room.

I'm not the woman I was before. I'm different, but I feel like, if I'm here, I have to be that woman again, and I don't want to be her. I don't want to be a naïve woman who pushes everything away to just exist.

"Sammy?"

"Yeah, I'm awake," I call out before clearing my throat.

"We need to talk," Mason sighs, sitting in the chair still pulled next to my bed.

"Okay . . ." I sit up, eyeing him cautiously. My muscles scream, but I bite back the pain.

"Do you remember last night?"

"I was a little emotional . . ."

"No, when you woke up in the middle of the night? You don't remember?"

I close my eyes, trying to dredge up memories, but all I find is more heartache.

"I think I have a concussion," I mumble.

"You woke up crying, calling out . . . well, I didn't know what else to do," he says, pleading with me to understand, but I have no idea what he's talking about.

"I'm sorry, Mason. These last few months . . . a lot happened," I try to explain. I can only imagine what or who I was calling out for, and trying to tell my brother why is too much of a minefield. I can't admit to him how much the Kings mean to me.

"Maybe you'd be better off . . . not here." Guilt clouds his eyes, begging me to understand what he's asking.

"Not here? But this is . . ."—the words stick in my throat, but I force them out—"this is my home."

"Is it? I'm not sure it is anymore. You're not the same."

Mason looks away, but I still catch the regret and sadness on his face. He's sent me away once before, when he couldn't handle me, after the coup. I understand he wanted me trained, but he sent me away, so he wouldn't have to deal with me, too. This feels eerily similar. I want to believe he's telling me I belong with the Kings, but how do I tell him they don't want me? They don't love me? They'd be here if they did. Other than glimmers of half-forgotten dreams, I haven't seen them for days. I assume Mason called them, since he knows Emma is okay, and they're alive, but how much did they reveal to him?

"Mason, I don't have anywhere else to go," I admit. It's something I never admitted to Ren or Shane. I didn't want to appear weak, but I don't care anymore. I am weak and strong and worthless and worthy. I am all those things and none of them, and I'm okay with that, but I still need a place to live. My chest tightens, nausea burning my throat.

"We both know that's not true, Sammy. You belong there. I don't know what it'll be like without you, but you have to go. You have to live. You can't be here and live," he whispers, meeting my eyes.

My heart leaps, immediately followed by a stabbing pain. I always thought Mason would lock me up and throw away the key if he knew I'd sought out the Kings. Him telling me he's fine with it when I no longer have the option. There's no way I'm showing up on their doorstep, begging for their love. I've chased after them for too long, and their absence speaks volumes.

"They don't want me," I whisper, tears filling my eyes.

Mason gathers me up, hugging me. "I love you, Sammy."

Then he's gone, and I feel like he's walking out of my life instead of just the room.

I bury my face in my hands, body shaking with my sobs, when arms surround me. They feel familiar, like home.

"Shh, it's okay, Bug. We got you," Alex murmurs, making me sob harder. I'm afraid, if I open my eyes, they'll disappear, and I'll be left alone.

"I don't know how you could think we wouldn't be here, Sam," Ren scolds, rubbing my back gently.

"Can we go home now? I'm sick of sleeping in a fucking chair," Shane grumbles, and I finally lift my head. He's standing next to the bed, arms crossed, but his eyes hold the worry he won't let out.

"It was your choice to sleep there, dumbass. You could have taken one of the guest rooms, you know," Alex says over his shoulder.

"Too far away," he responds, meeting my eyes. "You ready to go, Princess, or do we have to wait for you to pretty yourself up?"

The only thing I want is to fall into them, beg them to take me home, but I can't. Not without knowing for sure what we are. I can't live feeling temporary anymore. I want to know where they were, why they weren't here, why they didn't come for me.

I have to force the words out, but I finally whisper, "Where were you?"

Ren leans in, resting his forehead against my head. "We were right here the whole time."

I'm shaking my head before he's finished. I would have known. I would have seen them.

"You were out a long time, Bug. Your brother wanted you to make the decision for yourself, without us forcing you."

"How long?" I ask, fixing a stare on Shane.

He sighs. "You can take however long you need, Sam. I don't like being here, but we won't rush you. Another couple hours won't make a difference."

I huff out a laugh. "No, how long am I staying with you?"

"You've got to be fucking kidding me." Shane scrubs his hands down his face, tipping his head back.

Ren leans in, whispering in my ear again, "How about forever?"

"I don't understand. I thought . . ."

"You were never temporary, Sam. I don't know why the hell you thought you were," Ren grumbles before pressing a kiss to my head.

"Forever is a long time."

"Not nearly long enough, Bug."

I look to Shane, waiting for his words. No matter what the other two say, Shane's and my relationship has been the most volatile, and with how we left things, I don't know where he stands. I hold my breath, watching the emotions flit across his face before he pushes Alex aside and cups my face, bringing his forehead to mine.

"Princess, keeping you is the only thing I've thought about. I can't imagine our lives without you. You are irreplaceable. I should have told you long ago, and I know I fucked up. I know I said shit I didn't mean, and it hurt you. I should have pulled my head out of my ass and told you how I really felt. We should have begged you to stay. I spend as long as it takes to convince you how much I need you. Please come home."

I nod, but dissolve into a blubbering mess again. I don't know how long they hold me, whispering words of love, but eventually, they seep into my shattered heart and stitch me back together until I tell them to take me home.

* * *

Thank you so much for reading Samantha and the Kings story!
Not ready to leave the Shadows of Synd behind?
Pre-order Ryker Helms' story:

https://mybook.to/runningfromshadows

If you'd like to hear about the other stories that have been living in my head, sign up for my newsletter, visit my website, or follow me on social media visit:
emiliaabraham.com

Special Thanks:

K.B. Barrett Designs - Cover Artist
Tala Editorial - Developmental Editor
Miss Eloquent Edits - Line Editor, Proofreader, Formatter

ABOUT THE AUTHOR

After many years of dreaming of becoming a full-time writer, Emilia Abraham took the leap, bringing her words to print. From sweet contemporary romance to spicy reverse harem and everything in between, she focuses on the happily ever after.

Emilia lives in the Upper Midwest with her husband (who's probably sick of listening to her expound on fictional men) and three kids (who try to steal her post-it notes). When she's not writing, she enjoys reading, playing video games, and consuming copious amounts of energy drinks.